Gray's Promise

by

Anni Fife

King Security Book Two

Gray's Promise

Contact Information: info@thewildrosepress.com

Cover Art by *Kristian Norris*

The Wild Rose Press, Inc.
PO Box 708
Adams Basin, NY 14410-0708

Visit us at www.thewilderroses.com

Publishing History
First Scarlet Rose Edition, 2017
Print ISBN 978-1-5092-1880-6
Digital ISBN 978-1-5092-1881-3

Published in the United States of America

A jealousy that destroys everything in its path…
a love that refuses to die.

The porch door was open, letting a soft breeze move through the cottage. I breathed in the dewy dampness, and a faint pain echoed near my heart. If I closed my eyes, I could almost hear Mama chattering to my dad in the kitchen. She always got up early to make breakfast. The memories were buried but when they surfaced, they were mine to treasure. I drank my coffee and washed down the last of my cinnamon roll. And with it, gently nudged the memory away.

The breeze gusted and I brushed away a curl of hair fluttering in my face. Gray was cracking eggs now and a wave of lust crept over me. His easy—and mostly naked—confidence in the kitchen was weirdly heady. An image of his face when he came last night slipped into my mind. The dampness in the air transferred to my skin and I shivered, goose bumps prickling up my arms. *Jeez*. He was so sexy. Even more than I could have ever imagined. Rubbing at my goosies, I peeked at him through my lashes. A vague heaviness fluttered in my tummy. He was confident and seductive as hell, but he was also holding back. He might have had reason last night, but I wasn't going to let him get away with it for long. Gray's running days were coming to an end. Soon.

"Butterfly." His sexy growl demanded my attention. He was sipping coffee, his electric gaze focused on me. "You wearing panties?"

Dedication

This one is for you, Dani. My generous angel, my best
friend for life, and my dear sister.
Love always, Anni.

Acknowledgements

The great American Thoroughbred racehorse,
Secretariet, who won the Triple Crown in 1973, inspired
Morgan Magic, my miracle horse. Secretariat's 31-length
record-breaking win in the Belmont Stakes is still widely
considered one of the greatest races of all time.

I would also like to mention that I have enjoyed using
creative license in demarcating the locations of Walker
Ranch and Morgan Farm. Denton, Texas, of course, exists
as does Clear Creek and Hartlee Field Road. But the
existence of my characters' ranches in this area is purely a
figment of my imagination. Similarly, selected restaurants
and locations are based on actual places…and some are
not. I'll leave it for you to separate fact from fiction.
Enjoy!

To you, wonderful readers, thank you for your
amazing support. I hope you enjoy Gray and Zoey's story
as much as I loved writing it. It's always great to receive
your feedback. Please e-mail me, chat to me on Facebook
or Twitter, or leave a review on Amazon, Goodreads or
any site that works for you.

Thank you to my dear editor, Ally Robertson, and the
hardworking team at The Wild Rose Press, Inc. Working
with you all is always a delight. And to my darling
mother, my most valued beta reader. You are a one-
woman support team. I couldn't do it without you.
Love Anni

"People like to say that the conflict is between good and evil.

The real conflict is between truth and lies."

—Don Miguel Ruiz

Chapter One
I Don't Want To Miss A Thing

Texas Health Presbyterian Hospital, Denton, Texas
16 August 2001, 5:12 a.m.
Gray

Grayson Walker slammed through the entrance doors of the emergency department. His heart was pounding so loud and so fast he was momentarily disoriented. An acrid smell of antiseptic washed over him, making his stomach turn. The room spun and he blinked hard, desperate to push away the darkness clawing at his vision.

Get a grip, man.

He bent over and sucked in a deep breath. A shudder ripped through him and he clutched at his thighs. *Shit.* He needed to keep it together.

"Gray?"

He recognized Randy's voice but took another rough breath before he glanced up at his friend. Randy faltered to a stop, fidgeting with his Stetson. His face was twisted with concern.

"Tell me." Gray winced at the weakness in his voice. He squeezed his eyes shut and dragged in another long breath. The rushing noise in his ears slowly faded. His lungs pushed insistently, but still, he waited. When he sensed calm, he exhaled harshly and straightened to his full height. "Tell me, please."

"It looks like it was a house invasion." Randy's normally melodic Texas twang was gruff. He gripped the rim of his hat and edged closer. "Hell, Gray. They slaughtered the whole family."

"Zoey?" Gray stomach tightened like concrete.

"She's okay," Randy said in a rush, lifting his hands in reassurance. "Jesus, she's not okay, but she's alive."

"Where is she?"

"Sedated. She's got a broken wrist; doctor is busy setting it."

Randy's face was ashen. His eyes flickered unnaturally. Whatever he'd seen at Morgan Farm had gutted him. His deputy sheriff's uniform was creased, sweat stains under his arms, and yet the sun had barely risen.

"What else?"

"Busted ribs. She's taken a real beating. She's also been doped."

"Doped? What the hell?"

"Yeah. Jacks too. We don't know what it is yet. Doctors have taken blood."

Gray pushed his tongue against his clenched teeth, trying to force saliva into his bone-dry mouth.

"Jacks took a bullet to the shoulder," Randy continued. "Shit, Gray, it was right up close, the barrel against his skin when the trigger was pulled. Your brother was lucky, it's a through and through. Muscle damage is minimal. But whatever they doped him with, it knocked him out cold and he bled like a pig from the exit wound. They've sewn him up. He's stable. As soon as you're ready, I'll take you to see him."

"No. I want to see Zoey first."

"Doctor said she'll call me when she's ready—"

"Dammit, Randy! I want to see her now," Gray hissed and took a step toward the doors leading to the patient area.

"Gray! She's still out cold. Let me take you to Jacks first." Randy's fingers curled around his forearm. "Please, buddy. Speak to Jacks first."

Gray searched Randy's pleading eyes. Tingles of dread lit through his chest. "What aren't you telling me?" The fingers around his arm squeezed tighter and Randy looked away, but not before Gray saw him grimace. *"What?"*

"She was raped, buddy. Zoey was raped."

Everything inside Gray froze. He stared into his friend's tortured gaze, desperate to see something that said he was lying. But there was nothing. Nothing but truth. His breath wheezed. The buzz in his ears returned, this time howling. *No! No! No!* Sweat broke out on his brow. He tried to swallow. He could feel it building in his stomach, bubbling and thickening. *Jesus, please no! Not his beautiful, innocent Zoey.*

Gray ripped his arm from his friend's grasp and raced for the entrance. He slammed his hands against the glass door and spun around behind it. Poisonous sludge spewed from inside him and he bent over, bracing himself against the wall. The beer and tequila from last night's personal pity party burned his throat as it vomited out. He lost track of how long he stayed like that, crouched over, his stomach heaving, his mind blank.

"Hey. Here. Take this."

He looked down as something cold pressed against his hand. Randy was holding out a coke. Swallowing painfully, Gray reached for the can. It was ice-cold. He rolled it over his clammy forehead and took several steadying breaths. When he felt he had a handle on it, he cracked the can open and took a careful sip. The familiar sweet taste trickled down his throat and immediately helped settle the poison trying to bubble up inside him again. *Fuck.* He needed to do better than this. For Zoey. *Christ.* For Jacks too. He tipped back the drink and let the coke pour down his throat. Crushing the empty can, he wiped his sleeve across his mouth.

"Let's go." He stepped away from the mess he'd made on the ground and headed back inside. "Tell me again about the Morgans," he demanded.

"Her dad and brother were shot. Each took more than one bullet. They were dead at the scene."

James and Noah, both dead. Gray kept rigid control of the pain screaming inside him. "And Mary?" he asked gruffly.

Randy guided them back through the reception, down a corridor, and into the emergency patient area. Activity was limited. It was still so goddamn early. They stopped beside a closed curtain where Randy's police partner stood vigil. "Mary's alive. She suffered multiple stab wounds. She's still in surgery."

Warmth flared inside Gray and he blinked to stem the sudden onset of tears. *Zoey's mom was alive!*

"Don't get your hopes up, buddy. She's in bad shape."

He nodded and roughly rubbed his eyes. His throat still burned and he swallowed painfully before inclining his head at the curtain. "Jacks?" he asked quietly.

Randy dipped his head in acknowledgment.

Gray squeezed his neck and took a purposeful

breath. He needed to be calm. Or at least, he needed to look calm. His brother could be a handful, and with his patience frayed, if Jacks went off, Gray knew he'd lose it too. He stepped closer to the head of the bed and eased the curtain open. Jacks was propped up against a pile of pillows, eyes closed. He was shirtless, white bandages swathed across his left shoulder and chest. Dried blood was splattered on his chin and neck. Gray blinked hard, forcing back the tears suddenly blurring his vision. Jacks looked oddly peaceful and Gray hesitated to wake him.

Hurried footsteps approached. "Is Mr. Walker awake?" a voice whispered loudly.

Gray drew the curtain closed and stepped back. Three medical personnel were crowded around Randy and his partner. One of them, a woman, was obviously senior, and most definitely a doctor. They all had the same worried look on their faces.

Shit. That wasn't worry, it was panic.

"I'm Mr. Walker," he said firmly, cutting through their chatter. He was over six foot and didn't hesitate to use his height to impress his dominance on the group. "What's the problem?"

The nurse and junior doctor looked to the woman. She was older, calmer. "It's Miss Morgan, we need—"

"Zoey!" He stepped closer. "What's happened?"

Her head tilted back awkwardly to look at him, but she stood firm. "Are you family?"

"Yes."

"Her fiancé?"

What? "Yes."

She wore thin-rimmed glasses that in no way obscured the intelligence in her hazel eyes. Her dark hair was short, pinned neatly away from her face. Gray returned her steady gaze. She must have seen something acceptable because she nodded sharply. "I'm Doctor Wells. Come with me, we'll talk on the way." She turned and headed for the corridor leading to the elevators. Gray lengthened his stride to keep up with her, vaguely aware the other doctor and nurse followed close behind.

"Doctor, I need to know what's going on with Zoey."

She stopped at the elevator and pressed the up arrow. "We're having difficulty calming her." She turned to look at him. "When she arrived she was unconscious. This was most likely a result of the blunt force trauma to her head, as well as the drug she was subdued with."

"Shit!"

She ignored his whispered expletive. "We were able to administer a local to set her wrist. She also has a concussion and two fractured ribs. Neither presents a danger if she remains quiet and rested."

Ping!

The elevator doors opened. They all moved inside and the efficient woman pushed the relevant button before continuing. "She regained consciousness several minutes ago but she's become increasingly agitated. We've tried to talk her down but she's not responding." She frowned at Gray. "I need to be blunt with you. Between the trauma, her concussion, and the drug still contaminating her system, your fiancée is not doing well at all."

Gray's hands balled into fists. He wanted to punch the walls. "Take me to her. *Now!*"

"You need to control yourself, Mr. Walker."

Rage joined the sick fear churning inside him and he glared at the doctor. She didn't flinch. Her face held no judgment, but her steady gaze also gave no quarter. Gray found it anchored him, offering him no alternative but to deal with the reality slamming into him. The rigidity in his body eased. Doctor Wells nodded slightly, and in a cool, precise voice, continued. "Given Miss Morgan's concussion and the yet unidentified drug in her system, we would prefer not to administer any more sedatives."

Ping!

The doors opened and they stepped out. She led them down another corridor and stopped outside a numbered ward. "Mr. Walker—"

"It's Gray."

"Okay, Gray." She clasped her hands in front of her. "Zoey is extremely agitated. To calm her, you need to find the calmness within yourself." Her probing stare insisted on a response.

He nodded sharply.

"She's on the edge of hysteria and in danger of hurting herself. If you cannot calm her, we will be forced to sedate her for her own safety."

Zoey!

Gray's heart hammered wildly. He closed his eyes, and for the first time since he'd raced into the ED, let her image surface.

His beautiful red butterfly. Mercurial and brilliant. Her dark-copper hair alight with so many fiery streaks, he was constantly amazed it didn't singe his skin. The curly length was unexpectedly soft, so goddamn sexy when it slipped like satin through his fingers. But as much as he loved her hair, it was her eyes that endlessly beguiled him. Tapered like a cat, they were vivid-green with a golden ring around her pupil. A fascinating combination of sex-kitten and innocent, and such an integral part of her expressive nature. There were times he thought they were too large for her heart-shaped face, but then she'd laugh and they'd turn that intense jewel-like green. Wicked. Infectious. Or she'd whimper with desire, and the golden ring would leak into the green. Hot and slumberous. Untamed.

"Gray?"

He opened his eyes, forcing Zoey's image back into darkness. "Take me to her." He met the doctor's unblinking scrutiny. "Please."

****

Gray's chest felt like a ton of cement was buried inside it. Fear and fury battled for control as he waited for the last orderly to leave the room.

"Close the door," he whispered harshly.

He didn't check to see if his request was followed because his only focus was on his girl. *His girl!* So fucking traumatized, she was cowering in the corner on the floor. *Christ.* Erratic pants escaped from between her split lips. She kept knocking her head rhythmically against the wall, her face turned away from him. *Her battered face.* Her broken wrist was cradled against her chest. Her legs folded up tight to her body. Like an abused animal, she was curled into herself.

Instead of moving toward her, he sank to his haunches. The room was a disaster. Not surprising. When he arrived, he walked into terrifying chaos. Zoey, scrambling against the wall keening wildly, two orderlies and a nurse trying to get to her. Even though he knew their goal was to help her, it didn't stop wild rage igniting inside him, burning up his control. Thank Christ, Doctor Wells moved quickly and cleared them from the room. "Do what you can, Gray. But whatever you do, do it slowly." Those had been her only words of advice before she followed them out.

He scanned the small room. It looked like the aftermath of a brawl. Bed covers thrown onto the floor. One pillow, torn, was all the way across on the other side of the room. A trolley was knocked over, the contents of a breakfast tray spilled on the floor—scrambled eggs? Another trolley stood at an angle between himself and Zoey, whose broken whimpers were now shredding his heart.

How the hell was he going to break through her terror?

Gray knew he'd only get one chance. Ideas came, one after the other, and he discarded them all. Bile worked its way up from his rigid stomach, clogging his throat. Fear had him by the balls. He swallowed hard and tried to ignore her gut-wrenching whimpers. *Goddammit!* With two fractured ribs, she had to be hurting. But that hadn't stopped her fighting the medical staff trying to help her. She saw them as strangers, the enemy. And right now, he was that too: a stranger, the enemy.

But whatever you do, do it slowly.

Forcing air into his constricted lungs, Gray eased himself to his ass and closed his eyes. Several steadying breaths later, his eyes still squeezed shut to protect himself from the devastation in front of him, he began to sing. The lyrics of Aerosmith's only number one hit flowed from somewhere deep inside him. Zoey's favorite song of all time, the hit song from the movie *Armageddon,* "I Don't Want to Miss a Thing." She had played it to him so many times over the summer that the words came effortlessly. But the fear remained.

It wasn't until he hit the end of the chorus that he dared to open his eyes. Her head was still turned away, resting against the wall. But her eyes—they were slanted toward him. Watching.

His breath hitched, causing his voice to rise but he kept on singing. And singing.

It took until the final chorus before she looked at him. Really looked at him. Her eyes so stricken with agony they were nearly black, the green and gold eaten up by her dilated pupils.

He shifted to his knees, and slowly crawled toward her. She didn't move. He kept on singing, repeating the chorus of Steve Tyler's power ballad over and over again, knowing he did it no justice, but so damn grateful that somehow, it had cut a path to his girl's shattered soul. Working his way around the abandoned trolley, he eased himself alongside her and settled against the wall. When he reached for her she moved willingly into his arms. He gathered her into his lap, bent his knees and surrounded her with his warmth. And he kept on singing.

He heard the door open but he didn't look up, his eyes glued to the precious girl in his arms. It clicked closed, and he kept on singing.

He sang until his voice was hoarse and Zoey had drifted off to sleep. Her broken wrist, in its brand-new cast, lay limp against his stomach. Her other hand clutched at his shirt, over his heart.

He let the song slowly die on his lips and watched

as she slept, her head resting on his shoulder, her russet-tipped lashes fluttering restlessly against her bruised skin. His ass was numb from the cold floor but he didn't move. Time passed, and Zoey remained still. He prayed she was at peace, that the nightmares would give her respite and allow her the few hours escape she so desperately needed.

The door opened again and he looked up. He expected to see Doctor Wells but it wasn't. It was Jacks. His brother hovered in the doorway before taking a hesitant step inside. Somebody had brought him a clean shirt. Gray noticed his arm was strapped, and that he was pallid, his face almost as white as the bandages supporting his arm.

"The doctor said she's calmer now." Jacks' whisper was hoarse. He tried to fold his arms but ended up cupping the elbow of his strapped arm. "How's she doing?"

Gray pressed his lips together and shook his head.

"Why did you tell them she was your fiancée?" Jacks' voice rose, tight with accusation.

"What?"

"You told the doctors *you* were Zoey's fiancé."

"What the hell, Jacks? Who cares?"

"I care!" Jacks hissed, taking a step closer. "She's *my* fiancée and I care."

"Quiet!" He glared angrily at Jacks. When his brother's mouth clamped shut, Gray looked down at Zoey. She hadn't stirred. Jacks' words swirled around in his head.

His fiancée! What the hell was he on about?

Pain radiated from his gut. His stomach had been knotted tight ever since he received the call from

Randy, and the muscles were starting to cramp in protest. He wasn't in any state to handle Jacks' bullshit. And neither was the shattered girl lying trustingly in his arms. His eyes roamed her injured face. Dried blood encrusted her split lip. Her left cheekbone was twice its size, the eye swollen shut. *Sweet Jesus, it hurt to see her like this.* Lowering his head, he touched his lips softly to an angry bruise marring her forehead.

Even with a bullet in his shoulder, Jacks was up to his normal shit-stirring best.

Not trying to hide the disgust he was sure reflected on his face, he leveled his gaze at his brother. "Her fiancé?" he whispered harshly. "What are you talking about?"

Jacks edged closer, his finger pointing at Zoey. "That's my ring on her finger." His voice rose in triumph. "I put it there last night when she agreed to be my wife."

Gray's arms tightened reflexively, and Zoey mumbled. She shifted restlessly, and the hand that clutched his shirt loosened. A blue sparkle caught his eye. He cocked his head, trying to clear the ringing in his ears. *No way.* His brain fought to process the impossible as his gaze remained locked on the aquamarine ring sitting obscenely on her finger. *That finger.* "No way!" He jerked his head up at Jacks. "How? Why?"

"Because we love each other, you bastard!" An unhealthy red stained Jacks' cheeks.

"No—"

"Yes! And that ring proves it." He jabbed at Zoey's finger.

Gray's heart pounded erratically. He recognized

the ring. A cushion cut aquamarine surrounded by smaller diamonds. It had belonged to his maternal grandmother. His mother never wore it herself, but she always promised Jacks he could have it for his future wife. Gray was okay with that. He never liked the ring. It seemed cold to him, much like his mother. An icy clamminess settled over his skin.

No way. No fucking way!

He held Zoey tighter. Her warmth seeped into him. Wild copper hair spilled over his arm and he bent to breathe in her familiar honeysuckle scent. His Zoey. His beautiful, fiery butterfly. Constantly on the move, her brain like quicksilver, inquisitive and brilliant.

He loved her so damn much. And she loved him. Didn't she?

He ignored Jacks and slowly stood, careful not to disturb the sleeping girl held safely in his arms. Walking to the bed, he gently settled her down.

"Gray—"

"Not now." He reached for a pillow to support her broken wrist, and straightening the strewn covers, tucked them snugly under her arms. His eyes briefly strayed to the offensive bauble on her finger that screamed she no longer belonged to him. His chest burned, and he tore his eyes away. "Sleep, Butterfly," he murmured and stroked a burnished curl off her face. Stepping away from the bed, he bypassed the breakfast mess on the floor and glanced at Jacks. "Outside," he said curtly.

No matter what Jacks claimed, Gray swore to himself he'd get to the bottom of this. His brother could be selfish and petulant. Over the years, Jacks had allowed his obsessive jealousy to taint their brotherly bond. But this was different. This was Zoey.

Zoey, who passionately declared her love for him all summer.

Zoey, who insisted she had repeatedly explained to an obsessed Jacks he would never be more than a good friend to her.

Zoey, who breathlessly promised she would sort things once and for all with Jacks at her birthday dinner.

The dinner he refused to attend.

The dinner that ended with her beaten and raped and her family dead, or as good as.

The dinner that ended with his brother's ring on her finger.

What happened last night?
What the hell had Zoey done?

Chapter Two
What She Wants

Walker Ranch, Denton County, Texas
One Month Later
Gray

Gray rested his forehead on the window pane and stared out toward Morgan Farm. He couldn't see the house from here. Nor could he see the small gravesite hastily erected to bury James and Noah. He didn't need to close his eyes to picture the two graves set on a small hill amongst the grove of tall cottonwoods. How many times had he joined Zoey's family under the shade of those trees? His jaw clenched. *Too damn many to count.* It was Mary's special place to sit and read. From there she could look across the pasture, down to their family homestead. Or in the opposite direction, she could keep an eye on the path leading out of the forest and away from Davis Pond, the favored hangout of her kids.

And soon, if his screaming gut was worth a damn, she would join her husband and son in the open space alongside them.

The funeral was awful, crowded with friends and family stricken by the monstrous tragedy. Mary wasn't there. She remained in a coma. Gray thought it had done her a favor. Her soft heart, overflowing with so much love for her family, would have imploded, destroying her from the inside out.

Zoey was there. Maybe. It was the first time he'd seen her in a month and he barely recognized her. Too thin. Too still. And she never looked at him, not once. Squeezed between her Uncle Richard and Jacks, she stared fixedly at some spot over the graves. And when the earth dropped into the freshly dug holes, and every hair on his body raised in horror as it thudded against the coffins, she never flinched. Sobs and whimpers filled the heavy air, but her face remained dry. Frozen. Gray's stomach had curdled. She was like a bad hallucination of her former self. As soon as the ceremony was over, he wasted no time getting the hell out of there.

He pressed his head harder against the cold glass. His stomach still churned at the memory. Why had she done this to him? To them? Locked him out of her life. She refused to add his name to the hospital visitor's list. The same at the recovery center she was currently checked into.

"She chose Jacks. She wants to be with Jacks. Let her be, Grayson." Margaret Walker was nothing if not blunt. *"Zoey has enough pain to deal with. Your selfish needs have no place here."* His mother's sharp assessment had slammed into him, finally halting his repeated attempts to bypass the hospital gatekeepers.

He felt hollowed out. And at the same time filled with so much burning rage, he thought he'd go mad. Or was it pain? He didn't know anymore.

Turning away from Zoey's home, his gaze followed the path to the stables. The roof of the tack room was only just visible over the trees. His eyes drifted closed and her face shifted into focus. Eyes, golden with desire, tilted down to stare imploringly at him as her body arched greedily in search of his tongue. He wet his lips, the taste of her flooding his mouth—

"Fuck!" He pushed angrily away from the window and turned back to his bedroom. Sourness coated his mouth, pushing away the memory of her taste. There was nothing here for him anymore. Even his room no longer felt like his own. He had been a boy in this room. He wasn't a boy anymore. He needed to finish packing and get the hell away from here. Willing energy into his heavy limbs, he rubbed roughly at his face. *Get it together, man.* It was time to stop feeling so worthless and go where he could do some good.

There's nothing left to do here. Not a single damn thing!

Moving with increased determination, he filled the two suitcases lying on his bed. In less than half an hour, Randy would be here to fetch him. His buddy had been more of a support to him over the last month than his own family. He'd helped him keep his shit together. And over too many beers and endless tequila shots, he'd also kept him up-to-date with the case.

Randy's father, Shamus, was a Texas Ranger. The Rangers had been called in to support local police because the vicious attack on the Morgans was declared a major case. Randy said the police were stymied. On the one hand, the attack appeared to be a brutal house invasion. Items from the house were missing, presumed stolen. But there were certain factors that also seemed personal.

They figured the attack happened toward the end of Zoey's dinner party. Blood tests revealed the whole family, including Jacks, had been doped with ketamine.

They'd been sitting ducks, helpless to defend themselves. Nausea rose in Gray's throat like it did every time he let the ugliness penetrate his brain. Forensics revealed Zoey's birthday cake was laced with ketamine. *How much more personal could you get? A goddamn chocolate birthday cake!* Laced with so much ketamine that whoever ate a decent-sized portion—and James and Noah had done exactly that—would have been either knocked out cold or so out of it, they'd have been defenseless against the shooters. *Jesus!* They'd been shot sitting at the family dinner table eating birthday cake. Not a single indication they even knew what hit them. Nor a lick of evidence indicating who baked the cake or where it came from.

Mary was another story. She suffered a vicious knife assault, made worse by a slew of defensive wounds. The level of ketamine in her bloodstream was low. Police deduced from the slice of mostly uneaten cake on her plate, she was hardly affected by the drug. She was found on the floor of the dining room. Sweet, loving Mary, faced with the atrocity of seeing her husband and son murdered, had fought for her daughter like the protective lioness she was. *Was she conscious when Zoey was raped?* On all that was good and holy in the world, Gray prayed she'd not been a witness. Dear, gentle Mary would not be able to survive that.

Jacks, who Gray knew had an aversion to chocolate, suffered a high dose of the drug from the cake. Gray guessed he must have eaten it to please Zoey. He was little help to the investigation, insisting he had no recollection of what happened. What puzzled the police was that they could find no logical explanation for why Jacks had been left alive. It wasn't a mistake; the shot to his shoulder had been made close-up, controlled.

Zoey's attack, like Mary's, was also vicious. As hideous as it sounded, her rape was the least brutal part of her assault. The rapist used a condom, leaving not a single trace of DNA. Zoey had no defensive wounds and Doctor Wells said it was likely the beating she suffered happened while she was unconscious. Her head was bashed on a hard surface, probably the tabletop. She either fell or was pushed to the floor where she was kicked so savagely her ribs were fractured and her wrist broken. She only ate half her slice of cake, but according to the doctors, this was enough to put her into a dissociative state at the time of the attack. What puzzled the police was that when she arrived at the hospital she had such a high level of drug in her system that doctors searched and found an injection site.

For whatever reason, the murdering, rapist bastards had given Zoey a booster dose of the drug. This resulted in an out-of-body or as Doctor Wells described it, "a near-death experience." Randy said the police had several ongoing cases where ketamine had been used as a date-rape drug. How that information was supposed to make him feel better, he didn't know. Randy also said that Zoey still remembered nothing from her ordeal.

And during the whole heinous attack, nobody heard anything. Not a fucking thing! Including the two farm hands that lived on the farm. Their quarters were a ways back from the main house, and since the gun used was small caliber, it was unlikely they'd heard the shots.

The police came and took a statement from him

and his parents. His father explained he was out of town the night of the attack, looking at a new horse. But he learned from Randy, his mother had actually visited the Morgans earlier in the evening. She'd shared a glass of champagne with them. She left soon after, returning to the ranch because Norma-Rae, his father's prize breed-mare, was sick. Apparently, his mother and the vet's assistant had been with the horse most of the night.

The information she'd been there, drinking champagne, seethed inside him like a noxious gas. He got himself so riled up that a week ago he'd railed at his mother, demanding she explain what she was doing drinking champagne with the Morgans.

"Hell, Mother, you don't even like Mary Morgan!" he'd snarled.

"I wasn't there for Mary, I was there for Jacks and Zoey."

"Why would you do that?"

"Because Jacks asked me to. It was a surprise. He was planning to propose and he wanted me there to celebrate." His mother's hazel eyes raked over him with a disdain he had become inured to. "When I arrived they were already celebrating. My son was engaged to the love of his life. Why wouldn't I celebrate with him? I only left because of Norma-Rae. Otherwise…" Her brittle voice faded uncomfortably.

But Gray barely noticed because he was reeling, the shock of Zoey's betrayal finally penetrating his thick skull. Bitter cold spread through him, dampening his rage, numbing his heart.

Gray slammed his suitcase shut. He pushed at the clothes bursting out the sides until he could forcibly close the zip. Even now, his skin turned clammy when he thought about Zoey with Jacks. But who the hell was he to be furious with Zoey? What was he doing while she was being seduced by Jacks? Where was he when she was being violated by a monster?

Yeah, where was his stupid ass? Sitting in a fucking bar, feeling sorry for himself!

The police followed up his alibi. It checked out, as he knew it would, but they still insisted he submit to a gunshot residue test. They tested his whole family, including Jacks. And the ranch hands from both properties. They also confiscated every handgun from Walker Ranch and Morgan Farm for ballistics testing. And nothing. No clues at all to lead them to the possible perpetrators. Only questions. Randy said they suspected Mary was left alive by mistake. But why had Zoey and Jacks been left alive? Too many unanswered questions.

He scanned the room and checked the wardrobe one last time. The only thing left hanging on the rail was the navy suit he'd worn to the funeral. He shoved the wardrobe door closed. He couldn't stand the sight of that suit and he knew he'd never wear it again.

The sound of a car arriving reached him, and he crossed the room to look out the window. Jacks. *Shit! Shit!* He'd hoped to avoid him. His mother informed him this morning Jacks was going to fetch Zoey from the recovery center. She was coming to stay with them.

"It's best you're gone when they get here," she'd said.

"Why don't you want me to see her?"

"It's not what I want, Grayson, it's what she wants," she said pointedly.

What she wants.
What she wants.

21

He turned from the window. Time to go. Grabbing his suitcases, he walked out the bedroom, the same one he had spent his entire childhood in. He didn't bother to close the door. But his whole body flinched as a door slammed shut inside his mind. And his heart. His world had fractured. Little felt real to him anymore. But his eagerness to get out of this house was definitely real. Grimacing, he tightened his grip on his cases and headed quickly down the stairs.

"Grayson."

Fuck. He took a deep breath to counter the knot tightening like a noose in his stomach. "Mother," he acknowledged, uncaring how cold he sounded.

"You're leaving?"

Setting the cases down by the front door, he turned to face her. As usual, she looked impeccable. Cotton-khaki fitted trousers, a neat white shirt, equally well fitted, and a single row of pearls peeping out at her collar. His mother was a slim woman, fit, of average height. Her honey-blonde hair was wavy, falling just below her jawline. She had a classic face, angular with a high, wide forehead, a strong chin more square than pointed. He always thought it too prominent, exacerbated by a full lower lip which had a habit of enveloping her much tighter upper lip, especially when she was annoyed. Which was often.

"You sound surprised." Sarcasm underlined his tone.

She clasped her hands together, meeting his raised brow with a perfectly arched brow of her own. "You're leaving and even now, you can't help being rude." Her brittle voice sent a creeping sensation down Gray's spine, exactly the same effect as a floorboard creaking in the dead of night.

Dammit. He didn't need this confrontation, not now. "I'm sorry, I didn't intend to upset you."

Her light-hazel eyes flickered. "Of course not." She tilted her head. "So what is your plan? Straight back to Columbia?"

"No."

"Oh. When does your semester start?"

"It doesn't."

His mother's knuckles whitened as she squeezed her hands tighter together. Yeah, it didn't take much for him to annoy her.

"What are you saying? You're not going back to law school?"

"No point," he said abruptly. "I've enlisted. I'm on a transport from Dallas to Parris Island in South Carolina first thing tomorrow morning."

"Enlisted!" Her voice rose, her head tilting even farther to the side. "I don't understand, Grayson. What are you saying?"

He gritted his teeth. Why did she insist on calling him Grayson? Not once had she ever relented and called him Gray. "I can't just go back to law school like nothing's happened."

"You mean with Jacks and Zoey—"

"Christ, no!" His blaspheme was purposeful and loud, and he watched her upper lip purse. *Screw her.* He refused to hear the sound of their names joined together like a fucking couple. "It has nothing to do with them." He ignored the disbelief on her face. After all, it wasn't a complete lie. "The attacks in New York and Washington—I need to do *something*."

She continued to stare at him, seemingly

unperturbed by the uncomfortable silence between them. "Oh, I see," she said finally, sounding unconvinced.

Gray drew in a silent breath. He doubted she did see but he wasn't going to elaborate. He didn't want to share with her how the image of the towers collapsing was imprinted on his brain. How, even though he knew he couldn't compare the pain of Zoey's betrayal, and his family's betrayal, with what had happened days ago in New York, he also couldn't stop thinking that it felt like an external manifestation of the devastation ripping through his soul. Except with this he could fight back. He could take control of his life and fight the monsters back.

"Have you told your father?"

"Yes, earlier this morning."

"The army—"

"No, the marines."

"Oh. Well, what can I say?"

"Good luck?" He took no pleasure as he watched her wince at his sardonic retort. *Fuck this.* Turning away, he reached for the door handle.

"Grayson."

"What?" He turned back impatiently.

She stiffened, her shoulders going back. "Goodbye then." Her eyes probed his, but it had been years since his mother was able to see into his heart. "And good luck." She inclined her head, and without waiting for his response, walked off toward the kitchen. He waited a few seconds but she didn't look back.

"Mother," he called after her.

She stopped and turned to look at him.

"Why did you adopt me?" Gray's stomach rolled.

Why did he ask her that?

Her head cocked and she studied him.

Goddamn fool. What was wrong with him, to give her an opening like this? Angrily, he curled his hand around the brass door handle.

"Your grandfather brought you to me." Her brittle voice froze Gray's hand. His eyes flashed back to her. "You were a good baby," she said steadily. "As good as I could have hoped for. But you weren't mine." Her contemplative gaze held his for another fraction of time, and then she turned and walked out.

Gray blinked rapidly, his hand tightening on the cold brass handle. For a split second his throat closed and he couldn't breathe. *But you weren't mine.* The pain of his mother's rejection reverberated in his head. He thought she'd lost the power to hurt him. *He was fucking wrong!* Struggling to breathe past the burn in his throat, he yanked the door open. Sunlight spilled inside and he ducked his head, his eyes watering. "You weren't mine either," he whispered fiercely and roughly wiped his sleeve across his face.

Reaching for his cases, he stepped outside. Jacks' car was stationary. For some reason, his brother hadn't exited the car. He could see him through the windscreen sitting in the driver's seat, both hands on the steering wheel. Gray glanced at the passenger seat. It was empty. She wasn't here. Randy's truck approached. Breathing easier, he moved quickly down the steps and along the path leading to the driveway. He passed Jacks' car without looking his way. As Randy pulled up, he wasted no time lifting his luggage and tossing it in the back of the truck.

Time to go. Go. Go.

He reached to open the passenger door but stopped when he saw Jacks' car door open in the reflection of the truck window. His brother eased out of his car and stood, looking toward him. Gray stared at his brother's reflection and waited.

"You're leaving," Jacks called to him. It wasn't a question.

What she wants.

What she wants.

Gray reminded himself for the hundredth time that day, this was who Zoey had chosen. His precious girl had suffered enough. Her reason for betraying him no longer mattered. His pain and selfish yearnings also no longer mattered. The only thing he cared about now was that she was allowed to heal. The shadow he'd seen at the funeral was not Zoey. It would destroy him all over again if she let her grief lay waste to herself forever.

The sun beat down on him and rivulets of sweat trickled down his neck. He could do this. *Yes.* He couldn't leave without at least trying. Turning, he strode quickly back to Jacks. "Yes, I'm leaving." He left no room for doubt as he stopped close to his brother and stared intently at him.

Jacks was three years younger than him and much smaller in stature. That didn't mean he was weak. He might have been a scrawny teenager, but his frame had filled out and Gray knew he was deceptively strong. He had the same dark brown eyes as Gerald, their father, but they weren't deep-set like his. They protruded slightly. At school he wore thick glasses that had the effect of magnifying his eyes, giving him a startled appearance. Now, he wore contacts. Unlike Gerald's tanned, weathered skin, Jacks had Margaret's fair complexion. He hated it because during the worst of the summer, he invariably ended up burned. His round face had matured, losing its youthful softness. Except for his chin. It wasn't exactly weak, but it was recessed in such a way that it had a certain fleshy look. There was no doubt his brother had grown up in the six years Gray had been away studying in New Orleans and then New York. Even though he'd been back for brief visits during his study breaks, he hadn't paid attention. Zoey insisted Jacks had gone from nerd to chick magnet. Gray didn't really agree, but then, given what had gone down, he certainly wasn't the expert.

"It's for the best." There was an arrogant finality in Jacks' voice. He looked toward the house. "Mom agrees." His gaze slid back to stare unblinkingly at Gray.

"I don't care what our mother thinks," Gray snarled, heat flushing through his body. "I'm not doing this for her, I'm doing it for Zoey."

"Zoey!" Jacks snarled back. "She wants nothing to do with you."

Gray watched the familiar venomous jealousy eat away at Jacks' calm facade. Lashing out at each other wasn't going to get the job done. He had to keep it together. Swallowing hard, he forced down the anger. "Jacks. Brother. Listen to me, please." Jacks' mouth clamped shut. He took a half step back, the car preventing him from retreating farther. Gray lifted a hand toward him. "I need you to promise me something," he entreated.

Jacks leaned stiffly back against the car. "What?"

Gray let his arm drop to his side and leaned

forward instead. "I need you to promise to do whatever it takes to make sure she flies free and beautiful again. No matter what, don't let this cripple her." Gray wanted to say so much more but he could see the rage darkening his brother's eyes. He stepped back. "I'm trusting you to keep her safe and h-happy." His voice cracked. *Fuck*. It was definitely time to go.

He jerked his head at Jacks and then moved quickly to Randy's truck. Opening the passenger door, he chanced a quick look back. Jacks stood ramrod straight, his arms rigid at his sides.

"She's mine," he shouted at Gray, banging his chest with a fist. "Mine! You don't get to tell me what to do with her."

As his brother advanced, Gray jumped into the truck. "Go," he snapped, slamming the door closed. Randy didn't delay. The truck pulled away and Gray stared ahead, his brother's garbled vitriol lost in the rumble of the accelerating engine.

They drove away from the house, through the rolling green pastures lined on both sides of the road with white pipe and cable fencing. As they neared the gated entrance, he saw his father riding toward them.

"Want to wait?" Randy asked.

His father slowed his horse to a trot and then a walk. He lifted his hat from his head, using it to wave. *Yeah*. That was his dad. Gerald Walker. A quiet presence hovering in the shadow of his wife. Sometimes comforting but rarely more than that.

"No." Gray wound down his window. "No need." He waved briefly back at his father and then turned to Randy. "Let's go."

They turned onto the main road and Gray sank

down into the leather seat, letting the warm wind from the open window blow over him. It was done. Over. He doubted he'd return home for a long time. If ever.

Resting his head back, he closed his eyes. Home. He wasn't sure where that was anymore. But it sure as hell wasn't here.

Chapter Three
A Distant Echo

Rooms of Doctor Rose Martin, Psychiatrist, Back Bay, Boston
August, Fourteen Years Later
Zoey

Rose Martin's small reception area was exactly the same as I remembered it. Warm and inviting. But with a graceful elegance, much like the woman herself. Tall, sash windows looked out on the busy street. The thick glass allowed sunlight to brighten the room, but successfully muted the noisy traffic. I sat, precariously balanced on the edge of the tan leather two-seater, my fingers curled like claws over my knees. I was three minutes early. The door to Rose's office was closed but I knew in exactly three minutes it would open.

Breathe. She's never late.

I looked down. My knuckles were white from gripping my kneecaps, but it didn't disguise the faint trembling that lived like red ants under my skin. Real or imagined? *I didn't know!* Shoving my hands between my legs, I squeezed.

Come on. Come on.

Over the last few days, debilitating stress had hijacked every muscle in my body. I rolled my head from side to side, trying to ease the rigidity in my neck. A trapped nerve made itself known near my shoulder blade. Trying to ignore the twinge, I began to count the tiny orange and navy squares that made up the geometric pattern on the rug. I was on square fifty-eight when Rose interrupted me.

"Zoey."

I shot to my feet. "Rose!" I was momentarily breathless. I hadn't heard her office door open.

She beckoned to me, standing by the door. "Come in, child."

I smiled. I was thirty-three and she still called me "child." I entered her spacious office and glanced around. My muscles relaxed a tiny bit and I found myself blinking hard to hold back tears. I knew what it was. Nothing of consequence had changed since I'd last been in this room. A room where Rose helped me hang on to my sanity. And the comfort of that was overwhelming.

"Come, sit down. We have much to catch up on. It's been a long while since I last saw you."

"That's a good thing, isn't it?" I winced, embarrassed by my sarcastic tone.

"That depends on how well you're doing, my dear." Rose ignored my rudeness, her own tone gentle and inquiring. Again, exactly how I remembered.

I answered frankly. "That's a tricky question, Rose."

She smiled and gestured at her leather couch, a replica of the one in her reception area. "Sit, Zoey. Please."

I sank into the soft leather. It had been a long time since I'd last sat here, but it felt eerily familiar. During my student days at Harvard and then my residency at Boston Children's Hospital, my life spun out of control.

It was my sessions here with Rose that became the lifeline that pulled me from the dark, filthy hole I'd buried myself in.

"You're still at Boston Children's?"

I nodded, a smile tugging at my mouth. I loved my job. *Oh, God. What will I do if I lose my job?*

My head jerked and I winced, rubbing hard at the sharp pain that shot through my neck. *Dammit.* I was so distracted with my own crap, I'd given myself whiplash. And I'd missed Rose's question. "Sorry, what was that?"

Her warm-brown eyes narrowed. "I asked if you've remained with pediatric surgery."

"Umm, yes and no," I mumbled, gently rolling my neck. "I spent most of the last year in AFCC. I was offered a fellowship in neonatal surgery. It was good." I relaxed back into the couch. "I'm still there. They've offered me a permanent position."

"A challenging field."

I nodded, not sure if she was asking a question. With Rose, I could never be sure.

"Challenging enough?"

That was definitely a question.

"I save lives, Rose. Lives that haven't even been born yet." I surged upright and perched on the edge of the couch. "There are very few surgeons in the world qualified to do what I do."

"I know that." She lifted a placating hand.

I searched her face. The only sign I could see of the seven years passed since we last met were a few more lines around her eyes and mouth. Her hair was shorter, a neat bob tucked into her jawline. It was still a rich chestnut, any gray hidden by expensive hair color. She radiated calm and a generosity of spirit that had always succeeded in breaking through my fears. And my rage.

"Yes, I guess you do," I sighed.

"I had no intent to offend you," she said apologetically.

A guilty lump lodged in my throat. Rose was a leading psychiatrist, not only in Boston but also in the country. And she was my friend. Patronizing her intelligence was beneath me. "I'm sorry. Really. It's not you, it's me. I'm a little touchy today."

"A little?"

I grimaced at her wryness. "Okay. A lot."

"You're clearly upset. You wouldn't be here if you weren't."

My eyes flicked away. *Shit.* I wasn't ready to talk about it.

"Slow, deep breaths, Zoey. And tell me how you've been over the years."

I loved Rose. She always gave me an out. "Better." I sounded feeble. "A lot better," I repeated, adding some backbone to my voice.

"And this time of year, you still find it a struggle?"

"Not as much as I used to. I found a way to manage it." Her gentle scrutiny urged me to explain. "When I completed my surgical residency, I joined Doctors Without Borders. I spent a year in the field with them. When I came back to Boston Children's, part of my deal included consent for me to volunteer six weeks a year in the field with DWB."

"The same six weeks every year?"

I inhaled sharply. *Rose was quick.* "Yes." My tone was a challenge.

But she ignored it. "It's August and yet here you

are, in Boston?"

I grabbed a throw cushion and shoved it into my lap. "I can't leave right now. Our department head is on a personal leave of absence. His wife passed away." The cushion crumpled under my kneading fingers. "My backlog of patients is too long for me to get away."

"I understand. How are you coping? Still getting nightmares?"

"Not so much." A small line knitted her brow. I ducked my head and began to smooth out the creases I'd made in the cushion. "They're worse this time of year, but then you know that."

"No, I don't know that. It's been years, and it makes me sad you still suffer so."

A tic started to pulse behind my eyelid. I jumped up and moved across to the wide picture window. The view of Clarendon Street was picturesque. At this time of year, the trees lining the neatly paved sidewalks were lush and green, offering a patchwork of shade to the busy stream of pedestrians.

"Are you going to tell me what brings you here today?"

"I got a letter from Jacks." I studied the sprawl of tables under the red umbrellas on the opposite side of the road. It was a Snappy Sushi, overflowing with customers. I liked observing others. It made me curious to watch strangers focused on their day while I remained apart. A life interrupted. Again.

"Jackson Walker still writes to you?"

I turned at the surprise in her voice. "Yes. Not as regularly as he used to. It tapered off over time. He only writes once a year, now." I hugged the cushion. "On my birthday."

Her eyes widened. "A cruel reminder?"

Was it? I dampened my suddenly dry lips. "I don't think he means it to be. He sends me an update on the farm. A little about himself." I shrugged. "He always ends by wishing me a happy birthday."

"Why do you think he does that?"

A bead of sweat trickled down my neck. "I don't know, maybe to be polite?" She frowned in puzzlement, and I rushed on before she could say anything. "The panic attacks have come back. They're worse than they've been in years."

"I'm sorry, Zoey. I know how difficult they are for you." She shifted, settling her hands in her lap. "What do you think has triggered them again?"

"The letter."

"The letter?"

"Jacks' letter."

"But you said you receive them every year." Her voice held faint confusion. "What's different about this one?"

I turned back to the window. My neck was wet with perspiration, which was weird because my hair was up in its normal tight bun. I clutched the cushion and squinted into the sun. I could just make out the clock tower of the old Baptist church. "He's getting married," I said softly.

"And this upsets you?"

"No, I'm happy he's found somebody who loves him. Somebody to build a life with." I took a shaky breath and looked over my shoulder. "He wants to buy Morgan Farm."

"Aah," she sighed. "And that's what has upset you."

My knees trembled, and I clutched at the window frame. "I guess so."

"Come and sit down." My vision blurred, and I blinked fiercely. "Please, child. Sit before you fall."

Dammit. I'd shed too many tears in this room.

And I refused to shed one tear more. Resting my face against the cool glass pane, I sucked in a deep breath. And just as Rose taught me all those years ago, I let the air flow out, one slow puff at a time. When I was sure the threat of tears was gone, I moved back to the couch and sat.

"Better?"

I nodded and carefully placed the throw cushion on the seat beside me.

Rose clasped her hands in front of her. "In the last few years, have you had any gains in your memory loss?"

"No." Something ugly turned in my stomach.

"Have you tried—?"

"No!" I shoved out my palm, desperate for her to stop. "I'm sorry—"

"It's all right, don't be sorry." Her voice was soft, soothing. She leaned forward, her face creased with concern. "Remember, when you are here you can be as upset as you need to be. Always."

My brain stuttered. *Stupid. So stupid!* But I had no control over the ice-cold dread unfurling in my core and snaking out to infect every part of me, including my traitorous brain. It happened, without fail, every time I tried to remember. *I was such a joke.* The brilliant Zoey Morgan, child prodigy, reduced to a cliché. *Living in my own fucking purgatory.*

"I don't know what to do. You have to help me.

Yesterday, I had to leave the canteen. I was eating lunch and my hands started to shake. For God's sake! Where is the nightmare in eating lunch?"

"Buried in the chicken salad?" The corner of her mouth quirked.

For a second I froze, and then a ray of warmth pierced the cold. "Funny," I muttered.

"Not really." Her smile was rueful.

The warmth inside me turned tepid, and I shivered. "I'm frightened. Really frightened. This is affecting my w-work." My voice broke, and I snatched up the cushion. *My work.* The only place I was in control. Safe. "Fourteen years, Rose. It's been fourteen damn years. How much longer is my brain going to keep punishing me?"

"You know better than that, child!" Rose's chin lifted in exasperation. "We've spoken about this before. You have a severe case of dissociative amnesia. You understand what this means, and yet you insist on blaming yourself."

"You said I would remember, over time. That hasn't happened. Who else am I to blame?"

"I also said the first part of the process when trying to recover your memories, is to create a safe place for yourself."

I waved my hand, indicating her office. "This room is safe."

"No, it isn't. Not for you. It's a treatment room—"

"Where you've helped me so much. Why can't you help me with the rest?" I swallowed hard, trying to ease the pain in my throat.

"Because real safety is something you have to feel, deep down in your psyche. A place, a person—"

"A person?" My breath hitched. She continued to talk, but I only half listened.

"Yes. Somebody who represents such a sense of safety and protection to you, your mind can let go of the fortress it's built around itself." Her astute gaze narrowed, and I tried to focus my attention. "Every year around this time, you head overseas into one war zone or another."

"We've been through this already. It's my way of relieving stress." I waved a hand dismissively, struggling to let go of the unfocused image. It hovered in my mind, like a distant echo.

"No, it's you running. Running from your past. It's like you're still blaming yourself. Like you don't want to be innocent."

I shook my head, simultaneously pushing away the image and refuting Rose's claim. "I know better than that. Or should I say, my head knows better. But in my heart, in my dreams—" I shoved the cushion away and slid forward. "All the smarts in the world doesn't control that."

"And hiding away from it—that doesn't control it either, does it?" Rose's brow arched. I knew she was right, but that didn't stop my body tensing, readying itself for battle. "Why do you feel the need to keep punishing yourself? Don't you think you've suffered enough?" She reached toward me, her voice beseeching.

I cringed, teetering on the edge of the couch. "It doesn't matter how much I suffer; it can never be worse than what *they* suffered."

"You mean your family?"

"Of course. Who else?" I snapped.

"And do you believe they would want that from you? For you to be suffering all these years?"

My stomach cramped. *I needed her to stop.*

"Did you love them, Zoey?"

Love them!

Agony coated my throat. "How can you ask me that?" I croaked. "I loved them more than anything."

"So if Noah had lived instead of you, would you want him to suffer like you? Or for your parents to suffer?"

"*No!*" My denial was piercing. Rose flinched, but I didn't care. At that moment I hated her.

"So why do you believe they want you to suffer? They loved you, Zoey, didn't they?"

I nodded, my head jerking painfully. *Yes, they loved me. I knew that without a doubt.*

"So why have you made their love about suffering?" She looked at me searchingly. "About punishment for surviving?"

I gripped the cushion so violently I felt a seam give way. "Because as long as I don't remember, I can't bring their killers to justice." My eyes filmed over and I knew this time I wouldn't be able to stop the tears. "My own fear lets them run free," I cried. "How awful is that? *How fucking weak is that?*"

****

Zoey's Studio Apartment, Beacon Street, Boston
One Week Later

Oh my God! I nearly killed that baby.

A baby who hadn't been born yet. A tiny fetus still living in his mother's womb. A baby who had yet to take one breath of air, one single suckle at his mother's breast. And I nearly sliced him with my scalpel.

I hugged my knees tighter to my chest.

What am I going to do?

What the hell am I going to do?

My body rocked as terror swamped me.

This wasn't okay. This really wasn't close to okay.

I burrowed deeper into the chair and glared around my apartment. This was the only piece of decent furniture I owned, besides my bed. And calling it an apartment was overstating. It was a studio. One square room that housed my bed, a fireplace, a wobbly bookcase, a simple wooden table with one wooden chair pushed up against the window. And this armchair. There was a tiny alcove that pretended to be the kitchen. And another tiny alcove with a basin, a toilet, and a shower made for very small people.

I moved here twelve years ago when Uncle Richard and Aunt Sarah finally agreed I was healthy enough to move out of their house and into a place of my own. It belonged to a doctor friend of Richard's who bought it for his daughter. She had graduated and gone to work in Chicago, and rather than sell it, he wanted to rent it out. At the time I was a med student, and this was the perfect haven for me. I loved my aunt and uncle, and I loved their teenage kids. I was deeply grateful they all helped to pack me up, move me out of Texas and bring me to the sanctuary of their home in Boston, far from the demons that had slowly been winning the war for my sanity. But after a year of living with them, I'd been desperate to have my own space. A place where I didn't have to pretend I was perfectly okay.

So I signed the lease and moved in here. And I never moved out. Why would I when it was perfect for me? Close to the hospital, and close to great park areas where I was a regular runner and cyclist. It came with heat, hot water and electricity included. Good security. When I finished my residency I thought of moving to a better place. A bigger place. For about one second. Why did I need a better, bigger place? After all, I spent most of my time at the hospital. This place was just for sleeping. I did treat myself and buy a new bed. And a new microwave. That was it. And it was perfect.

Or so I convinced myself.

But I wasn't a complete halfwit. I knew I stayed because it was familiar. And because it wasn't a home. It was never going to be a home. I didn't want one. Home was for family and I didn't have one.

I grabbed my cell phone from where I'd tucked it under my leg and swiped it open. I started scrolling through contact names, but my hand was trembling so severely, I kept going past the number I was looking for.

Dammit!

I shoved the phone into my lap and stared blindly around the room. It was getting dark, but I had no urge to get up and switch on a light. If I closed my eyes, I knew his image would appear. It had strengthened over the last week, gaining an addictive sort of clarity.

As soon as I left Rose's office, the distant echo I'd tried to ignore had mutated into a loud clamor. I'd broken into a jog when a reel of images flashed into my head, moving too quick for me to focus. By the time I arrived home, I was sprinting. Heart pounding and sweat soaking through my neat white blouse, I unlocked and relocked my door, and moved quickly to sit on the edge of my bed. Like a damaged piece of film, the spool in my head stuttered to a stop between two frames, flickering from one image to the other, and back again.

Images of him.

Grayson Walker.

Gray!

My heart beat so painfully it felt like it had doubled in size, filling both sides of my chest. The moment Rose talked about a person being a safe place, she triggered images of Gray. In my head. In my heart. *In my goddamn soul!*

But I couldn't go to him.

No. I didn't deserve him.

But what else was I going to do?

I nearly killed my patient this morning. The panic attack was so bad, my hand started to tremble during the critical surgery I was performing on a seven-month pregnant mother. On her tiny, baby boy still resting in her belly. *Jesus!* I'd tried so hard to get a handle on it but the harder I tried, the more my hand trembled. For the first time in my surgical career, I had to step away from the table.

No. I might not deserve him, but I refused to allow that to stop me. I was losing my mind and he was the only person I could think of to help me. There was nobody else I trusted.

I needed to face my demons.

I needed to remember.

I sucked in a deep, shaky breath. *I needed to go home*. And the only person I trusted to take me there was Gray.

Help me, Gray. Please.

I squeezed my eyes shut and immediately saw his

face. It flickered. The same two images. Over and over again. In the first he was watching me, his handsome face taut with hunger. His normally, clear blue-gray eyes a deep smokey storm, so wickedly intense they inflamed the desire already scorching through my body, heightening the unimagined pleasure of my first real orgasm. *So hot.* My first orgasm that didn't come from my own hand. My first orgasm with Gray. *Jeez, I was so innocent.*

I trapped my tongue between my teeth, forcing saliva into my dry mouth. His beautiful face faded. Replaced by the other image. This one didn't make my stomach tingle, it made me want to curl up and disappear to a place where the pain stopped. It was how his face looked seconds before he walked away for the last time.

I'm so sorry, Gray. So damn sorry. But I need you. Please, if only in memory of my family. Help me.

My hand was still shaking and it took several attempts before I managed to hit the right number. Resting my cheek on my raised knees, I waited.

After six long rings, he answered. "Yes, hello." His deep Texas drawl sounded so close, he could have been standing in front of me.

"Hello, Gerald? It's Zoey. I need your help."

Chapter Four
Hoping For Fireworks

King Security Headquarters, DUMBO, New York City - Five Days Later
Zoey

It was nearly nine-thirty and I was outside King Security, the company where Gray worked. A taxi dropped me off fifteen minutes ago but I was still there. Cowering against a pillar, staring at the impressive red-brick building on the other side of the cobblestone street. A rich aroma of freshly baked chocolate chip cookies wafted out the door of a nearby café, Pascal's Chocolat! I'd left my breakfast uneaten on the hotel tray this morning. Even the whiff of coffee had sent my stomach into a nervous spasm. But now I was tempted to go inside and treat myself. Anything to delay meeting with Gray.

Gerald refused to give me Gray's home address or cell phone number. I had to push him hard to give me anything at all. He finally caved and sent me the address and telephone number for King Security. I decided not to call and try to talk with Gray. What was the point? He'd probably hang up on me. I needed to see him in person, catch him off-guard.

It was already warm, the sun high enough to prickle my skin. But I snuggled into my lightweight jacket, shivers raising goose bumps all along my arms.

Gray hasn't been home for fourteen years.

This shocking news only made me more nervous. Gerald said the last time they saw Gray was when he returned to Denton for Randy's wedding. I knew when that was. I knew exactly when that was because it was the last time I ever saw him.

I blinked hard, the tic starting up behind my eyelid again. The memory of Gray's last visit was as clear to me as if it happened yesterday. It was two days before Randy's wedding. As was Gray's way, he didn't call ahead, he just showed up. I think he knew if he called, I would find a way to avoid him.

He'd come to see me four times over six years. Each visit we spent no more time together than it took to eat a meal. We would chat, like strangers, until Gray lost patience and began to ask questions. Questions I didn't want to answer. But he would push, and keep pushing until I had no choice but to shut it down. I did this by going mute. Yes, I wouldn't say a word. Eventually, he gave in and let me be. Until the next time, when we would do the macabre dance all over again. He never gave up, not until that last time.

I was in my final year of residency at Boston Children's when he showed up again. He was different this time. Well, more different than the rest. I'd noticed each time he came to visit that he was leaving the gentleness in him behind. I guess the military had that effect.

He never said much about it, but this time I could see a new hardness in him. An edge of steel. His eyes were the same. Always filled with a familiar lightness whenever he looked at me. A searching intensity, more blue than gray. I knew what he was searching for, and I also knew I would never give it to him.

When he came I was at the end of a long shift. He surprised me with a take-out coffee and insisted I talk with him outside. I was working in the ED and didn't want to make a scene. I also didn't want him to see how his unexpected presence devastated me. His visits always shook me deeply, sending me into a whirlpool of self-destructive behavior. This time was much worse. I'd recently fallen off the deep-end and was in intensive therapy sessions with Rose. He had no idea how much I wanted to fall into him, let him hold me, love me. *No fucking idea.* And I needed it to stay that way.

So I was a tight mess as we stood outside in the parking area. He didn't waste time with small talk. He just jumped right in and asked me to go to Randy's wedding with him. I stared, mesmerized by the magnetism of him. He was so goddamn beautiful and I ached for him. Yes, I actually yearned for him. But I also hated him. I hated him for reminding me of what I couldn't have. So I lashed out. Bitter vitriol spewed from my lips, and my chest burned as I watched his eyes shutter. That special light that seemed exclusively for me faded until there was nothing. The pain in my heart was so intense it felt like I was dying. And I was. Because I knew he'd given up on me. I could see it plain as day.

Goodbye, Zoey.

That was all he said before he turned and walked away.

And I hadn't seen him since.

Gerald said Gray was not the same man. "He's built a fortress around himself," he said. I probably contributed to that. But I was desperate, so I took the time to explain to Gerald some of what I was struggling with. I told him I truly believed Gray was the only person who could help me.

"I've run out of options," I said. "Please, Gerald. Maybe if he can help me find my way, I can help him too."

God, who did I think I was? Me, help Gray? What a joke.

"It's time for you both to come home," Gerald said, and I could hear the strain in his voice. "Face the past. So you can heal and move forward with your lives."

So here I was, standing across the way, and it was time to move. My nostrils twitched. Before I could weaken at the temptation wafting from Pascal's, I pushed away from the pillar and crossed the street. The entrance door was made of one-way glass. It was bigger than a standard door and it was locked. There was a small numbered panel with a buzzer. A camera was set discreetly into the brick wall about three feet above it. I steadfastly ignored the churning in my stomach and reached for the buzzer.

And was forced to jump up against the wall as the door swung open.

"Shit! Sorry, sugar. Didn't see you there."

Oh my Lord! Tawny eyes gleamed down at me. I knew I was gawping but there was nothing I could do about it.

"Can I help you, sugar?" His voice was a deep rumble. "You looking for somebody?"

I couldn't get my tongue to work. The man had an otherworldly beauty, his skin a rich copper-brown and his lips—*oh my*—thick and sensual. And smirking at me.

Talk, woman. "Uh…I'm uh…looking for Grayson Walker."

"He expecting you?"

"No." I gulped, still trying to unstick my tongue from the roof of my mouth.

"What's your name, sugar?"

My jaw tightened. *You may be gorgeous but you're too damn forward.* "What's yours, *sugar*?" I drawled.

Golden eyes pinned me in place. *Holy moly.* He was like a cat, not a pussycat, a mountain cat.

"This should be entertaining," he muttered and held the door open. "C'mon inside. My name's Tane. I'll take you to him."

I sucked in a breath and careful not to touch him, stepped inside. The door swung shut, and he led me to the elevator, which must have still been on the lobby because it opened as soon as he pressed the button. Indicating for me to enter ahead of him, he followed close behind and used a card to swipe against a security panel. As he pressed the button for the first floor, a man's voice called out.

"Hold up!"

The mountain cat who called himself Tane reached out to stop the elevator door closing.

"Thanks, man. I'm already late for the meet with King."

I took an involuntary step back as a very tall, very hot, hulk of a man stepped inside. His eyes glanced over me and then snapped back. They were deep midnight-navy, striking and perfect—like the rest of him. Even his hair was hot, dark-blond and pulled back in a rough ponytail. *Jeez!* He looked like Thor.

"Who's this?" His eyes sparkled with curiosity.

I pressed against the back wall of the elevator.

"She's here for Gray."

"Really," he drawled.

Yes, really. I was obviously the brunt of some inside joke. Gritting my teeth, I studiously ignored them and stared sideways at my reflection in the mirrored wall. My unruly hair was sleeked back into its usual bun, pinned at my nape. Not a tendril out of place. I took in my outfit. Dark skinny jeans, a simple white shirt with a lace collar, and a lightweight black blazer. Neat. Boring? I flicked a glance at the two men who were doing nothing to hide their frank appraisal of me. *I looked so plain standing next to them.*

The elevator stopped and the door slid silently open.

"After you." Tane waved, a slight quirk pulling at his sensual mouth.

I stepped out and immediately forgot about the hot distractions behind me.

Gray!

He was behind the reception desk, leaning over a computer screen, and discussing something with the receptionist. He glanced up to check who was exiting the elevator. I had no doubt he knew me immediately because his brows snapped together, recognition clear on his face. His eyes tracked me as I approached.

"Good morning, may I help you?"

I tore my gaze from Gray's to stare at the receptionist. He was slim, dark-eyed, and so perfectly groomed he looked like he'd been airbrushed for a GQ cover. His brow arched, waiting for my response. I ignored him and looked back at Gray, who remained frozen. Like a still-life, one arm resting on the back of the receptionist's chair, the other bracing himself on the desk. Only now, his face was blank. My stomach tried to launch into my chest. *Blank*! I didn't know how else to describe it. *Dear God, please let my face be blank too*. But I knew it wasn't.

Gray!

My heart raced. It was a cliché but it was true. I could feel it pumping in my chest. Gray was even more handsome than I remembered. His dark hair was short, but not military short. It was sleekly styled, like his clothing. Practical, but his jeans were definitely designer. He was more built than I remembered, the power in his body clearly defined by the silky black T-shirt hugging his torso. He'd always been confident; now it was something else. Something that lifted the hair all over my body. But my heart didn't care. It beat wildly. Recognizing him. Wanting him.

But his face was blank.

"Hello-oo! Do you have an appointment?"

"Cool it, Blake, she's here for Gray."

It was the hunk who looked like Thor that spoke. But like Gray, I paid him no heed. I was locked in a silent battle of wills with Grayson Walker. And I was losing.

Shit. I should have made an appointment.

I sucked in a long breath. *One-one-thousand, two-one-thousand, three-one-thousand…*ever so slowly, I breathed out, never breaking eye contact with him. My heartbeat settled. *Yes.* I could do this; I was a master at control.

Acid trickled up my throat as he pushed away from the desk and straightened to his full height. His fixed gaze never left mine. My hands curled, fingernails digging into my palms. I always remembered his eyes more blue than gray. Gentle and glinting with wicked humor. Not anymore. Now they were slate. Cold and lethal, like the scalpels I used to cut through human tissue.

"How did you know where to find me?"

No greeting? No "lovely to see you, Zoey"?

"Gerald," I croaked.

I swallowed hard, pushing down the pain. My voice was normally husky and low-pitched. Gray used to say it was sultry. I loved that, especially since the huskiness was a result of baby colic. I was a chronic crier as a baby and developed nodules, which in turn created calluses on my vocal cords. So sultry sounded nice, sexy.

I didn't sound sultry now.

My skin goosed as I watched his lips set into a hard line. His mouth was one of the thousand things I loved about him. His upper lip a perfect cupid's bow. His lower one, full and sensual with a marked indent. I used to tease him that he had the mouth of a porn star. And he did. *God! The indescribable pleasure—*

"Do you want?"

What did he say? As usual, I'd let the past smother the present. "I'm sorry—"

"What are you doing here, Zoey?" he repeated, clearly impatient.

Yes, what was I doing here?

He stepped around the desk and my body clenched. It took a lot for me not to retreat. He was imposing. It wasn't his size or height. It was his coldness. He was as compellingly attractive as he was cloyingly terrifying. *Stop it. What was I thinking?* Gray wouldn't hurt me.

Gray would do whatever it took to keep me safe.

"Zoey—"

"I need your help," I blurted.

His lip curled unpleasantly. "You need *my* help?"

I dropped my gaze and made eye contact with the elegant receptionist. He was alert, his dark eyes ablaze with curiosity. I didn't turn to check, but I had no doubt Tane and the blond hunk were also watching. If the situation wasn't so important to me, I'd be amused too.

But this was important. It was everything.

I squared my shoulders. "Look, I'm sorry to surprise you like this, but could we talk privately?"

"That's not necessary," he said bluntly. "Speak to Blake. He'll make an appointment for you to see King. I don't meet with new clients."

What? I gripped my elbows, hugging my arms to my body. "I'm not a client. This is personal, Gray. Please. I need your help."

His lethal gaze narrowed, and I understood what people meant when they say time stopped. Our curious onlookers faded away, and there was only Gray and I. And the years of pain between us.

Who was this man?

He was not the caring, protective boy I grew up with. Neither was he the wildly sexy man I fell in love with. Or the smitten man who fell in love with me. The hair on my neck stood on end and my awareness heightened. This wasn't even the man who kept visiting me in those early years, trying repeatedly to connect with me.

This man was unflinching and totally indifferent to me.

"I can't think of anything I could possibly help you

with. Or want to help you with," he added, like an afterthought.

He sounded so remote, I stepped back before I could stop myself. His eyes flickered. Gray's eyes were the window to his emotions. Another cliché but also totally true. I used to be able to read them and know exactly what he was thinking. Feeling. But not anymore.

My stomach rolled as his beautiful mouth twisted. "For chrissake's, woman! The last time we spoke, you begged me to leave you alone. You accused me of bringing back your worst nightmares." He stabbed a finger at me, his expression hard and unforgiving. "You want more nightmares, Zoey? Is that why you're here? To punish yourself."

Bile shot up my throat and I swallowed desperately.

He'd never know how close he was to the truth.

I took another small step back. His hands were fisted at his sides, and his eyes—they were like tempered steel.

Jesus! He looked like he was ready to attack.

I squeezed my eyes shut, blocking him from sight. Forcing air into my constricted chest, I forced down what felt like burning coals lodged in my throat.

Damn him! If I didn't look at him, I'd be okay.

I kept breathing. Short, sharp breaths. And I just stood there, my eyes closed tight. An image floated just out of reach. Gray, his hand reaching out to me. My pulse quickened. That was the Gray I wanted, needed. Mentally, I reached back, trying to catch his hand, hold on to him. But it was a mirage, a dream. And like all dreams, it fractured into a million different pieces and was gone. Nothing.

It could only have been seconds that I zoned out, but it was all the time I needed. I opened my eyes. This was a stranger standing in front of me. This was not a man I could ever trust to keep me safe. He was absolutely right. There was nothing this Gray had to offer that could help me.

I swallowed again, the pain in my throat becoming a distracting burn. "You're right, this was a mistake." I was grateful my voice wasn't a croak. "I'm sorry for interrupting your day." I felt empty. And filled to the brim with terror of the nightmares I knew were waiting for me. "Goodbye, Grayson." Even I could hear the finality in my voice.

God, I was tired. Too tired for this.

Without meeting his gaze, I nodded at him and turned away. I absently acknowledged the gawkers, and then walked quickly to the elevator. When I pressed the button, it opened immediately. Thank goodness for small mercies. I stepped in and hit the button for the lobby.

"Tane!"

My gaze shot to the big blond who had growled the command. His midnight eyes were locked on me, and he wasn't smiling. Just before the doors closed, the man called Tane slipped between them and joined me inside. The doors shut but the elevator didn't move. I stared at the man that reminded me of a mountain cat. Sweat trickled down my neck but I was freezing. Wrapping my arms around my waist, I tried to hide the full body tremors rippling through me.

"So Tane is it?" I raised an eyebrow and he nodded. "On a scale of one to ten, how entertaining was that for you?"

He flicked his security card over the panel and pressed the lobby button again. "Well, sugar. I was hoping for fireworks."

Fireworks? Not a chance. "When did he get so cold?"

"He's been like that for as long as I've known him." He leaned against the mirror and folded his arms. "I'm guessing you had something to do with that." His tawny eyes glowed, not in accusation but with an unexpected gentleness. Empathy radiated from him and I looked away, fighting back tears.

"Maybe," I muttered. "But the Gray I knew was never ice-cold. He would never turn down somebody who asked him for help." Tears escaped, and I used both hands to roughly wipe at them. "He's become like that all on his own."

"Has he?" The doors slid open and Tane stepped forward, blocking my way. "Come to think of it, he was more of an asshole today than usual." His golden gaze ran over me with unnerving thoroughness.

A pulse of hot anger shot through me. "And it's your business because—" I glared at him but he didn't answer. "Please let me pass."

He waited a moment, and then his far too sexy mouth tipped into a wry smile. "Okay, sugar," he drawled and moved aside.

I slipped past him and hurried out. *Out!*

Somebody upstairs must have been watching from a camera because the street door buzzed open. I didn't stop to think. I pulled the glass door and quickly stepped outside.

I needed to get out.

I needed to get as far away from this place as I could.

Far far away!

****

Gray

Gray sat through King's thirty-minute briefing on the Far East job, listening to every word. But he didn't hear a thing. The ensuing discussion on the best approach to the job was the same. He listened. He participated. But his head wasn't in it. King noticed. So did Luke. Neither brought attention to it. But it wouldn't last. As soon as the war-room emptied, he knew Luke would pounce.

"Gray!"

"Yeah." Mira's dark eyes glowered at him. "I got it," he reassured her. "I'll speak to my CI, and get right back to you."

Her eyes flattened, black and dispassionate. She held his gaze for a long moment, and then without another word, stalked out. He squeezed the back of his neck and grimaced. *Dammit.* She had every reason to be pissed at him. This job was important to her. She'd been chasing leads for years and one had finally popped. If he was going to help her, he needed to be on his game.

"You waiting to get a piece of me too?" Gray eyed Luke who was leaning against the center table, arms folded.

"Not before we get some coffee."

"Fuck coffee. I need a drink."

"It's not even midday," Luke said mildly.

"And so?" Gray's chest burned. *Zoey! Fuck.* "You coming or staying?" he challenged Luke.

"What do you think?" Luke pushed away from the table.

The constriction in Gray's chest lessened as he left the building with Luke. He didn't want to talk about Zoey, but he also didn't want to be alone. *Christ.* The shit rolling around in his head—he could feel the pressure building. Being with Luke wasn't exactly sharing the load, but it went some way to alleviate the pressure, to have his best friend, the man he considered his brother, at his side.

In no time at all, Gray opened the door to The Overhang, their preferred drinking spot in this part of town. It was at the end of Water Street, a block from the Brooklyn Waterfront—and it always had Belgium beer on tap. Like a lot of places in historic DUMBO, there was an upstairs area that included rooftop seating with views over the East River. He didn't even consider that option. The last thing he gave a shit about was fresh air and a scenic view.

Instead, he headed to the far side of the circular bar dominating the room and slid into a discreet corner booth. Luke settled opposite him, relaxing back against the burgundy leather. Gray wasn't fooled. He could read every nuance of Luke's body language, and his friend was anything but relaxed. It didn't matter. Luke was patient. He'd remain silent until Gray gave the signal he was ready.

He was never going to be fucking ready.

He gripped the thick muscle in his neck, trying again to force tension from it.

"Hey, fellas. What can I get you?"

Gray didn't recognize the barman. But it was early in the day, and he couldn't remember a time when he'd been in before midday to drink. *So fucking what!* "Two Belgium's-on-tap. Whatever you've got. And a shot of *Tezón Blanco*."

"I'll take an Americano, black," Luke added.

"Coming right up."

Gray tracked the man as he returned to the bar and went about filling their order. In his peripheral vision, he could see Luke tapping the table with one finger. But he kept his gaze glued to the barman, breathing a silent sigh of relief when he made his way back to them.

"Here you go." He placed their order on the table. "Coffee's on its way."

Gray brushed the slice of lemon off the glass rim and raised his tequila. "Cheers, brother," he said sardonically and knocked back the shot. The drink burned a familiar trail of heat down his gut. The last time he needed a drink this bad was when Luke got shot. And even then, he'd not been anywhere near as desperate for the alcoholic burn as he was now.

He carefully placed his empty glass on the coaster and picked up his cold beer. He indicated to Luke's frothy glass. "You going to look at it or drink it?"

Luke smiled grimly and picked up his beer. His navy eyes narrowed, darker than midnight. "Cheers, brother," he said equally sardonically and took a long swallow.

Gray tipped his own glass and brought it to his mouth. The bile that kept trying to work its way up his throat had left him parched. Closing his eyes, he drank. And didn't stop until the glass was empty.

"Black Americano."

He opened his eyes as the barman placed the steaming mug in front of Luke.

"Thanks, man," Luke murmured.

"Same again." Gray waved his hand at his empty glasses. "Hunt?"

"I'm fine."

Gray shrugged. "Just me, then," he said to the barman.

"You going to talk to me?" Luke asked.

Gray again tracked the barman as he retreated behind the bar. "Nope. Not about this."

"I know you, Gray. And I know what I saw in your eyes when you first caught sight of her—"

"Christ, shut it!" He slammed his hands on the table and glared at Luke.

Neither spoke. Silence reigned while the barman served Gray another round. And then continued while he tossed down his second shot of tequila. Gray wasn't concerned. The silence wasn't uncomfortable. Luke knew what he was about and would wait.

"She's the same girl who fucked you up all those years ago, isn't she?"

Guess Luke wasn't so patient after all.

Gray lounged back against the booth, waiting for the tequila to work its magic.

"In the Marines," Luke persisted. "Every break you'd disappear. Come back all fucked up. Never speak about it. She do that to you?"

"It wasn't her fault." *Dammit.* He still instinctively jumped to her defense. "Really bad shit went down. The worst."

Luke sipped his beer and waited. Gray knew he'd wait all day if that's what it took. He might as well get it done.

"She got engaged to Jacks. I left home, joined the

marines. She broke off the engagement, went to Harvard. I'd go and visit, try and break through. She'd keep sending me away." *Hell, he sounded like a whining teenager.* But his stomach ached like a son-of-a-bitch. "The last time I saw her, it got ugly." He shrugged and picked up his beer. "It was best not to go back again."

"Best for who?" Luke asked.

Gray hesitated, holding his beer aloft. "Both of us," he said after a while.

"She's in trouble. You gonna do nothing?"

"*Fu-uuck!*" He banged his glass down and raked his hands through his hair.

"Yeah," Luke sighed. "Listen. You're not going to believe this, but she's staying at The Palace."

"You're shitting me?"

"Nope. Tane followed her."

Gray sat back, folding his arms. "You're like a bunch of old crones, always sticking your noses where they don't belong."

"Happy to be of service," Luke quipped.

Gray shook his head. "You're serious, The Palace?"

"Yeah. Crazy shit." He leaned forward, pushing away his cooling coffee. "My crap with Katya started with that damn shootout at The Palace—"

"Bullshit! Your troubles with Katya started well before she arrived at The Palace."

"And yours didn't with Zoey?" Luke waggled his eyebrows. "They started eons ago."

"Fuck!"

Luke grinned at Gray. "Oh yeah, bro. I get the feeling you're gonna be doing a lot of that."

Gray's jaw clenched. It wasn't funny.
Bloody hell!
It was anything but funny.

Chapter Five
That Was Then and This Was Now

The New York Palace Hotel, Madison Avenue, NYC
Zoey

I pulled the last blouse from the wardrobe and moved back to the bed. My clothes were spread chaotically across the decorative bed cover. *Darn-it!* Why had I bothered to unpack all my stuff last night? *Because you thought you'd be here for a whole lot longer.* I gave an imaginary finger to the irritating voice in my head and flung the blouse alongside my barely-packed suitcase. *How could I have gotten it so stupendously wrong?*

Turning away, I yanked at the pins securing my tight bun. I had a whopping headache. My hair uncoiled and I gently combed my fingers through it.

I'd started to pull clothes from the wardrobe the moment I returned to the hotel. I was leaving for Texas, with or without Grayson Walker. And based on this morning's fiasco, it was obvious I would be traveling alone. But my brain was mush, and I seemed unable to complete the simple job of packing my suitcase. Pushing a load of T-shirts aside, I slumped down on the bed.

Okay, Zoey. Think.

Who was that man? Did I do that to him? *No!* I hurt him, but that was years ago. Why would he hang on to that hurt?

I did. The truth whispered through my head. *I still can't let go of the pain.*

But he was mean!

Okay. Yes. He was mean. But maybe I deserved it. Of course he was pissed at me. I accused him of causing my worst nightmares. I sent him away and told him to never come back.

Dammit!

Dammit. Dammit.

I jumped up and grabbed a hair-tie from the bedside table, roughly securing my hair in a loose ponytail. Gerald had warned me about how much Gray had changed and I'd ignored it. *I was a selfish bitch.* I strolled into his workplace without any warning. I could actually see his defense mechanism slot into place. It was when his face went blank. But instead of fighting hard to break through to him, I turned tail and ran, like the coward I was.

Knock. Knock.

Who was that?

Knock. Knock. Knock.

"Okay, I'm coming." Maybe it was an early turndown. I opened the door. "I don't need a...oh!" *Gray*! Adrenaline spiked through me.

"You going to let me in?"

I clung tightly to the doorframe, keeping my other hand firmly on the half-opened door.

"Zoey?" His face tightened with impatience. He'd put on a navy-blue tailored jacket. It smartened up his jeans and T-shirt. It also brought out the blue in his eyes.

"Are you going to be mean to me?"

His brow arched. A sliver of emotion glinted in the depths of his gaze. "Open the door. We need to talk."

My toes curled into the carpet. I looked a mess. "The room's a m-mess." I coughed, clearing the frog from my throat. "I'm…uh…busy packing." His eyes drifted down to my bare feet then slowly retraced a path to my face. *Crap.* I was blushing. The corner of his mouth turned up. It was only the teensiest-tiniest little bit. But it was still a smile.

I stepped back and opened the door wide. His eyes narrowed and he hesitated for a moment. My warm flush cooled as I watched his mouth harden, obliterating all trace of that tiny quirk. Before I could change my mind, he stepped past me and walked inside.

Okay, then.

I closed the door and took a fortifying breath. He gave the chaos on my bed a cursory glance before moving over to the window. My room was fairly high up, so the view over Midtown Manhattan was something special.

"The last time I was in one of these rooms, it was a bloodbath." He turned to face me.

"Excuse me?" I stood behind the dressing-table chair, gripping the back of it.

"My brother's woman got caught up in some bad shit. Some of it went down here."

His brother? "Is she okay?"

"She is now."

"Your brother? You're not talking about Jacks—"

"Christ, no!"

"You said your brother—"

"I meant my real brother." He took a step forward. "The man who has my back. Not that piece of shit!"

I sucked in a harsh breath. Hostility poured off him, from his balled fists to his taut neck. Even his language was aggressive. Gray rarely cursed, and never in front of me.

But that was then and this was now.

And as I'd already deduced, this was definitely not the same man. Just as I wasn't the same woman. Not by a long shot. My grip on the chair loosened. "I'm sorry," I said softly, not knowing what else to say.

"You're leaving?" It sounded like an accusation.

I stared at the mess on my bed. "Um…yes."

He jammed his hands on his hips. "You said you needed help."

"It doesn't matter, Grayson."

"The name's Gray, you know that, Zoey. Always Gray." He took another step closer, and my heart stuttered. "What trouble are you in?" he said gruffly.

"It really doesn't matter," I insisted. "You were right, there's nothing you can help me with."

"You obviously thought differently or you wouldn't be here in New York."

"I was *wrong*," I said loudly. "I should never have come."

His eyes narrowed. "You're never wrong about anything."

Heat flushed through me and I leaned over the chair. "Really, Gray. You of all people can say that!"

"*Christ*, woman!" He stepped right up to me. "I'm here. I'm prepared to listen. Isn't that what you want?"

His scent slammed into me. *Oh, my God.* It was musky and spicy and something else.

"Zoey. What the hell?"

"I need a moment." I'd been wrong. His eyes

weren't cold. They were dark-slate again, but far from cold. A storm seethed in their depths. "I'm sorry but you have to give me a moment. I need the bathroom," I lied.

"Jesus Christ! Fine, go." He waved impatiently.

I let go of the chair and literally scampered into the bathroom.

Holy shit!

I wasn't lying. I might not need the bathroom, but I did need a time-out. I sat on the toilet seat and sucked air deep into my lungs.

One-one-thousand, two-one-thousand, three-one-thousand...

My breath stuttered. My calming trick wasn't working, and I needed to think this through fast. Gray's patience was obviously shot. If I didn't get out there soon, he'd probably leave.

Good riddance.

If he left, I'd never see him again.

No! I hugged my stomach.

Okay. Okay. He's aggressive. Hostile. But he was here. I hugged my stomach tighter.

I didn't want him to leave.

Gray was here. He was offering to listen. That was a good start. Wasn't it?

I stood and flushed the toilet. Rinsing my hands at the vanity, I stared at my left hand. I did that a lot, the memory of that ring on my finger taunting me.

Why? Why did I betray Gray?

Nausea swirled and a familiar fear rolled up from that dark place that lived inside me.

Dammit. Not now.

I hunched over the vanity and flicked water on my

clammy face. The knots in my stomach eased, but I didn't move, letting the cool water continue to run over my wrists. Everything was going to be okay. I might be broken, but I had a strong sense the man in my room was also broken. And I'd had a lot to do with that. I promised Gerald I'd handle Gray with care. And I would.

I turned off the tap and reached for a towel.

Once, a long time ago, I was his perfect butterfly. I wasn't that anymore, and I couldn't fix that. Familiar despair hollowed my chest. *I'd never be his butterfly again.* But like in my dream, Gray was reaching out, even if his hand felt an ocean length away. And for the sake of both of us, I needed to reach back and try to connect with him.

I dried my face. *Yuck.* The towel was soiled with makeup so I tossed it in the bath. Using my fingers, I quickly wiped away the smeared mascara under my eyes, and taking one more deep breath, exited the bathroom. Gray was at the window again.

"I'm sorry about that," I said.

He turned, his eyes immediately zeroing in on my face. "You okay?"

I grabbed onto the concern in his voice. "I'm fine. I just need some time to sort myself out."

He crossed the room. "How much time?"

The storm clouds in his eyes had faded, but his gaze was still intense. Searching. My knees wobbled because I had an inkling of what he saw. "How about dinner?" I said huskily.

He didn't hesitate. "Sure, dinner. I'll pick you up at seven-thirty."

Thank you.

"Finish unpacking," he ordered, nodding at my suitcase.

Whatever.

He gave me another penetrating stare. "Seven-thirty, Zoey. Don't be late." Then he walked past me. Opened the door. And was gone.

Chapter Six
Strands of Fire

King HQ Building, DUMBO
Grayson Walker's Apartment
Gray

Son-of-a-bitch!

Gray reached back, grabbed his T-shirt, and yanked it off. He tossed it in the wash-basket and quickly stripped off his jeans.

Zoey. Shit.

Seeing her was like being hit by a high-speed bullet train. He desperately needed a long, hot shower to put all the pieces of himself back together. And to rebuild his defenses before he had to face her again at dinner. He pulled off his underwear and reached into the luxurious glass cubicle to flip on the hot water. He loved his shower. *Hell.* He loved his bathroom. Walnut-brown flooring, dark-wood cabinetry, gleaming copper taps, and polished white marble tiles. King spared no expense when he kitted out the residences in his building. When he'd moved out of Luke and Katya's house in February, King immediately offered him an apartment. Gray knew he offered the apartments to key employees only. He was a key member of King's elite team, but he was still grateful to the arrogant asshole. The apartment rocked.

He stepped under the pounding hot water and

groaned. *Yeah.* Lowering his head, he closed his eyes. Immediately her image slid into his mind. She'd changed. And not for the good. He'd recognized her the moment she stepped from the elevator. Even with her hair scraped back and those godawful demure clothes she was wearing, he knew exactly who she was. But that woman was not his Zoey. She was too slender. Too neat. And too damn still.

Christ!

He rolled his neck and shoulders, trying to loosen the taut muscles. Yeah. She was too damn still and it made him hellish uneasy. Zoey was never still. She constantly paced when she talked, gesticulating in earnest. Teasing. Laughing. She was a slip of a thing at five-foot and a bit, but her energy was larger than life. It flowed from her so naturally, it gave the impression she was taller than she actually was. Well, that's what he had always thought. The nervous woman clutching at the chair in her hotel room—so fucking fragile. No, that was not his Zoey.

Gray braced himself against the wall. Hot water pounded his chest. *Fuck-it.* Who was he kidding? She had never been *his Zoey.*

Even now, after all this time, she still had the power to fuck with his head. Just like the summer he'd fallen for her. He'd stopped by the Morgans to let them know he was home, and Zoey opened the door. She flipped her unruly flame-red hair and peeped at him through thick, golden lashes. POW! In an instant, he was gone for her. *Totally fucking gone.* His sweet Pippi Longstocking, the kid he loved like a baby sister, was no more. Like a butterfly emerging from its silken cocoon, Zoey had shed her gangly immaturity and blossomed into a beautiful, sultry woman.

She was nineteen years old, five years younger than him. A captivating butterfly. His butterfly.

Or so he'd believed.

****

Walker Ranch, Denton County, Texas
14 August 2001. Just Before Midnight
Gray

"I love you, Gray."

Gray pulled Zoey deeper into his embrace. He loved hearing that timbre in her voice. Low-pitched, husky, like an erotic whisper. And when she uttered those words to him, his cock always responded. Hardening. Demanding. He gazed into her upturned face. So cute and adorable. And bewitching. She was like the girl next door and yet nothing like the girl next door. A sensual contradiction.

"I love you too, pretty butterfly," he whispered against her lips.

Her tongue darted out and flicked over his lower lip. Saliva flooded his mouth. He groaned and covered her lips with his own. She immediately went on tiptoes, arching into him. *Oh yeah.* He loved her body. She was so much smaller than him, but each soft curve was a perfect cushion for his harder frame. And he needed more. Cupping the back of her head, he bunched his fingers into the silky weight of her hair. She obliged his urging, angling her head, opening her mouth to him. *Yes.* His tongue entwined with hers, the heady taste of her sinking into him. A sweet intoxication. Incendiary. *Shit.* He had to stop.

Tightening his grip, he eased her head back. "Enough, sweetheart." Her eyes fluttered open. Vivid.

The green so intense they gleamed like precious emeralds. *His tempting witch.* She was panting, her breath a hot tease on his lips. He couldn't resist and gently nibbled her bottom lip, soothing the small bite with his tongue.

"Gray," she sighed into his mouth, her arms tightening around his neck.

The sound of a horse snorting, accompanied by a faint whicker, echoed into the room. It was enough for him to reach up and circle her wrists, pulling them slowly from his neck. "Butterfly, it's late. And we're in the barn."

She let him take a small step back, her wrists resting loosely in his hands. "Can I tell you something?" Her mouth curved into a smile. They were in the tack room, a walled-off extension of the main twelve-stall barn. He hadn't switched the light on, not wanting to alert anybody they were there. But there was no need. There were skylights cut into the high rafters throughout the barn, allowing moonlight to flood the room and bathe Zoey's face in pale beams.

"You can tell me anything." He stroked her inner wrists with his thumbs and smiled. He could feel her pulse. It was beating fast. Like his own.

"I love being here, in the barn with you." Her husky voice wrapped around him. "I saw you once at one of our Fourth of July barbecues. You came out of the hay barn with Sally Ryan." Her pert nose crinkled. "She had hay caught up in her hair. She was laughing, her clothes all mussed."

Darn! He remembered that day. He pulled Zoey closer to him, flattening her hands against his chest.

"You winked at her. I hated her. I wanted to be

her."

"You must have been all of thirteen years old."

"So what." She tilted her head back and pouted. "I didn't care. I still wanted to be her."

Heat radiated from her hands, sending a warm tingle through his chest. *Jeez, he loved her.* "You're her now. What you gonna do about it?"

"Make love to me," she pleaded, leaning into him.

Her eyes were huge, upturned. But she was a kitten, not a cat. "You're so innocent, sweetheart." He brushed her lips with his own.

"No, I'm not," she said. "I made sure of that."

Gray's breath hitched. His fingers circled her wrists. "What the hell are you saying?"

"Don't swear at me!" She lunged back, trying to pull away from him.

His fingers squeezed. "Zoey, what are you saying?"

Her eyes blazed with sudden fury. "Why are you angry? You're always telling me I'm too young for you. Too innocent. Well, I'm telling you, that isn't the case anymore." She strained against his grasp and he let her go, cold dread seeping into his chest.

"Did you give yourself to Jacks?"

"No! I told you, I don't belong to Jacks."

He searched her furious gaze. *Okay. Okay.* Tension leached from him. He believed her. "*I* know that, and *you* know that," he said gruffly. "Jesus, even your father made it clear to me that you and Jacks are only friends." He reached out to cup her cheek. "But Jacks doesn't get it, Butterfly. He's my brother, and I need you to help him understand he has no future with you." Caressing her cheekbone, he watched the fury fizzle from her expressive face.

"I know. It's just that he's been a really good friend." She covered his hand with hers, nuzzling her cheek against his palm. "You've been gone a long time, and he got good at keeping me company."

"I bet." He pulled his hand away.

"It's not like that. Even Noah's been too busy with his girlfriends. The only one who's been around is Jacks."

"What about friends at college?"

"You know how it is." She moved restlessly in front of him. "I was sixteen when I went to UNT. Too young to hang with other freshmen." Her hands moved in agitation. "I'm not whining, it's just how it was. But added to that, I worked like a dog to finish pre-med in three years. That didn't leave time to make friends. And now, my graduating class is celebrating in bars and I'm still nineteen." She moved close to him, her hands on her hips. "Too young to drink. And according to you—" Her chin jutted up. "Too young for sex."

He stared at her. She was pissed. Laughter bubbled inside him but he made sure to check it. *Darn!* She wasn't just pissed, she was horny. Her apple cheeks were flushed. Her wide mouth pursed in a seductive pout. He could relate. He'd had a constant erection for the past six weeks. Even when he wasn't with her, thoughts of her addictive sensuality kept him hard.

She poked out her tongue.

Sweet Jesus!

He bent to eyeball her, and it took every ounce of control not to suck her tongue into his mouth. "Keep that tongue in your mouth if you don't want to find it in mine," he said, his voice rough.

"Damn you, Gray! I'm technically a virgin but I'm not innocent."

"So you keep saying." An unpleasant sensation unfurled in his gut. "Tell me, Zoey, if it's not Jacks, and you insist you're a social misfit, then who's been sniffing around you?"

"Jeez! You don't have to get all riled up," she protested. "There's such a thing as hooking up, you know."

"You hooked up? With who?"

She shuffled uncomfortably and his gut twisted. "Umm...other guys around campus." Her chin jutted up. "It was nothing serious."

What the hell! "Why would you do that?"

Her eyes were huge. Beseeching. "I didn't go all the way."

"That's means nothing." His chest burned but he sucked down his rage when he saw the hurt confusion on her face. Like always, his instinct was to protect her. Shelter her. In so many ways, Zoey was not like other nineteen-year-olds. "Butterfly, help me understand here." He cradled her face, his fingers sliding into her hair. "How can you not value your body, not know how special you are?"

Tears filled her eyes. "But I didn't go all the way. I would never." Gray's insides hurt as her slender fingers curled around his wrists. "That's yours, Gray. Even when you didn't know you loved me, it was always yours."

"I'm happy to hear you say that, sweetheart." He kissed away a tear trailing down her cheek. "But what happened before doesn't matter. Even if you weren't a virgin, it wouldn't matter. Not to me." He kissed her other cheek, her tears a salty burn on his tongue. "It only matters you share yourself with somebody who means something to you. You understand?"

Her mouth quivered.

"C'mere." He wrapped her into his arms. She slipped her hands behind him, clutching handfuls of his shirt. "I'm easy on a lot of things, but not this," he said softly. "From now on, this body belongs to me. And I don't share. Tell me you understand."

She hugged him tighter but didn't answer. He needed her to get this. "Zoey?"

She sniffed and lifted her head, her lashes wet with tears. "Okay, Gray. I understand."

He searched her face. It was open and filled with love for him. He brushed her lips with his. "Okay," he murmured. Then he kissed her.

Long and deep.

His tongue licked against hers, absorbing the sweet essence of her taste. Honeyed nectar. As vital to him as the air he breathed.

Her nails dug through his shirt, into his back. "Gray—" His name was a whimper.

He eased back, gliding his lips along her jawline. "Mmm," he sighed, breathing hot air onto the sensitive skin of her ear.

"Come to my dinner tomorrow night," she pleaded. He sucked her lobe into his mouth and bit down. "Oh Lord!" She sagged against him, and he tightened his arms to support her weight. "I can't think when you do that," she groaned, letting go of his shirt to bury a hand in his hair. "Please come, I want everybody to know we're together."

"We already talked about this." He trailed his lips

down her neck. "Jacks has been at your birthday dinner every year since I've been gone." His tongue traced over her wildly fluttering pulse. Her fingers tightened their grip on his hair and he smiled. It ramped him up to know how much she loved his hands on her. His mouth on her.

"But you're back now. And I spoke with Dad and Mama, and they love that we're together."

"I love that they're happy about us," he said sincerely. "But I'm not going to sit at a table and watch my brother make a play for you." He pressed his thumb against her kiss-swollen lips. "He did that last week and it makes me nuts. You've been promising to talk to him—"

Her tongue darted out and swirled around his thumb. "And I will. I'll talk to him after dinner tomorrow night." She nipped at his thumb. "The dinner you're not coming to."

It was torture to ignore her blatant tease, the hot promise of her hungry tongue. But she had stubbornly avoided a confrontation with Jacks all summer. It had to end. "I love your mouth on me, but it's not gonna work." He leaned in and replaced his thumb with his mouth, gently nibbling her lower lip. "No more family dinners. Not until you sort things with Jacks. I know you don't want to hurt him, but the longer you leave it, the harder it's going to get. And you'll end up hurting him worse."

"You're right. I know you're right. I'll do it, I promise." Sincerity radiated from her, melting his unease. It melted further when she let go of his hair, and brought both hands around to cup his face. "I love you, Gray Walker. For as long as I can remember, you're the only man I've ever wanted."

Heat unfurled. *Jesus.* She looked at him with such adoration. Like he was a king amongst men. "Zoey," he groaned, folding her into his body. "You make me feel like there's nothing I can't do, nothing I can't achieve. Hell, Butterfly, I hope I'm the man you believe me to be."

"Show me. Make love to me."

"Soon, but not while Jacks is in the picture."

"Gray—"

"And definitely not in a tack room in a barn." He tightened his hands around her waist and hoisted her up. Her legs instinctively wrapped around his hips. "I promise, when I take what you're offering, we're gonna be in a king-size bed, and you're gonna be smiling, completely free to give me everything you've got." Her legs squeezed and she rubbed her heat against him. "Such a bad girl," he growled, sliding his jean-clad erection along her core.

"Gray." Her legs locked and she buried her fingers back in his hair.

He slowly ground against her. "You're gonna be so hot and wet, pretty Butterfly, you're gonna be begging me for it. And I'm going to spend all night giving it to you." He licked her lips, circling her mouth with his tongue. "And you're going to have all night to give it to me," he promised hoarsely. "My beautiful butterfly. All mine."

"I like that picture," Zoey gasped, her mouth greedily stroking against his.

"It's not a picture, sweetheart, it's a promise."

A horse whinnied, the sound drifting clearly over the rafters. A couple of horses nickered in response.

Gray stilled, cocking his head.

"What is it?" Zoey whispered.

"Shhh." He listened but heard nothing except some restless stomping. Maybe the horses sensed their passion. "It's nothing." He smiled at the gorgeous bundle in his arms.

She smiled back. "About that promise, Mr. Walker. I'll take it," she said huskily. "But what about now?" She pressed her forehead against his, her breath feathering over his lips. "I'm so hot, I ache."

Gray caught his breath when she pushed against his cock. *Yeah. He ached too.* He teased her mouth with his own, slowly walking toward the single bed up against the wall in the corner. It was used by ranch hands who stayed overnight to watch over a sick or pregnant mare. Right now, he had other plans for it.

"Now?" He dropped one knee onto the bed and lowered her to the mattress. "Now we're going to do something about that ache." His voice was deep, full of intent.

"Gray, don't you dare tease me—"

"I'm not teasing." He lifted her body farther up the bed, and moved between her legs, careful to support his weight. "You're going to lie back and trust me to take you where you need to go." Moonlight washed her face, catching the excitement glimmering in her wide gaze.

"What are you going to do?" she said breathlessly.

"I'm going to taste you." Propping himself on his elbows, he trapped her face between his hands. "Everywhere." The erotic vow echoed between them as he claimed her willing mouth. No longer in a teasing mood, he sank his tongue past her lips. Swirling. Licking. Loving how her tongue danced up against his own.

She arched into him and he growled into her mouth. He could feel her heat burning through their clothes. Ripping his mouth from hers, he started to move down her body.

"Gray?" Her hands tried to pull him back.

He easily shrugged off her grasp and continued to slide down her body until he was sitting at the end of the bed. "I said I was going to taste you everywhere."

"What?" She pushed up onto her arms.

He slipped off her shoes. "Everywhere, sweetheart, means everywhere." He reached up and flicked her trouser button open.

"Oh!" She gasped and fell back against the pillow.

"Mmm. Oh." Standing, he leaned forward and unzipped her pants. "Lift up." She immediately complied and heat flushed through him. *Fuck, he loved that she took direction.* "Good girl," he praised, quickly sliding her cotton trousers down her sleekly muscled legs, and taking her tiny white panties with them.

Her skin was luminous in the pale moon rays. A scattering of copper curls beckoned between her legs. Gray's heart raced. *She took his breath away.* Her hands fluttered and he could see she was undecided about whether to cover her exposed pussy. "Nu-uh, Butterfly. Don't hide from me. You're too damn beautiful." He waited until she flattened her hands on the old, Indian-style bedcover. "There you go. Now spread for me." He circled her calves, nudging her legs apart, showing her exactly what he wanted.

"Gray—" Her voice was deliciously low-pitched.

"That's it," he encouraged, crawling between her legs. He stroked her thighs, holding them open, trailing his mouth along their velvet smoothness. Her musky scent mingled with the warm aroma of fresh hay.

She was exquisite.

Sweat coated Gray's brow as his lips hovered over the heady promise of her.

He couldn't wait to savor her taste.

To let the essence of her heat coat his mouth.

Zoey!

****

Grayson Walker's Apartment
Present Day
Gray

"Zoey!" Gray groaned and came hard in his hand. Hot water rained down his back. Images of Zoey flickered in the billowing steam. Her body supine, open. The memory of her addictive heat coating his mouth.

Goddammit!

He shuddered, bracing himself on the slick shower wall. The last time he'd shot his load this hard was during that long-ago summer.

He'd teased Zoey in the barn, repeatedly taking her to the edge until she begged him to let her come. And he did. With his fingers and tongue, he'd made love to her until her body exploded beneath him, the taste of her flooding his senses. Owning him. It had taken every bit of his control not to explode along with her.

"What about you?" she'd murmured. Her green eyes turned golden, languorous. Like a sated cat.

"I'm a grown man, I can wait." He'd gently kissed her mound. "For you, I can always wait."

After dropping her home, he'd raced back and stripped. If his memory served, he'd been so rock hard it had taken only a few firm strokes before he erupted. It had also been with his hand. Alone in the shower.

Gray pushed away from the wall and turned off the water.

They'd had their whole future ahead of them. Or so he thought.

How fucking wrong he'd been!

He wrapped a thick bath sheet around his waist and stood in front of the vanity. The mirror was steamed up. He wiped it with his fist and examined his reflection. *Shit.* He looked tired. No, not tired, freaked out was more like it. And he was freaked out. Jacking off to the memory of Zoey did not bode well. And it certainly didn't succeed in shattering the concrete block that had taken up residence in his chest. Nor did it melt the mountain of ice freezing his gut.

Gray searched his eyes. They were dark, the gray swirling. His grip on the basin tightened. That was fear lurking in their depths. Because Zoey Morgan was his nemesis. His own liquid kryptonite. One taste and he would be fucked.

Over the years he'd had a lot of women. And he enjoyed most of them. But not one of them had filled the devastating hole created by Zoey when she forced him out of her life. She hadn't only been his heart during that hot summer, she'd been an integral part of his world for most of his young life. His confidant. His friend. Even her family had been closer to him than his own family.

Losing the Morgans was beyond his and their control. A monstrous tragedy.

Losing Zoey. That was a pain he would never understand.

Gray ran a hand over his short beard. It could go another couple of days before it needed a trim. Drying off, he made a vow to himself. He wasn't going to let her play him again. He'd come a long way from the poor sucker who needed so badly to be loved. There was something wrong with Zoey. He could see that. He'd hear her out and do what he could to help her. But he would never allow himself to be fooled by the promise glittering in her green eyes.

To let her back into his life would be like taking heroin—a sure path to self-destruction. And he wasn't going to let that happen. Not again.

Chapter Seven
Rainbow Trout

Le Parisien Bistrot, Murray Hill, NYC
Zoey

"Top-up?" Gray held the wine bottle ready to pour.

I gulped the last of my Bordeaux, and put down my glass. "Sure."

I studied him while he poured. There was no trace of that teeniest-tiniest smile I'd seen earlier. In fact, there was no sign of anything. His face was blank again. It had been that way since he fetched me from the hotel. The only words he'd muttered were to explain where we were going. "Le Parisien Bistrot in Murray Hill. It's not far from the hotel," he said.

Was blank his default expression? Stealing peeks at him from the corner of my eye, I rubbed at a spasm in the side of my neck. What a pity if it was because he was noticeably good-looking. That's the best way to describe Gray because whenever I was with him, I didn't notice anybody else. It had always been that way, even when I was eight years old. Nothing had changed. My chest beat hollow, and I picked up my glass.

If anything, I found him more alluring. A more potent version of his younger self. Tonight, he was dressed in dark jeans and a white, fine-lawn linen shirt. It was faintly transparent, offering teasing glimpses of his powerful body. But what I liked best was his beard.

He'd often carried a couple of day's growth. Now, he had a full beard covering his cheeks and jawline. Dark like his hair, it was short, neatly trimmed. Only a light smattering on his chin below his lip. He had a mustache, also short and neatly groomed. My fingers tingled. I wanted to stroke his beard, it looked so damn touchable.

Oh, for goodness sake!

This morning I thought him cold. Too cold. I sipped more wine. Who was I to judge? I was also cold. Except when I was with my patients, I was as cold as ice. Or at least, that's what my colleagues said behind my back. I sipped again. The rich blackberry flavor slid down my throat. Maybe we could be good for each other after all. Two ice-blocks, chipping away at each other.

"Zoey?" A faint scowl dented Gray's brow.

My spine prickled. I knew his blank look was a defense, but now I could see it slipping, a storm gathering behind his eyes. Ice-cold? I licked the taste of wine from my lip. Maybe I was wrong again. Maybe his type of ice was dry. So cold, it burned hot.

"We've placed our food order," he said impatiently. "Are you going to just sit there knocking back wine or are you going to tell me what's going on?"

His tone was sharp, aggressive. And it pissed me off. "Tane was right, you're an asshole." I pushed my glass to the side. "Were you always one or is this a new thing?"

His porn star mouth thinned into a furious line. "Tane should keep his mouth shut."

"What. About you being an asshole?"

He gripped the edge of the table and leaned forward. "What do you want, Zoey? A trip down memory lane?"

Anger flushed through me, quadrupling the warmth from the wine. I mirrored his action and leaned across the table. "Maybe a little bit of catching up would be nice. Is that too much to ask before I spill my guts to a virtual stranger?"

"I'm not a fucking stranger!" His angry gaze sliced over me. Our faces were inches apart, his denial a simmering heat hanging between us. Then the corner of his mouth twitched, and he sat back, his gaze sweeping over me. "I forgot about that red-hot temper of yours," he murmured.

Oh Lordy Lord!

Butterflies went berserk in my stomach. I thought I knew everything I needed to know about Gray, but it had been such a long time. And I'd forgotten. Forgotten how compelling he was. Dangerous. To my senses, to my heart. He was the enchanter who knew every magic combination to ensnare me. Own me.

He picked up the wine and refilled our glasses. Half the bottle was gone. I wanted to empty my glass again but resisted. I hadn't eaten much and I was already feeling lightheaded. Gray sipped his wine, his gaze more assessing than threatening. The fury that had stifled the air between us slowly dissipated. And the giant knot twisting my insides loosened a fraction, because I felt like I'd won a small victory. The dreaded blank look was gone from his face. I eased back in my chair and drew in a long, silent breath. His expression was difficult to read, but it wasn't blank.

"So what would you like to ask me?" he said.

I could still decipher a faint honeyed tone in his drawl, but most of his Southern Texas twang was gone. Had he dropped his home accent consciously? My brain raced. There was so much I wanted to know. "When did you leave the marines?"

"About eight years ago."

"Why didn't you go back to law? You only had a year left before you graduated."

He shrugged. "I was a different person by the time I was discharged."

"But you loved the law. You wanted to join the FBI."

"Life changes. So do dreams."

I stiffened. *Had I done that to him?*

"Zoey, it's not a bad thing." He studied me with unnerving thoroughness. "After discharge, Luke and I were recruited into a special task force. We took down a lot of bad guys."

"Luke?"

"Luke Hunter." Gray's face relaxed. He took another sip of wine. "We met early on, during basic training. Served together for most of our tours. Went through Force Recon training together. We were seconded to the Rangers as a sniper team."

Gray was a sniper! "Thor," I murmured.

"What?"

"The hunky blond at your office—he's Luke?"

Gray's brow knitted. "He's married."

My breath hitched. "Uh…okay."

"He met his wife, Katya, on the job. Things got messy for a time, but it turned out okay. They've got a kid, Lily." His voice deepened. "A ray of sunshine."

"You guys are obviously close."

"Yeah."

I fiddled with the stem of my glass. "And you're both at King Security now?"

He nodded. "Yeah. Joined four years ago." His fingers drummed the table. "You stay in touch with my dad?" His tone was difficult to read.

"Not regularly, but he likes to check up on me from time to time." I worried at my lower lip. "Gerald told me you haven't been home—"

He slapped the table. "No!"

I jumped in my seat. "Sorry. I didn't mean—"

"No, I'm sorry." His hand curled into a loose fist. "I shouldn't have snapped."

I nodded jerkily. *To hell with it.* I snatched up my wine and took a healthy swallow. His eyes tracked my movements.

"I don't go to Texas, but we stay in touch." His tone was more cordial. "Actually, I saw Dad last year when I was in New Orleans. We didn't have a lot of time but it was good to see him."

"And your mom?" I said nervously. They'd always had a strained relationship.

He looked away, his gaze skimming over the tables in the small restaurant. The place was packed. Gray said he was a regular here, and I could see why. The decor was charming, typical of a small bistro. Tables huddled close together, but far enough apart to invite private conversation. The walls were covered in French paraphernalia, a reflection of the classical French menu. There was an authentic mood to the place, romantic for lovers, but comfortably warm for friends.

"We talk on birthdays," he said finally. "She used to reach out, but I shut her down."

"You did?"

He shrugged stiffly. "My mother's brand of toxicity is not one I favor."

I could understand that. "And Jacks?" I said hesitantly.

His face hardened. "I saw him last at Randy and Sheila's wedding. We barely spoke." He sipped his wine. The poignant voice of Edith Piaf drifted through the restaurant. My chest ached with sadness. Or was it guilt? I chugged down more wine. "What about you?" Gray said.

"Well, you know I left Denton after my mother died." I put down my glass. "And I haven't been back since."

He frowned. "Not even to see Jacks?"

I shook my head.

"You're kidding! You haven't seen Jacks at all?"

My hands balled into fists. "We keep in touch by email."

"That's all. You don't speak?"

"No." Incredulity was written all over his face. And I hated it. "I think he's changed, matured."

"Really." His lip curled. "How so?"

I shifted in my seat. I wished I could wave a magic wand, wipe away the past. Change it. Anything that would stop the horror from replaying. Instead, I tried to explain. "He was pretty messed up when I ended the engagement and went to Boston. First he phoned, but I wouldn't pick-up." I looked down, picking at the napkin in my lap. "He started sending emails but when I didn't respond, they stopped too." I wanted a sip of wine, but my hand was trembling. "A year or so later he wrote again. He wanted to lease the farm." I looked at

Gray. He was listening closely. "He and your dad were already keeping an eye on it for me, so I wrote back, gave him permission. I didn't want to charge rent but he insisted." My nails bit into my palms, and I finished in a rush. "The money goes into an account. I never touch it."

"Sorry for the delay folks. We're pretty jammed tonight." I smiled gratefully at the waitress as she placed a steaming plate in front of me. "Rainbow trout for you." She moved to Gray. "And another trout for you, Mr. Walker." She grinned down at him. "Be back with the sides."

"Thanks, JoJo. Some iced water would be good as well."

"Coming right up."

"Why don't you touch the rental money from Jacks? It's yours."

I blinked rapidly. The chef had cooked the trout whole. There was a black hole where its eye had been removed.

"Zoey." Gray's voice was impatient. "Zoey, you okay? *Shit!*"

I flinched at his soft curse. Sweat beaded my upper lip. *Why didn't I want that money?*

"Chili yogurt sauce for the trout, french beans, fingerling potato salad and two waters." The efficient waitress found room for everything on the table. "Can I top up your wine?"

"I'll take care of it, JoJo," Gray said. "Thanks. That'll be all for now."

"Okie dokie. Enjoy folks."

"Here, drink some water." Gray pushed a cold glass against my hand.

I was trembling. *Shit. Fuck.* I used both hands to pick up the glass. Cool water trickled down my throat. Thoughts of Jacks drifted away, and my stomach slowly settled.

"Better?"

I nodded.

"You don't like trout?"

"Sorry?"

"You looked like you were about to be sick." His gaze shifted from me to the trout.

"No, I love trout."

His brow furrowed. "Drink some more water, and then eat a little. You'll feel better."

I arched my brow. *So bossy.* But I picked up my water and emptied the glass. The trout's eye socket glared at me. "It's still got a head," I said.

"It's French."

"This is America."

"You're a surgeon. You gonna let an itty-bitty fish get one over on you?" His eyes twinkled, the blue beating back the gray. I scowled at him, but a smile tugged at my mouth. "Eat, Zoey. You're too thin."

"And you're rude," I snapped, no longer smiling.

He shook his head and began to eat.

I watched him furtively, but I picked up my knife and fork. "Rude, and too damn handsome," I muttered under my breath.

"What did you say?"

"Nothing." I stared determinedly at my fish.

"You need me to cut the head off for you?"

"No!" I could hear the laughter in his voice. I bit my lip, trying not to smile. But as I gingerly cut into the fish, I couldn't stop the warm tingle spreading through my chest.

The trout was delicious. The skin perfectly crusted, the meat fresh and lightly smoked. We sipped wine and ate. In spite of everything, I was having a good time. I liked being with Gray. There was so much distance between us, but also, so much beautiful familiarity. So beautiful, it made me want to cry.

****

Gray

Gray lingered over his last piece of trout while he surreptitiously studied Zoey. He couldn't deny she was still a striking woman. He'd noticed more than one set of male eyes follow her when they walked through the restaurant. It irritated him that his hands had ached with a need to touch her, to stake his claim. *What the hell was with that?*

She had her hair gathered in a loose knot at the side of her neck. He preferred it hanging free, but at least it wasn't scraped back in that godawful nun's bun. She was dressed in white, slim-fitting pants, and a pale-green sleeveless top embellished with heavy beading. It looked pretty on her, the pale green setting off her luminous eyes. It also fell loosely over her hips, but not before hugging her full breasts. Zoey had lovely breasts. *Thank fuck that hadn't changed.*

He watched her stab her fork into french beans, coating them in the chili sauce. Watching her enjoy the food calmed Gray in a way he wasn't used to. He shoved that thought away and sipped his wine. *She really was too damn thin.* Gray had no problem with slender women, but there was a fragility to Zoey he didn't like. He couldn't miss the trembling in her hands. Or how skittish she was. Especially when she talked about Jacks. *Yeah.* She didn't like to talk about Jacks.

He took the last mouthful of trout and chased it down with red wine. Zoey's eyes drifted to him. They were slightly unfocused, distant. A faint pang whispered in his chest. He recognized that look. She was thinking. Buried inside her head. When she was a young girl, it would fascinate him how she'd lose herself, forget where she was. He never tried to keep up with her mercurial intellect. His only wish, like her family's, to be her buffer against a sometimes harsh reality.

She blinked and the bottom of Gray's spine tingled. Her eyes were focused on his mouth. "How's the food?" He smirked when her head jerked, her gaze snapping up to his. A faint blush crept up her neck. "The trout?" He nodded at her plate.

"It was very good." She gave him a small lopsided grin. "An epicurean feast," she teased. He remembered how much she used to laugh. *Christ.* He missed her laugh.

She placed her knife and fork together. He was tempted to urge her to eat more but forcibly clamped his mouth shut.

She's not yours to take care of.

Gray caught JoJo's attention and held his silence while the waitress cleared their plates. He wanted to talk more about Jacks. The way Zoey shut down on him earlier, he had a feeling his brother was pivotal to why she'd come to New York. But he needed to tread with care; he had no desire to watch her withdraw again. Observing her closely, he made sure to keep his tone light. "You mentioned before you thought Jacks had changed. What did you mean by that?"

Her smile faded. She nervously smoothed a non-existent lock of hair behind her ear. "He writes me every year. Updates me on the state of the farm. Tells me a little about his life." Her hand fluttered restlessly. "How he's become a regular at the church. His letter this year was different. Unexpected."

"How so?"

Her eyes locked with his. "He's getting married. A couple of years ago he met a woman at the church, Wendy somebody. They're planning to settle now, have a family." Her lashes swept down, but not before he glimpsed something disturbing in her eyes. When she spoke, her voice was so low he had to strain forward to hear. "He wants to buy Morgan Farm."

Gray gripped the side of the table. "How do you feel about that?"

"Happy for him." Her lashes lifted. The table edge cut into Gray's palm as his grip tightened. Her beautiful eyes were shadowed with loss. Bewilderment. "He deserves that, don't you think?"

Motherfucker.

Zoey was begging. And he knew it had nothing to do with his brother's impending marriage vows. "Do you want to sell the farm?" He fought to keep his voice steady.

Zoey shoved her hands in her lap. Her breathing had quickened and she shifted restlessly in her chair. Gray's tension rocketed. He had the sense that at any moment she was going to fragment. Disappear.

He pushed her wine glass forward. "Drink," he urged. Her gaze shot to him, and she squinted sharply. She did that when he bossed her. *Good.* At least the ugliness had faded from her eyes. He emptied the rest of the bottle in his own glass and took a generous gulp. "You still at Boston Children's?" She nodded. The rigid tension across her shoulders seemed to ease. Yeah. She needed a break from talk about home. "You stayed in surgery?"

"Yes." His own tension lessened as she took another small sip. "I specialize now, in fetal surgery. I love it." Her face lit up.

"What about research projects?"

"I've been approached. A lot. But it's not for me."

"Why not? You could manage both, easily." Gray frowned as he thought back. "Isn't that what you always dreamed, to invent something life changing?"

"No!"

His pulse jumped. Zoey's vehement cry raised the hairs on the back of his neck. Taking care to move slowly, he leaned closer to her. The color drained from her face. "What's going on, Zoey?"

She blinked slowly. "My brain is broken. How can I work on ground-breaking research when I don't trust my own brain?"

Gray's stomach clenched as he fought to keep his expression neutral. "How can your brain be broken?"

"It won't remember." Her voice was painfully raw.

His skin prickled. *Surely not?* "Zoey, are you talking about the attack on the farm?" She nodded jerkily. "But that was a long time ago. You have no memory because you were drugged."

"But not so much I can't remember."

He scrambled to understand. "You remember now?"

She leaned close, her hands gesturing urgently. "No. That's the problem. I get flashes. Nightmares. But

I can't remember. I've been to doctors. Psychiatrists. They all say the same thing. Dissociative Amnesia." She waved a hand dismissively. "It's complicated, but basically it means my brain won't let me remember."

Gray stared into her earnest face. Everything around him slowed, faded. His reality stilled. Shifted. *Son-of-a-bitch.* All this time she'd been punishing herself. *Sweet Jesus.* Punishing herself for something that wasn't her fault. His throat burned. He wanted to grab hold of her, shake her. Comfort her.

"Gray?" Her uncertainty squeezed his heart.

"You still get nightmares?"

She worried at her lip. "The panic attacks are worse. They went away but recently they came back worse than ever. It's affecting my work."

"Why did they come back? Was it Jacks' letter?"

"Maybe. I guess it didn't help." A derisive smile twisted her lovely mouth. "I get jittery around this time of year."

Gray sucked in a harsh breath. He felt like he'd been hit on the side of the head with an invisible battering ram. How was he supposed to reconcile what she was telling him with what he thought he knew about her? Slowly, he sat back.

Zoey Morgan was his nemesis. His liquid kryptonite.

The reminder reverberated in his head. He needed to tamp down his emotion or she'd suck him right back into her world. "Why me, Zoey? Why do you think I can help you?"

Her body stilled, emerald-green eyes boring into him. It took a lot for him not to look away. His gut twisted. He knew what she was looking for. He also knew she wouldn't find it. He was a master at hiding his emotions, showing only what he wanted people to see. But his gut twisted even more when her own face shuttered, her lashes sweeping down to mask her eyes from him.

"I had a bad experience in surgery, a panic attack." She spoke quickly, her voice raspy. "I've made a lot of fuck-ups in my life, but I've never doubted my ability to be a doctor. A surgeon." Her hands curled into fists, and bunched the tablecloth. "I can't let my past take this away. I won't!"

Gray forced himself to ignore the desperation pouring from her. "You didn't answer my question. Why me?"

Her body jerked like he'd cut her. Gray's ears rang, and he had to swallow hard to hear her response. "I went to see a psychiatrist who helped me before. She said going home wasn't enough. That regaining my lost memories would only have a chance to happen if I felt I was in a safe place."

Adrenaline tingled through Gray. "And you believe I'm your safe place?"

Zoey's hands flattened on the table, her gaze drifting over his shoulder. "In the hospital…after everything happened…I remembered being in your arms."

Gray couldn't stop himself. He reached out and gently touched her hand. "You remember that?"

She looked down. He could feel her fingers trembling beneath his. "I felt safe," she whispered. "I need you to come home with me, Gray. Home to Denton."

Chapter Eight
Before The Pain

Tattoo Parlor, Bushwick, Brooklyn
The Next Morning
Gray

Careful not to spill the four coffees precariously balanced in the cardboard holder, Gray used his shoulder to push the tattoo parlor door open. If he didn't know it was a tattoo shop, he'd have walked straight past. There was no signage, no blinking neon light shouting out "Tattoos!" According to Luke, Val the owner was an iconic inker. And like a secret membership, anybody in the know had no problem locating the place. Gray wasn't in the know. Hence, Luke had sent him clear directions. He stepped inside and nudged the door closed with his foot.

"Hi there."

He winced at the chirpy greeting. It came from a tiny Asian girl perched behind the reception counter. She had indigo blue hair cut short, and styled like she'd recently been electrocuted. Her tight red tank showed off intricate, full-color ink covering both arms.

"Yay, coffee! You must be Gray." She grinned, but her eyes were glued to the coffees he gingerly placed on the counter.

"Yeah."

"Give me a sec to check with Val. See if it's okay

for you to join them."

She hopped off her swivel stool and skipped across the well-worn wooden floors to the corner of the shop. Luke was there, sprawled face down on a tattoo bed. A tattooist, who Gray assumed was Val, was bent over him, obviously at work. The cute receptionist whispered something to Val. Gray couldn't hear his response but understood the shake of his head. Cutie-pie made her way quickly back to him.

"Val says can you give him five minutes? My name's Yuki by the way. Why don't you take a seat over here?" She pranced over to a chocolate-brown velvet couch. It was strewn with turquoise and mustard patterned cushions. "They really won't be long. And thanks for the coffee. I was getting desperate. Our machine conked out."

Gray winced again. The girl was cute but too bloody chatty for seven in the morning. Especially when he spent most of the night awake, his mind locked in a constant replay of his dinner with Zoey. He grabbed a coffee and walked over to the couch. "Thanks, darlin'. Go back to whatever you were doing. I'm fine."

"Okay, sure thing. Call if you want anything. There are magazines here. Maybe you'll decide you want some ink." She beamed at him, dark eyes twinkling.

"Don't think so, darlin'." He smiled at her. He couldn't help it; her sparkle was infectious. She winked and skipped away. Gray's smile died, and he sank gratefully onto the deep velvet couch.

There was a faint smell of stale cigarettes. But more bothersome was the disinfectant. Yuki must have been cleaning because it was thick in the air. He drank down half his coffee, washing away the acrid taste. The shop was actually pretty cool. The walls were a combination of face-brick and antique-style paint-technique. They were plastered with ornate mirrors and framed photographs depicting spectacular tattoos. Each of the four work booths had a circular railing with a deep-purple velvet curtain hanging from it. The artist could pull the curtain closed if a client required privacy. Tattoo sketches were tacked to the wall of each booth. Even from a distance, Gray could easily identify the differing style of each artist.

He'd never hankered to be inked. In the military, they'd been advised not to get platoon-identifying tattoos if they planned to pursue undercover work as a career. In a drunken stupor a couple of years ago, Luke explained what the inked violets on his inner arm represented. For one crazy minute, Gray was tempted to get a red butterfly inked on his own skin. A permanent reminder of lost love. Or a warning never to forget. He'd quickly chased away the temptation with another inch of Luke's bourbon.

Gray drank down the rest of his coffee. Normally he was a morning person, like cutie-pie over there. He eyed the wide-awake girl, happily tapping away on her phone. Not today. He'd slept like shit. Suppressing a yawn, he stretched his legs out and rested his head against the cushions.

I'll help you, Zoey. I promise.

His words had mocked him all night. He'd been too fucking arrogant to admit he didn't have the slightest clue how to help her. Her plea for him to return to Denton had sent a ghostly chill down his spine because her desperate fragility reminded him of her mother. The last time he'd visited Mary, the day before he left Texas, still haunted him. She'd been conscious but catatonic. Her eyes drowning in so much pain it had been unbearable to witness. He sensed Zoey was close to the same edge, and if she toppled over, she could lose herself like her mother did.

I'll help you, Zoey. I promise.

Gray crushed the coffee cup in his hand. He was furious he'd made that promise to her. It was stupid and reckless. After her revelations last night he'd bought himself some time. Told her he needed the night to think things through, and that he'd call her this morning.

Well, now it was morning, and he wasn't any closer to knowing what the hell he was going to do. Exhaling heavily, he again combed through the bits of information she'd offered up during dinner. Why was she still carrying around so much shit? What had he missed?

"Gray!" He jerked upright and raked his fingers through his hair. Luke was twisted on the bed, beckoning to him. "Come on over. Bring the coffees."

"I've got them," Yuki chirped.

He stood and followed her across the room. She handed Luke and Val a coffee.

"Thanks," Val muttered.

"You need anything else?"

"No thanks, Yuki." He emptied half the coffee cup. "Man, I needed that," he sighed, and closed his eyes in pleasure.

"Yeah. Thanks, bro." Luke drank back his coffee from his prone position on the tattoo bed. "Been here since six, and no fucking coffee," he groused.

"Why so early?"

"Ask Val." Luke pointed at the tattoo artist. Gray knew Val was a man, but if he hadn't heard his deep voice, it would be up for debate. He was slender, medium height, with a narrow face and sharp cheekbones. His hair was pulled back into a complicated updo with decorative oriental sticks holding the strands in place. Thick black eyeliner exaggerated the slant to his almond-shaped eyes.

"I'm busy." Val tossed back the rest of his coffee and threw the cup into a bin at his feet. "You wanted to be fitted in. So I fitted you in." He picked up a tattoo machine with a four-needle configuration and bent over Luke's shoulder.

Gray could see he was making progress shading in the extraordinary tattoo taking shape on Luke's body. He studied the trail of lilies winding up and over Luke's shoulder. The detail in the petals and pollen-coated stamens was intricate and stunning. There was a sense of masculine power in the black and white design that defied its feminine subject matter. "You got a thing for flowers, Hunt?"

"*Abso-fucking-lutely!*" Luke smiled, resting his chin on his hands.

Gray also smiled. Yeah. Luke loved his girls. "Lily seen this yet?"

"No. It's a surprise. She'll see it when it's finished."

"Shit. Is that a skull?" A perfectly inked skull, the same size as one of the lily blossoms, was nestled at the base of the design.

"Yeah. A reminder to watch over what's important to me."

A year ago, Luke nearly lost his daughter, and the woman he loved, to a madman. In his quest to keep them safe, he took a bullet to the shoulder, and one to the head.

"You're inking over the scars?" Gray asked Val.

"Working the design around them mostly." He wiped away excess ink. "Scar tissue holds ink differently to healthy tissue. So I'm minimizing the shading on the actual scars."

"You're a wizard, man." Gray could barely make out the bullet scar on the back of Luke's shoulder.

Val nodded, supremely indifferent to his praise. Not surprising. Luke said he was considered one of the finest inkers of his generation. The photographs and awards plastering the walls around them reinforced this sentiment.

"So you get much sleep last night after we spoke." Luke looked over his shoulder.

"Not much."

"Yeah. You were pretty clammed up. You ready to spill?"

Gray spotted a chair in the opposite corner and dragged it over. He sat astride, resting his arms on the chair back. "The whole story is insane," he said morosely. "I don't even know where to start."

Luke's shrewd gaze assessed him. "Why don't you backtrack for me? To before the pain. Tell me about your connection to her."

Gray consciously slowed his breathing. He found the steady buzz of the tattoo machine oddly comforting. "We were neighbors. Morgan Farm and Walker Ranch butt right up against each other. But it wasn't always that way. It used to be, the land was all Davis land."

Luke frowned. "That's not your father's name."

"Uh-uh." Gray shook his head. "My grandfather was Jackson Davis. He bought the land in the nineteen-fifties. Developed it into one of the first horse-breeding ranches in the area. Thoroughbreds and racehorses." Luke rested his face on his hand, his eyes on Gray. "He did okay. James Morgan, Zoey's dad, used to work for the old man when he was a kid. Had a real knack with the horses. When he finished school, my granddad took him on full time."

Luke hissed in pain.

"You need a break?" Val asked.

"I'm fine. Keep working." Gray's mouth twitched when Luke's gaze landed back on him. "Hurts like a motherfucker," he cursed. "Keep talking, I need the distraction."

"The story's an urban legend in Denton," Gray continued. "Hell. In all of horse country."

"I grew up in LA and Jersey." Luke's face grimaced in pain. "No horse stories there, brother."

Gray laughed quietly. "Once upon a time, there was a new-born foal—"

"Funny."

Gray smirked but picked up his story. "According to my granddad, the foal was a runt. A breeding error with a rogue stallion. He wanted to flog it at auction. But Zoey's dad, James, he was nuts about that foal. Convinced my granddad to sell it to him. Only, he didn't have any money. But that didn't stop him." Gray clasped his hands loosely. He'd heard the story countless times when he was a kid, but he still loved it. "He makes this crazy-ass deal. Talked Granddad into cutting his wages in half for two years, in payment for the foal. The old man shakes on it. And the legend of Morgan Magic begins."

Luke's chin jerked up. "You're shitting me. Morgan Magic!"

"Yup."

"*The* Morgan Magic?"

"There was more than one?" Gray arched a brow.

"Fuck me," Luke breathed.

"You wanna hear the rest?" Gray said impatiently.

"Fuck yeah."

"Fuck yeah," Val echoed.

Luke's head dropped again. "Don't mind him. He's like a lawyer. We've got tattooist-client privilege."

Val winked at Gray, and tossed an ink-stained towel on a dirty pile. Gray smiled inwardly and carried on. "Over the next year, the foal grew. Lost his gangly, sickly look. And soon, it's time for James to find a trainer." He gave a half shrug. "But he has to get creative because Davis Ranch is primarily for breeding, and James has zero cash to outsource training. Enter Gerald Walker, my father."

"No kidding?" Luke muttered.

"Yeah. Dad was the assistant trainer at a nearby facility. James reckons him. Offers him half of all Magic's winnings if he'll train Magic for free. They strike a deal. Two years later, it's 1973, and Magic wins the Kentucky Derby. The rest is racehorse history."

Val reared up, his mahogany gaze wide with awe. "He won the Triple Crown!"

Gray grinned. "That he did."

Luke turned to scowl at Val. "Hey, you, why am I hearing your voice in this conversation?"

"Be cool, Luke, my man. It's Morgan Magic. That

horse was a fucking legend." Val waved the tattoo machine in excitement.

Luke smiled. "Shit, Gray. The artist is right. That horse was *epic*."

Both Luke and Val fell silent. The eclectic chill-out music of Buddha Bar quietly filled the room.

Yeah. The legend of Morgan Magic was a beautiful thing.

Several moments later, Luke broke the silence. "I'm guessing James Morgan was now cash-rich. What did he do to convince your granddad to sell him a piece of Davis land?"

"The old-man had made some bad calls. The ranch was struggling. The same year Magic won the Triple, Granddad had a heart attack." Gray flexed his hands, cracking his knuckles. "My mother's mom died when she was five. Granddad never remarried. Brought my mother up on his own. After his heart attack, he was worried about the ranch, about my mother's security. To secure their future, he traded James the piece of land that became Morgan Farm."

"Traded?" Luke looked confused.

"Yeah. Instead of a cash sale, Granddad traded the land for life-long breeding rights to Morgan Magic. Turned out to be a good deal. With Magic, and my dad running the breeding program, the ranch bred a Horse of the Year, a Preakness winner, and a string of broodmares in high demand."

"Your dad left his job, joined up with your granddad?"

Gray nodded. "From what I understand, my mother had a thing for James. But he wasn't interested. He'd met Mary, and was gone for her. After Magic won the

Triple at Belmont, James and Mary got engaged." Gray shifted in his chair. "From what I gleaned over the years, my mother went apeshit. Refused to attend James and Mary's wedding. Wouldn't even greet them if she bumped into them in town." Gray rolled his neck, trying to loosen the tension beginning to build there. He suddenly wanted this story over. "But my dad was in love with my mother. He courted her, weathered her tantrums. A year later, they were married. I think my granddad encouraged it." Gray's eyes met Luke's. "After he made the breeding trade with James, he sold half the ranch to my dad. Renamed it Walker-Davis Ranch. He promised the other half to my mother, a dowry of sorts. He signed it over to her on the day she married my dad."

"Christ." Luke's brow arched. "He practically sold her to your father."

"I don't think it was as cold as that," Gray denied. "My mother was skittish. I think he believed she needed taking care of. But there's no doubt business was involved." Warmth prickled his chest as he thought about his granddad. "Turns out, he lived another fifteen years before his heart gave in." Gray smiled. "Fuck, I loved the old bastard. He could be cranky but he was a great grandfather. Real hands-on. Things went to shit after he died." He abruptly stood.

Luke lifted his head. "So you knew the Morgans your whole life?"

"Sort of." Gray folded his arms. "They lived next door but we didn't have a lot to do with them at first. It remained unspoken, but there was bad blood between my mother, James and Mary. I know my dad had an all right relationship with James, but we were never encouraged to play with the Morgan kids. And it stayed like that until I was thirteen." He moved restlessly to the wall and studied the sketches pinned there. Inching closer, he noted some of them were of Luke's intricate tattoo.

"What happened then?"

Gray kept his back to Luke. "Granddad died. I was cut-up. Brooding. Had nobody really to talk to." His chest constricted. "Dad was distant like he always was. Things with my mother were pretty screwed up. Then she told me she wasn't really my mother. Of course, she did that in front of Jacks, made no bones about who the real crown prince was."

"That was all sorts of fucked up," Luke growled.

Gray turned to face him. "It was what it was." He shrugged. "Being adopted has a way of putting you on the outside."

"Bullshit!" Luke shoved up, bracing himself on his forearms.

"Whoa!" Val reared back, his tattoo machine held high.

Luke ignored Val's cry, his gaze burning into Gray. "It doesn't have to be like that. And you fucking know it!"

"Yeah, well." Gray balled his fists, his arms hugged tight to his chest. He neither agreed nor disagreed with Luke. But he did know how much his best friend cared about adoption. His aunt and uncles had taken him in when he was twelve years old. They saved him from a brutal life in Los Angeles. "You wanna hear the rest?" His tone was a soft challenge.

Luke's fierce gaze burned a moment longer before he sighed. "Yeah. I wanna hear the rest."

Gray ducked his head and blew out a silent breath. Luke could be badass but he was the best friend a man could have. He moved back to his chair, swiveled it to face front, and sat down. "It feels like forever ago." He rubbed his hands over his face, casting his mind back. "It was summer. Baking hot. Jacks had his school buddies over, and they were hanging at the pool. I wanted to be alone. There's this big pond at the bottom of the ranch where it meets up with Clear Creek. It's so big, my granddad used to call it Davis Lake." His mouth twitched and he looked at Luke. "The name stuck. The pond crosses over both properties. The Morgans always used to swim there. Hell. It's probably why my mother had our pool built. To keep us far away from them."

"Sounds like you're stretching, bro."

"You don't know my mother, Hunt. Anyway, that day her ploy didn't work. I rode to the pond and came face to face with a Morgan family-day picnic. Changed my life." He briefly closed his eyes, the memory of that day as clear as if it happened yesterday. "I don't know what Mary saw, but she wasted no time welcoming me into the family fold. I spent the whole afternoon with them. And over the next five years, hundreds more."

"Zoey must have been a little kid," Luke said quietly.

"She was." His mouth quirked. "Eight years old. All red hair and freckles. Laughing green eyes. Shit. That girl loved life." Gray's smile faded. "And she loved me." He winced inwardly, hearing the rawness in his voice. "After that day, she shadowed me everywhere. I started to spend a lot of time with James. Liked how his head worked. Unlike my own dad, he

109

always found time for me. And Zoey was always by my side."

"What about her brother?"

"Noah? He was a great kid. And a great brother to Zoey. Never made her feel like a pest." His jaw clenched. *Shit.* Even after all this time, he missed the guy. "He was always gentle with her, even when she was a pain in the ass. Which was often because she was too damn clever for her own good." He leaned forward, resting his arms on his thighs. "Noah and I got on. But even though there were only a couple years between us, my bond was with Zoey. It didn't matter she was five years younger than me. She got me, you know?" Luke nodded. "Knew what was going on inside my head. Knew when to talk, and when to keep silent. A miniature sage." Gray smiled wryly.

"She was like your baby sister?"

"I guess." Gray clasped his hands tightly. "But once she hit her teens, things changed. I knew she had a crush on me. I was careful around her. Kept my distance. I think it hurt her, but she didn't show it. When I was eighteen I left for New Orleans. I was at UNO for four years but went home for most of my breaks. I didn't see a lot of her. I think she was avoiding me. And I was focused on college pussy."

"And that's changed?" Luke smirked. "Except for the age of said pussy of course."

"Fuck you," Gray said with little heat.

"No thanks."

"Christ. How does your wife put up with your shit?" Luke's smirk changed into a Cheshire grin.

"Fuck," Gray groaned.

"Exactly," Luke said smugly.

Gray shook his head. But he wished he had what Luke and Katya had. Once, a long time ago, he thought he did have it. *How had he been so blind?*

The humor faded from Luke's face. "So when did it change between the two of you?"

"Summer she turned nineteen," Gray said. "I finished my second year at Columbia, came home for the summer. And there she was."

"Definitely not your sister, yeah."

"Definitely not my fuckin' sister." Gray's voice had deepened.

"So how the hell did she end up engaged to your brother?"

Gray sighed. "If I could tell you that, Hunter, I'd offer my own services as a sage." Heaviness settled over him, eating into his tired mind. He glanced at Val. The guy was listening, but his focus was on the ink. It didn't bother Gray. Luke trusted the androgynous genius, and that was good enough for him.

Luke half raised his head. "Look, I'm not downplaying what your girl suffered. It was godawful. But in real time it was a long time ago." His gaze was searching. "She should have got over it by now. At least enough to live her life without nightmares."

"Agreed. But it's not happening." Gray shook his head. "She's so close to the edge that no matter what I do, I'm not sure I'm going to be able to pull her back."

"What the fuck is going on with her? You said she received some email from your brother?"

Gray's insides shrank. *That jealous prick was not his brother.* "Can you believe that little fucker moved to her family's farm? Leases it from her."

"She okay with that?"

"She says he takes care of the place for her." His teeth mashed together, sending a bolt of pain through his jaw. "Don't know how he sleeps peacefully in that house."

"Maybe he's moved on," Luke mused.

Gray rubbed his aching jaw. "Would seem so," he muttered. "He's engaged to be married. Says he wants to buy Morgan Farm."

"And that freaked her out?"

"So she says." He stared blindly down at the floor. "But there's gotta be more. I know it."

"How so?"

He looked up. "Something happened, Luke. Something I didn't see. Why does a warm, vivacious girl, beautiful inside and out, turn into something she's not?" He punched his fist into his palm. "Why does she betray the man she claims to love?" His bitter question echoed across the wooden floor. Gray's mouth twisted, and he slumped back in his chair. "I don't get it, man. She tossed me out like overripe garbage. Never even offered an explanation."

"I hear you, brother." Luke looked over his shoulder. "Hey, Val. Let's take a break. Ten minutes. Yeah?"

Val glanced at Gray. "Sure, Luke. No problem." He gave the tattoo a final swipe, and efficiently stowed his tattoo machine. "Call me when you're ready. I'm going to grab a smoke."

Luke sat up, swinging his legs to the floor. He folded his arms and studied Gray. "Her experience was hellish brutal."

"I know that. But her betrayal came before the attack." Gray jumped up and shoved his hands in his pockets. "She had his ring on her finger and was celebrating with champagne well before the violence hit that night." Remembered fury tightened his voice. "For fuck's sake, even my mother shared a glass of champagne with them."

Luke's brows drew together. "What about now. Do you trust her, or you think she's still bullshitting you?"

"I don't know. And it makes no bloody difference." He took his hands from his pockets and jammed them on his hips. *Dammit*. He was breathing too fast. He turned his back and sucked in several deep breaths. When he had control, he turned back to Luke. "If there's even the slightest chance she's telling the truth, I need to help her." His throat thickened. "If nothing else, I owe it to her family."

"I get that." Luke's gaze was steady. "You mentioned Zoey hasn't been back to Texas since she left."

Gray nodded.

"Neither have you."

Gray swallowed. "I don't have much to go home to. You know that."

"It sounds like you both don't have much to go home to. Yet you both have ghosts haunting you." Luke's expression hardened. "Go home, Gray. Take your woman. It's time to stop living a half-life."

Gray's skin prickled. "*My* woman?"

"Isn't she?"

No!

The denial screamed in his head, but his tongue stuck to the roof of his mouth. Vivid-green eyes danced with his resolve, sending his pulse racing. Gray blinked hard. *Fuck, no.* It could snow in Texas during midsummer before he trusted himself to another woman. Especially Zoey Morgan.

"What about Eva?" Luke said.

Gray cleared his throat. "What about her?"

"Bring her in. Let her do an assessment." Luke shrugged. "If Zoey's such a loose cannon, get Eva to give you some perspective. She might even be a help to Zoey."

Gray shook his head. Luke's suggestion had merit, but Zoey would never go for it. "Zoey will never agree to meet with a stranger."

"Then don't give her a choice." Luke's midnight-blue stare drilled into him. "From what you've said, you two have a really fucked up history. That woman would never have come to you unless she had nowhere else to turn. Use it."

"That's cold."

"Maybe," Luke grunted. "But you know I'm right."

Gray's jaw spasmed. "Fucking hell."

"Yeah." Luke broke eye contact and looked over to the reception. "Yuki, sweetheart. Tell Val I'm ready."

"Sure thing, Luke."

He turned back to Gray. "Hey, you wanna hear some good news? Looks like you could use some."

"Sure, what's up?"

"Katya's pregnant."

Warmth shot through Gray. "Holy shit." From the wide smile on Luke's face, Gray knew his friend was over the moon. He reached to shake his hand. "Really happy for you, man. You guys deserve it."

"Thanks."

"Katya happy?"

"Oh yeah."

"Lily?" Luke and Katya's daughter had a special place in Gray's heart.

"We haven't told her yet. Katya wants to get to the three-month mark."

Gray nodded. "Good thing I moved out."

"Babies don't take up much room, brother."

"I know, but it was time. You guys needed your space to become a family."

"You are our family." The challenge in Luke's voice left no room for doubt.

Gray inclined his head.

"The glitterbug misses you." Luke smiled wryly. "Hell. We miss you. Keeping that kid out of our bedroom is a damn nightmare."

Gray grinned. He loved looking out for Lily while Luke and Katya got it on. "Teach you to take me for granted." He chuckled.

Val joined them, slipping smoothly onto his swivel chair. Gray wrinkled his nose. The tattooist reeked of cigarette smoke. "Whatever happened to that horse?" Val said, taking another clean towel from the pile on the trolley.

"He was poisoned with a Ketamine overdose. About five years after he won the Triple," Gray said.

"Shit. I remember seeing something about that in a documentary." Luke resumed his prone position. "They ever find out who did it?"

Gray shrugged. "Not as far as I know. James would never speak about it. Dad neither."

"What a shame. A great horse like that."

"It's jacked up, my man. Not so magic after all." Val set the tattoo machine buzzing and bent over Luke's shoulder. Gray watched as he quickly lost himself in the artistry of his work.

Yeah. Not so magic after all.

****

Piccolo Cafe, Gramercy Park
Zoey

I'll help you, Zoey. I promise.

I slept like the dead. And when I woke, I didn't have that exhausted feeling like I hadn't slept a wink. Gray called around eight. He was with a friend and running late. He asked if I could meet him at the Piccolo Cafe in the East Village at nine o'clock. Something had cropped up at work, and he didn't have a lot of time. He wasn't short with me or anything, just apologetic.

I grabbed a taxi at the hotel. The Piccolo Cafe was on Third Avenue, just down from Stuyvesant Square. I people-watched as we stopped and started down Lexington Avenue. I found it weirdly satisfying to watch commuters rush to work when I had the rest of the day at leisure. I'd decided a shopping spree was first up. I had plenty of clothes, but they were all wrong. Dull. I needed some color in my life. Excitement tingled through me. Maybe even something a little sexy. My foot moved in rhythm to the West African beat filling the taxi. The suffocating anxiety was gone. My breathing was still a little quick, my tummy a little fluttery. But it didn't feel like the strangling panic of the last few weeks. I cracked the window and breathed in the busy smell of New York. I was impatient to hear what Gray had to say.

The taxi pulled up alongside a tiny Italian eatery. I paid my fare and walked inside. The aroma of fresh-brewed coffee hung in the air with a welcome richness.

People were perched on small round stools, crowded around wooden tables crammed close together. I made my way to the front counter. It was piled high with croissants and a variety of breakfast paninis with mouth-watering fillings.

"Eat here or takeaway?" I dragged my eyes from the tempting display. A barista-come-server was busy at the expresso machine.

"Eat here, please." I smiled.

He glanced over my shoulder. "*Cinque minuti.*" His accent was a seductive mix of Italian and American. "You wait?"

"Yes, I can wait."

"*Bene.*" He winked.

It turned out to be less than five minutes when a table freed up. I quickly staked my claim, eyeing the new arrivals already queuing up. Just as I sat, he walked inside.

Gray.

Electric eyes slammed into me and my heart surged. I sucked in an impatient breath. *Would there ever be a time my heart didn't soar at the sight of him?* A desolate cry echoed in my head. *Never!*

"Sorry I'm late." He slid onto the stool opposite me. "Subway was held up."

"You took the subway?"

"Yeah. Quickest option. I was in Bushwick. The traffic into Manhattan is murder." His eyes scanned the restaurant. Volatile energy poured from him.

"I could have met you at your office." I sounded breathy.

His attention sliced to me. I swallowed the lump threatening to strangle me. His eyes were gunmetal-gray today. And they missed nothing.

"You look better. Sleep well?"

"Better than I have in a while, thanks." *Blast. Still breathy.* I smiled tentatively. He was making me nervous.

"Good for you." His mouth twisted. It wasn't pleasant. "Let's order," he said curtly. "I don't have a lot of time." Butterflies lifted off in my tummy, taking my smile along with them. I glared at him. He drummed his fingers on the table. "You decide what you want to eat?"

My breathiness was gone now. "Toasted croissant with smoked salmon and avocado," I snapped. "And a double-shot cappuccino."

His brows swept up. "You sure that's all?"

I folded my arms and balanced stiffly on my stool. *A'hole!* "I'm sure," I said sweetly. His eyes glinted, but for the life of me, I had no idea what he was thinking. Without a word, he got up and went to the counter. It took a lot for me not to crane my neck to keep him in sight.

Minutes later he returned with our food. He handed me my order and suggested we eat first then talk. With a mumbled "fine," I bit into my croissant. I thought Gray's *a'hole* mood would kill my appetite, but I was wrong. I ate so quickly, I literally inhaled my food. Gray also wolfed down his panini. I was halfway through my cappuccino when he deigned to speak.

"I'll help you out. Come to Texas with you." My breath caught and I nearly choked on my coffee. "But I've got two conditions." He chugged his expresso in one mouthful, then pushed the cup aside.

My eyes filmed over, and I carefully put down my

cappuccino. *Oh my God! Gray's coming home. To Texas. With me.*

"Two conditions, Zoey."

I ignored his blunt tone. I didn't give a damn what his conditions were. *Gray's coming home.*

"Zoey!"

"Yes. Okay. Two conditions." I blinked rapidly. The threat of tears passed, and I looked up. He looked pissed. "O-kaay," I stressed. "I get it. Two conditions."

His beautiful mouth flattened. "I want you to meet with a friend of mine. She works with our team."

My skin prickled. The crappy blank look he favored was back. "You want me to meet your girlfriend?"

He waved a hand impatiently. "Eva's not my girlfriend. She's a friend and colleague. And a damn good psychologist with solid instincts. Her profiles are rarely off."

A spurt of adrenalin shot through me. With difficulty, I kept my voice steady. "You want her to profile me?"

"She's by trade, a psychotherapist." He laid his hand flat on the table and leaned forward. "And yes, I want her to profile you."

I froze. He was too close. Electric heat sizzled through me. My body clenched, but I took meticulous care not to retreat from him. "Do you think I'm a liar? A fraud?" I waited. He held himself rigid. Seconds ticked by, and a different heat stole over me. "You don't trust me," I whispered.

"Let's just say I don't trust. Full stop."

"But you trust her?"

His expression tightened. "You were the one who

came to me, Zoey. If I'm going to help you, this is what I need." I broke eye contact and picked up my coffee, pretending to take a sip. For a moment his gaze settled on my mouth, then he sat back and folded his arms. "I'm not doing this to be a bastard. There's a lot of shit screwing with your head. I need to have some idea of what to expect."

I swallowed a faint pang of nausea. "You're worried I'm going to freak out on you?"

"I'm worried you're going to freak out on *you*." His brow furrowed. "Look, it's up to you, but I'm not going into this blind. I need to know what's safe for you. How best to help you."

He thinks I'm heading for a straightjacket. I put down my coffee and clasped my hands tightly in my lap. They were rock-steady. But I knew the tremors were only one panic attack away. "All right," I agreed softly. "I'll do what you want. But I want to see my own therapist."

He shook his head. "That's not going to work for me. I know Eva. I trust her."

But you don't trust me.

My knuckles whitened. I thought of Rose and the countless therapists I'd visited before finding her. *Oh, God.* Could I put myself through that again? The pain. The humiliation. Gray's face remained like granite. But something flickered in his eyes. I couldn't read it, but my injured soul clung to it. I cleared my throat. "Tell me about her. Who is she?"

"Scarlett Eva Young. Only uses the name, Eva." His mouth curved into a faint smile. "Don't make the mistake of calling her Scarlett." I instantly wanted to know more, but he carried on talking. "She grew up in

LA where she got her doctorate in clinical psychology. Her specialization was trauma counselling and victimology." The tendons in his neck stood out and his gaze flicked sideways. There was something he wasn't telling me. "She moved here around three years ago. Now she only consults with us, and when she has time, she assists local law enforcement with victimology profiles."

I frowned. "And patients?"

"Nope."

I ignored his curt tone. "Why?"

"Do you think you're the only person who's suffered a tragedy, Zoey?" His eyes were a storm of accusation.

I flinched. It seemed I was pushing his buttons without even trying to. "I'm sorry you think I implied that."

"Shit." He ran a hand roughly over his beard. I swallowed the acid slowly leaking down my throat. Gray caught my gaze. "I shouldn't have said that." His tone was contrite. "It was out of line."

I didn't know what to think. Or say. I nodded stiffly.

He rested his hands on the table. "Look. I've worked with Eva for over two years. She's saved our asses more than once."

I tore my gaze from his. My coffee was cold, but I drank down the dregs anyway. My relaxed mood was gone, swallowed up in a Grayson ice storm. And it hurt. "You had two conditions," I said. "What's the second one?"

He tapped his fingers on the table. "You're not going to like it."

I pushed my empty cup aside. *Like that made a difference*. "Just tell me." A tinge of anger colored my voice.

"I want you close to me. In the King HQ building. It's where I live."

My breath hitched. "You want me to move in with you?"

"No. You can move in with Eva. She has an apartment there as well."

"Are you crazy?" I hissed. "I'm not living with a total stranger."

"Then you can move in with me."

"You're nuts!"

He jerked forward. "I need this, Zoey." His voice deepened. "I need to get to know you again. I can't go back to Texas and be your safe place if I don't know who you are."

Bulldust. Even with his hooded eyes and blank face, I could see he was hiding things. "Do you know what you're doing, Gray? Forcing us so close together?"

"We won't be," he said firmly. "I'm snowed under at work. You'll be in my guest bedroom, and we'll grab time to talk when my schedule allows." His chin jutted. "And you'll be close to Eva."

I rolled my eyes at him. "You're poking a hornet's nest, Gray. Be careful you don't get stung."

His mouth twitched. "Maybe I'm banking on it."

An unexpected tingle caught me by surprise. I squeezed my legs together and looked away. *This was nuts.* I drew in several deep breaths before I turned and leveled him with what I hoped was a cool gaze. "If I agree to both your conditions, how long before we leave for Texas?"

His brows snapped together.

Way to go, girl. My answer had stunned him.

"Work's busy," he murmured, his stormy gaze drifting over my face. "I need time to sort my schedule."

"How much time?" I pushed.

His mouth thinned. "Until Eva gives me the green light."

I lifted my chin. "One week, and then I'm leaving." My heart thumped. "With or without you," I said firmly.

I yearned with all my heart that it was with him.

But I prayed my face didn't tell him that.

I prayed it didn't tell him anything at all.

Chapter Nine
A Dead Ringer for Scarlett Jo—

Brooklyn Bridge Park, DUMBO
The Next Day
Zoey

Scarlett Eva Young.

She was a stunner. And if she wanted, could easily moonlight as a stand-in for Scarlett Johansson. I sneaked a glance at her as we walked side-by-side, and tossed the thought aside. There was too much intelligence in her ice-blue gaze to be anybody's stand-in. I sighed heavily. Brooklyn Bridge loomed in front of us. The picturesque view should have lightened my mood, but it didn't. I think Eva surmised this because instead of forcing conversation, she left me to my thoughts.

"I'm sorry you got stuck with me," I said abruptly. "I'm sure you've got better things to do with your weekend."

"It's no problem." She gave me a quick smile. "We're all working this weekend."

Bitterness leaked into my mouth. "And I'm *your* work."

"Yes," she said without hesitation. "Gray wanted my help."

"And you always do what Gray wants." I didn't try to hide my sarcasm.

She stopped in her tracks. I carried on a couple of steps, but she didn't move. Sighing with impatience, I pivoted to face her.

"What are you trying to say, Zoey?"

Her blunt question made me cringe. Heat crept over me and I slowly walked back to stand in front of her. "I'm angry with Gray and I'm being a bitch," I admitted. "I'm sorry."

Her eyes widened and a faint smile flirted with her mouth. "Apology accepted." She inclined her head in the direction of the bridge. "Let's head for the park. We can grab an ice-cream and sit by the river. Okay?" Her voice was sweetly seductive. Not as husky as mine, more breathy like Marilyn Monroe.

I found myself hooked. "Okay," I said.

We walked under the bridge and wound our way through a growing crowd. Noisy chatter mingled with excited laughter from children playing nearby. The immensity of Brooklyn Bridge as it arched over our heads, and stretched out across the East River, was both impressive and humbling. My chest eased, and the black cloud that had been smothering me since I arrived at Gray's offices this morning began to lift.

"Why don't you go find us a bench by the river, and I'll buy ice-creams?" Eva said.

I looked at the queue outside The Ice Cream Factory. It was only a few people deep. "Okay."

"Any flavor preference?"

"Vanilla with something. Surprise me." I gave her a faint smile and walked off.

The crowd thinned as I moved farther down the pier toward the river. When I was some distance away I found several empty benches, but I opted to stand by the railing. Lower Manhattan stood across the river, and in the distance, I could make out the Statue of Liberty. I closed my eyes and breathed in the briny smell of the river. Faint music from a carousel blended with the sound of waves splashing on the rocks beneath me. I tried to lose myself in the peaceful setting, but annoying thoughts of Gray intruded.

I'd warned him he was poking a hornet's nest when he demanded I move in with him. I gripped the railing and my mouth twisted. Instead of warning him, I should have warned myself. He'd been a complete bastard this morning. It started even before breakfast when he sent a curt text saying Tane would fetch me from the hotel. No explanation. And it got worse when I arrived at his office. He was waiting in the reception, but he barely greeted me. "Take her upstairs to my place," he said to Blake, the slick assistant I'd briefly met during my embarrassing showdown with Gray. "Show her around and give her a set of keys and security card. Make sure she's downstairs to meet with Eva by ten." He'd given these orders without looking at me. My throat had burned. I wanted to believe the burn was anger, but I knew it was hurt. When I tried to speak with him, he cut me off with a cold "We'll talk later." Before I could respond, he'd stalked off, disappearing down a passage.

"Here you go." Eva's voice jolted me from my thoughts. She was holding out an ice-cream cone. "Vanilla and butter pecan." She smiled.

"Thanks." The ice-cream was already starting to melt and I quickly took a lick. "Mmm. This is good."

She licked her own cone, joining me alongside the railing. We stared out at the view, silently enjoying our ice-creams. Eva didn't seem in a hurry to talk. I liked that about her, finding her calmness and direct manner reminded me of Rose.

"This was a good idea," I said.

She nodded. "This is one of my favorite places to visit. It helps me clear my head."

"I can see why."

I finished the last of my cone and wiped my hands on the serviette provided. A gentle wind swirled around us, bringing the sound of children's shrieks. Eva walked over to an empty bench. Yes. It was time to talk. I ignored the tightening in my chest and moved over to join her. The quicker I gave Gray what he needed to hear from Eva, the quicker we could head to Denton.

I sat and puffed out a determined breath. "Where do you want to start?"

Over the next half hour, I brought Eva up to date with my history. She didn't push me on details, accepting only what I offered. But I didn't kid myself. Eva was like Rose, and I knew it was only a matter of time before she punched a hole through my already flimsy emotional guard. I wasn't wrong. It came when we were discussing my dissociative amnesia. She crossed her legs, angling toward me.

"Do you understand why your memories are blocked?"

I reached for the correct medical jargon. "Apparently, what happened to me was so traumatic my brain forced my mind to separate and compartmentalize the trauma."

She frowned. "You sound skeptical."

"I am." Shifting uncomfortably, I crossed and uncrossed my legs. "Look. I know what happened was bad. But there are a lot of people who experience

violence and even rape, and they find a way through it."
I shook my head, meeting her cool gaze. "Why can't
I?"

She frowned in thought. "Perhaps it's not the
violence that caused your memory to be disrupted—"
Her voice trailed off.

My skin prickled. "Go on."

"Perhaps it's something else." She searched my
face. "Something totally incompatible or unacceptable
to your Self."

I knew what she was getting at. I tore my gaze
away, staring blindly at the river. "You mean something
I witnessed, don't you?"

"Yes." Out the corner of my eye, I saw her hand
lift as if to reassure me, but then it dropped back into
her lap. "It would have to be something so abhorrent to
you, your mind refuses to accept it."

I nodded jerkily. "You want to know something?" I
whispered huskily.

"Whatever you want to tell me, Zoey."

My fists clenched so tight, my palms ached. "In the
night, when the nightmares come, I wake terrified,
knowing absolutely that what's hiding in my brain is an
evil I don't ever want to see."

She bent closer. "So why are you here, looking for
answers?"

I jumped up. "Because the longer this shit ferments
inside me, the more damage it's doing." Eva remained
silent, but deep lines creased her brow. "I have to be
able to work, Eva. To do that, I've got to put my past to
rest."

Her eyes suddenly narrowed. "And is Gray part of
the past you want to leave behind?"

My spine jolted upright, sending a hot pain shooting through my neck. "I already did that," I said harshly. "A long time ago." I whirled around and paced over to the railing. A gust of wind swirled, and I squeezed my eyes closed. *'Cause I'd miss you, baby.* The sound of Gray's voice singing to me sent goose bumps racing over my skin. *Oh, Jesus.* I hadn't remembered that in so long.

"Zoey?" Her voice was at my shoulder.

"I betrayed him," I whispered. "Forced him to leave."

"Why would you do that?"

I spun around, shattering the ghostly memory. "I have no fucking idea why I did anything," I shouted.

Eva reached out, and I stiffened. But her hand only curled around the railing. "This isn't about Gray," she said softly. "And you know that. It's about yourself." She inched closer but she didn't touch me. "You have to find a way to forgive yourself."

I sucked in a calming breath. "How do I do that when I can't remember what I did, or why?"

Her flawless face softened. "You go back to the beginning."

I glanced away. A small boy ran by. His parents weren't far behind, and I noticed the pier getting more crowded.

"Let's sit," Eva urged.

We moved back to the bench. Eva waited until we were seated before she spoke. "There are various methods of approach, but my preference in your case would be light hypnotism." I visibly flinched. She calmly continued. "Zoey, it's simply a form of deep relaxation. We wouldn't delve too deep. I believe it's healthier for your memories to surface on their own."

I exhaled noisily. "My therapist in Boston thought the same. But she also said I'd have far more chance of success if I felt safe."

"I'm sure she told you that safety means different things to different people."

I met her chilly gaze. It no longer fazed me. In its depth, I recognized a steely core of compassion. And something else. Something so hauntingly sad I knew I daren't intrude. Shrugging off the thought, I reached for something lighter. She really was remarkably gorgeous. With her thick platinum-blonde hair, perfect D-cups—which at this moment peeked lusciously out of a fitted T—and a bee-sting mouth, she must drive the men in her life crazy. I smiled inwardly. She might not be a "tits-and-ass" woman to be underestimated, but I couldn't stop myself from teasing. "You're a dead ringer for Scarlett Jo—"

"Don't!"

It was a furious hiss. Laughter tickled the back of my throat. Her eyes narrowed, and I bit my lip. But the more she glared, the more my lips quivered. "You're a wicked girl, Zoey Morgan." I grinned, and she shook her head and smiled.

People meandered past, many exclaiming on the lovely view. After a while, her gaze shifted back to me. "Does Gray represent safety for you?"

My breath hitched and I took a moment before I replied, "You don't miss much, do you?"

"We might be similar like that." She raised a single brow minutely.

I held her gaze. "So what now?"

"That's up to you. What do you want from me?"

I straightened. "It's not what I want, it's what Gray wants." I shrugged stiffly. "Or needs."

She flicked away a stray lock of hair. "I don't think Gray knows what he needs, but he's not my patient."

"Neither am I," I snapped. Her mouth pursed, but she inclined her head in acknowledgment. I drew in a slow, shaky breath. "Can you help me?"

"I can try to guide you, but only you can help yourself." She looked away and seemed to gather herself. My stomach clenched when she looked back, her gaze leaving me nowhere to hide. "And if you feel Gray is part of your healing process, then you need to demand his presence."

I blinked, my vision suddenly blurry. "I'm not sure Gray is who I remember him to be."

"And what about you, Zoey? Are you who he remembers you to be?"

Chapter Ten
Blue As a Texas Sky

Pascal's Chocolat! DUMBO, Brooklyn
Four Days Later
Zoey

In three days I was leaving for Denton.

I slurped iced-chocolate cappuccino and licked away the milky foam that coated my lip. I'd promised Gray a week. Four days had passed, and the amount of time he'd spent with me—a big fat zero. Likewise with Eva. The day after we met she called and canceled our session, explaining she'd be tied up for a while. A while turned into three days. Something was going down at their office, and her and Gray were caught up with overtime. I understood the priorities of a demanding job, so I wasn't annoyed. But suddenly I was faced with days of free time. Days with little to do but shop, explore—and think. I rarely went on holidays, making use of all my leave to go on field trips with Doctors Without Borders. I thought I liked being busy, having a purpose. *What a crock of poop!* That blunt truth slammed into me while I was walking through Central Park. I'd been kidding myself for years. I only hated holidays because I'd checked out of my life. I'd given in to fear, allowed it to eat up my joy, and drain away any ability to love. To love others. To love myself. My life was barren. It was a damning revelation.

I drank down the last of my decadent coffee and used a spoon to scoop up the drops of melted chocolate. Richness coated my tongue and then was gone. The time would come for me to grieve for the life I'd retreated from. To rebuild. But first I had to beat the fear.

In three days I was leaving for Denton.

I pushed my empty cup aside. No matter how much chocolate I drank, it couldn't fill the yawning hole in the pit of my stomach. Eva said if I needed Gray to help me heal, I must demand his presence. I couldn't do that. I'd given up the right to demand anything from Gray a long time ago. I yearned with all my heart that he'd come with me. That he would help catch the monsters waiting for me. But if he didn't, I would face the monsters on my own. Even if I lost myself in the process.

I stared out the window of Pascal's Chocolat! Loneliness was now a constant ache, and it was because of Gray. Because last night he woke the devastated young girl buried deep inside me. It was around one in the morning, and I'd been too restless to sleep. I got up to make tea and found Gray in the kitchen. He was standing at the window drinking a beer. His hair was mussed, his clothes wrinkled. He turned as I approached, and I stopped breathing. So freaking handsome. But he looked exhausted. He apologized for not being around and invited me to have breakfast with him. He'd cook. I said okay, but he kept looking at me, his beautiful eyes holding such stark loneliness that goose bumps had raised all over my body. His loneliness called to a secret place inside me. I was used to spending time alone and I never felt lonely. Not until today. Of course, when I'd come downstairs to meet him for breakfast, he was gone.

A hand tapped me on the shoulder and I jumped. Twisting my neck, I looked up. "Blake, hey."

"Mind if we join you?"

"Of course." I looked curiously at the woman beside him.

"Hi. I'm Katya, Luke's wife."

"I'm Zoey." I reached out and shook her hand. "Gray's mentioned you."

"Well, it's more than he's said about you," she grumbled.

She was extraordinarily beautiful. Not bombshell sultry like Eva. Rather, she had a timeless beauty like a movie star from the 1950s. Her hair was long, a deep blue-black glossy curtain. I'd never seen eyes the color of hers. They were violet and surrounded by the longest black lashes.

"It's your turn to order." Blake pecked her on the cheek and nudged her toward the counter. "I want an iced coffee, please. No chocolate." She glared at him but he ignored it, sliding gracefully into the chair opposite me.

"Don't you dare ask her about Gray until I come back." She dumped her jacket on the empty chair next to me and stalked off to place their order.

They reminded me of snarky siblings. I bit my lip and looked at Blake. He was a picture of sleek elegance. Dressed in a killer navy suit with a lavender silk tie, his short black hair was styled like he was prepped for a hair-product commercial. But a weird danger whispered beneath his coiffed surface that disturbed the hair on the back of my neck.

"How you doing, Cinderella?" he said. "You look like you've lost your Prince Charming."

I pointed to myself. "Cinderella, really?"

"You don't agree?" His onyx eyes twinkled.

I snorted. "Cinderella was a miserable slave girl."

"And Prince Charming saved her from her plight."

I looked at him curiously. "Is that how you see me? Helpless. In need of a man to save me?"

His perfectly tweezed brows drew together. "Perhaps not." He leaned back, his gaze hooded. "Something's changed from that first day when you came looking for Gray."

"How so?"

"Hmm. I'm not sure."

I gritted my teeth. "Different enough to drop that tawdry nickname?"

He gave a delighted smile. "You really don't like it?"

"No!"

He burst out laughing.

"What are you laughing about?" Katya placed Blake's iced-coffee in front of him, and put down her own steaming mug. She looked from Blake to me. He shook his head, and I gave her a wide-eyed look. She snarled something indecipherable and slipped into her chair. I ducked my head to hide my smile. These two people were as good as strangers to me, but both were connected to Gray. And because of that, my loneliness eased.

Blake leaned forward conspiratorially. "So tell us, darling, how is that man of yours?"

"Who?"

He scowled impatiently. "Gray, of course, who

else?"

I jerked upright. "He's not my man!" I denied hotly.

He threw his hands in the air, nearly knocking over his coffee. "Goodness, girl, who are you kidding?"

"Blake!" Katya slammed her chocolate concoction on the table, glaring at him.

He glared back. "You haven't seen how that man looks at her." A smirk hovered around his mouth. "I've never seen the charmer all rattled like this."

My heart thumped double-time. *Gray rattled.* "Well, you're wrong. Gray's definitely not my man." I looked away. *Not anymore.*

Katya cleared her throat. "Are you going to Mira's party tonight?"

"Of course she's going," Blake said.

I frowned and looked from Katya to Blake.

"Oh, my Go-od!" Blake waved his hands dramatically. "That alpha cretin forgot to tell you, didn't he?"

"Tell me what?"

"It's Mira's birthday," Katya said softly. "King's throwing a party for her at his penthouse." She fiddled with her cup and glanced at Blake. "I guess it's Mira's penthouse too since she also lives there." Her pretty gaze returned to me. "We're all going. I'm sure Gray was supposed to invite you."

"He didn't," I said flatly, and tried to ignore the ugly heaviness creeping over me.

"Because he's a cretin," Blake said. "I heard King ask Gray to invite you."

"Well, he didn't."

Blake reached across and squeezed my hand. "He's

been busy, sweetkins. It probably slipped his mind."

"Luke also hasn't been home early for days." Katya rested her arms on the table. She had a faint chocolate mustache on her upper lip. "That must be it."

I pressed my hand against my stomach. "I don't think that's it—"

"Yes, it is," Blake interrupted. "I'm King's man-Friday, and I'm telling you, you're invited." He picked up a napkin and passed it to Katya. "Wipe your mouth, princess. You look like Lily after she's guzzled a chocolate milkshake."

My throat thickened. The chocolate cappuccino was beginning to make me faintly queasy. It was time to go. I reached for my bag, but my phone vibrated in my pocket. I pulled it out and looked at the screen. "It's Gray," I murmured and tapped the screen to connect the call. "Hi."

"Where are you?"

It was a tight accusation. I gripped the phone. "Pascal's."

"What?"

"I went for a run," I said with more force. "And then I came here for coffee." Silence echoed down the line. My scalp prickled. "Gray?"

"I thought you left."

I sucked in a shallow breath. Raw vulnerability colored his voice. "I didn't leave," I said carefully. "I just went out."

"I get that."

A fine sweat broke out on my forehead. "Gray—"

"I left early. Work. Came back to make you breakfast."

"Make me breakfast?"

"Yeah. I said I would." He sounded more like himself. "Been busy. Not had much time to talk with you."

I squeezed the phone, my hand clammy. "I didn't know you were coming back."

Katya burst out laughing. I looked up. She was playfully punching Blake in the arm.

"That Katya?" His voice rumbled in my ear.

"Yes."

"You've met?"

"Blake's here. He introduced us."

"How's the glitterbug?"

"What?" I was struggling to keep up with him.

He chuckled, and I closed my eyes. "Lily, her daughter."

Without answering, I handed my phone to Katya. "Gray wants to know about Lily," I said.

She smiled and took the phone. I barely listened as she chatted with him.

Since I was a little girl, I'd been sensitive to Gray. His moods were like a picture storybook to me. He'd often remark I knew what he was thinking before he uttered a word. Back then, he'd loved this about me.

Katya finished her conversation and handed me the phone. "Gray says to wait for him, he's on his way."

I nodded. "Are Gray and Lily close?"

Her face lit up. "Gray adores her, and she loves him right back. According to Lily, that man can do no wrong."

I laughed quietly. "I believe it. I was like that with Gray when I was young."

She rested her chin on her palm. "You've known him that long?"

I nodded. "We were neighbors in Denton. The first time I saw him, I was eight years old."

Her eyes rounded. "He must have been a teenager. What was he like?"

I smiled. *Gray at thirteen astride his horse.* "Breathtaking."

Her eyes sparkled wickedly. "And do you still find him breathtaking?"

My breath trapped in my throat. Katya watched me steadily. An awkward silence hung between us, but I refused to fill it. A moment later, her gaze skated over my shoulder. "Here he is," she said.

Blake snorted. "Saved by Prince Charming."

Before I could bite his head off, Katya rose to her feet. "Come on, Blake, it's time to go. Luke's waiting for me." She collected her jacket and handbag, and winked at me. "We'll see you tonight."

I didn't know what to say, so I nodded stiffly.

She bent down and whispered in my ear. "I think he still makes you breathless." With a squeeze to my shoulder, she hurried off. I swiveled and watched her greet Gray. He smiled warmly at her, and I quickly swiveled back.

Blake pressed his hands to the table and rose. "Mira's difficult to buy for. I'll make you a list."

"What?"

He leaned forward, his elegant face stopping inches from mine. "Get out of your head, sweetkins. Mira. Birthday present." I stared at him, bug-eyed. "She's complicated. I'll make a list of gift suggestions. Text them to you."

I nodded. *Jeez.* I felt like a puppet, and these crazy people were pulling my strings.

His dark gaze flicked past me, and then came back. My breath caught when he leaned in another inch. "When that man smiles, and his eyes go as blue as the Texas sky—" His mouth relaxed into a sensual smile. "Definitely breathtaking."

****

Gray

Gray waved off Blake and Katya and moved through the chocolate emporium. The aroma of chocolate was strong, but not enough to dilute the scent of honeysuckle still clinging to his senses. His mouth tightened. His heart was still in overdrive from this morning. The woman used the same goddamn honeysuckle shampoo that drove him crazy fourteen years ago. He knew he was thinking like an asshole, but it felt like she was taunting him. His sleep was disrupted by the memory of her taste, and the tantalizing scent of honeysuckle that was uniquely Zoey. With every day she lived in his space, her scent became more pervasive. This morning when he went to look for her, he found her bedroom empty except for that lingering scent. It was so powerful, it triggered memories of his loss and drove him from her room.

Gray ruthlessly shut down his thoughts and slipped into the chair opposite Zoey. Her green gaze swept over him, and she smiled hesitantly. Her hair was in a ponytail, but several tendrils had escaped, curling around her face. Their obstinacy hinted at the untamed beauty she kept intentionally muted. Her fair skin had a new golden sheen to it, illuminating faint freckles across her nose and cheeks. He guessed she'd been taking advantage of the warm weather.

Gray pulled his chair closer to the table, and

surreptitiously flexed his shoulders. He had a cluster of growing knots that were compounding the headache he'd had since Zoey made her dramatic entry back into his life. But he could deal with a headache. What he was fighting against was desire. In his mind, he had a giant red cross plastered over everything Zoey. But his cock wasn't paying attention. He was sitting in a cafe piled high with chocolate treats, and he was semi-hard. And it wasn't the fucking chocolate.

He crossed his arms and leaned on the table. "Blake reminded me about Mira's party tonight," he said gruffly. "I'm sorry. I should have passed on the invite."

"It's okay."

"It's not okay. Work's been a bitch and it slipped my mind."

She shrugged.

Gray shifted uneasily. He couldn't decide if she was pissed or not. Guilt pricked his conscience. He'd insisted she move in with him, then ignored her and buried himself in his work. "I guess you've had more free time than you planned, huh?"

She smoothed an errant curl. "I understand the demands of work. Schedules don't always pan out the way you want them to."

He looked away, his gut squirming. Zoey didn't miss much. And he was a moron who didn't deserve her understanding. The case he was working might be personal to King and Mira, but he knew if he asked, they would have cut him loose to give him the time he needed. But he hadn't asked. "This case heated up quicker than we anticipated." He forced a smile. "But everything's getting sorted, and I should have some free time."

She bit her lip, and his dick jumped. "If it's easier, I can move out, give you some space."

"Fuck, no!"

Her head jerked up, surprise clear on her face.

Gray shoved his chair back, jamming his ankle across his knee. "You don't have to do that. As I said, I'll definitely have more time."

Her astute gaze searched his face. There was a tiny freckle at the corner of her bottom lip. And he wanted to taste it. He forced his gaze away. How could he hate her scent when the first thing he did when he got home was breathe deep, inexplicably relieved to have her sleeping under his roof?

She cleared her throat. "Will Eva have time to meet with me soon?"

"Yes. Tomorrow. And as I told you, if she's good, I'm good."

Her face tightened. She looked like she was about to say something but then ducked her head.

"What?" he said.

She shook her head firmly. "It's nothing."

"I obviously said something to piss you off."

Her chin lifted. "It's nothing, Gray. You said nothing." Her eyes locked with his, then sliced away.

"Zoey—"

"Are you going to order something to drink or can we leave?" Her arms were braced on the table, her hands balled into fists.

He dropped his ankle to the floor. "I promise I'll have more time tomorrow. I'll make an effort—"

"Don't!" Her hand shot out. "I don't want you to do anything you don't want to do."

"For fuck's sake, Zoey, that's not what I said."

She cocked her head, emerald eyes blazing. "Do you remember that day when your mother told you about your adoption?"

He reared back in his chair, only just catching himself.

"You came to the pond. It was the first time we met properly, but we connected immediately." Her voice was low and husky. "It was like we'd known each other forever. At the end of the day, you told me about your mom." She leaned forward, her intensity hypnotic. "You put on a brave face but I could see you were broken. You said it was over with her. That you were going to lock everything about her into a box and throw away the key."

Gray didn't need to close his eyes to picture that day. He could still see his mother sitting rigidly on the couch, Jacks held close to her side. He'd sat alone in the chair opposite. Then, in her clear precise manner, she'd proceeded to shatter his world.

"When you were born your birth mother gave you away to the church." Her unblinking hazel gaze froze him in place. *"The church gave you to your father and I."*

Gray looked at his brother, trying to grapple with what his mother had said. "Did the church also give you Jacks?"

She yanked Jacks against her, wrapping her arms tightly around him. "How dare you suggest such a thing!" Her voice was shrill. "Jacks is a special gift from God. He's our miracle child."

Gray was thirteen, but he still couldn't compute what she was saying. He looked at his mother and

Jacks. "Then what am I?"

"Adopted," she hissed.

The word had hung starkly between them. The bitter way she said it a clear rejection of all he was to her, all he could have been to her. Gray knew right then he would never be "son-enough" for her. It didn't matter what he did to try and please her, or how much he loved her. With one word she'd shifted his reality, and he understood she would never love him like a mother should love her son. And he accepted it. Like Zoey said, he put her in a box, sealed it up, and kept her far away from his heart. And mostly it worked. His mother never had the power to really hurt him again.

"I was there, Zoey," he bit out. "You don't need to remind me what happened."

"Then tell me something, Gray. Is that what you did with me? Shut me in a box after my engagement to Jacks?" Her eyes drilled into him. "Am I still in that box?"

He dropped his gaze. Her hand was flat on the table. Pale and slim. Pain rippled through his jaw when he saw it was trembling. *Too fucking fragile. But not too fragile to save lives.* He leveled his gaze back on her face. "Butterflies don't do well in boxes, Zoey." His voice was cold.

"Butterflies!"

Her cry was stark, and it shot like a speeding bolt deep into his chest. But Gray forced himself not to flinch. "They flutter against the sides until they rip their wings to shreds."

Raw pain moved across her face. "Is that what you want, for me to be battered and bruised?"

His breath ceased. He ran a hand roughly through

his hair. "Don't be dramatic," he said gruffly. "You know better than anybody I would never hurt you." He clattered forward in his chair, gripping the sides of the table. "I'd lay down my life if it meant you could fly free. And you know that."

"How would I know that, Gray?" Her pupils flared, eyes suddenly too large for her face. "Who you are today is not the man who called me his butterfly."

The pain he'd been trying to hold back erupted. He leaned forward until he could feel her breath on his face. "And you, Zoey—you're not the woman I called butterfly either, are you?"

Her face contorted and suddenly her eyes were swimming in tears. "No, I guess I'm not."

His breath strangled in his throat. "What the fuck, Zoey?"

She shoved her chair back, jumping to her feet. Grabbing her bag, she impatiently swiped at her cheeks. "Stir up a hornet's nest, Gray, and you're going to get stung." Without looking at him, she spun and walked away.

Gray watched her exit the cafe and move rapidly across the street.

Stir up a hornet's nest, and you're going to get stung.

She was right about that.

But it wasn't the hornet doing the stinging. It was him. He'd struck at the heart of her. And it sure as hell didn't feel good. His heart was pounding, and the back of his throat felt like razor blades had slashed at it.

No. It didn't feel good at all.

Chapter Eleven
Snake Charmer

Grayson Walker's Apartment
Zoey

Who was that woman?

I stood in front of the wardrobe mirror, trapped by the wide-eyed gaze of the woman staring back at me. She was an older version of the carefree, innocent girl I used to be. I tossed my head. I'd planned to pin my hair in an elaborate updo, but every time I finished, I ended up yanking it loose. I tossed my head again and watched as my hair tumbled in a curly mass down my back. My breathing quickened, and electric tingles spread from my chest, flowing like fine champagne right to my toes. I twirled, and my flamboyant new dress flared around my thighs.

When I stormed away from Pascal's, it had taken me several blocks of energetic stomping, and a subway ride to Fifth Avenue before the pain of Gray's verbal attack began to fade. But as my breath came easier, so did the clarity of my thoughts. And I didn't need to be psychic to know that Gray was conflicted. He might say it was work keeping him busy, but I knew that was bulldust. He was avoiding me. Who could blame him? I hurt him then spent years pushing him away. A blind person could see he was struggling with me being back in his life. Even when he was younger, Gray could be aloof and sarcastic, but he only lashed out if he felt threatened by those he loved. Or if he was hurting. This thought had stopped me in my tracks. I'd propped myself against a street lamp, and replayed the morning's incident over and over in my head. For Gray to sting me like that, it had to mean he felt something.

And something was better than nothing.

I whirled around again. I loved my dress. I found it in Bloomingdales. It was a vibrant red, a color I rarely wore because I thought it clashed with my hair. Large poppies in purple, pink and white drifted across the upper half of the one-shoulder neckline, and down the dramatic flutter sleeve. The dress was made of airy silk that skimmed my body and fell just above my knees. It had an asymmetrical finish, allowing the hem to swing flirtatiously when I moved. I'd matched it with high-heeled purple sling-backs.

I allowed myself one final look at my reflection. My tummy quivered, and I quickly turned away. There was no time for doubts. Grabbing my velvet evening bag, I left the room. In the kitchen, I poured a small glass of white wine and sat in the sitting room to wait for Gray. It was nearly eight o'clock. Eva called earlier to say if he's not here by eight-ten, to text and she would drop by and fetch me. I sipped my wine. Eva understood what all women do; no matter how confident we might be, none of us wants to fly solo to a party filled with strangers.

The chilled wine helped my dry mouth, but it did nothing to steady the faint tremors in my hands. I was weirdly excited about the party, but the familiar dread in the pit of my stomach was becoming difficult to ignore. It was dark and malignant. Memories were tearing loose, snaking their way through my subconscious. Soon. Soon the monsters would escape into the light of day.

I would lay down my life if it meant you could fly free.

I stripped away the anger coating Gray's vow and wrapped it around myself. Its truth acted as a buffer against the fear. So did living in his home. From the moment I arrived, I liked being here. The apartment was an industrial-style loft spread over two levels. And a screaming contradiction to my desultory student digs in Boston. Exuding modern sophistication, the windows were dramatic and oversized, with soaring ceilings and oak herringbone floors. It was furnished with cream leather couches, and chrome and wood coffee tables. Scattered rugs introduced color, and a selection of intriguing photographs in simple black frames covered the walls. I particularly liked a set of three that dominated the sitting room. They were moody shots of New Orleans. When I peered closer, I could see the photographer's name written in tiny print in the corner. It was Luke.

But it wasn't the plush sleekness of Gray's loft that comforted me. It was the intimacy of being surrounded by his personal effects. Like the photographs displayed on the narrow side table in the hall. One was of Gray with Luke in the marines. Another of Luke, Katya, and Lily at their wedding. Gray with Lily on a beach somewhere. And then there was the photo that brought me crashing to my knees. Thank heavens I'd been alone because I'd sat on the floor with that photo clutched close to my face, tears streaming down my cheeks. Gray, his arm crooked around my neck, and both of us surrounded by Noah, my mama, and Dad. I cried until my throat burned and wracking hiccups stole my breath. But the crazy thing was that when my tears stopped, I knew they were cathartic because they washed away another layer of the black slime living like a parasite in my brain.

I finished my wine and took my glass back to the kitchen. Gray might rarely be home, but I knew he was close. Close enough to catch me when the monsters came calling.

At least that was until I left for Denton.

I worried at my lips, licking away the remainder of my favorite bronze-berry lipgloss. It was eight-fifteen. I tried to ignore the hollow pang in my chest. The silence was beginning to drain my confidence. I reached for my bag lying on the granite kitchen island and rummaged inside for my phone. Time to text Eva.

Beep-beep!

My phone clattered onto the island. That was the sound of the security system unlocking the front door.

Gray was home.

My chest rose and fell in rhythm with his footsteps.

"You're still waiting for me."

I sucked in a deep breath and stepped around the island. "I was about to text Eva."

His eyes widened. And traced a slow path down my body before returning to my face. The tingling in my blood heated to a boil. "I'm sorry I'm late."

"That's okay," I said breathlessly. "I was late getting ready."

His smokey gaze drifted over me again. I fiddled nervously with my hair, trying to smooth the wild curls. His brows knitted together, and I dropped my hands. He ran a hand roughly over his jaw. "I need a shower," he said gruffly. "You okay to wait ten minutes?"

I nodded jerkily.

Tiny blue shards glinted in his eyes. Before I could convince myself they were real, he turned his back and moved to the staircase. He stopped in the hallway and stared at the gaily-wrapped gift I'd left on the table. "Dammit. I forgot to buy Mira a birthday present." Exhaustion exposed his southern drawl.

My heart skipped. "If you want I can give her that from both of us."

He half turned. His gaze was an intimate caress, stroking over my exposed skin. "It's a good present," I blurted. "Blake sent me an ideas list."

His mouth twitched. "Then it must be good." It was a honeyed drawl. "And yeah, if you could add my name to the card, that would be good too." He looked down at the gift and flicked one of the trailing gold ribbons. "Let me know how much you spent, and I'll cover it." He stepped away and headed up the stairs.

"It's fine, I've got it," I called.

I could hear him pause on the stairs. "Not fine, Zoey. Let me know, yeah?"

I rolled my eyes. "Whatever."

"And Zoey—"

"What!" I said impatiently.

"You look good."

I stopped breathing.

"Beautiful."

I teetered on my high heels. Only when I heard his footsteps resume up the stairs did I let go of my breath.

Beautiful.

My knees wobbled. A bark of hysterical laughter

escaped and I clapped a hand over my mouth.

Beautiful.

Wildness bubbled inside me and I clung to the edge of the island. When my knees stopped shaking, I fetched Mira's gift and sat at the dining room table. Slipping out the card from the envelope, I read my brief birthday greeting. I'd signed it "Best wishes, Zoey." Before I could chicken out, I added "and Gray."

Zoey and Gray.

Our names blurred and I quickly closed the card and slid it back into the envelope. Over the next five minutes, I freshened my lipgloss and drew on all my breathing techniques to try and settle the wild fluttering inside me. It was a wasted effort. Because when Gray reappeared downstairs, he sucked the calm right out of me. His hair was mussed and still damp. But it was his freshly showered scent that stole my breath. It mingled with his familiar spicy aftershave and sent my heart tripping over itself.

"You ready?"

"Yes." I sounded strangled.

"Everything okay?"

"Of course." I jumped to my feet and jerked my head in the direction of the front door. "Shall we go?"

He nodded at the gift. "You put my name on the card?"

"Yes," I said brightly.

"Good. Thanks." He looked at me quizzically, like he was going to say something else, then shook his head and turned away. "Let's go."

I quickly followed after him. King's penthouse was in the same building. At the elevator, my eyes kept straying to him. He looked nothing like the young cowboy I grew up with. He was dressed in off-white slim fitting jeans, and a pale-gray silky T-shirt that hugged his broad chest. A light charcoal linen jacket finished off his stylish attire. I swallowed the lump in my throat and looked up at him. "Your dress style has changed."

His eyes crinkled. "You nostalgic for cowboy boots and a dusty Stetson?"

I grinned. "Maybe."

Ping!

The elevator doors opened and we stepped inside. Gray swiped a card and hit the button to the penthouse. Then he casually leaned against the mirrored wall and studied me. Heat crept up my neck. "You...um." I cleared my throat. "You look very nice tonight," I said in a rush.

He pushed off the wall and turned to face the doors. "Thanks." His tone was offhand.

I cringed inwardly. I could feel my blush spread over my cheeks.

Ping!

The doors slid open, and we were looking directly into King's impressive penthouse. I guessed the whole floor must belong to him. The party was already well underway, and surveying it from inside the lift, it looked both surreal and alluring. Gray held the door open waiting for me to exit. Instead, I inhaled deeply, then slowly breathed out the awkward discomfort his moody behavior had caused. Stepping into his space, I said in a low-pitched voice, "Have fun, tough guy." And brushed past him.

Blake immediately accosted me, kissing the air on both sides of my cheeks. "You look divine, darling, like an exotic red butterfly. Maybe that's what I'll call you—"

"No!"

Gray's denial was so vicious it froze Blake in place. And made me crush the prettily wrapped gift held in my hands. I took a rapid step backward and stared at Gray. An ice-storm raged in his eyes.

"Gray?" Blake said softly. "Something wrong?"

My gaze cut to him. His onyx eyes were locked on Gray. All sign of his previous teasing was gone. I swallowed with difficulty.

"You don't call her butterfly," Gray said.

My scalp prickled. A deadly quality emanated from him, turning his statement into a threat. In my peripheral vision, I saw Luke approach. But I ignored him and rested my hand on Gray's arm. "Gray?" He didn't react. Squeezing his steely bicep, I stretched up and whispered into his ear, "Hey, tough guy, take a breath."

"Everything okay?" Luke loomed on the other side of Gray.

"It's fine," Blake said firmly. His gaze shifted from Gray to me, and back again. "Everything is fine. Yes?" He raised a brow at Gray.

I looked at the beautiful but complicated man standing by my side. His bicep flexed beneath my fingers. My pulse raced, but abruptly he inclined his head. Then without another word, he settled his hand firmly in the small of my back, and urged me past Blake and into the hub of the party. I chanced a quick look back at Blake. Both he and Luke hadn't moved. "Sorry," I mouthed.

The next several minutes slipped by in a fog. Gray

introduced me to Mira and King. It was a hazy conversation because all I could hear was the pounding of my confused heart. And all I could feel was the burn of Gray's hand searing through my silk dress. At one point a waiter dressed in a tuxedo floated a tray of classic cocktails under my nose. I zeroed in on a vodka martini, and by the time Mira left with her crumpled gift in hand, and King had moved off to join another group of guests, my glass was empty.

"Would you like another?"

"Sorry?" I stared dumbly at Gray.

"A drink." He pointed at my empty glass. "You want another?"

"Sure." He reached for my glass, but I jerked it away. "I want the olives." I fished one out and popped it in my mouth. His face was blank except for his eyes. Blue and gray battled restlessly, neither victorious. I chewed my olive but nearly choked when his gaze drifted to my mouth.

"Feel free to mingle," he murmured. "I'll send over the cocktail waiter."

For the second time that night, I thought he was going to say something more. But his mouth hardened, and he walked away.

Sweat trickled down my neck. I clung to my glass so it wouldn't slip through my damp palms. Out the corner of my eye, I caught sight of Blake watching me. Fishing out another olive, I sauntered casually in the opposite direction.

I stuck to the outer rim of the party. There were easily forty or fifty guests, all of them strangers except for those I'd met at Gray's office. I smiled and here and there offered an absent nod. My stomach churned, and my brain scrambled, trying to make sense of what had happened.

You don't call her butterfly.

Freaking hell. I could still feel the heat from his hand imprinted on my back.

"Vodka martini, ma'am." A tuxedoed waiter intercepted me and proffered a silver tray holding a perfect cocktail swimming in olives. "With extra olives," he said with a flourish.

I searched for Gray. He was on the opposite side of the room talking with King and a group of sophisticated strangers. He had his profile to me. I waited, but he never looked my way. "Thank you," I said brightly, turning back to the waiter. He smiled, and I swapped my empty glass for the fresh one.

Sipping the gratifying coolness of my martini, I continued my solitary circling of King's impressive home. The double volume open-plan space was stunning. Half was a living area with the entire river-facing side made up of floor-to-ceiling windows. The other half was a sumptuous dining room that flowed into a state of the art kitchen. A central floating wall created a focal point, housing a 360-degree wood-burning fireplace. Light wooden floors and Persian rugs brought a warm classic touch to the industrial-style loft. Clusters of modern pendant lights hung on wires of varying lengths, creating warm pockets of intimacy. The furniture was sleek, mostly white and chocolate brown. Eclectic art covered the walls, and a variety of Asian and African sculptures were artistically scattered about. Thane Kingsley had remarkable good taste. The vast penthouse was a clear display of his wealth, but subtlety and restraint were abundantly evident.

Bowls of fresh white roses and irises and hundreds of candles made the room look festive but elegant. And a constant stream of jazz and easy listening music created a relaxed mood without inhibiting conversation. I was definitely impressed. I popped another olive in my mouth, and nearly swallowed it whole when I caught sight of an explosion of color dominating the dining room wall. I rapidly moved nearer and stopped dead when I read the name scrawled on the bottom corner. Jackson Pollock.

"Something to eat, ma'am?"

I jerked around and just managed to save my cocktail from spilling down my dress. A demure young waitress was holding out a tray loaded with what had to be the coolest designer snacks I'd ever seen. My stomach rumbled unexpectedly. "It all looks delicious." I smiled. "Which one is your favorite?"

She grinned, revealing the cutest dimples. "The marinated shrimp is popular." She pointed at baby shrimp pierced with tiny wooden forks. "And these are my favorite too. Crab ravioli with tarragon."

I was suddenly ravenous. "I want to taste everything," I said.

She giggled and nodded toward the dining room table. "There's a pile of plates over there. Taste one of each and see what you like."

I did exactly that, helping myself to a rosemary lemon chicken ballotine, a fingerling potato with pancetta and artichoke, a shrimp, a ravioli and a tiny newspaper parcel filled with baked cod and some sort of Japanese dressing. Taking my plate, and nearly empty martini glass, I edged back into the living area. I was careful to keep the fireplace between Blake and myself, who I noticed was slowly circling the room toward me.

Snacking on my food, I studied the interesting crowd. This was definitely not a jeans and beaded top kind of party. Gray stood with Luke and Katya. She looked ultra-feminine in a cream midi-length tea dress overlaid with black embroidered mesh, and baroque-style lacy cap sleeves. Luke wore a cobalt-blue dress shirt that was the perfect offset for his midnight eyes. It hadn't escaped my attention that he remained in close proximity to Gray. I also noticed his unsmiling gaze frequently strayed to me. My fingerling potato lodged in my throat, and I washed it down with the last of my martini.

"Hello Zoey," Eva's breathy voice greeted at my side. "I love your dress. You look fabulous tonight."

I smiled but my eyes bugged out as I waved a martini-hand at her own killer dress. "You too," I gasped. Her long-sleeved bodycon hugged her curvaceous figure like a pair of Spanx. It was a geometric design, predominantly white with bold patterns of black, pale-green and burnt orange. "Jeez, Eva. You look freaking hot."

She gave a bark of laughter. Then she huddled closer. "I notice Gray hasn't taken his eyes off you."

"Bull," I muttered and fished an olive out with my tongue. Eva blinked in surprise. I chewed my olive and swallowed. "Wherever I happen to be, he makes sure he's several people away. Look." I pointed at Gray who was now talking with Tane and a man with long dreads.

"He's trying not to show it, but he's keeping an eye on you." Her voice was firm. My chest tightened, but I just shrugged. Eva wrinkled her nose. "It sounds like things haven't improved between the two of you." She peered hungrily at my plate.

I moved it out of her reach. "If you promise to shut up about Gray, I'll give you one of my shrimp."

Her blue eyes widened. I teased her with my plate, and she shook her head wryly, a smile breaking out. "Deal," she muttered and snatched the shrimp away.

The music faded, and King's voice cut through the room. He was standing by the fireplace, ready to make some sort of announcement. King had the kind of magnetic aura that could not be ignored. He was dressed in a designer charcoal suit and black shirt and tie. As I circled the party, I'd watched him glide effortlessly from one group of guests to another. Smooth and hospitable, but always aloof. He reminded me of an apex predator marking his territory. And like Luke, I frequently felt his gaze targeted at me, even though when I tried to catch him in the act, he was always looking elsewhere. Guests began to gravitate toward him, but Eva and I hung back.

"Good evening." His clipped English accent easily silenced the party chatter. "First off, I want to thank all of you..."

"A refresh, ma'am." The waiter's voice was hushed as he presented me with a glistening martini filled with olives.

I smiled my thanks and again swapped my empty glass for a full one. Automatically, I searched for Gray. And found him standing next to Mira, whispering in her ear. My smile faded.

Mira was an enigma. Blake's list of gift ideas had been an eye-opener, but I really knew nothing about her. What I did know was that in a room full of beautiful people she stood out. She wasn't exactly beautiful, but her exotic appeal made her impossible to ignore. She was dressed in a super-tight, super-sexy, long-sleeved cat suit. It was made of metallic-silver and black leather, with wide, cutout fishnet panels running from her ankle, all the way up her sides, and under her arms. Not only did the leather sheath show off her seriously toned body, the fishnet panels screamed to all who cared that she was commando. Seriously high black stilettos and oversized chunky silver earrings finished it off. But she succeeded in looking even more striking because her outlandish outfit was offset by an aloof air, much like King's. I wondered if they were lovers.

"Please join me in wishing Amirah a happy birthday." I tore my gaze away and tuned back into King. "I won't ask you to sing or she'll have my scalp." Laughter spread through the room.

I leaned into Eva. "Amirah?" I asked.

"It's her full name," Eva said in my ear. "But only King calls her that."

"Please join us on the roof deck, and share a special birthday gift I've arranged for Amirah." King moved toward her and held out his hand. I gulped when she hesitated. But a second later she acquiesced, and together they moved to the tall glass doors leading outside.

Eva and I joined the crowd drifting after them. "Are they together?" I asked softly.

Eva slipped her arm through mine. "Depends on how you define together. When Mira turned up a few years ago, King gutted this place and redesigned it to include a separate wing for her."

My curiosity was stirred. But Eva's easy gesture of friendship was far more impactful. I glanced at her and felt my smile return. I didn't have close friends, but I had a feeling that was about to change.

We walked onto the roof deck, and my jaw dropped. Thousands of fairy lights interspersed with hanging lanterns had been strung up to enclose the deck in a magical Arabian Nights theme. Low Moroccan tables and colorful cushioned chairs surrounded a central wooden dance floor. The exotic atmosphere was heightened by stained-glass tabletop lanterns and Arabic-style rugs strewn everywhere. Decorative pagoda-style tents were scattered along the edges of the deck, providing a variety of tempting foods.

The pièce de résistance was a huge sound stage that took up the entire far side of the deck. This was King's birthday gift to Mira. A live performance by her favorite band, Pink Martini. I clapped along with the announcement even though I had no idea who the band was. But when their lead singer let rip with a spine-chilling opening note of *Armado Mio*, I immediately became a devoted fan. The orchestra-style band was made up of ten musicians, all dressed in tuxedoes. China Forbes, the glorious singer, wore a sensational hot-pink bustier that flowed into a floor-length skirt made of cascading pink and purple roses. Their repertoire was wonderfully diverse. One moment we were caught up in a samba parade in Rio, and the next we were transported to a romantic Italian palazzo.

Mira ignored King and snapped her fingers at Tane. The two glided onto the dance floor and began to dance with such effortless grace, they held everybody spellbound. Like mating shadows, their fluidity was breathtakingly erotic. I'd never seen anything like it before. I looked for King, but like Gray, he'd melted away into the crowd.

The party was blow-your-mind brilliant. Eva stayed glued to my side until a friend dragged her onto the dance floor. Within seconds, Katya had me down on the chair next to hers. She was sweet and non-intrusive, but soon Luke dragged her onto the dance floor too. Blake, who'd been lurking nearby, immediately slipped onto her seat. I tensed, but I needn't have worried. He pretended like Gray hadn't turned assassin on him, and in no time, we were huddled like co-conspirators, him pointing out interesting people and sharing the latest hot gossip about them.

I frequently caught glimpses of Gray swallowed up in the partying crowd. He was always chatting. Smiling. Flirting. I laughed and smiled too, working hard to hide the dark mood slowly creeping over me. A number of strangers invited me to dance. I declined. Time passed. Gray flirted. And Gray danced. I declined a fourth martini and tried to lose myself in the music and friendly banter. But snatches of Gray's glib patter kept intruding.

"It's good to see you, darlin'…"

"Would you like a drink, darlin'…"

I gritted my teeth and wished I'd taken that last martini. Why did he have to address every woman as darlin'?

"Dance with me, darlin'…"

I hated that one most of all. I wanted to rip off my silk dress and crawl inside my skin because he danced with every woman there that night. Every woman except me. A man called Matiu joined our table and he was a good distraction. He was the man I'd noticed earlier with the long chocolate brown dreads. He had the same otherworldly beauty as Tane, and Blake whispered to me that they were twins. Matiu set up a *hookah* and taught me how to smoke it. I was a quick study and was soon puffing away on cherry-flavored nicotine-free smoke.

And that's when it happened.

I was giggling at my failed attempts to imitate Matiu's perfect smoke rings, when my gaze strayed across the dance floor. And slammed into a roiling storm. My throat closed like a noose was pulled tight around my neck. Because at that moment I could see right into Gray's soul. And it was haunted. I choked on the smoke, and Matiu leaned forward, offering me his beer. His body cut my connection with Gray. My coughing fit got worse and I took a gulp from Matiu's glass, spluttering to him that I was okay. But I wasn't okay. *And Gray wasn't okay!* It was a scream that rattled my brain. But it also loosened the noose around my neck, because knowing Gray was in pain too, somehow lessened my own.

It took several minutes for my throat to stop burning. I was just deciding how to make a discreet exit when a hand brushed my shoulder. "Come on, sugar, dance with me." Tane held out his hand.

I shook my head firmly. "Are you crazy? I can't dance like Mira."

"You don't have to." His hand closed around mine, and he smoothly pulled me to my feet. "You only need to dance like you."

The band began to play a bluesy number, and China Forbes' seductive voice peeled into the glittery night. A smile spread across my face when Tane spun me out, his arm fully extended, then spun me back, and gently pulled me to his body. "Blake's right." His melodic drawl was a rumble near my ear. "You do look like an exotic red butterfly."

"You heard us," I said breathlessly, trying to keep a little distance between me and his rhythmically swinging hips.

His sensual mouth quirked. "Sugar, everybody heard you."

You don't call her butterfly.

My hand spasmed on Tane's shoulder. Gray's warning had been deadly. "And you still want to call me butterfly?" I said skeptically.

His unusual topaz eyes gleamed before he spun me out again and back. "You want me dead?" His fluidity and innate strength stole my breath. As did the striking tattoos that covered both his arms. He was magnetic, but meshed with his mysterious beauty was a streak of elusive savagery.

"Are you afraid of Gray?" I panted, trying to keep up with his smooth dance moves.

The music slowed, and he met my curious gaze. "When Walker's motivated, he's deadly. And you, sugar, motivate him." He pulled me into a loose embrace and twirled us around. "See that smile?" He inclined his head toward the side of the dance floor. My eyes followed, and my stomach twisted. Gray. Flirting with a tall blonde. Tane bent closer to my ear. "That smile is the last thing I'll see before he takes me down."

I forced myself to look away. "That smile is just another weapon he's honed."

His eyes glittered. "You see right through him,

don't you?"

"You mean the snake charmer act?" I tossed my head, sending my hair flying around me. "If he tries that shit on me, I'll punch him in the face."

Tane threw his head back, laughing out loud. I smirked, and the knot in my tummy eased. "Come on, bruiser," he teased. "Katya's made a surprise birthday cake for Mira."

He slung an arm around my shoulders and guided us in the direction of the central pagoda. There was already a crowd several people deep. Tane let go of me as we sidled closer, and I glimpsed Katya bent over a large cake lighting rows of birthday candles. A chill tingled down my spine. I hesitated, but the gathering guests pushed me forward. A couple in front of me parted, and I stepped closer. Mira was planted in front of the cake, hands elegantly plastered to her hips. Her obsidian gaze was locked disdainfully on Katya.

"Lily helped me bake it." Katya lit the last candle with a flourish and glared at Mira. "I promised to get a photo of you blowing out the candles."

"Hrmph!"

I jerked in surprise at Mira's childish grunt. And was even more surprised when she sashayed forward and bent to blow out the candles.

"Wait! I have to get a photo for Lily." Katya scrambled for her phone, pushing guests back so she could capture a better angle. Mira remained frozen in place. Her hair was swept up in an oriental style chignon, but a few glossy black tendrils had escaped. They were brushing against the cake. Chocolate cake.

"Okay, I'm ready," Katya called.

Chocolate cake.

I stepped back. Mira deftly blew out the candles. People clapped and began to sing. I bit my tongue to hold back my scream.

Leave. I have to leave.

A sludgy darkness edged my vision.

Leave.

Snippets of "Happy Birthday" hammered into my skull.

LEAVE!

Thick slime slithered through my brain. I tried to move backward, but I couldn't tear my eyes from the cake.

"Hey, sweetkins. You ready for cake?"

"I have to leave," I croaked.

Blake shook his head and grabbed my hand. "You can't leave. Not before you have a slice of cake."

"No!" I yanked my hand away. Blake's mouth moved but all I could hear was the thrashing of my heart. Darkness crept closer. And with it, came the smell of roses.

Oh, God. So many pink roses.

Powerful arms wrapped around me, pulling me against a rock hard body.

"Zoey."

Help me, Mama.

"Zoey!"

Gray. His voice reverberated in my head, drowning out the monsters scrabbling to be heard. I grabbed onto his wrists, my fingers digging into his skin. His arms tightened, cocooning me against his warmth.

"Is she okay?"

"She's fine, Blake. Zoey doesn't eat chocolate cake." His steely tone left no room for discussion.

Untangling his wrists from my grasp, he gently turned me into his chest. I was trembling and I knew he could feel it.

"You ready to go, darlin'?"

I flinched. His eyes narrowed. Eyes that, for the first time since I'd arrived in New York, glinted with a familiar blue intensity.

"Zoey?"

"I'm ready," I whispered.

Chapter Twelve
Steel Threads

Grayson Walker's Apartment
The Next Day
Zoey

I pressed my forehead to the windowpane.

Low clouds were threatening rain, casting a dull haze over the East River. The weather matched my mood. I'd spent the best part of the night trying to stay awake because I knew from experience this was the only way to keep my nightmares at bay. Being a doctor, I was practiced at staying awake, but last night I kept drifting off. Each time it happened I would jar awake soaked in sweat.

Gray had my back at the party. I don't know how he did it, but without making a scene, he exited us from the penthouse and brought me downstairs. My way of showing gratitude was a mumbled plea of exhaustion, and the sight of my back as I hightailed it to my bedroom. He followed and knocked softly. I crawled onto my bed fully clothed and curled into a tight ball. I could hear him pacing outside. After a while, he knocked again. I hugged myself until my arms ached. He knocked several times more, then I heard his footsteps retreat.

I was awake when he left this morning. But like a coward, I didn't venture out until I was certain he'd gone from the apartment. When I came downstairs, I found a note by the coffee machine. He was helping Mira prepare for a trip. I should call him when I was awake.

I didn't call him. Instead, I called Eva.

"You're tired, Zoey. Maybe we should continue this tomorrow."

I breathed in slow and long, and then looked over my shoulder at Eva. "You said you want to try a different approach. Please, I'll talk about anything except what happened last night."

Eva searched my face. After a moment she gave an acquiescent shrug. I breathed a sigh of relief and pushed away from the window.

"I want to talk about your life before the attack on your family," she said.

"How far back do you want me to go?"

"It doesn't matter. Whatever springs to mind."

I sank into the corner of the L-shaped couch. "Gray," I said firmly.

"How so?"

"That summer we fell in love." I made a face. "Actually, it was Gray who fell in love. Me—" I pressed a hand to my chest. "I always loved him."

She smiled and nodded for me to continue.

As I cast my mind back, I slipped off my shoes and tucked my legs beneath me. "Gray had a lot of pain to deal with growing up, especially after his grandfather died. His mom was cold and her favoritism of Jacks bordered on psychotic." I took a moment to let my thoughts unravel. Eva didn't interrupt, waiting patiently for me to continue. "It ostracized Gray, ruined any chance the brothers had of being close. Gerald was kind, and I think he did his best. But his best really wasn't good enough." I grimaced. "I always believed it was a miracle Gray grew up like he did, that his family didn't corrupt his ability to love."

"Do you still believe that?" Eva said.

"Gerald said Gray's built a fortress around himself." The band of knots at the base of my neck throbbed. "He implied it was my fault."

"And what do you say?"

I kneaded a knuckle into the spot where it throbbed the worst. "Gray built a wall around his heart long before me. And he was always very selective about who he allowed behind that wall."

Her head tilted. "He let you in?"

"He let Butterfly in," I said harshly, dropping my hand. "His perfect innocent Butterfly."

"You were Butterfly?"

"Yes. But I wasn't perfect, far from it." I looked away. "Deep down, I think he knew that." *And he held back because of it*. I didn't say that out loud.

Eva pursed her lips. "Is it possible you might be projecting? Assigning feelings to Gray that you really feel about yourself?"

I shifted uncomfortably. "I don't know. Maybe."

She slid forward and perched on the front of the couch. "I know you grieved for your family, Zoey. And with Rose Martin's support, you learned to heal from your rape. But did you ever grieve for yourself? For all *you* lost."

"What do you mean?" I said huskily.

"Zoey, you didn't only lose your sense of safety. You lost the life you had been living. You lost your dreams. And most of all, you lost the life you planned to live." She held out her hands. "You're only focused on bridging the gap in your memories. But what happens after that?"

I jolted upright, kicking my feet to the floor. "What happens!" I cried. "I finally get to understand what the hell happened that night. That's what happens." I leveled her with a glowering look. "And maybe I get to catch the monsters who did this to my family. To me!"

"And then what?" she said softly, her intense blue eyes never wavering. I flinched. Her question hung in the air like a giant vacuum sucking up oxygen. She leaned forward, her voice earnest. "To fully heal, you need to accept what happened to you and integrate it into your life. No matter the horrendous nature of the attack, it's shaped who you are today." She paused, her gaze searching. I gave a faint nod, and she took that as her cue to continue. "But it's important you understand that it no longer has to be the focal point of your life. Not anymore."

I hugged my waist, digging my fingers into my bony frame. Eva's reasoning made perfect sense. But her words didn't fill the bottomless pit inside me. That dark and slimy place full of unexplained terror and suffocating nightmares.

"What do you want from life, Zoey?"

I hugged myself tighter. "You don't mean work do you?"

"Not really." She smiled encouragingly.

I looked away, staring blindly around the room. Rose's voice filtered through my mind. *Breathe in through your nose, out through your mouth.* Slowly my heartbeat steadied. I felt his arms circle me, pulling me against his heat. "There's only one thing I'm certain of, one thing that's never changed." I drew in another steadying breath. "And that's Gray. Even on my darkest days, he's my sun." My gaze flicked back to Eva.

"Have you told him?"

"Of course not. He thinks I betrayed him." I waved a hand. "Threw him away."

"Did you?"

Acid pooled in my throat. I swallowed with difficulty. "No, I didn't betray him."

She looked puzzled. "How do you know if you say you can't remember?"

"I just know." I leaned forward, clasping my hands in front of me. "Like I know which scalpel to select from a tray. Or that I loved my mother and father and Noah." My knuckles whitened. "I know I would never choose somebody else over Gray. Never."

Her eyes met mine. "Maybe you need to tell him that."

"Maybe." I bent to slip my shoes back on. "One day."

"Are you angry with him for leaving you?"

"How can I be angry with him? I betrayed him with his brother." I straightened and shoved my hair back. "Jesus, Eva. What the hell else was he supposed to do?"

"Stay."

I froze, my hands bunched in my hair. That single word sounded like an accusation, and it set my heart pounding.

"If you would never willingly betray him, don't you think he should have believed that about you too?"

I jumped up and stumbled into the sitting room table. "No!" I gasped, regaining my balance. "It wasn't his fault. I'm the one who put his brother's ring on my finger." I smacked my chest hard. "I did that. Gray had nothing to do with it." I whirled around and walked quickly to the kitchen.

Eva gave me some time and then joined me. Without speaking, I poured us both a glass of water. Just before leaving, she dropped another bombshell.

"You need to talk to Gray. I think he knows more than he realizes," she said. "After all, he was there too."

****

Late afternoon.
Gray

Gray closed his front door softly and paused to rub his temple. His head felt like it was going to explode. He could no longer deny that however entrenched his self-defense mechanism was when it came to Zoey, his need to protect her was stronger. Thousands of tensile steel threads bound them together. Over time, they might have been stretched to their limit but they had not broken. It was like she was burned into his DNA. And when Zoey hurt, Gray felt the same hurt deep inside himself.

Throughout the night, and most of the day, he'd replayed what happened. *That fucking chocolate cake.* He couldn't reach her fast enough when he saw her distress. Jesus. He could still feel her trembling against him, her eyes dilated with fear. And after her gut-wrenching retreat when they returned to his apartment, it had taken all his control not to kick her bedroom door down.

Today, he'd checked his phone repeatedly. And nothing. Not even a damn text message. He'd distracted himself by snapping at Tane. He was still pissed the smooth asshole had danced with Zoey. If that made him an asshole too, he didn't give a shit. He also didn't care that he'd danced with several women himself. Hell. He'd made sure of it. The only woman he stayed clear of was her.

And then an hour ago he got a message from Eva. *I spent time with Zoey today. You need to do the same!* In Eva-speak, that was an order.

Gray sighed wearily and turned from the door. He dumped his keys on the hall table and glanced over the sleek railing to the living room. It was a half level lower than the open-plan kitchen and dining area. Zoey was curled into the corner of the long couch, her gaze glued to the wall of windows. She had her legs drawn up close to her body, her chin resting on her knees. His chest tightened. Her air of fragility, which had not been in evidence last night, at least before the fucking cake, had returned full force. He gripped the railing. "Hey," he said quietly.

She twisted to look at him. "Hey."

"I'm getting a drink. Can I get you something—a glass of wine?"

"Sure," she murmured. "White wine would be good."

Her skin looked pale and clammy. And she had deep blue shadows beneath her eyes. His hands tightened. "Difficult session with Eva?"

She shrugged, her bruised gaze drifting over his shoulder.

"Zoey," he called, his voice deep. Her gaze snapped back to him. "If I go and sort drinks, am I going to find you here when I get back?"

Her eyes widened, then a faint smile began to play

around her mouth. "Where are you going to make drinks, Uptown?"

"Nope." His lips twitched. "In the kitchen."

"So where do you think I'm going to go while you do that?" she snarked.

"Your bedroom." He arched a challenging brow. She snorted in disgust and dropped her legs to the floor. The boulder pressing down on his chest shifted. She was adorably unladylike when she snorted like that. "So you going to keep your ass on the couch?" he pushed her.

"Yes!"

"Good."

He spun away, hiding his smile. When he returned a few minutes later, she had her legs up again, this time tucked beneath her. He passed her a glass of wine and settled himself a little farther down the couch. Sampling his favorite bourbon, he watched her take a big gulp of wine.

"Eva wanted me to talk a little about how my life was before, um…before the attack." Gray pretended to sip his drink. This was the first time she'd volunteered anything about her talks with Eva. Her forehead creased. "I don't know if I'm remembering right."

Gray waited. Her luminous eyes flickered, and she stared fixedly at her wine. *She was disappearing inside her head.* He injected a bossy edge to his voice. "Talk to me, Zoey. What are you trying to remember?"

Her chin jerked up, and she squinted at him. "Am I wrong about how good it was between us?"

He gulped his drink. The burn gave him time to catch his breath. He wanted to scream; instead, he spoke through gritted teeth. "Being with you was the most beautiful thing that ever happened to me."

She shook her head, looking troubled. "Why didn't you want to make love to me?"

Gray paused. Her husky voice was laced with pain. And it carried a subtle accusation. He tossed back his drink, anger picking up where the whiskey burn ended. "We did make love—"

"No!" She interrupted harshly. "You stopped. You always stopped."

His fingers cramped around his glass. He remembered how she was, naked, spread out for him to taste. "Why are you asking me this now?"

Her lashes swept down.

Gray could see she was hiding again. He slammed his glass on the table and jumped to his feet. The rage he'd kept bottled up for what seemed like forever erupted. "Why the fuck would you do that, Zoey?" He loomed over her. "How could you play me like that?"

She recoiled against the back of the couch. "I didn't play you!" Her wine splashed, and she shook drops from her fingers. "How could you accuse me of that?"

He jabbed a finger at her. "The same day you claimed to love me, you put his ring on your finger. For fuck's sake!" he shouted in her face. "How could you do that?"

For a moment she remained frozen, her face ashen. Then her green eyes flashed, and she reared up in his face. "I. Don't. Know." She thrust closer to him. "I don't fucking know!" Her mouth twisted, and acid burned in Gray's gut. "Don't you think I would tell you if I knew? But I don't remember!" The muscles in her neck strained. "I don't remember Jacks proposing. I don't remember saying yes. And for the life of m-me—" Her voice broke, and Gray had the sudden desire to wrap her in his arms. "I do not remember him sliding a ring on my finger." Her liquid gaze begged him to believe her. But before he could say a word, she slumped down and slid her fingers into her hair. Her eyes squeezed shut and she began to rock. "I don't remember anything. So please, for pity's sake, stop hammering me with it."

Her anguished cry faded, leaving Gray's skin raised and crawling. An ugly sensation began to slither through him. Zoey sucked in a shaky breath, and slowly untangled her hands. Gray struggled with his own breath and stayed silent. She sat back on her knees, wrapping her arms around her waist. "What?" she mocked, exhaustion making her voice raspy. "You don't believe me?"

Lines of defeat cut into her beautiful face, each one scoring a line of pain through his heart. "I do believe you." He ignored her jolt of surprise. "I need a minute to think." He reached out and slipped the wineglass from her loose clasp, and collecting his own glass, walked away. "I'll get us a refill," he said, without looking back.

Gray refilled their drinks on autopilot. His rage had fizzled out, but in its place was a sickening suspicion. Why had he not seen this before? *Because it was a truth too evil to consider!*

I don't remember anything!

Her despair rang in his head. He braced himself on the counter. Shit. It hurt to breathe. His chest felt like he was never going to breathe easy again. But Zoey was waiting for him, so forcing himself upright, he picked up their drinks and walked out the kitchen.

She was standing by the window and turned to watch him approach. He avoided her questioning look and handed her the chilled wine. Moving to stand beside her, he stared outside. It was drizzling. He finished half his drink before he turned to her. He didn't mince his words. "If you don't remember something so important like putting an engagement ring on your finger, have you ever considered that it might not have happened?"

Confusion clouded her pale face. "What do you mean?" she whispered.

"I mean exactly what I say. What if Jacks' proposal never happened?" He tossed back the rest of his drink.

"Are you saying he made it up?" She sounded bewildered.

He raised his brow.

"Why?" she gasped. "Why would he do such a thing?" The last of the color drained from her face. "My God. Is he even capable of doing such an awful thing?"

"Capable?" he said darkly and reached for her glass before she dropped it. "Yes, he's capable." A surge of forgotten fury flared. "He was always a jealous obsessive prick, especially when it came to what belonged to me."

"I never belonged to you," Zoey hissed.

"Really?" he barked and leaned down to her. He was so close he could smell the wine on her breath. "You can say that?" Her beautiful cat eyes went round. "You always belonged to me, Zoey. Surely *that's* something you remember?"

Emotion contorted her face. "Damn you, Gray Walker. *Damn you.*" She whipped around and walked rapidly away.

Gray let her go. Her footsteps raced up the stairs, and he turned to face the gloomy view. It was pouring with rain now. But the weather wasn't the cause of the insidious chill cooling his skin. Poisonous bile coated his tongue, and he emptied Zoey's wine glass.

If Jacks lied about that ring, what else did he lie about?

Gray broke out in a clammy sweat. Why hadn't he had more faith in Zoey?

Jesus Christ.

Had he walked away from her when she needed him the most?

Chapter Thirteen
They Were Robbed

Grayson Walker's Apartment
After Midnight
Gray

Gray slipped from bed and glided through the dark room. He'd been awake only seconds, but was fully alert. He closed his eyes and reached out with his senses. Nothing. But he knew it was something. With his gun held weapons ready, he moved silently out the door. As he hit the passage the hair on his body raised. There was a low whimpering. It sounded like an animal bleating in distress. And it was coming from Zoey's room.

He moved fast and approached her door. Another whimper. Quietly turning the handle, he crouched and went in low. A light from the adjoining bathroom spilled into the room, and he instantly had a clear picture. Moving slowly, he lowered his gun to the floor and pushed it behind him. Zoey scrambled back, hugging the headboard. He took a small step toward the bed. Her strangled whimper shattered years of military training and he lunged forward.

"No-ooo!" She cringed back, kicking her legs at him.

He held out his hands. "I'm not going to hurt you."

"No…please, no—" Terror devoured the luminous

179

green of her eyes, leaving behind inky pools of darkness.

Gray stopped moving. "Zoey," he said hoarsely. Her face contorted and she began to rock, knocking her head against the upholstered headboard. His throat burned. He felt like he was trapped in a time warp, wrenched back inside that goddamn hospital room with Zoey, broken and beaten, cowering on the floor. Being careful not to startle her, he moved away and picked up his gun. "I'll be back in a second," he whispered and backed out the room.

Gray raced into his dressing room, secured his weapon and hastily threw on a T-shirt. There wasn't time to put on jeans; the boxers he was wearing would have to do. Heading out, he had second thoughts and quickly turned and grabbed an extra T. His heart was pounding. The fear inside him was like a malignant mass, clawing to get out. He exited the room and ran downstairs. With singular focus, he grabbed what he was looking for, and sprinted back up the stairs. When he reached Zoey's door, he forced himself to stop. Breathing hard, he lifted the mobile speaker and turned on the mounted iPod. Spinning through his personal playlists, he stopped on "Melancholic." His hand felt clumsy, and he cursed when it took precious extra seconds to find the song he wanted. There!

He slipped through the door. Zoey was still pressed up against the headboard, curled into herself. He stopped a few feet away, and holding the speaker aloft, hit play. The opening bars of the song filled the room. Her head lifted. Steve Tyler's voice sang out and Zoey blinked. Gray hardly dared to breathe. When the power crooner sang "I Don't Want to Miss a Thing" for the second time, Zoey slumped, her arms dropping to her lap. Her eyes flickered, the dark sludge slowly bleeding away, letting in the vivid green he loved so much.

Gray's breath came easier, but he stayed where he was. He let the song swirl around them, and slowly it chased the malevolence from the room. At the end of the third chorus, his patience was rewarded. Zoey lifted her chin and her mouth curved into a crooked smile. "You're a big fake." Her voice was low and raw.

Moving with caution, he propped the speaker on the bedside table. She didn't flinch away. "What d'ya mean?" he said and sat on the bed.

"You know."

He maneuvered against the headboard, taking care not to touch her. Stretching out his legs, he tilted his head to look at her. "Tell me."

She searched his face. "You still listen to this song?"

"Of course." He feigned a smile. "Save the world, win the girl. Every boy's wet dream."

She rested her head against the plush headboard. His stomach clenched. He hated those dark circles under her eyes.

"They were robbed," she murmured.

"Who?"

"Diane Warren and Steve Tyler." She wrinkled her nose. "They were robbed of the Oscar for Best Song."

He snorted, his smile coming more naturally. *She loved this fucking song.* The chorus repeated, and he waited until the last note faded. "Will you let me hold you, darlin'?"

She bowed her head abruptly. "Don't call me that."

"What?"

"That," she said irritably.

"Darlin'?"

She nodded jerkily. In the low light, her hair was a copper mass of curls. Several tendrils clung damply to her face. His hand itched to smooth them away. "You don't like it?"

She shook her head.

"Then what do you like?"

"I don't care, just not that."

"Okay." He worried at his beard to stop his hand from reaching out. "Will you let me hold you now?"

She drew her legs to her chest, holding herself tight. "You'll only let me go."

His heart lurched. "I won't let you go, Zoey."

"You will." Despair roughened her voice.

Shit. He needed to change tack. "Is this about what happened at the party last night? Or what I said about Jacks?"

She gave a jerky half shrug. "I told you I get nightmares. But generally they only get this bad around my birthday."

His jaw locked. For most people, their birthday was a day of celebration. For Zoey, it was a day of bloody nightmares. "It's not your birthday," he pointed out.

"But it was last month." She shrugged again. "Normally, I go away for six weeks over this time. I have a standing contract with Doctors Without Borders." She looked up. Her haunted eyes were breaking his heart. "This year I couldn't take leave."

"Why Doctors Without Borders?" He frowned.

"To help where I can." She smiled wryly. "And I get the side benefit of focusing on other people's pain."

"That's fucked up."

Her jaw jutted stubbornly. "What, helping people who need helping?"

"No, Zoey." He thrust his face close to hers. "Climbing into other people's nightmares to escape your own. That's fucked up!"

She jolted upright. "It's better than climbing into stranger's beds!" she yelled.

"I'm not a fucking stranger!" he yelled back.

She shied against the headboard. "I wasn't talking about you."

Gray wrestled with his temper. He wished she wouldn't shy away from him like that. "Then who?" he said more quietly.

"It doesn't matter."

"Who, Zoey? What stranger are you talking about?"

"Nobody."

"Who!?" he shouted.

"*Everybody!*" Her scream blasted into him. Every muscle in his body went rigid as he watched her face contort. "So many of them I don't remember," she cried.

Heat coursed through him. Her pain was killing him. *Fuck it.* He reached out and scooped her into his lap. Her eyes flew open. For the first time that night, he could see the mysterious gold ring that circled her pupils. He could also see the wet sheen of tears she was fighting to hold back. With perfect timing, the iPod clicked to Tracy Chapman. Her no-frills, indelible lyrics to "Baby Can I Hold You" wrapped around them. Gray folded Zoey in his arms and held her to his chest. As he'd thought, her camisole was soaking wet.

For about a second, Zoey resisted. Then she sagged against him, her head falling to rest on his shoulder. Gray closed his eyes. His throat thickened and he found himself fighting back his own tears.

Too long. Too fucking long.

She fit into his arms like she belonged there.

Why the hell had he stayed away from her for so long?

He held her close and breathed in her honeysuckle scent. As Chapman's song faded, he lifted his head. "We need to get this off." Not giving her a chance to react, he slipped his hands under her wet camisole and pulled it up and over her head.

"What—"

"Here you go." He grabbed the extra T he'd slung over his shoulder and settled it over her head. Her arms were clumsy, and he helped her get the T-shirt on, before tugging her back against him.

"Thank you," she mumbled into his neck.

He rested his temple on the crown of her head. "Talk to me, Butterfly, please." She flinched, and he could hear her catch her breath.

"Don't call me that." Her fingers curled into his side, gripping his T. "I'm not that girl anymore."

The old endearment had just slipped out. He hadn't meant to use it. Gray stroked her hair out of her face, relishing the touch of the satin tendrils against his skin. "But you don't want me to call you darlin'—"

"You call every woman that!"

Gray's blood pressure spiked, and a smile tugged at his mouth. *Well shit.* His arms tightened around the precious woman lying against him. "And Butterfly?" he whispered close to her ear. "You don't like that either?"

"I'm not your butterfly anymore." She shifted restlessly. "I can never be that innocent girl again."

"That's bullshit." She started to struggle in his arms. "Don't, Zoey. Please." *Christ, he was begging.* She glared at him but she stopped moving. He expelled a silent breath. *Jesus. If begging stopped her fighting him, he'd beg.*

Her head dropped back to his shoulder. "It's not bull," she said.

"It is. You have your innocence in every way that counts." He threaded his fingers through her hair. "That motherfucker gave you pain and broken bones, but he took nothing from you that couldn't heal."

"I was a virgin, Gray."

His hand fisted involuntarily. "I know."

"I wanted you to have that."

He closed his eyes, tucking her even closer to his warmth. "Zoey, your innocence belonged to you. Nobody could take it if you weren't offering it." He lowered his mouth to her temple. "I know those monsters stole your family from you, but they could never steal the beautiful, innocent butterfly I fell in love with." He cupped her jaw, gently lifting her face. "They couldn't take that from you, Zoey, because it always belonged to me."

Her liquid gaze searched his. "You don't understand—" She seemed lost for words.

"Then tell me," he said.

Her lower lip trembled. Gray was about to stroke it with his thumb when her fingers curled around his wrist. "He might not have taken it that night, but for years I gave it away." Her short nails dug into him. "God, Gray, I went with so many different men I can't even remember their faces."

Everybody!

Her shrill scream echoed through his mind.

Gray pressed back against the headboard. Ugly images twisted in a macabre dance in his head. He moved his hand from her face, but Zoey's fingers kept their fierce grip on his wrist. Staring at her tortured face, he willed the images into oblivion. "I know you were hurting, but why would you do that to yourself?"

"Because I didn't care. I needed to feel something. Anything." Her eyes shimmered, a bottomless pool of green. "Anything except that godawful pain that owned me. As long as I had control, I let them have what they wanted. But the more I did it, the more numb I became." A single tear escaped, and she let go of his wrist to jerkily brush it away. "After a while, I didn't feel anything."

"Is that why you stopped?" *Please, say you stopped.*

"I kept putting myself in more and more dangerous situations. One day, I woke up—" She sucked in a shaky breath, her hand trembling against her chest. "God, I've never felt so dirty in my life." Gray's heart pounded as more tears escaped down her cheeks. Unable to stop himself, he used his thumbs to brush them away. "I found this awesome woman," she said huskily. "She helped me. It took a long time, but eventually, I understood why I did it. And learned to forgive myself." Her hand reached for his wrist again. "Do you hate me?"

He drew her closer, holding her head tucked into his neck. "It doesn't matter what you do, Butterfly, or what you did." He intentionally used the endearment.

To convince her. To convince himself. "I could never hate you."

She hiccupped. He stroked his hand down her back. She let go of his wrist and rested her hand flat against his chest. Gray breathed her in. For long moments they stayed like that, their breaths kissing each other, the music soft around them. Then the yearning began to grow, their intimacy turning into a familiar ache.

"Gray." It was a soft whisper.

He slid his fingers into her fiery hair and tilted back her head. Her gaze was filled with longing.

"Gray," she mouthed silently.

He settled his mouth over hers. For one interminable second, she didn't respond. Gray touched his tongue to her bottom lip. And like a genie rubbing a magic lamp, they parted. Gently, he ran his tongue over her mouth, nibbling and kissing. Her breath hitched, and electricity sizzled through his body.

"Zoey," he groaned.

She pushed up against him, her mouth opening to invite him in. He couldn't resist. Gliding his tongue past her lips, he searched for more of her taste. Her tongue welcomed him, kissing up against his own. And still, he couldn't get enough. Their tongues entwined, dancing and teasing, licking and savoring. Gray shuddered when her hands stroked up his neck. She kept going until they were buried in his hair. He pulled her flush against him and deepened their kiss.

So fragile. And so fucking perfect.

He kissed her until they were both breathless, clinging to each other. Her need matched his, a burning desire that ignited his own. The fire was going to consume them, and they weren't ready.

He wasn't ready.

He eased away, smoothing her hair from her face. "Zoey." Her lashes lifted, and Gray's cock surged. Gold and green stared at him. Hot and slumberous. He lowered his mouth and caught her swollen lip between his own. And sucked. She whimpered, and heat pooled at the base of his spine.

Shit. He had to stop.

Dragging his mouth from hers, he cupped her head and tucked it into his neck. Her hot breath puffed against his hammering pulse. He held her tight, gently stroking her back. Soothing her. Soothing himself. When he felt like he could move without exploding his load, he gently separated them. She blinked, her eyes heavy, clearly exhausted. He cradled her face. "I think it's time we went home to Texas," he said softly. "Both of us. It's time to find the truth."

Her hand covered his, and she pressed her face against his palm. "I'm scared," she whispered.

So was he.

"Don't let me go, Gray. Please."

His hand tightened on her face, and he pulled her closer. "I'm not letting you go." His mouth brushed hers, feather light.

"Make love to me," she said in a rush, her breath puffing against his lips.

Gray shivered. "Christ. Don't ask me that, not now. Not tonight. You're too vulnerable."

"Gray—"

"We can wait, Zoey. At least until you're thinking clearly." He tightened his arm around her waist and lifted himself up. Snatching the bed covers from beneath them, he shifted them both lower on the bed and stretched out. Then he fitted her snugly against himself.

"Gray—"

"Shhh, Butterfly. We're going to sleep now." He yanked up the covers. She muttered something he couldn't hear and shifted to rest her head on his pec. "What was that?" He pulled the duvet around her shoulders.

Her hand crept up to curl around his neck. "Butterfly is dead," she whispered.

Gray froze. There wasn't a breath of space between her body and his own. He could even feel the beat of her heart fluttering against his chest. "That's not true," he whispered gruffly. "Because if Butterfly is dead, so am I."

"What?" She sounded groggy.

"Go to sleep, Zoey. Please."

"You'll stay?" Her hand pressed against his nape.

"I'm right here. I'm not going anywhere."

Gray stared at the ceiling. Her breath was a warm caress across his throat. After a time, her hand slipped from his neck to rest on his chest. Her breathing deepened. Only when her body slumped against him, did he let his eyes close.

Yeah. It was time to go home. Time to heal.

And time for those responsible to get what they deserved.

Justice was coming.

And he was going to be the one fucking bringing it.

Chapter Fourteen
Hold Onto the Light

The Next Morning
Zoey

I woke alone and reflexively hugged the pillow pressed to my chest. Somewhere outside the window, a pigeon squawked loudly. I listened closely but heard nothing else. Tentatively, I stretched out a leg. The empty side of the bed was still warm.

Gray.

I buried my face in the pillow and drew in his spicy scent. It slowed my breathing and sent liquid warmth flowing through my body. A quiet calm settled over me, and my mind stilled. The deep ache of fatigue I went to sleep with was gone. I was alone, but I didn't feel lonely. A faint clatter echoed up the stairs from the kitchen.

Gray.

A lazy flutter tingled in my belly. I licked my lips, searching for his taste. Memories trickled in. My godawful nightmare, Steve Tyler, Butterfly—

No!

I shoved them away. There was time enough for that stuff. By the end of the day, we'd probably be in Texas. But for now, I wanted to hang onto the light. To the memory of Gray's arms around me, his mouth pressed to mine. I drew up my legs and hugged the pillow tighter.

My determination to be happy held for the next several hours.

Over breakfast—toasted muffins with real butter and honey and homemade cappuccinos—Gray brought me up to date. We were flying to Texas midday. He'd already spoken with his father, and Gerald wanted us to stay with them. My stomach rolled at this news, but I gritted my teeth and held fiercely to my happy. It helped when Gray announced we were flying on King's private jet. I decided to play it cool, not letting on I was wildly impressed with the slick generosity of his boss.

The whole time, Gray and I were cautious with each other. The ugliness between us had vanished, but nothing had replaced it yet. I think we both knew the powerful bond between us had been awakened. But it was still ephemeral. Fragile. By unspoken mutual consent, we kept things light. Every so often our eyes would meet. Hold. The blue shards swirling in his gray depths would stir up my earlier flutters. And each time I'd be the first to look away, unable to hold his gaze.

We were traveling private, which meant we were able to bypass Fort Worth and land at the smaller Denton Airport. The novelty of flying a luxury jet was wasted on me. For the entirety of the flight, my eyes were glued to the sky outside my window. I played mind games, seeing images in the passing clouds, recalling complicated surgical procedures in my head. Whatever it took to cling to the light. And to keep the insidious creeping fear out of my mind. Gray seemed to read my mood and let me be. But by the time we landed in Denton, my neck was a solid wall of knots. And the fear was a hammering ache behind my temples.

Denton. The heart of North Texas horse country. The place where Norah Jones and Don Henley honed their musical brilliance. Home to my alma mater, UNT, the Mean Green football team, and an eagle named Scrappy.

Home to Gray.

Home to me.

Before I had time to assimilate I was there, we were flying down the 288 Loop toward Clear Creek. Toward Walker Ranch.

Hold onto the light.

Gray was driving. He'd hired a nondescript sedan that was waiting for us at the airport. His posture seemed relaxed but from the white-knuckled grip he had on the steering wheel, I knew he wasn't. In twenty minutes we were going to drive into a past neither of us was ready for.

Hold onto the light.

I turned from the view that was moving in a blur past my window. And giggled. Gray glanced at me, his brows arching above his sunglasses. "What's up?"

I shook my head, smirking.

His gorgeous mouth curved into a smile. "C'mon, share."

"You're too much for this li'l car." I sniggered.

"Come again."

I swallowed my silly laughter. "You're suited to your giant SUV much better."

His gaze whipped back to me. "Zoey Morgan. Are you saying I'm too sexy for my car?" I clamped my lips together but only succeeded in snorting. He grinned and looked back at the road. "Too much man for my sedan?" he drawled.

I burst out laughing. "Gray Walker, rap artist. That's funny."

He shook his head, but his mouth kept twitching. My laughter slowly faded. The miles swept past.

I smoothed my hair into its tight ponytail. "How do you feel being back in Denton?" It was a question I avoided asking myself.

He didn't answer immediately. I worried at my lip. His gaze never left the road ahead. It was several miles before he broke the silence. "Walker Ranch may seem like paradise for a kid to grow up in. But for me, it was a place to bide my time until I was old enough to leave."

He slowed the car and turned left into Sherman Drive. Hartlee Field Road was just ahead. I rubbed uneasily at the knots in my neck.

"It's familiar but not," Gray said thoughtfully. "Like a life that belonged to somebody else."

I shifted restlessly. "Or maybe you in a different life."

"Maybe." He pushed his sunglasses up and looked at me. "Is that how you feel?"

"A little."

His brows drew together. "You okay?"

I jerked my head to stare out the window. A pain shot up from my neck into my skull.

"Zoey?"

"I'm fine," I whispered, my nails biting into my palms.

We turned into Hartlee Field Road. He reached across and pulled my hand from my lap. Uncurling my clenched fist, he linked his fingers with mine. My throat thickened. His hand was warm. Rough. Strong.

We drove for a while longer. The road took a couple of familiar sharp turns before it straightened out. My fingers tightened around Gray's.

Two signposts.

Walker Ranch, 0.12 Miles Turn Left. And below it: Morgan Farm, 0.2 Miles Turn Left.

"You want me to stop?" Gray said softly.

I couldn't tear my gaze away.

"Zoey?"

I shook my head. Walker Farm was just ahead. My nails gouged into his flesh. But he didn't flinch. And he never let go of my hand.

"Okay, then. Here we go."

He braked, and with one hand on the steering wheel, turned into the entrance leading to his family's ranch. The imposing gates stood open. They were made of white wrought iron, each inlaid with a rearing horse. We drove through and followed the road winding through the green pastures. Each side of the road was lined with white pipe and cable fencing. Without wanting them to, my eyes strayed to the right. Morgan land. We were driving along the border between Walker Ranch and my family's farm. In the distance, I could see the trees leading down to Clear Creek. The river and thickly forested reserve were a natural boundary to our land. The family homestead was hidden behind a small hill. A hill where a grove of soaring cottonwoods stood vigil. Watching over my family.

I can't do this.

I wrenched my gaze away and stared straight ahead. Beads of sweat lined my brow. We were fast approaching a fork in the road. The right led to the pond. It was a point of contention that my family always referred to it as The Pond, whereas the Walkers always called it Davis Lake. Gray explained it was a family joke, but I never got it. To me, it was the pond where my family idled away scorching summer days. And it would forever be the pond where I first met Gray.

We followed the fork to the left, to the Walker Ranch homestead. The main house was situated on a small rise on the far northwestern side of the ranch. On the far side, a line of trees led down to the Creek. And on the other side, there were acres of grazing pastures.

My heart skipped a beat the moment the house came into sight. And then another. It was an elegant colonial double-story, painted a pale buttercup yellow with white trim. The roof was charcoal slate, and three dormer windows dominated the upper story. A wide porch with elegant white balustrades ran the circumference of the ground floor. I tugged my hand from Gray's. My fingers were trembling. I smoothed back imaginary tendrils and fiddled with my ponytail. Gray's gaze flicked to me, and then away. His mouth was tight.

The gravel gave way to a circular pebbled driveway. Gray brought the car to a crunching halt beside the bricked pathway that led to the front door. It opened just as he pulled up the handbrake, and Gerald and Margaret walked out. Air caught in my bone-dry throat. My lungs screamed.

Oh, God!

Gerald's face broke into a welcoming smile. Gray's mother had remained slim. But her hair was shorter and more platinum than I remembered.

Oh, God!...Oh, God!

I couldn't breathe.

Go!...Go!...

My voice was trapped in my paralyzed throat.

Oh, God, please!

Sweat burst from my pores, soaking the back of my shirt. I grabbed at the dashboard, black spots beginning to dance in front of me.

"Zoey?"

Breathe. Breathe. My throat was a burning desert. Air finally scraped past and filled my lungs. "*Go-ooooo!*" My ragged scream erupted into the car.

"What the fuck!" Gray reached for me.

I jerked away. "Go. Go." It was a weak whimper. Forcing another painful breath, I clutched at his arm. And screeched. "Please *go-oooo!*"

Gray released the handbrake and threw the car into gear. In a hail of flying stones, he tore out the driveway. I could hear him talking, but the wail in my ears was too loud to hear what he was saying. I bent over and yanked out my ponytail. My teeth were chattering. Hot sweat coated my skin, but I was freezing.

Oh, God, help me, please.

I sank my fingers into my hair, pulling at it until my scalp burned. The black sludge was here and it was eating into my brain.

"Zoey." His warm hand cupped the back of my neck. "Take your time. Deep breaths."

I reached back and gripped his wrist.

And we stayed like that. Gray's warm hand at my neck. My fingers like claws, holding onto his wrist. I was breathing like a freight train. Gray's breaths came hard, but they were steady.

It took me a while to realize the car was stationary. I slowly straightened and coughed to clear my throat. "Where are we?"

He gently stroked damp hair from my face. "Davis Lake."

His voice was so deep I turned my head. My vision filmed over. His eyes were filled with dark-gray storms like an angry tornado had him in its grip. "Pond," I croaked.

The corner of his mouth twitched, but there was no matching gleam in his turbulent gaze.

Ring. Ring.

I flinched. "Answer it." I reached for the door handle. "I'm going to get some air."

****

Gray

"*Fu-uuck!*"

Gray's harsh expletive filled the silence as his phone rang off. He watched Zoey walk down to the pond, and rubbed his arms. *Jesus Christ*. He was still covered in goose bumps. The terror in her scream would haunt him to his dying day. Whatever the hell he thought they were up against, it was a cakewalk compared to the reality of the situation. *Fu-uuck.* He raked shaky hands through his hair. This was far worse than he could ever have imagined.

His phone vibrated in his pocket, and a second later started ringing again. He unhooked his seatbelt and reached back to pull it out.

Gerald.

Gray sighed and lifted the phone to his ear. "Hey, Dad."

"Gray. What the heck, Son?"

197

"I'm sorry if we scared you. Zoey had a panic attack. I had to get her out of there." His gaze never strayed from where she stood, staring out across the pond. Silence echoed down the line. Gray's hand tightened around his phone. "Dad?"

"Did we do that to her—your mother and I?"

Gray's jaw clenched. He could hear the anguish in his father's voice. "I don't know. She hasn't been good lately. I think the house is a trigger for her."

His father took a noisy breath. Then silence.

Dammit. He needed to be with Zoey. "Dad—"

"Where are you now?"

"Davis Lake." Gray's mouth twisted. Even shaking with fear, Zoey had the strength to tease him.

"Is she okay?"

"She will be," he said steadily, wincing as his jaw spasmed.

"Listen, Son. I'll open Granddad's cottage for you. You can stay there."

"Christ, Dad. It's been years since anybody stayed there—"

"No it hasn't," his father interrupted. "I did some work on it a while ago. I stay there sometimes when I want some time alone. You know—"

Gray could picture the beseeching look on his father's face. "Yeah, Dad. I get it."

"Yep, well. It's nice. Zoey will like it. Give me an hour to air it out. Your mother will bring some fresh linen and supplies."

Gray gripped his phone. He couldn't think what the hell to say.

"It'll be good, Son. Trust me."

All Gray wanted to do was take Zoey by the hand,

and run as far and as fast as he could. He watched as she looked over her shoulder. She noticed he was still on the phone, and turned back to the water. He closed his eyes. If they left now, she would never be free of the darkness holding her hostage. And neither would he. His father's suggestion was a good one. The cottage was on the farthest side of the pond near the stream. Still on Walker land, but far enough away from the main homestead for Zoey to feel safe.

"Okay, Dad. We'll see you in an hour."

"Good. Your mother will be pleased."

He gritted his teeth. "Yeah. Apologize to her for us, will you? Tell her Zoey's not ready yet, but we'll be by soon."

"I'll do that."

"Right. Gotta go."

"Yes, right. See you—"

His patience shot, Gray hung up and tossed the phone on the dash. He opened his door and climbed out. Zoey's head turned, and she watched him as he walked down to join her.

"That was my dad."

"They must think I'm crazy as a loon." She gave him a distracted smile.

"They're okay." He wanted to smile back, but couldn't. Instead, he told her about his father's suggestion. She appeared to listen but Gray could see her mind was elsewhere. "You going to be okay with that?" he asked.

"Why did you leave me?" She sounded strained. Adrenalin tingled through him. She turned, folding her arms across her middle. "Back then. Why did you leave?"

199

He resisted the urge to fold his arms too. "You asked me to."

"I never did that." She shook her head emphatically.

"For fuck's sake, Zoey, you accused me of causing your nightmares!" She took an involuntary step back, and Gray balled his fists. *Goddammit.* Forcing his hands to relax, he reached for a more controlled tone. "The last time I saw you in Boston, you said every time you saw me, I brought back your nightmares. How was I supposed to stay after that?"

She rubbed nervously at her arms. "I meant the first time, after…after. Shit!" She threw her hands up in distress. "I can't even fucking say it!"

Her anguish leeched Gray's anger. He took a cautious step closer. "After you were raped?" he said softly.

"Y-yes." She cleared her throat. "After I was raped and my family was murdered." It came out in a rush, her words meshing together. "Why did you leave me alone after that?" Pain mixed with confusion shadowed her eyes.

Perspiration trickled down Gray's spine. They were standing in the shade of two Cottonwoods, but he felt uncomfortably hot. "I didn't leave you alone. I left you with Jacks." Her mouth went slack. "He was your fiancé!" he snarled. A bolt of pain shot through his jaw when she reared back. The image of that ring on her finger flashed into his mind, making his skin crawl. "I didn't leave you alone, I left you with your fiancé," he repeated through gritted teeth.

Zoey blinked rapidly. A deep frown creased her forehead. Then she whirled around and stood with her back to him. Gray heard her whisper something. But his heart was beating a loud tattoo in his head, and he wasn't sure he heard right. "What did you say?"

"I missed you," she whispered again.

Jesus, he thought she said that. "I couldn't stay." He gripped the back of his neck. "I couldn't stay and watch you with him. And my mother—shit, she was beside herself to get me out the house."

Her shoulders hunched. "I still missed you."

Gray rocked back on his heels. "He was my brother, Zoey. You chose *him*."

She twisted round, her haunted eyes slamming into him. "Did I?"

His chest burned. He wished he could give her the answer she needed. "Come here." He held out his arms.

She shook her head. "If you felt like that, why did you keep coming to visit me in Boston?"

His arms dropped to his sides. "I needed to know you were okay."

Her head tilted sharply. "I sent you away again and again, but you kept coming back."

"Yes."

"Why?"

He pressed his lips together. Why the hell was she pushing this? He met her searching gaze. "Your words told me to leave, but what I heard was you begging me to stay."

"Until that last time?" Her voice was hoarse.

"Yes." He shrank inside. "When you said what you said, I couldn't come back after that." Her red-tipped lashes swept down. "It's different now." He took a half step closer. "You've changed. You need me—"

"Nothing's changed!" she shouted, her head

rearing up.

"Dammit, Zoey—"

"I mean I haven't changed." She pummeled her fists to her chest. "I don't want to lie to you anymore, Gray. Don't you get it? Every time you came to see me, I lied." Her raised voice rippled over the pond, sending a group of wood ducks into flight. Their harsh quacking seemed to echo her anguish. Gray watched them disappear over the forest before he looked back at her. She stood frozen, her face stricken.

"What do you mean, you lied?"

"You were right. I was telling you to leave but I was desperate for you to stay. That last time—" She squeezed her eyes shut, then opened them again. "It wasn't you bringing back my nightmares, it was me. You were a reminder of everything I lost. Everything I didn't deserve." She punched her fist over her heart. "I survived! Everybody else d-died." Her voice broke.

He moved closer and lowered his face to hers. "That was never your fault."

"And what about Jacks?" she sobbed. "I betrayed you with him. Was that also not my fault?"

Acid seared his throat. "I don't have the answer to that, Zoey. But I'm going to help us find it." Her eyes squeezed shut again, but not before he saw her tears. "Let me hold you, Butterfly, please." He lifted his arms.

For a single breath, she stood still. Then her eyes blinked open and she stepped hesitantly toward him. Gray's heart skipped a beat. He circled his arms around her and folded her slight body along the length of him. She was trembling. Her hands clutched at his shirt. Threading his fingers through the hair at her temple, he pressed the side of her face to his chest. "It's going to be all right. I promise, we're going to work it out."

****

Zoey

Gray held me to his warmth. Slowly, my erratic breathing began to steady. With each stroke of his hand, another shudder faded. I lost track of how long we stood there, my cheek pressed close to his chest. Soaking up each other's warmth. Soaking up each other.

Finally, he whispered in my ear, "You feeling better, Butterfly?"

My chest spasmed, and I pushed against him. "I feel like a fraud every time you call me that."

He cupped my jaw, urging me to look at him. "A fraud?" he queried mildly.

"Don't you see?" I circled his wrist. "Every time you call me that I remember how I used to be. Who I used to be to you." My voice was hoarse and I swallowed with difficulty. "I told you, I'm not that person anymore."

He shrugged off my hold and sank both hands into my hair, effectively holding me prisoner. "I'm not the same man I used to be either." His eyes sparked with twin blue flames. "It's time we both accept that and move the fuck on." He shook me firmly, and frissons of heat tingled through my scalp. He wasn't wrong, but I still found myself challenging him.

"What if I don't want to move the fuck on?" My chin lifted obstinately.

His hands tightened. "Then I'll beat on your pretty ass until you do."

I jerked against him. Wicked intent filled his gaze, and awareness sizzled through me. I could feel my own eyes widening. "I'm shocked," I drawled huskily. "Gray Walker wants to spank my butt." I licked my bottom lip and cheered silently when his breath caught. "Is that what turns you on, tough guy?"

A sensual smirk stretched across his face. "Actually, sweet-thing, everything about you turns me on." He untangled one hand and dropped it to my butt. "And I only spank when you're bad." He gave my cheek a soft squeeze.

"Gray!" I wheezed as crazy heat ignited with his bold touch.

"But you present your naked ass to me, and let me do whatever I want with it." His drawl curled around me, deep and delicious. "I can't deny that picture gets me really fucking hard."

"Oh!" I gasped. I could feel a hot flush reddening my face.

Laugh lines creased his eyes. "Mmm, oh." He brushed a few damp tendrils from my heated cheeks. But slowly, the humor faded from his face. "Listen to me, Zoey." My heart skipped a beat when he brought both hands to my face. They were warm and rough, but strangely cool against my hot skin. "You are not a fraud." His fingers threaded into the hair at my temples. "You will always be my butterfly. Nobody, including you, will take that from me." He shook me gently. "Or from you."

Chapter Fifteen
A Brotherly Warning

Granddad Davis' Cottage, Walker Ranch
A Short While Later
Zoey

Gray eased the car into a small forest clearing. A dusty white pick-up truck was already parked and we stopped alongside it. Gerald was standing by a narrow path that disappeared into the trees behind him. He was wringing his hands, and my chest ached at the worry lining his already deeply grooved face.

Gray killed the engine. I quickly hopped out the car, but Gerald hesitated to come over to me. My eyes prickled, and I slowly made my way to him. "Thank you for helping me with Gray." I kept my voice low. His nervous gaze swept over me. I closed the gap and reached up to hug him. His shoulders were stiff, but I only hugged him tighter. A lump lodged in my throat. He smelled of sweet hay and horses. Like my father used to.

"I'm sorry we scared you, Zoey," he said gruffly.

"I don't think it was you. Sometimes, I just get freaked out."

His arms twitched, and he returned my hug. The car door behind us slammed, and Gerald gently let me go. "Hello, Son."

"Dad."

I stepped aside, and Gray greeted his father with a brief handshake. My throat thickened, and I had to look away. I didn't need to be a surgeon to see the pain and longing in Gerald's eyes. But he brushed it aside and urged us down the path. I'd never been to the cottage before. As far as I knew, the last person to live there was Gray's grandfather. But it was immediately apparent the place had been cared for. It was nestled in a small wood alongside a stream that was probably an offshoot of the main creek. It looked like it was hand-built, but I could see no sign of disrepair. Even the roof looked well maintained.

Gerald eagerly pushed open the door. "Come inside. Come." He ushered us in, and let the door close behind us. "I've done lots of work," he said proudly. "Let me show you around."

The cottage was lovely. The living room was down-home style, centered around a ventless gas stove fire. There was a concealed flat screen TV, a DVD player, a music center and an eclectic collection of CDs and DVDs. I bit my lip when I saw the movies ranged from *Secretariat* and *Phar Lap*, to a full boxset starring John Wayne. Turning away, I took in the leather two-seater couch that was brightened with a colorful throw. There was also a reading chair that looked like it had been chosen for comfort. Gerald explained he'd had some of the furniture custom made, and the rest he'd purchased from local auctions.

The kitchen was surprisingly well equipped with up-to-date appliances. There was a handcrafted backsplash made of colorful pottery shards. When I questioned Gerald about who made it, Gray snorted, muttering something about one of his granddad's ladies.

There was also a full supply of dark roast coffee, creamer, biscuits, and even several bars of dark chocolate. Gray commented on this, and Gerald shifted uncomfortably, admitting he'd recently been spending a lot of time at the cottage. I hung back when Gerald painstakingly pointed out each custom-built change. He was addressing both of us, but I knew he was really talking to Gray. I compared how he looked now, to how I remembered him.

To me, Gerald had always been a quintessential man of the land. He was tall and angular, holding himself aloof, but invariably polite and softly spoken. With his strong square jawline and dark intelligent eyes, I'd thought him conservatively handsome. He had a furrowed brow that seemed to me to reflect a man who spent a lot of time thinking. Through my teen years, the grooves on his face had deepened, but I always thought they added to his gravitas. His hair had been dark-brown and wavy, and when not stuck under a hat, it was indented with the shape of his Stetson, like he had been born wearing it.

I crossed my arms and lightly rubbed my knuckles against my chest. Gerald had aged. Now his hair was streaked with gray, and ruthlessly combed back. A small paunch hung over his western-style belt buckle. It seemed out of place on a man I remembered as being so lean and strong. His eyes were puffy and his face carried an ashen strain that marred his handsome weathered features.

"Zoey." I blinked as Gray walked over to me. "Why don't you unpack while I see my father off?" He looked tense. I smiled and nodded, and quickly went to say goodbye to Gerald. Gray collected our bags from the front door and carried them to the bedroom.

The one and only bedroom.

He dumped them on the floor, and clearly distracted with his own thoughts, walked out. I pushed the door closed and drew in a shaky breath. A king-size bed dominated the room. My stomach quivered, but I ignored it and looked around. The bedroom was small, but dappled light filtered through the curtains, giving it a lovely rustic warmth. The cottage theme continued with a freestanding wardrobe, a hand-carved antique oak dresser, and two small bedside tables with pretty brass lamps. I wandered over to the window and looked out.

You will always be my butterfly.

I inhaled the woodsy smell. Gray's conviction swirled in my head. I wanted to believe him, and maybe one day soon I would. But for now, there was too much drama weighing me down. I still hadn't processed the panic that erupted when we drove up to his parent's house. If Gray hadn't driven off and taken us to the pond, I think I might have gone mad. I swallowed down my tears as I remembered his face when I confessed my pathetic lies to him. God. He'd brushed it aside like it meant nothing. Like I hadn't hurt him to the core when I pushed him away. My eyes blurred. So much pain.

I spun away from the window and stared at the huge bed.

I only spank when you're bad.

I snorted and brushed away my tears. The man was incorrigible, and too potent for my own good. *Holy shit.* My heart had nearly pounded out of my chest when he teased me like that in his honeyed drawl. I stroked a hand over my jean-clad ass. Gray always had a bossy streak, especially when it came to sex. I guessed some things hadn't changed. I shook my head impatiently, but it was hard to ignore the tingle that throbbed between my thighs. Pushing away my crazy thoughts, I unpacked my clothes and toiletries. When I finished arranging and rearranging my stuff, I stood and stared at Gray's black bag. It sat like a squatter by the door. Did he expect me to unpack for him? I worried my lip, trying to decide what to do. The bedroom door swung open, and Gray jerked to a halt when he saw me standing there. Before he could say a word, I jumped in. "Has Gerald left?"

His brows rose at my breathless tone, but then they drew together. "Dad's gone, but Jacks is here." I involuntarily sucked in a loud breath. He stepped inside, and gently pushed me back as he closed the door. "My mother called him. He says he's worried about you and wants to say hi."

"Oh." My heart thrashed.

"You've been through a lot today. You don't need to do this now." His gaze was probing. "Jacks can wait."

"No." I crossed my arms and hugged them to my chest. "There's no point putting it off."

"Zoey—"

"You won't say anything to him, will you?"

"Dammit—"

"I don't want to accuse him of anything, not until I'm sure. It's too heinous—"

"Butterfly, I'm not going to say anything."

"I need more time." I met his concerned gaze. "And you and Jacks are like oil and water."

His hands curled around my arms. "I'm all grown

up now. If I say I won't say anything, I mean it. Okay?" Blue shards glittered in his tender gaze. I nodded jerkily. He pulled me to him and his head lowered. A lump lodged in my throat when he brushed his mouth over mine. "But I do want to call Eva." His breath was a whisper on my lips. "I think she should come and join us."

I closed my eyes, shutting out his magnetic beauty. "No, I don't want that. Not yet," I added with more conviction.

He let go of me and cradled my face. "Zoey," he coaxed.

"No!" I grabbed his wrists and tugged. It was like trying to separate welded steel. I glared at him, and with a wry shake of his head, he let me go.

"You're a stubborn witch."

I tilted my head and batted my lashes. "I wonder who I learned that from?" He didn't answer, but his eyes gleamed. I ducked around him and walked to the door, pulling it open. "Are you coming?" I smiled when he snorted. But as I walked out and his footsteps followed behind me, a new warmth filled my chest.

****

Gray

Gray's fleeting humor evaporated when Zoey walked out onto the screened porch. And straight into his brother's arms. No hesitation. If he didn't know better, he'd believe she was relaxed and happy to see Jacks. But his gut twisted.

Because he did know better.

He leaned against the french doorframe and watched Jacks go through the motions of a friendly reunion with Zoey. He was still broad and thick with muscle, but he'd gained roughly forty pounds. The weight had settled around his chin and gut, giving him a soft, chubby appearance. He was back to wearing glasses, and with his short scraggly beard and a hairstyle that looked like it was cut by his fiancée, Gray thought he looked like a typical middle-aged man. Not un-groomed exactly, but like he was comfortable with his life.

Gray's gut tweaked. Nervous humility seemed to have replaced Jacks' youthful arrogance, but Gray found it impossible to assess his brother without his suspicions distorting his judgment. The one thing he could tell was that Jacks was definitely keyed up. His voice was strained with it.

Jacks' gaze left Zoey and shifted to Gray. "It's good to have you home again." His smile looked forced.

Gray stepped forward. "Thanks." But rather than shake his brother's hand, he put his arm around Zoey. Jacks' head bobbed. An awkward silence ensued. Gray cared fuck-all to fill it, but Zoey shifted, subtly digging her elbow into him.

"So congratulations are in order," she said brightly. "Have you and Wendy set a date?"

Jacks switched his attention back to her. "No!" He exhaled in a rush. "I mean yes, thanks for the congratulations, but no we haven't set a date yet. Hopefully soon." Zoey nodded vigorously. Jacks shifted from one foot to another. "We heard about your scare earlier, and Wendy's fit to be tied. She made me promise to invite you both to church tomorrow, and after, you're to join us at the farm for Sunday lunch." He blinked several times, the soft fleshiness under his eyes making him look a little toad-like.

Zoey tucked closer to Gray. He tightened his hold on her. "I'm sorry, Jacks, but Zoey isn't ready—"

"It's only us." Jacks cut him off, clasping his hands together earnestly. "I promise, it'll be only Wendy and me." He looked from Gray to Zoey and back again. "Please, Wendy really wants to meet you."

Gray slipped his hand around Zoey's nape, resting his thumb on her racing pulse. "I'm sorry—"

"No, don't." She turned in his arms, her hand curling gently around his wrist. "I want to go," she said huskily. "I have to face the farm sometime." Her fingers squeezed, and a fire started in Gray's chest. Desperate courage poured from her. "Tomorrow is as good a time as any. And if Wendy's to be your sister-in-law, I want you guys to meet." Her gaze implored him.

"You sure," he murmured. She nodded, and his thumb brushed along her throat. Her lips parted, and Gray found himself swallowing to clear his throat. The intimate moment lasted a second longer, then she let go of his wrist and turned to Jacks.

"We'd like to join you for lunch, but if you don't mind, we'll give church a miss for now. Too many familiar faces." She smiled.

"I get it. No problem. Lunch is good." He shuffled restlessly. "Um, Zoey, listen." His hand lifted. Gray instinctively stiffened, and Jacks' gaze sliced to him. Whatever he saw made him jerk his arm back. "I'm sorry." His gaze flicked back to Zoey. "I want you to be prepared. We've made some changes." He gestured awkwardly. "The farm may not be like you remember."

"It's okay." Zoey's hand lifted to placate Jacks.

Gray breathed silent thanks when she stopped short of touching him. "You've kept me updated about everything you've done. And anyway, my memory's a pile of garbage." She laughed wryly. "That's one thing that hasn't changed."

Jacks smiled stiffly, but he didn't laugh with her. A sliver of ice trickled down Gray's spine. "Don't want to be rude, but Zoey needs to unpack. It's been a long day and we still need to get something to eat." He ignored Zoey's wide-eyed look and urged her back inside. "Thanks for coming, man. We'll see you tomorrow."

"Yep. Good." Jacks followed on their heels. "Come early. Around twelve-ish. It'll give us time to show you around."

"We'll do that," Zoey said.

"Go unpack. I'll walk Jacks out." Gray stared at Zoey, daring her to contradict him. He smiled inwardly when she rolled her eyes.

"Bye, then." She smiled at Jacks and walked off to the bedroom.

Gray shoved his hands in his jean pockets and showed Jacks out the cottage. He felt torn. There was a time when he'd adored his baby brother. They'd been close in their early years, but his mother's twisted possessiveness had slowly corroded their relationship. His granddad understood her best, and repeatedly tried to intervene, but nobody was a match for Margaret's masterful manipulations. After her cold reveal of his adoption, Gray realized she wanted Jacks all to herself. Her constant pandering to his brother's every need had warped Jacks' carefree, loving nature. By his early teens, he was a hot mess, plagued with self-doubt and paranoid sibling jealousy. Seeing Jacks in the flesh again, especially all grown up, it seemed far-fetched to think him capable of taking such hideous advantage of Zoey.

As he followed Jacks down the path, Gray's chest constricted. He knew there was a kid buried inside him who was still desperate to be loved. A young dumbfuck who fell in love with a butterfly, and refused to believe his girl would ever willingly put on someone else's ring. Especially his brothers! *But he wasn't that vulnerable kid anymore.* And he damn sure wasn't going to accuse Jacks unless the facts pointed in his direction.

They walked into the clearing, and Jacks stopped by his dark-blue Chevy. He fished his keys from his pocket and beeped the locks. Gray drew in a quick breath. He may refuse to entertain paranoid accusations, but that didn't mean he couldn't prod Jacks' memory. "Before you go, would you mind if I ask you something?"

"Sure, whatever you need."

"It's about the night of the Morgan attack." Gray braced when Jacks abruptly turned around. "I know you gave a police statement at the time, but have you ever remembered anything new from that night?"

Jacks' heavy-lidded eyes blinked. "Like what?"

"Something that's not already in the police report."

He frowned quizzically. "Don't you think I would have told them if I had?" His face tightened. Gray couldn't decide if it was anger or confusion. "Why are you dredging this up again? It was fourteen years ago. So much pain but we've healed now." His chin jutted. "It took a long time, but darn-it, Gray, we healed!"

"Speak for yourself!" Jacks shrank against his

truck as Gray jabbed a finger at him. "Maybe if you heard Zoey whimper in terror when nightmares rip her from sleep, you'd bloody understand not everybody is as lucky as you are. Not everybody healed."

"Zoey still has nightmares?" Jacks looked stricken.

"Yes!" Gray hissed.

"That's why you've come home." For a moment he held Gray's gaze, then his eyes darted away.

Gray stepped back, giving him some space. "Her memory is still blocked about what happened that night."

Jacks' gaze darted back. "But I thought the drugs did that."

"Partly. But Eva thinks it's something else."

"Eva?"

"She's a friend, a colleague. She's talking with Zoey, helping her."

"Helping her? How?" His voice rose.

Gray's gut twitched again. "She's a psychologist. She's good."

Jacks' chin jerked up as a flock of Red-winged Blackbirds landed in a nearby tree. "Maybe remembering isn't such a good idea," he said vaguely.

"Zoey believes it's the only thing that's going to help her heal."

Jacks nodded, but his gaze remained locked on the chattering birds. Gray waited. Seconds ticked by before Jacks seemed to realize he hadn't answered. He looked away from the birds and frowned at Gray. "Do you agree?"

"I think for Zoey, she needs to understand the past before she can start to heal and move forward."

"With you?"

"What?"

"Move forward with you?"

Gray stilled. "What the fuck, man?"

Jacks quickly raised his hands. "I meant to say, is there a Gray and Zoey again? From what I saw in the cottage, there is."

Gray and Zoey.

Hot sparks spread from Gray's chest until even his fingertips tingled. "Listen carefully, Jacks." He squared his shoulders and loomed closer to his brother. "There has always been a Gray and Zoey. If you think you're going to get between us again you're outta your motherfucking mind."

Jacks shook his head wildly. "I'm glad for you guys. Really! I've got Wendy and I would never do anything to hurt her." He pressed his hands together, holding them in front of him. "I love her, man. She's the best thing that ever happened to me."

Gray's nostrils flared. *Christ*. He was breathing like a charging bull.

"I've gotta go. Wendy's waiting for me."

Gray dipped his chin.

Jacks fidgeted with his car keys. "Listen. Maybe you should think through this thing with Zoey." He looked away from Gray. "I don't think Denton's the best place for her anymore."

"What are you saying?"

His mouth twisted, making the folds under his chin bulge. "Violence has hurt her here before. I don't want it to hurt her again."

"I'm not getting you," Gray growled. "Is that a threat?"

"No!" His voice rose in a squeak. "Of course not.

It's just a brotherly warning."

"And are you still my brother?"

Jacks' eyes rounded, looking huge behind his thick glasses. "Of course I'm still your brother," he gasped.

The birds in the tree squawked, and as one, took flight. Gray watched for a moment. It was getting late, and Zoey was alone in the cottage. He had the sudden need to feel her warmth up close. He abruptly nodded at Jacks. "Thanks for coming, we'll see you tomorrow."

And without waiting for his brother's response, he turned and jogged back to the cottage.

Chapter Sixteen
Did You Just Call Me Buddy

"Moms on Main", Aubrey, Denton
Saturday Evening
Zoey

I wanted a burger with all the trimmings and homemade fries. Gray insisted I go sit while he placed our order at the counter. I was still stuck on what went down with him at the cottage earlier, so I didn't argue. Choosing a side booth, I slipped into the wooden bench and looked around. "Moms on Main" was a typical small town family diner. Kitted out in the style of a general store, it was hometown rather than rustic, offering instant comfort and friendliness. Chalkboard signs shouted that "Moms" was the first place winner—four years in a row—at the Annual Taste of North Texas Event in the "Comfort Food Category." Performing stars were their Chili, Pot Roast, and Corn Chowder.

When Gray asked where I wanted to have dinner, I stalled over going to a restaurant in town. Denton felt like another life ago, one I wasn't ready to step back into. Gerald had mentioned to Gray about a diner he frequented in Aubrey called "Moms on Main". He said they did home-cooked food, North Texas-style, and it was only a fifteen-minute drive. Perfect.

Gray looked over his shoulder, his eyes scanning

the restaurant before they stopped on me. I gave a little wave, and he winked before turning back to the counter. My stomach tingled. I could still feel every inch of his powerful length pressed against me.

When he came back to the cottage after seeing Jacks off, I was curled up in one of the cane chairs on the porch. Without so much as a word, he stood in front of me and held out his hand. His eyes were filled with silver storms and blue lightning. I didn't hesitate. I took his hand, and he pulled me from the chair and folded me in his arms.

Warmth.

Strength.

And the heady scent that was uniquely Gray.

My arms crept around to grip his shoulders. His muscles flexed. One hand cupped my head, the other circled my waist, and he urged me closer. I pressed against him, nestling into his neck, hungry for his scent. He buried his face in my hair. And breathed deeply. And that was how we stood. Locked in each other's arms, our hearts beating in rhythm, each against the other. And I was reminded of what I'd believed since I was eight years old. That there was an inevitability about Gray and I. That no matter what life threw at us, we would never escape each other. Our bond was our destiny. What it meant for our future I didn't know. Like it had in the past, I had an inkling fate might have a hand in that.

I shook off my thoughts as Gray approached. The man was deliciously handsome. He was wearing a pair of jeans that looked so old I guessed they must be his favorites. They molded to him like a second skin, fading to patches of white along his muscled thighs.

He'd thrown on a slate-blue Henley. The thin fabric clung to his toned physique. But best of all, the sleeves were rolled up to reveal his ropey forearms.

"Food will be ready in ten," he muttered, sliding into the booth opposite me. "I got a beer for you, that okay?" He held up the chilled bottle.

"Thanks."

He poured my beer into a glass and pushed it across the table. Taking his own bottle, he raised it. "Cheers, Butterfly."

I quickly reached for my glass and clinked it with his bottle. "Cheers, tough guy."

His mouth twitched, and then he raised the bottle to his lips and drank. And drank. I froze with my glass halfway to my mouth. The muscles in his neck were taut, his throat rippling with each swallow. My nipples tightened. And nerves that had only started to wake since my reconnection with Gray, tingled between my legs.

Holy shit. I was going to have an orgasm sitting in a booth in "Moms on Main."

Gray brought his bottle down. "You look a little flushed." His head tilted, and his porn star mouth curved into a wicked smirk. "Better drink up, sweet-thing, before you overheat."

Sweet-thing!

A vision of Gray, licking me up like sugar candy, popped into my mind.

"Zoey!" It was a growl.

I squeezed my legs together and quickly brought my glass to my mouth. The beer was ice-cold, and I didn't stop drinking until I emptied half the glass. Gray lounged back, fiddling with his bottle. His eyes ate me up, but he didn't seem inclined to chat. I liked that about him, his ability to be present without the need to talk incessantly. My father was the same.

"My dad loved you," I said impulsively. "You were the only one he trusted me with, even more than Noah. If we were all going out together, he'd say, 'stick with Gray, he'll take care of you.' "

Gray hunched forward. "He was wrong. I didn't take care of you, did I?"

My heart beat painfully. "I didn't stick with you, did I?"

His brows drew together. They were dark and straight. Neatly groomed. Not by any barber or his own hand, but by the unknown genetics that had been so generously bestowed on him. I reached for his hand, clasped it between both of mine, and pulled it toward me. My lips settled on his knuckles, rough and callused, a reminder of his lethal skills. I kissed each one before I looked up. "I'm so sorry about what happened with Jacks." Sincerity made my voice more husky than normal. "I don't remember what I did or why, but I'm so goddamn sorry."

He reached across, and gently extricated himself. Then he captured my hands in his. "It was a long time ago, Zoey."

"That doesn't make it better."

His hands squeezed. "You still want Jacks?"

"No!" I tugged away. "I never wanted him. Never!"

"Okay then."

I stopped tugging. "Okay?" I croaked.

"Yeah, Butterfly. Okay."

The waitress arrived with our order, and Gray let

me go. I immediately missed his touch.

"Burger with fries?"

"That's me."

She placed a plate in front of me and slid another plate in front of Gray. "Catfish and shrimp. Corn chowder side coming right up," she chirped.

I lifted the top half of my bun and brought it to my nose. *Mmm.* Definitely not your regular factory bake. And my burger—lettuce, tomato, onion and a dill pickle. Classic. My mouth began to water.

"Here you go, handsome—fresh corn chowder." The waitress beamed at Gray. She must have been at least sixty, and was sporting a mile-high blonde beehive. Gray winked at her, and I smiled and ducked my head. A red bowl of steaming onion rings landed next to my plate. "Onion rings for the burger."

"Thanks." I immediately snatched one up and bit into it. "Oh my God, you have to try one." I shoved the rest of the ring into my mouth. "Homemade," I said with my mouth full of crispy batter. "Definitely not frozen." I swallowed and licked my fingers.

Gray's eyes crinkled. "Pass me one."

I picked up the bowl—

"No, sweet-thing, with your fingers."

My hand wobbled, and the bowl clattered back to the table. Electric heat raged in his eyes. Fire erupted in my belly. I trapped my lower lip between my teeth, and deliberately taking my time, selected a golden ring. My breath stuck in my throat as I stretched across the table. Holding my gaze, he leaned forward and bit into the fried crispiness. When I would have withdrawn my hand, he moved, predator fast, and circled my wrist. Then, he proceeded to suck first my finger, and then my thumb into his mouth.

Hot damn!

Heat exploded between my legs. His mouth was burning hot, and I could feel the sensual roughness of his tongue. When he was finished, he turned my hand over and pressed a soft kiss in my palm. "Delicious," he drawled, his voice deep and rich. Then he let me go, picked up his cutlery, and dug into his food.

I picked up a fry and jabbed it into some ketchup. My heart was pounding, and my "I-want-to-fuck-Gray-right-now" meter had shot up into the red. I peeked at him through my lashes while pretending to nibble on a fry. He was busy with his meal, but he looked damnably smug. I nabbed my beer and took a healthy swallow. Laughter bubbled up, and I mashed my lips together. Then I steadfastly ignored the hunk of gorgeous in front of me and forced myself to eat.

My burger was juicy, tasting the exact opposite of the cardboard-flavored fast food I tended toward in Boston. Chomping on another fry, I tried to remember when last I devoured a meal with such relish. The tastes and smells of the diner evoked bittersweet memories of my family. Mama had a rule that if you were home, you sat your butt at the table and partook of family mealtime. Much like this diner, her talent was comfort food. Because that's what she was, a treasured comfort giver.

Pushing away my empty plate, I watched Gray scoop up the last of his chowder. "I miss Mama," I said, as he set his bowl aside.

He grabbed a napkin and wiped his mouth. "I know you do, Butterfly." Instead of prodding me, he waited patiently for me to continue.

"You know how my family was. They were my anchor. But it was Mama who understood me best. She could always see when I started to unravel."

He leaned forward, resting on his arms. "You mean when you go deep-sea diving in your head?"

I glared at him, but he winked, and it took the sting from his words. "It's more than that." I twisted my napkin into a tight ball. "I have a bad habit of allowing a million different realities to run-a-muck in my mind. Sometimes to a point where they start to feed on each other, skewing things. Mama had this way about her; she could set things right without me even realizing it." I looked at Gray, his face so familiar it was imprinted on my soul. "You had that same way," I said softly. "When she died, and you went away, I think I lost my way."

His eyes narrowed. "The men?"

Acid trickled up my throat. "That." My hand fluttered. "And running into war zones that were so chaotic, the reality in my head seemed tame by comparison."

"And the rest of the time? What do you do?"

"I work." I shrugged, but I was so stiff it was more like a spasm.

"Jesus. You've tied yourself up so tight you can barely breathe."

"Like you're doing any better!" I hissed.

He shook his head impatiently. "Dammit, Zoey. This isn't about me, it's about you. And I know you." He leaned across the table. "This is not who you are."

"All finished, folks?"

Oblivious to the tension, our bustling waitress cleared the debris from our table. Gray and I remained locked in silent combat.

"Another round of drinks?" She held up our empties.

"No thanks." Gray tipped a questioning brow at me.

I tore my gaze from his. "I'm fine, thanks." My teeth were clamped together so all I could manage was a half-smile.

"It's your lucky day," she simpered. "We offer all our newcomers a free piece of Mom's homemade chocolate cake. How about that! You folks up for a treat?"

My heart hiccupped. Gray's eyes closed, and his face screwed up in a hilarious grimace. I clapped my hands to my mouth, wild hysteria threatening to break free.

"How 'bout you change that cake for a coconut cream pie?" Gray choked out, his voice sounding strangled.

I rolled my eyes, struggling to contain my laughter.

The waitress' gaze darted between us, her wide forehead puckering in suspicion. I think she finally cottoned on all was not as it should be at "Moms on Main." "I can do that," she said hesitantly.

"Great." Gray grinned at her. "We'll take it to go."

Her face brightened. "No problem, handsome. Coming right up." All at rights again, she bustled away.

"It's fucking macabre. Chocolate cake is stalking us."

I giggled. "And you're my Galahad, riding in to save the day."

His amusement abruptly faded and he dropped his head, raking his fingers roughly through his hair.

"Gray?"

"*Fu-uck!*" It was a harsh whisper. Several moments passed, and then he lifted his gaze. I inhaled sharply. His agony blazed so brightly, it sucked oxygen from the air. "I wish with every cell in my body I was there that night to save you."

"I don't."

He flinched, disbelief clear on his face. "What the fuck—?"

I pushed onto my forearms and leaned halfway across the table. "If you were there, you'd probably be dead too." His eyes devoured my face. I could deal with a lot of shit thrown my way, but the world without Gray. *No fucking way.* "You made me a promise a long time ago," I said huskily.

He blinked slowly. "Remind me."

I flopped back on my bench. It consistently annoyed me how easily I recalled everything. Word for word, I could regurgitate streams of conversations I'd participated in or factual documents I'd read. But try and remember the most awful night of my life. Not happening.

But the night in the barn? Oh, yes. I remembered that.

I closed my eyes and cast back. Tiny flares of heat flickered over my body. That night in the barn, Gray painted a picture I would never forget. Doing my best to imitate his lazy drawl, I leaned forward and recaptured his gaze. "I promise when I take what you're offering, you're gonna be so hot and wet, pretty Butterfly, you're gonna be begging for it. And I'm going to spend all night giving it to you."

His tongue snaked out to lick sensually at the

indent of his lower lip. "Crazy beautiful," he breathed. "You remember every word."

I swallowed hard. *My beautiful butterfly. All mine.* He said that too, but I couldn't find the courage to remind him.

"Say it again," he demanded.

"Why?"

"Because it makes me so fucking hard hearing those words fall out of your mouth." A dull flush stained his cheekbones.

I pressed my thighs together. "No!"

"No what?"

"No, I'm not saying it again."

He leaned forward. "You don't want to make me hard?"

I squirmed in my seat. "Jeez! You're even more annoying than I remember."

He grinned. "You used to find it charming."

I still did! How to tell him I craved him. That I wanted nothing more than to lick up every potent inch of him.

He reached out and stroked his thumb feather light across my knuckles. "You know, there's a part of that promise you're forgetting."

Tingles traveled up my arm. "Oh?"

"Yeah." His thumb kept stroking. "The part where I said I'll only claim you when you're free to give me everything you've got."

I jerked my hand from his grasp. "I am free."

"You're a prisoner, trapped by fear and nightmares." His voice softened. "You can't tell me it's not affecting your judgment."

Dammit. I hated when he did that. Spoke in dulcet

tones while still dictating terms. "I might be caught up in a difficult time but when it comes to you, Gray Walker, my judgment has always been crystal. It's you who's trapped in the past. Always looking for a reason to hold yourself back."

"That's shrink bullshit!" He surged forward. "I made you a promise a long time ago and nothing's changed."

I surged forward too. "There was a time when holding back didn't stop you from pleasuring me."

His nostrils flared. "You got an itch, Zoey?"

Awareness flushed through me. "And if I did?" His smoky-blue eyes dropped to my mouth. Like he flicked a switch I licked my lips.

"Christ!" His whispered curse made my stomach tighten into a hard ball, but I met his scowl and blinked innocently. He shook his head, his gaze mocking. "I'm not the person to tap, sweet-thing, if all you want to do is scratch."

I felt my face flush. "I'm not a kitty cat, buddy!"

His brows shot up. "Did you just call me buddy?"

I clamped my lips together. Disbelief was frozen on his face. I returned his stare bug-eyed. My body started to shake. I swallowed but as hard as I tried, the laughter gathered.

"Zoey!" he growled.

Uncontrolled giggles burst from me. "S-sorry." I held up a hand. "So sorry." I spluttered again and bent over double, giggles turning into snorting laughter.

"Fuck. Now I know what Luke means by Katya being a pain in his ass."

I hugged my aching stomach and squinted at him. "Jeez, tough guy, what's with you and asses?"

He glared at me. "You need yours spanked."

"Is that a promise?" I was aiming for blasé but my wheezing snort ruined the effect.

Gray stood and grabbed my hand, tugging me to my feet. "Let's get out of here. This isn't the place for this conversation."

"What?" I giggled. "A spanking conversation." The idea of Gray reddening my butt made me clench it. *Yikes!*

"No, sweet-thing." He swung his arm around my shoulders and whispered in my ear. "A conversation about your itch. That conversation."

"Oh!" My breath quickened. And my laughing fit instantly died.

Lordy.

It was hot in here.

Chapter Seventeen
Coconut Cream Pie

Granddad Davis' Cottage
Saturday night
Zoey

Hot. Cold. Pissed. Peaceful.

Safe.

Hot.

Did I say hot?

Being with Gray was like riding the world's wildest roller coaster. From one moment to the next, he hit my emotional triggers. Sometimes he was calculating about it, but mostly I think we just sparked off against each other.

I should have found it draining. I didn't. I was exhilarated.

During the drive back, the air was thick with sexual tension but neither of us spoke to break it. As soon as he opened the cottage door, Gray asked me to choose some music while he made coffee. I flipped through Gerald's CD collection and kept a frustrated eye on Gray. He seemed distracted, not once looking in my direction as he went about putting on the coffee machine. Tension began to squash my earlier tingles. I noisily flicked the CDs together. *Maybe it was better to just duck and go to bed?* I spotted "City of Angels," one of my all-time favorite soundtracks. *To hell with it.* I slipped the disc from the rack and inserted it into the deck. Bono's voice filled the cottage and I dropped onto the couch. Gray was still clattering in the kitchen. My foot started to tap the air, following the beat of the music. Gray sliced the single portion of coconut cream pie in half and meticulously placed it on two *separate* plates. My foot started to tap faster, missing the beat altogether. He picked up the plates and walked over to me. For a second his gaze settled on my tapping foot, then he held out a piece of pie to me. I ignored it and glared at him. "You don't like to share?"

He looked from the pie to me. Nobody could say Gray wasn't sharp. It took him only seconds to cotton on. His mouth curled suggestively, sending a shiver of desire licking over me. "You want me to feed you, Butterfly?" He sat and I quickly scooted over to give him space.

"No." His smoky-blue eyes made me breathy. I tore my gaze away and looked at the pie. "But I don't mind sharing a plate—" I scooped up a dollop of cream with my finger and met his startled gaze. "Or a spoon." Sinking my finger into my mouth, I licked it clean.

Heat exploded in Gray's eyes, burning away the smoky-gray, and leaving behind clear Texas-blue. My heart flip-flopped. He leaned forward and placed both plates of pie on the low oak table. Then, in the blink of an eye, he grabbed my wrist. My heart stuttered. For the second time that night he brought my hand to his mouth. "You like to live dangerous, sweet-thing?" His tongue flicked over my finger. "Who needs pie when you taste as sweet as you do?" He sucked my finger into his hot, wet mouth. His tongue swirled, and desire arced straight down between my legs.

God, I wanted more of that mouth.

Pop! He withdrew my finger. Cool air drifted over my damp skin.

"I like feasting on your fingers, Zoey, but I think you have sweeter treats for me to taste."

I gulped. "You said I'm not ready."

"I changed my mind." His face was tight with arousal. Warning prickles lifted the hair on my neck.

Don't mess this up.

I tugged gently at my hand. When he reluctantly let me go, I leaned into him and cupped his face. His short beard was surprisingly soft against my palms. "You're not an itch, Gray. You've never been that." I felt a muscle pulse in his cheek. "I want so much more from you." *I wanted everything.* "But that's too much for me to deal with right now."

He eased my hands from his face. "That's why we're going to wait."

"Jeez, tough guy. Make up your mind."

He stood, pulling me up with him. "You want to play, so we'll play."

"I don't get it."

His mouth quirked. "Maybe I wasn't clear. There are a hundred ways to play and make you come without taking you with my cock." He tugged me to him. "You remember some of them, don't you?" Electric heat radiated from his body, and I sprang back. He chuckled but didn't let me go. "Yeah, you should be nervous."

Beads of sweat popped out on my upper lip as he began to herd me backward. I gasped when my back hit the small passage wall leading to the bedroom. "When I'm finished with you, your throat is going to be raw." He bent to my ear. "First from begging. Then from screaming." He gently nipped my earlobe, and I arched into him. He was rock-hard.

"Awfully sure of yourself." I was panting and it ruined my brazen challenge.

He grinned. "Oh yes, sweet-thing, of that I am."

I slid restlessly against him. "Um, what about you?" I said nervously. "Are you still so generous about giving and not taking?"

Excitement lit through me when he lifted my arms and held them against the wall. He crossed my wrists and grasped them in one hand. His mouth hovered over mine. "Is this what concerns you?" He leaned back and my blood boiled over. His hand was resting over his jean-clad cock. "You think playing is still all about your needs." I bit my lip as he slowly began to stroke. With each firm touch, I imagined his rampant erection throbbing in pleasure.

"Gray—" I moaned.

"Sorry, but you're a big girl now, and I'm not as generous as I used to be."

My raspy breaths mingled with the bluesy brilliance of Jimi Hendrix. His sultry voice sang out about his baby, and before I realized what Gray was doing, I was in his arms and plastered against the wall. Instinctively I clung to his shoulders, wrapping my legs around his waist. He ground against my heat, and I whimpered when the seam of my cropped pants rubbed against my clit. Gray's warm breath washed over me. "This time I get to come too, and it's not going to be on my own in the fucking shower." Using his body to support me, he buried his hand in my hair. "This time, Butterfly, your hands and mouth are going to get me where I need to go."

Then he kissed me.

It wasn't gentle. His lips pressed hard against mine, forcing them open so his tongue could plunder. He kissed me like he was starving. Ravenous. And greedily, I kissed him back.

Gray!

I couldn't get enough. His taste. His feel. Like a magic elixir, it consumed me. Demolished me. Completed me. I grabbed onto the back of his head. More. I wanted more. Our tongues swirled. Entwined. His hand in my hair fisted, forcing my head to tilt so he could kiss me even deeper.

Yes.

Tingles raced over my scalp and spread like lightning through my body. I groaned into his mouth and began to writhe against his hardness. He thrust back, his movements an erotic rhythm in sync with his plunging tongue. I shuddered. I was burning up.

Lordy. I was going to come.

Gray tore his mouth from mine. "Don't you dare!" he growled.

"What?" I gasped.

He stopped moving, his pelvis pressed hard against mine. "You don't get to come yet." Before I could answer, he nipped my lip sharply.

"Ouch!"

He kissed a damp trail to my ear. "When you come I want your heat on my hands and your taste in my mouth." His tongue licked and more heat exploded in my belly. Then his arm tightened around my waist and the walls spun as he stalked with me into the bedroom. Stopping near the bed, he loosened his hold. "Drop your legs, Zoey." Command deepened his voice.

I dug my heels into his butt.

"Now, Butterfly."

I squirmed. His eyes crinkled, but there was no wavering in their gleaming demand. The ache between my legs began to throb. "You're bossy," I said huskily.

He untangled his hand from my hair and cupped my face. His thumb stroked over my kiss-swollen mouth. "You get off on it," he said gruffly. His brow rose in challenge. Alpha dominance poured from him, and I couldn't deny, it got me off. Big time!

I wrinkled my nose.

"Stop thinking so hard." His thumb stroked again. "Trust me with your pleasure, Butterfly. You won't be sorry." He jostled me gently. Texas-blue swirled, merging with stormy gray. A dull ache blossomed in my chest. I let my legs slide down his body until my feet touched the floor. He supported me until I was steady and then he let me go. "Strip for me. I want you naked."

A shiver rippled down my spine. *Strip for him while he watched?* My chest heaved with unsteady breaths. I took a small step back and began to unfasten my pale-green and pink floral blouse, one pearly stud at a time. My pulse beat madly, but I let the sleeves slip down my arms. Gray stood soldier still, his scorching gaze tracking my every move. My blouse fell to the floor and I sent up silent thanks I was wearing lingerie from my recent shopping splurge. My designer bra was a balconette-style in ivory lace, and showed off plenty of creamy cleavage. I heard Gray suck in a breath and I peeked at him through my lashes. His hands were curled into fists at his sides. I knew he could see my nipples through the fine lace. Saliva flooded my mouth.

I fiddled with my bra strap, but had second thoughts and dropped my hands to my belt-buckle. I loosened it and wetting my lips with the tip of my tongue, diligently unthreaded my belt, one loop at a time. I flicked a glance at Gray and my racing heart went berserk. He was loosening his own belt-buckle, the corner of his mouth twitching in a half-smile. I froze as he left his belt hanging loose, and popped the top button of his jeans.

"Just making room," he drawled lazily. "Don't let me stop you."

I squeezed my legs together and sucked in a giant breath. *One-one-thousand, two-one-thousand.* Gray's hand slipped into his jeans and he casually repositioned himself. I puffed out a strangled breath. "You're killing me," I wheezed.

"And you're still dressed." He winked and withdrew his hand.

Toeing off my white low-top sneakers, I quickly unzipped my pants and shoved them down my legs. My hands were clumsy and suddenly I was hopping around, my pants tangled up around my ankles.

"Jesus!" Gray burst out laughing and lunged forward, his arm swooping around me. "Fucking gorgeous but definitely not a stripper." He chuckled and pulled me against him, his warm hand settling squarely on my bare butt.

My panties were a matching set with my bra. They were ivory lace with a narrow satin thong pretending to cover my ass. Gray's hand was rough against my skin. He squeezed my cheek and an arrow of heat blazed to my core. My hand flew up and curled around his neck. "Gray—"

"Still want you naked, Zoey, but I think it's safer if you finish stripping on the bed." He swung me up and deposited me gently in the middle of the huge bed. I scrambled to my knees. *Jeez.* The man tossed me around like I weighed nothing at all. "I want to see those pretty breasts," he teased and bent over, bracing himself on the bed. "And I wanna taste those dusty-pink nipples peeking at me."

Arousal flushed through me. Gray was too devilish for his own good. And I loved it. Holding his wicked gaze, I thrust my chest out and wound my hands behind my back. "What about you?" I said huskily.

He reached up, fisted his Henley and pulled it over his head. Muscles rippled across his broad shoulders. My lips parted. *So freaking sexy.* Still braced on one arm, he began to pop the buttons on his jeans. I couldn't tear my eyes away. His fly was open and the tip of his hungry cock was pushing above his briefs.

"Your turn," he growled.

My gaze shot to his. I fumbled with the clasp of my bra until it unhooked. Before I could catch it, the silky fabric dropped forward. Gray's gaze lowered. My already sensitive nipples went taut. I shrugged my bra the rest of the way down my arms and tossed it to the floor. Gray slowly straightened. He shuffled and I knew he was toeing off his shoes. Cupping my aching breasts, I grazed my thumbs over my pebbled nipples. An electric charge streaked down to my pussy, and I gasped loudly.

"Fuck! I'm gonna watch while you make yourself come."

"What?" It was a breathy squeak.

Gray shoved down his jeans and navy underpants

and kicked them off. When he straightened, I nearly orgasmed on the spot. His hand was wrapped around his cock and he was lightly jacking himself. A tiny drop of essence was seeping from the glistening head.

"I see you like to touch yourself, sweet-thing." He flicked his thumb over the head of his cock, and saliva flooded my mouth. "So you're going to take yourself there while I watch." He braced himself on the bed. "And after, I'm going to lick all your creamy beauty up." He rubbed his thumb over my parted lips. My pussy screamed and I knew I was soaking wet. Because his thumb was coated in his taste.

I licked my lips.

Gray.

He watched me take his essence into my mouth then closed the gap and kissed me. His tongue quickly invaded, swirled. I angled my head, but with only another flick of his tongue, he withdrew. I stared, transfixed by his powerful sensuality. This was not the Gray I remembered from when I was a teenager. I might have caught a glimmer of him once, in the barn, but that was a shadow of the man standing in front of me now. Besides his innate sexuality, Gray oozed physical strength. His muscles didn't bulge. They were hard and ropy. Beautifully sculpted. His stomach was flat, tight. He had those clearly defined v-shaped lines where his lower abs met his hips. My doctor's brain recognized it as low body fat, combined with freaking high levels of strength and fitness. I swallowed, savoring the last of his taste. Who gave a damn about scientific cause and effect?

"Show me what you got, sweet-thing."

Burning need lanced through me. His body wasn't

the only thing changed. His youthful charm had transformed into a seductive weapon. And I was addicted. I eased off my knees and lay back against the pillows. Bringing my knees to my chest, I slipped my panties over my ass and down my thighs. "You going to be a gentleman and help me with these?" I straightened my legs.

A slow smile stole over his face. "That I can do." He put one knee on the bed and slid my panties the rest of the way down my legs. I stopped breathing because his gaze was locked on my pussy. And he wasn't smiling.

Shitsofuckit. I forgot.

"What the fuck?"

I propped myself up on my elbows and looked down my body. Gray was riveted on the tiny red butterfly tattoo nestled in the corner of my neatly groomed triangle.

"When?" he asked hoarsely.

I hesitated.

He crawled closer and settled his mouth feather light on the spot. My vision blurred and I reached down, threading my fingers through his hair. He didn't need to know the details. Not now. "When I graduated from Harvard," I said softly.

He breathed deeply and pressed his lips to my skin. I closed my eyes. Now wasn't the time to tell him the tattoo was a reward to myself after my last session with Rose. It was a promise never to sink back into the darkness. Never again to devalue myself or my body. One day soon I'd explain it all to him. But not now.

I stroked his hair. "I thought you said you were going to make me scream?"

His lashes lifted. My stomach fluttered as his beautiful mouth twitched. "I said first I was gonna make you beg."

"How you gonna do that if I have to do all the work?"

The encroaching weight in my chest receded as his devilish smile chased the sadness from his face. Rising to his knees, he moved between my legs. "Look and learn, sweet-thing." His hands circled my calves, and he gently urged me to bend my knees. My heart kicked as he spread me open. "Now, isn't that a pretty sight."

My pussy clenched. Heat erupted, and I broke into a damp sweat. "Gray," I panted.

He sat back on his haunches, spread his thighs, and rested my legs over his. "Play for me, pretty girl." He stroked my thighs, his fingers spreading a trail of wildfire up my legs. I trembled. Gray soothed me with gentle strokes. Hesitantly, I began to glide my fingers between my breasts, and then slowly down my stomach. Gray's lips parted. Holding my breath, I settled my hand on my mound. "Let yourself go, Zoey." Desire laced his voice, making me shudder. I'd pleasured myself a million times. I knew where to touch, how fast to stroke, which nipple to squeeze and how hard. But doing all that in front of Gray—it ramped my arousal into another stratosphere. His hands curled around my thighs. "C'mon, Butterfly, show me how you fly."

His velvet voice tugged at me. My eyes drifted closed, and I let myself drown. In his voice. In his touch. In his heady scent. My fingers started to move. I was already achingly wet, and wound so tight it wasn't going to take much to set me off. Spreading myself open, I slipped a finger between my folds. Like I received an electric charge, my pussy spasmed. Nerves flared, sending exquisite ripples of pleasure flowing through my body.

"Gray!"

"Right here, Butterfly. Show me more."

I dipped my finger, coating it in my slick heat. Then using firm strokes began to circle my aching clit. I brought my other hand to my breast and roughly grazed my nipple with my palm.

The more I let go, the more I wanted to let go.

"Fucking beautiful."

My eyes opened. *Gray*. I wanted to fly for him.

Catching my nipple between my thumb and finger, I squeezed. My clit pulsed and I started to undulate, my finger circling faster.

"Gray!"

"Tell me what you need?"

"You!" I wailed.

"You want my fingers?" His voice was a deep growl.

Oh God. My pussy spasmed. "Please, Gray, I need your touch."

He lifted my leg and placed a wet kiss on the back of my knee. I arched up, my fingers strumming desperately.

"Gra-aay!" It was a drawn out groan.

He moved up beside me. "Give me your mouth," he demanded gruffly. Desperate, I turned my head. His mouth covered mine, hungry, seeking. Starved for his taste I licked against his tongue, dancing, feasting. His hand glided between my legs. I stopped stroking when I felt his finger slide inside me. I wanted to weep at the feel of him filling me. Fucking me.

He paused.

My eyes shot open.

"You stop, I stop," he growled into my mouth.

I wanted to bite his luscious lips. But I wanted his fingers more. My legs were shaking. Sweat ran down my neck. Burning need was a live flame flowing from my core. I needed to come. *Lordy*. I needed to come bad.

Panting into his mouth, I closed my eyes and started to strum.

His finger didn't move.

I arched up, searching. But still, he didn't move.

"Ask nicely, Butterfly." His guttural demand whispered over my lips. I opened my eyes and stared into twin flames of blue. His face was flushed, his body taut.

Holy shit. It really turned him on to hear me beg. I squirmed and began to brush my fingers firmly over my soaking heat. "Please, Gray," I panted. "Please, I want to come."

His finger began to thrust. "More," he whispered.

"Yes, more," I gasped. "Please. More." My body bucked frantically. *"Ple-eease!"* I screamed.

His fingers filled me. They moved, plunged. I stroked. My rhythm picked up, and so did his. I arched up, trying to catch his mouth.

"That's it, Butterfly. Fly."

His lips slammed down on mine. I thrust my tongue against his, slaking my thirst. But it was coming, and it was going to be huge. Tearing my lips away, I cried out. "Help me!"

His fingers plunged, hitting a spot deep inside me.

A million sparks of heat exploded at once.

And I fragmented.

Gray's arm snaked around my shoulders, pulling me to him. Pleasure like I'd never known washed over me. Cocooning me. I was where I belonged. In his arms. Safe.

It took long moments for my frenetic pulse to slowly return to normal. My limbs were heavy, melted by the sweetest languor. I burrowed closer to Gray. His skin was damp. Musky. I stroked his nape, running my lips over his taut neck. His arm tightened as I settled my mouth over his pulse, and licked. Salty. Male.

He groaned.

His pulse was racing beneath my tongue. His beautiful body, rigid beneath my sprawled torso. I stilled. His hand was still between my legs, cupping my heat. Calming me.

But Gray wasn't calm.

Trailing my lips over his jaw, I kissed the corner of his mouth. "Hi," I whispered.

His heart-stopping gaze twinkled. "Hi. You okay?"

I nodded.

His hand glided up my back and bunched into my hair. "I like how you beg, Butterfly."

Lazy arousal stirred in my belly and I shifted against his hand. "It's your turn now."

He grinned. "To beg?"

I caught his bottom lip between mine and laved it wetly. His hand in my hair tightened. I raised my lashes and let his lip go. "No, tough guy. It's your turn to come."

His body moved, and quick as a flash, I was on my back, Gray hovering over me. "Not yet. First I get to taste." His hand stroked provocatively between my legs. I squirmed as sated nerves sprang awake.

"But I want to pleasure you."

"Everything you do pleasures me."

I lightly slapped his shoulder. "You know what I mean."

He moved his hand away, and immediately I felt the loss. He trailed it up my belly, and gently cupped my breast. His thumb brushed my nipple. A quiver of desire spiraled, and my nipple hardened.

"Yeah, I know what you mean." He lowered his head and circled my nipple with his tongue. "But if you touch me now, I'm gonna explode. And I've waited to taste you again for too fucking long."

He looked up and I inhaled sharply. Blue shards glittered in his eyes. My mind raced. Gray was stubborn but so was I. Holding his gaze, I smiled languidly. Then I reached down and dipped two fingers in my creamy heat. Gray's eyes widened. Unhurriedly, I brought them to my mouth and coated my lips. "So taste," I invited huskily.

His cheekbones flushed a dark red. "Jesus Christ." He cupped my face, his fingers sinking into the hair at my temples. "You're fucking perfect." Holding me still, he lowered his mouth. His tongue flicked out, and he licked along my parted lips. "So erotic," he growled. A flame of wicked arousal scorched through me, and I arched into him. His cock brushed against me. Rock-hard and velvet smooth.

I wanted to touch. God! I needed to touch.

My hand moved. Gray's moved faster. He caught me by the wrist and rolled to his back, taking me with him. Letting go of my hand, he circled my waist and ab-curled upright. My legs parted, falling to either side of him.

"What—"

"Just getting comfortable." Twisting around, he stacked pillows then reclined back. "There we go."

Suddenly I didn't give a damn what he was doing. I was mesmerized by his hungry cock standing erect between my legs. With the tip of my finger, I dabbed a pearl of glistening cream. Already addicted to his taste, I sucked my finger clean.

"Fuck!" My gaze flew to his. "You do that again, I'm going to come before you touch me."

"Oh. I get to touch you now?" I raised a sardonic brow.

His eyes narrowed. "If you prefer, you can watch." I stopped breathing when his hand snaked down and fisted his cock. Like he was teasing me, he languidly caressed his hand up and down.

It was the sexiest thing I'd ever seen.

"You need to make a decision, Zoey. Watch or touch?"

"Touch," I said breathlessly. "I want to touch."

"With your hand or your pussy?"

What?

I looked up. My eyes must have been giant saucers because he ab-curled again, and kissed me hard. His knees lifted and parted, nestling me deeper astride him. I clung to his shoulders as he gripped my hips and guided me over his cock.

"I think I just decided." His voice was thick and deep.

"Gray—"

"I was gonna let you choose to get me off with

your hand, or like this." His hands bit into my hips, and I slid over his cock. "You up to riding me, Butterfly?"

"But I thought—"

"Not gonna fuck you, Zoey." He rocked his hips, sliding his cock through my wet folds. "Want you to get me off just like this." He rocked again. I shuddered as the tip of his cock nudged my sensitive clit. "Oh yeah," he groaned. "This is gonna be good for both of us." Loosening his grip on my hips, he relaxed back against the pillows. "Come here." He tugged me forward. "I want to suck on these pretty little nipples while you do your thing."

His voice was a seductive spell, weaving all around me, trapping me. I braced on his chest and moved until my breasts hovered over his mouth. His lips closed on my nipple and I bucked up. "Gray!"

He sucked, and molten desire exploded.

"Oh, God."

He sucked harder.

Aching need spasmed between my legs, and I dropped down onto his pulsing cock. Gray grunted but continued to feast on my breasts. Rocking my hips, I began to move on his velvety length. My pussy was swollen, and so tender I could feel the thin ridge running along the underside of his cock. *Oh Lordy.* It was wild. Sublime.

Gray's hands slipped to my hips. "Faster." He nipped my erect nipple, sending another bolt of electricity searing through me. I reared up, my heart beating wildly, my breathing totally out of control. His cock was slick with my juices. Iron-hard. Pulsing. Demanding.

"Oh God." My nails dug into his pecs. Each time I

rocked, the ridge around his head rubbed against my clit. I was throbbing now. Frantic.

"Wait for me, Zoey."

"Gray!"

"Wait!" His grip tightened, and he lifted me off him.

"Gray—"

"You're gonna finish on my hand."

Oh, Lord!

Steadying me with one hand, he buried the other between my legs. His fingers plunged inside me, and his thumb hit my clit. My pussy went wild.

"That's it, fuck my fingers."

Greedy. Feral. I did as I was told. Waves of heat erupted when Gray let go of my hip, and wrapped his hand firmly around his turgid cock. His biceps rippled, his stomach went taut. And he began to jack himself. He was rough and fast. Running his hand from base to tip. Rotating. Tugging. A drop of semen leaked. And another.

"Now, Zoey." His fingers thrust. His thumb pressed.

And for the second time that night, I came apart.

"Gray!" Wondrous heat exploded. Spread. Moving through me. Incinerating me.

"Fu-uck!"

I forced my eyes open. Gray was stretched rigid, his hand still moving, thick essence spurting from him. His eyes were closed, head thrown back. His face twisted in pleasure.

Beautiful. Primal.

Mine.

Chapter Eighteen
Nothing!

Granddad Davis' Cottage
Sunday Morning
Zoey

I was only half awake when Gray dropped a feather light kiss on my temple and slipped silently from the bed. I heard a shuffle of clothes, and then the door click quietly closed. I didn't hear Gerald arrive.

When I wandered into the kitchen a while later, Gray said Gerald had brought over fresh cinnamon rolls, orange juice and tomatoes from the garden. I had a momentary pang of regret I hadn't been around to say thanks, but it quickly melted away. I wanted to be with Gray. Alone. Especially when I found him dressed in his faded jeans and nothing else. Not even shoes.

My mouth went dry, but the rest of me went wet. Achingly wet! Squeezing my thighs together, I leaned over the island. I was wearing his Henley and a pair of panties.

His smoky-blue gaze raked over me, but besides a small smile, he didn't comment. He was busy with the fixings for omelets. Pointing to the fresh coffee and rolls, he said to sit and relax while he cooked. I happily complied and retreated with my goodies to curl up in the sitting room.

The porch door was open, letting a soft breeze

move through the cottage. I breathed in the dewy dampness, and a faint pain echoed near my heart. If I closed my eyes, I could almost hear Mama chattering to my dad in the kitchen. She always got up early to make breakfast. The memories were buried but when they surfaced, they were mine to treasure. I drank my coffee and washed down the last of my cinnamon roll. And with it, gently nudged the memory away.

The breeze gusted and I brushed away a curl of hair fluttering in my face. Gray was cracking eggs now and a wave of lust crept over me. His easy—and mostly naked—confidence in the kitchen was weirdly heady. An image of his face when he came last night slipped into my mind. The dampness in the air transferred to my skin and I shivered, goose bumps prickling up my arms. *Jeez*. He was so sexy. Even more than I could have ever imagined.

Rubbing at my goosies, I peeked at him through my lashes. A vague heaviness fluttered in my tummy. He was confident and seductive as hell, but he was also holding back. He might have had reason last night, but I wasn't going to let him get away with it for long. Gray's running days were coming to an end. Soon.

"Butterfly." His sexy growl demanded my attention. He was sipping coffee, his electric gaze focused on me. "You wearing panties?"

My jaw gaped.

"New rule, sweet-thing." He calmly took another sip of coffee. "No panties in the cottage." His gaze swept to my breasts. They were heaving. "No bra either," he added. My nipples hardened, easily visible beneath his thin Henley.

Was he nuts?

The words screamed in my head, but they didn't leave my lips. Challenge burned in his gaze. I sucked in an excited breath. He put down his mug and began to chop tomatoes. "Slip them off and bring them to me." His voice was low, steady, but edged with steel.

I stopped breathing.

"Fuck you" was on the tip of my tongue, but his seductive energy silenced me. He was chopping tomatoes, his stance casual, but I knew he was totally focused on me. And I loved it. Last night Gray pushed me, first to strip for him, and then to make myself come while he watched. Twice he'd thrown down the gauntlet and then backed off, trusting me to make my own decision. And asking me to trust him with my pleasure. My pussy clenched. If I was flippant I knew he'd back off. And I didn't want that.

Moving to the edge of my chair, I lifted my butt and slid down my underwear. They were also part of my New York collection, a lacy Brazilian seamless-cut in the palest mint-green. And they were damp. I stood, and even though I knew his Henley covered my ass and lady-parts, it took every bit of self-control not to tug at the hem.

Gray's hands stopped moving and his head lifted. I teetered on suddenly weak knees. His eyes were gleaming, blue glints swirling. My mouth moistened and I licked my lips. Then using one finger to hold my lacy underwear aloft, I swayed slowly toward him. I was barefoot so it wasn't easy getting my hips to swing, but I think I did pretty good because by the time I walked around the island and stopped in front of him, a revealing flush stained his cheeks.

"So, tough guy," I said huskily. "If I don't get to

wear panties, why do you?"

"Panties?" he drawled, his brow arched.

"You know what I mean."

He leaned into me and gently brushed his lips over mine. Then like it wasn't enough, he came back for more, his tongue tracing the seam of my mouth. Heat tingled down my spine. My lips opened wanting more, but he moved back and the corner of his mouth lifted. "This isn't about me, it's about you. But just so you know, I'm already commando."

My eyes dropped to his zipper. And my pussy began to throb. I could see he was hard beneath his jeans.

"You going to give me those?"

I tore my eyes away and collided with his twinkling gaze. *Oh, Lord.* I was way out of my depth with this man. Gripping the island to stop myself collapsing into a mess at his feet, I held up my pretty green panties. His warm hand closed over my wrist, and he tugged me closer. His mouth pressed over my madly beating pulse. His tongue swirled, and he gently bit me.

"Gray!"

He let go, and at the same time slid my panties from my finger. *Oh, God.* I knew what he was going to do. Mesmerized, I watched as he brought them to his face and inhaled deeply. His gaze kept mine anchored to him as he slowly bunched up my underwear, and slipped them into his pocket.

"On a scale of one to ten, how wet are you right now?"

"A hundred," I gasped.

He grinned, and then without saying another word, went back to chopping tomatoes. I gritted my teeth to stop my jaw from hitting the floor. I was on fire, desperate for more of his touch…and he was making breakfast.

I studied him. His hands were steady but a deep flush marked his cheeks. My gaze dropped to his zipper. *Oh yeah*. He was as steamed up as I was. I traced a fingernail down his muscled arm. His bicep went taut. "If you're trying to distract me from our lunch with Jacks and Wendy, it's working."

He lifted his head and winked. "You wanna fetch me the cheese?"

I grinned. "Sure."

I wasn't lying. Gray's sensual play had totally checked my trepidation about going home to Morgan Farm today. Grabbing the cheddar from the mostly empty fridge, I turned back to him. He was leaning with his back against the island, arms folded.

"You have any hard limits?" His expression was difficult to read.

My fingers dug into the cheese. "Is there something you're not telling me?" I stepped closer. "Are you a dominant, Gray?"

A smile flirted with his mouth. "I have a bit of the sexual dom in me. I tried it out for a time."

My brain and my heart stuttered. "BDSM you mean?"

"Yeah."

"And?"

"And you wanna give me that cheese before you destroy it?" He held out his hand. I thrust the cheese at him.

"And!" I said impatiently.

"I liked some of it." His gaze was wicked. And

assessing.

"Only some?"

"You curious?"

Hellooo! "Absolutely."

"Good." He turned back to the island. "Grab me the grater. I think it's in that cupboard over there." He pointed behind me.

I searched the cupboard and found the grater. I was tingling, and a light film of perspiration covered my skin. Surreptitiously I wiped my upper lip. "Hey, tough guy?"

Gray turned and seeing I was holding the cheese-grater, eased it from my hands. He placed it on the counter and gently pulled me to his chest. His arms wrapped around me and I immediately slipped mine around him. His skin was warm, velvet-smooth beneath my palms.

"Am I freaking you out, Butterfly?"

"Not really." I rested my cheek against his naked flesh. I wanted to run my tongue over his tempting nipple. Instead, I looked up and caught his eyes. "It's just, I don't think I'm a submissive."

He combed back my hair, leaving one hand buried in my curly mass. "No. But you enjoy elements of sexual control."

Maybe I should have been pissed at his arrogance, but I was much more curious. "Why do you say that?"

"Because when I give you instructions it makes you wet." He lowered his head and nipped my lip. "And when I take your choice away, it makes you even wetter."

I began to wriggle.

His hand fisted in my hair, and his arm tightened

like a steel band around my waist. "Don't be embarrassed." He shook me gently. My scalp zinged from his tight grip and I stilled because the zing ratcheted the ache between my legs. "It's fucking hot how you respond to me." He pushed his erection against me. "But it's more than that." His warm coffee-breath whispered over my face. "When you give up some of your control or even better, all of it, that allows you to be free of your head. You don't need to think, you don't need to be scared. You just need to feel."

His body was iron-hard, chiseled. But his eyes were swirling mists of gray, filled with glints of infinite blue. I relaxed into him. "That's a lot of trust," I said quietly.

"Yes." He hugged me, before gently disengaging himself. Then he moved back to his prep board littered with chopped tomatoes and broken egg-shells. Picking up the cheese, he peeled off the wrapper.

"I don't have any limits. Not with you."

His head jerked.

"I trust you to take care of me." I waited, my patience rewarded when he turned his head and caught my gaze.

"That's a shitload of trust, Zoey." His voice was deep, rich like dark syrup.

"Yes, it is." Time slowed. A sense of fullness grew inside me but I didn't feel heavy. For the first time in as long as I could remember, I felt like I could fly. "Does that make you nervous?"

His beautiful gaze devoured me but he didn't answer. After what seemed like forever, he lifted a hand and tucked an errant curl behind my ear. Then, still without a word, he turned back to the island and started to grate the cheese. I swallowed a soft lump lodged in my throat.

"Do I have time to shower before omelets?"

He nodded. "Sure."

I smiled and headed for the bedroom. His retreat didn't bother me. I was starting to understand this new Gray. Strong. Sexy. Sensitive. And protective of a heart that had been shattered.

"Zoey."

His gruff call stopped me in my tracks.

"When we leave this cottage, unless I say otherwise, you always have your panties on."

I burst out laughing, and waving off his barked command, headed for the shower.

****

Morgan Farm
Sunday Midday
Zoey

Nothing.

I felt nothing.

For the first time in fourteen years, I was home. And I felt nothing.

After the spine-tingling awareness and sense of joy ignited by Gray's sensual play, to feel nothing but dull detachment in a place where I should be full to bursting with emotion, was therapy-worthy. At least I think Rose would think so, Eva too, most likely.

As we wound our way down the long gravel road to the homestead, I could feel Gray's protective gaze. I ignored it in favor of the passing view. The farm had reverted to much of its natural wooded state, getting denser as it neared the river. But the rolling pastures to my left were as I remembered. Mostly open and green, with a meandering wood-pole fence that followed the contour of the land.

When Magic died, my dad slowly shut down his breeding program. I asked my mama about it once, and she said that Magic's death broke his heart. "When that horse perished, he took your dad's horse spirit with him," she said. So my dad poured his heart into his family, and his energy into hydroponics. And what started out as a hobby ended with him becoming a key supplier of herbs and micro vegetables to the local market.

We neared the homestead and I couldn't help searching for the hydroponic tunnels that used to stand alongside the barn. A faint pang pierced my numbness. They were gone. I knew they would be. Jacks had written two years ago to ask if he could take them down. We drove by and I craned to look. The tunnels had been replaced with a large riding arena.

"You okay?"

"Sure." I faced forward again and dragged in a ragged breath. There it was. Nestled in amongst a spread of soaring elms, my childhood home. A single-story house built of natural stone with a high charcoal-slate roof. My father used to say it looked like an English cottage, especially when my mama lined the pathway with giant blue hydrangeas and a multitude of garden-variety roses.

Today there were no flowers, just an assortment of green shrubbery. And Jacks and Wendy waiting at the end of the path.

The return of the prodigal daughter.

Well, sugar. I was hoping for fireworks.

Tane's sarcastic retort from days ago drifted

through my mind. Once again I'd disappoint. There would be no fireworks.

When Jacks and Wendy proudly showed us around the renovated paddocks, my breathing was steady. I had no expectation of my father or Noah appearing around the corner. It was like the life I used to live here had simply vanished. Or maybe it had belonged to someone else. They showed us two simple chalets they'd built amongst the edge of the tree line. One was for counselling staff, and the other for kids who did camp sleepovers. They'd started a community program running camps for traumatized children. Wendy explained that learning to ride and care for the horses helped these kids heal. Her dedication was touching, even impressive. I smiled and nodded. But a giant hollow had settled in my gut and I felt empty. Nothing.

Wendy surprised me. She wasn't the typical leggy-type blonde I remembered as being Jacks' preference. While she did have blonde hair—Texas-big and wavy—she leaned toward the curvy and buxom. Her wide smile oozed country-homeliness, and her light-brown eyes were direct and filled with warm honesty. She seemed honey-sweet, her care for Jacks written all over her face. She stayed close to him, constantly touching his hand and stroking his arm. And although I guessed he'd told her a lot about me, she held her silence. But the worry showed in the numerous anxious glances she sent my way.

Worry for me or worry about their future?

I wanted to care more, ease her anxiety. But I didn't. I pretended not to notice her sensitive glances. And I didn't respond to Jacks' subtle references to their ambitious plans. I chose instead to let an awkward silence hang between us, like a giant sucking leech that could find nothing to attach itself to.

When we headed to the main house, Jacks and Wendy were a little in front murmuring between themselves. Gray was by my side, a protective shadow.

"You okay?" His eyes were creased in concern.

"Sure." I lengthened my stride, straining to catch up with Jacks and Wendy.

How many times was he going to ask me that today? He probably had a straightjacket stashed in his trunk.

Dammit! I shook the stupid thought from my head and slowed. Gray matched his pace to mine. A deep frown grooved his forehead and I reached for his hand, linking my fingers with his. "I'm fine, really."

He tugged at my hand and brought us to a stop.

"What?" I squinted at him, impatient again.

"You guys all right?" Jacks called. He and Wendy were waiting for us by the front door to the house. My family's home. My home.

"We're fine!" I yelled back, my eyes locked to Gray's.

"We're not fine," he murmured. "But we're going to be."

The faintest touch of butterfly wings brushed against the emptiness inside me. "I'm fine," I whispered huskily.

A wry smile twinkled in his eyes, smoothing away his frown. Then, keeping his hand linked with mine, he guided us up the path.

When we entered the house, I knew everybody was holding their breath. Their anxiety reached out and circled my throat. But it didn't strangle me. I breathed deep, and there was nothing. No scent of cut roses that used to adorn the hall table, and every surface my mama could find. No aroma of freshly baked afternoon scones, or mouth-watering smells from Mama's roasts. No sound of classical music escaping the confines of my dad's study. No rhythmic beats of country rock echoing down the corridor from Noah's bedroom.

There was nothing.

Nothing.

I breathed easy.

The house was different. The furnishings were different. This was no longer my family home. I was a stranger in this house.

The only time I balked was when Wendy finished showing me around and walked toward the dining room. Gray had gone outside to take a call from King. Lunch was to be a barbecue out on the pool terrace. I knew Wendy was heading for the dining-room doors that opened to the pool, but every muscle in my body froze, including my brain. I stood there like I was chipped out of solid marble. It was Jacks who noticed. He took me by the arm and gently led me away. My tongue was ten times its usual size, stuck to the roof of my mouth. He didn't say a word, just guided me through the sitting room and out the side door to the terrace. He took me over to Gray who was still on the phone and then went back inside to help Wendy.

Gray quickly wound up his call and asked me if I was okay. "I'm fine," I said. I could see by the storm brewing in his eyes that he didn't believe me.

Jacks came out to barbecue the chops and ribs. I wandered inside, via the sitting room, and sliced cucumber and spring onions while Wendy nattered away preparing warm potato salad. I ignored the faint tremor in my hands and did my best to play the role of friendly guest. But I could feel it welling up. A roiling cloud of venom, shaping itself into a silent scream. Threatening to pierce my veil of Nothing.

Jacks called. Lunch was ready.

The four of us sat, and like old friends dug into the family-style barbecue. Jacks and Wendy chatted about the farm, detailing more of their plans. I nodded and bit into a sticky rib. I wanted it to taste of Texas, but instead, a bland gunky mess coated my dry mouth. I sipped an iced cola. Nibbled on a chop. I smiled. Washed my food down with more cola, and grimaced. The ice had melted, leaving my drink warm and watery.

Gray spoke reservedly, filling some of the silence. But he remained watchful. Vigilant. And frequently caught my furtive glances. Glances I never ever allowed to stray over his shoulder, across the green pasture, and up the small hill to where the grove of tall trees stood sentry.

We finished with possum pie. Wendy's mother came from Arkansas and the pie was a family tradition. It was filled with decadent chocolate custard, sliced peaches, and sour cream cheese. And to finish it off, a layer of toasted pecans spread liberally over the top. It was wonderfully rich and delicious—and sat like a cloying weight on my chest. I had to breathe through my nose and take frequent sips of strong black coffee to stop myself heaving.

Gray's phone rang again. It was Mira. He excused himself to take the call. Wendy refused my help to clear the table, insisting I take myself off for a walk.

Bless your heart, sweet Wendy.

The darkness was hovering, the pain gathering. I needed to be alone. To feel nothing.

Oh God, please.

I needed to feel something.

My body was stiff and clumsy as I headed back toward the paddocks. I followed the same wood-pole fence my dad had built and stopped when I reached the new training arena. I clung to the fence and tipped my head back. Warm Texas air and the familiar smell of horses filled my lungs. My gagging nausea slowly dissipated.

"You okay?"

My lips curved but I kept my face turned up to the sun. "How many times are you going to ask me that today?"

"As many times as you lie to me and say you're fine." His warm lips brushed my neck.

"I'm fine."

"Liar." He yanked a curl that had escaped my loose chignon.

I wrinkled my nose and dipped my head to look at him. "What's with the phone calls?"

He shrugged. "The case I was working on with Mira has gone south."

"Do you have to go back to New York?"

"No."

"If you have to go I understand—"

"No," he said forcefully, and lightly rested his forehead on mine. His warm breath puffed against my lips. "There's nothing that will take me from you. Not today. Not ever." He cradled my face. Heat flowed from his hands, chasing away the cold detachment that had held me hostage since we drove up to the farm.

Gray.

I soaked him in. His promise of today. His promise of tomorrow.

A warm breeze mingled with his hot breath, and the fine hairs on my skin sprang to attention.

"You ready to go?"

I nodded.

"You want to visit with your family before we leave?"

I flinched.

His hands tightened.

I shook my head, and his clamped palms brushed against my ears. The loud rustle helped mute the silent scream inside my mind. He released me, but instead of stepping away, he took my hands and settled a soft kiss across my knuckles. "If your dad was alive, he'd hate that you haven't moved on, that you've punished yourself like this."

"I know," I whispered.

He gave me one last squeeze, and then linked his fingers with mine. We started to walk back toward the house. I wanted to explain how terrified I was, but the words remained locked inside me. What if the hollowness returned? What if I felt nothing when I stood over my family's graves? Thick bile shot up my throat. My fingers locked around Gray's and I continued to walk silently beside him.

"Y'all on your way?" Jacks met us as we reached the path leading to the house. He had changed into old jeans and a T. They were dusty, obviously work clothes. A well-worn Stetson sat comfortably low on his brow.

Gray untangled his fingers from mine and stepped

forward, holding out a hand. "Thanks, man, we're gonna take off now." They shook hands. My eyes watered when Gray clasped his other hand over Jacks', a familial warmth that had to date been absent.

Jacks cleared his throat. "It was good having you here." He blinked rapidly, his eyes shifting to me. "Both of you." He removed his hat, raking his fingers through his hair. "Wendy had to take a call. There's a problem with one of the kids for the camp next week. She said to tell you not to wait."

"Okay. You'll be sure to tell her thanks for us." I smiled hesitantly at him.

"Of course."

We walked to the car, and Gray beeped the locks. I nodded awkwardly at Jacks. I wanted to hug him, but my skin crawled at the thought of somebody touching me right then. Somebody other than Gray. I climbed into the car and Gray shut the door. Jacks stood by my window, restlessly playing with his hat. His Adam's apple bobbed erratically in his thick neck. He seemed agitated. Gray got in and started the car. "Hang on a second." I pressed the button to open my passenger window. "Hey, Jacks. Is everything all right?"

He shuffled closer and bent to look at me. "Yep. Yep. All good."

"You sure?"

He leaned in and rested his arms on my windowsill. "You remember we have all your furniture packed up, stored in the barn." He gripped his Stetson in one hand; the other gestured at me. I stared at his inner wrist. "You still want me to hang on to that for you?"

A shrill wail filled my ears. Burning cold spread

out from my core, like evil was consuming me. I ripped my gaze from the thin white scar that ran along his wrist. I could see his mouth moving but I couldn't hear a word. I nodded. He smiled and moved back from the window. I forced a smile in return. Icy slime slid through me.

Gray eased the handbrake off and we drove away.

"Zoey?"

His hand covered mine, big and warm.

"Butterfly—"

I shook my head hard and stared blindly out my window. If I spoke, I'd lose my battle with the burning bile clogging my throat. The nothing feeling was gone. Obliterated by an oozing evil that stripped away years of therapy and survival, and left me with blank memories, and a primal fear for what was yet to come.

The monster had escaped and it was coming for me.

****

Granddad Davis' Cottage
Late Sunday Night
Gray

"It's like we've regressed fourteen years."

"She kicked you out?"

"No!" Gray gripped the phone. His gut burned like Zoey had punched him with a hot metal fist. "But she's withdrawn, shut me out."

"There's gotta be a reason," Luke said calmly. "What flipped her?"

Gray stopped pacing. Luke's question punctured the balloon of self-pity he'd wrapped around himself. *What the hell was wrong with him?* He didn't need to be a genius to clock that Zoey was freaked the hell out.

He inhaled sharply, a wave of queasiness rolling over him. She was so deep inside her head, she barely noticed when she slammed the bedroom door in his face.

"From the moment we arrived at her family's place she was calm. Too fucking calm." Gray raked a hand through his hair. "Before we left I asked her if she wanted to visit her family's gravesite."

"Shit."

"Yeah. She froze. Didn't want anything to do with that."

"You push her?"

"No." He sat on the edge of the reading chair. "She'll go when she's ready."

"How'd it go with your brother?"

"Like I was living in a parallel universe."

"It's been a while. Must feel like you're strangers."

"Yeah. Too long." Gray rolled his neck, wincing at his tight muscles. "Or not fucking long enough," he muttered.

"He behave like a prick?"

Gray's chest tightened as he pictured Jacks. "Nope. He was good."

Luke didn't respond.

Gray let the silence stretch. It was more than Zoey's retreat that was making his gut scream. The whole thing just didn't add up. "Jesus Christ, Luke. He's living in her house with his fiancée, building guest chalets like they own the joint. For him, it's like nothing ever happened." His knuckles turned white around his phone. "Zoey's alone. She's got no family, no ranch, a shadow of a life. And she's haunted by nightmares that leave her shaking like a terrified child."

"What are you telling me?" Luke's voice deepened. "You suspect he was involved?"

"I don't know what I'm telling you," Gray said impatiently. "All I know is when I think back to how Zoey and I were together. When I think about the person she is, then and now, I don't buy her playing me like that. It's just not who she is."

Luke sighed. "You were the one who walked away, brother. She was brutalized, her family murdered, her mother barely alive, and you walked away because you felt wronged. Was that about her or about you?"

"Fuck. You sound like Eva."

"Doesn't change the question, bro."

Gray took several deep breaths. "When we drove up to my parent's house, Zoey had a panic attack. But it was nothing I wasn't feeling myself. Bloody hell, Hunt. I saw my mother and it felt like fire ants were crawling over me." He jumped to his feet and started to pace again. "All my old shit is flaring up. This place is a trigger to every insecurity I had as a kid." He stopped at the kitchen island. "But I'm not that dumb kid anymore."

"You weren't a kid when you left either."

"No. But I was young and insecure, especially when it came to where I fitted in with my family." He paced down the short hallway and stared at the closed bedroom door. "I let myself be steamrolled. I got so screwed up seeing that ring on her finger, I let them get into my head." He turned and paced back into the kitchen. "I'm not the same man, Hunter. I won't let Zoey down again."

"I know that. Now you need to make sure she knows that too."

Gray moved the phone from his ear and cocked his head. *Fuck!* He brought the phone back. "Luke. I gotta go. I'll call you tomorrow." He was already moving toward the bedroom.

Toward the terrified whimpers reaching out to him through the door.

Chapter Nineteen
So Much More than Nothing

Granddad Davis' Cottage
Monday Morning
Zoey

I coated my fluffy pancake in thick maple syrup and stuffed it in my mouth. Yum. Ignoring the tight band of knots stiffening my neck, I stabbed the last piece of pancake on my plate. It was also dripping with syrup, and I quickly closed my mouth around it before any could escape.

Mmm.

Gray's pancakes took the edge off my dark mood. I was drained after last night. When I woke from that damn nightmare, I'd been shivering like an abandoned kitten. Gray didn't need any coaxing tricks to lure me into his arms. The moment he slipped onto the bed, I'd burrowed into him. His protective strength had swept away my icy shivers. But even he wasn't strong enough to clear the murky shroud smothering my memory.

I put down my fork with a clatter. "I thought it was my turn to cook breakfast."

Gray's eyes glinted. "Hard to do if you're curled up in bed asleep."

I scrunched up my face. "Sorry."

"Don't sweat it. You needed the shut-eye." His smoky gaze dropped to my empty plate. "Enjoy the pancakes?"

I drew my finger through the pool of syrup on my plate and stuck it in my mouth. "Yum."

His mouth twitched. I breathed a silent sigh of relief. Even though my cowardly retreat yesterday must have confused the hell out of him, he seemed relaxed. We were standing opposite each other at the kitchen island. I studied him, and a sense of completeness resonated in me. He was beautiful. Not only on the outside but through all the complicated layers that made him who he was. And he got me. Always. Like this morning, instead of talking our situation to death he made pancakes. I tilted my head at him. "Cinnamon buns. Pancakes. I thought you liked to keep it healthy?"

He chugged the last of his coffee and set his mug on the countertop. "I do, but it's nothing a good ride won't work off."

A flash of heat shot through me.

"Not that sort of ride, Zoey." He braced himself over the counter. "We're going horse riding." He grinned.

His smiling face stole my breath. "Horse riding?" I squeaked.

"Yeah. It's been a good while for me, and I'm guessing for you too?" A different kind of excitement unfurled in my belly. He reached out and wound a lock of my hair around his finger. "You look like you could do with blowing out the cobwebs." He tugged gently. "You up for it?" I nodded vigorously. He let my hair slip away and straightened. "Good. You need to change. We're due there in half an hour."

"Where?"

"I called Randy. He and Sheila are working, but he

left word with his ranch hand that we're coming. Says his dad's horse needs exercise and so does Sheila's."

For a frozen moment, I stared at Gray. Then I dashed around the counter. "That's great!" I cried and leaped at him, flinging my arms around his neck. "That is really great. Thank you—"

His mouth slammed down on mine, quickly smothering my ear-to-ear smile. I melted into him. He held me close as his tongue danced with mine. Kissing Gray was better than pancakes. I pressed into him and he sucked my tongue deeper into his mouth. *Lordy.* Kissing Gray was way better than pancakes!

His mouth eased away. Hot coffee-breath wafted into my face. "Plan for a long shower after riding." His voice was husky as he stroked his thumb over my madly fluttering pulse. "I wanna explore those riding thoughts you had that made you blush so pretty."

Heat zinged through me. "I can't wait," I said huskily.

His tongue glided over my lips once more before he let me go. "I called Eva while you were asleep."

I drew in a sharp breath.

His eyes narrowed. "You agreed last night, Zoey."

I searched his face. *Shit.* Beneath the sexual flush, he was tight with worry. I flattened my hand on his chest. "It's okay."

He covered my hand with his. "She's flying in late this afternoon. Be here by early evening."

"Okay."

Seconds ticked by, then he blew out a heavy breath. "C'mere, Butterfly." He tugged me close again. I snuggled into him, and he rested his chin against my temple. "Things in your head are unraveling fast."

I curled my fingers over his shoulders and pressed them into his strength. "I feel like I'm holding my breath, waiting for the tiniest puff of wind to blow and then I'll see it all."

"Eva will help you."

"I know."

Last night I'd argued about the need for Eva to join us. But it was more from habit than not really wanting her here. When Gray said, "I've got a bad feeling danger is stalking you, Zoey. If it takes Eva to help you untangle your head, then that's what we need to do." I immediately gave in. Gray was frightened for me. And if I was honest with myself, I needed someone like Eva to help me. To take me where my brain was resisting with all its power for me to go.

"My dad called." Gray lifted his head and looked at me. "He wants me there today for lunch. I have to go, I can't put it off anymore."

I leaned back in his arms. "Okay."

"My mom invited you too."

I stiffened. "Good."

He squinted skeptically. "I don't think it's good. Too much too fast."

"It's what I came here for." I brought my hand around and stroked the lines creasing his brow. "Anyway, I want to see your dad."

He rubbed his bearded cheek against my palm. "Two days ago you panicked so badly you couldn't catch your breath."

"I'll know what to expect this time around."

He quirked an eyebrow.

I braced myself against his chest. "I need you to help me remember. To help me crush the fear that lives inside me." My fists curled into his T. "If you're going to keep protecting me from it, then you're not helping me." I stretched up and softly pressed my mouth to his. He returned the pressure, and then lifted his head.

"I'll call my mother, let her know there'll be two for lunch."

God. He was beautiful.

"It's going to be fine," I tried to reassure him.

His mouth twisted. "It's going to be fine when you stop waking up screaming in terror."

"It's not so bad anymore. Now, when I wake up, you're there to catch me." I smiled wryly. "I've lost the dreadful urge to run and hide."

"You ran yesterday," he grunted.

I pulled a face. "I'm sorry. A nasty habit, but I'm here now." He didn't look impressed. I studied his porn star mouth. I wanted him to smile. "Come on, tough guy. We're going horse riding."

"Yeah," he muttered. "And don't forget the shower." He leaned down and nipped my bottom lip. "I need that more than the horses."

I grinned. "You got it."

He scowled, but I didn't care. His lips were twitching. And Texas blue was gleaming from his eyes.

Beautiful.

Just crazy beautiful!

****

Zoey

Horse riding with Gray was like eating coconut cream pie followed by a dash of bitter lemon. Deliciously memorable and bittersweet at the same time.

Once we were saddled up, we headed out to a well-

272

trodden track in the direction of the creek. The humid breeze was a familiar whisper, reminding us of long-ago times from the past we'd both left behind. We didn't talk much, but the silence between us was rich with understanding. My body soon acclimated to being back on a horse, and I was able to relax into my saddle and let my mind drift. A blurry memory shook free from the bungled mess in my head. My dad, riding strong and upright, and always a horse-length in front of us. Noah, his non-stop chatter and snorting laugh a constant challenge to my dad's patience. And me, dawdling at the back but never left behind. All of us riding full gallop alongside the creek. My mama, waiting at the pond with thick chicken and pickle sandwiches, and ice-cold colas. And Gray. From the time I was eight, he joined us so often it wasn't long before it seemed he'd been a part of us forever.

I'd been so intent on burying the pain, I'd buried the good stuff too. Gray was right. My dad would be so disappointed.

We broke into a canter and I tipped my head back, loving the warm wind blowing through my hair. I looked across at Gray and a surge of regret burst in my chest. *Why had I pushed him away?* His smiling gaze caught mine and he winked. My spirit lightened and I laughed out loud, urging Sheila's thoroughbred mare to go faster. We burst from the woods and raced side by side across the open field. My laughter peeled out and with it, a chunk of my pain was gathered up and scattered into the wind.

When we arrived back at the cottage, Gray grabbed my hand and led me into the bathroom. My skin prickled and I had to fight the urge to resist him. An ominous dread was beginning to eat away at my happy mood. I opened my mouth to explain but before I could utter a word, he stripped me naked and gently shoved me into the stall. He turned on the shower and warm water rained down on me. I stood stiffly. Seconds later, his arms slipped around me and pulled me to his naked length.

I held my breath but nothing happened.

His hard body surrounded me, his skin hot and alive against mine. Water poured over us. Steam gathered and merged intimately with our breaths. And we stood. Together. My resistance melted and I turned my head, resting my face against his sculpted chest. The clean smell of the shower mingled with his unique musky scent. I rubbed my cheek against his slick skin.

This wasn't nothing.

This was so much more than nothing.

At some point, he urged my head under the spray, and took his time washing first my hair, and then my body. His hands soothed me, his powerful presence smoothed my jagged edges. And by the time I got dressed, his perfect understanding of what I'd needed gave me the strength to climb into the car, instead of running like the coward I'd been for most of my adult life.

****

Walker Ranch
Zoey

When we left the cottage, we were nearly half an hour late. Gray called his father to tell him we were on our way, and when we pulled into the drive we found him standing at the end of the path. He was alone but clearly agitated, wringing his hands and shuffling on the spot.

"What now?" Gray sighed.

"Lunch is canceled?" I said hopefully.

He snorted. "Don't think we're that lucky, Butterfly. C'mon, the quicker we do this, the quicker we can leave." He unclipped his seatbelt and opened the door.

I followed suit. As I stepped from the car, I took a moment to adjust the wrap-around neckline of my dress. It was a navy-and-latte floral with a swingy skirt and cap sleeves. There was a fine tremor in my hands but I ignored it, and instead gave myself an imaginary pat on the back. At least this time round I managed to get out the car instead of pulling my hair and screaming like a crazy person.

Gray pressed Gerald and we discovered his anxiety was caused by Margaret's demand that Jacks and Wendy join us for lunch. He appeared a little calmer when I hugged him and insisted it was okay. I didn't add that my palms were damp and I felt like I was going to be sick. He herded us up the path but as we reached the front door, he abruptly stopped and turned to Gray. "It's good to have you home, Son." His voice was deep and gruff.

Gray nodded, his face giving little away. But the tendons in his neck were taut. I tore my gaze away and looked back at Gerald. His eyes were locked on his son. *So much sadness.* My stomach knotted and I slipped my hand into Gray's. His fingers contracted and I did my best not to wince.

When we walked into the house I instantly began to distance myself. It wasn't conscious. But with every step, I shrank further into my head. It was like a fine gossamer veil floated down and settled over me. Protecting me. Gerald led us into the sitting room and my gaze immediately went to Jacks. He was sitting next to Wendy on a couch. He rose to greet us, and I snatched up my ghostly veil and gathered it around myself. But other than a tentative smile, he stood where he was. Wendy smiled and I smiled back.

And then Margaret swept into the room.

"My dear Zoey!" She closed the gap and folded me into a tight embrace. I hugged her back but made sure not to let go of a single inch of my magic veil. I knew if I let it go, I'd bolt for the front door and not stop running until I hit the creek. After a moment she stepped away with seeming reluctance, and turned to Gray. I sucked in a sharp breath when all expression smoothed from her face. "Grayson." It was said in such a way that it was both a question and a sufferance.

"Mother." Gray bent and touched his lips to her cheek.

When he straightened, I glimpsed something flash in her eyes but before I could look further, she retreated to stand next to Jacks.

After that, the afternoon slipped by in a cacophony of polite conversation and food I forgot as soon as I put it in my mouth. I sat opposite Jacks with Gray next to me, and Margaret to my left at the head of the table. Gerald was seated to Gray's right at the other head, which gave them an opportunity to chat quietly together. It was difficult to follow their conversation because Wendy kept up a non-stop one-way gabfest directed at me. She chatted endlessly about the farm, and the kids she and Jacks were helping. Her eyes were filled with such needy expectation, it left me with an unpleasant sensation crawling in my stomach. A number of times I felt Jacks' gaze on me, but each time I looked, his eyes would slice away. Margaret was unusually quiet. I studied her as much as I could without appearing rude. She had aged in a disturbing way. There were more lines around her eyes and mouth. And there was a dry, brittle quality to her hair that was now bleached platinum rather than the honey color she used to have. She seemed to hover somewhere between the handsome woman I remembered, and a sicker, gaunter version of her younger self. She reminded me of the homeless women in the city who spent their days slipping between the cracks of life.

The afternoon ticked by awkwardly, and slowly my protective veil began to unravel, one ghostly thread at a time. Tiny goose bumps broke out on my arms and traveled out until they spread like a virus over my whole body. By the time dessert arrived—a vanilla and hazel ice-cream concoction with cherries from Beth Marie's Old Fashioned—a vicious poison had gathered inside me. I stared at my slice of ice-cream cake. If I picked up my spoon to tackle it, I feared I might splat it across the table.

"Zoey!"

I jerked. Jacks' call was sharp, cutting through the conversation around the table. In the sudden silence, his gaze finally met mine. My stomach heaved. A familiar arrogance shone in his heavy-lidded eyes. It was the arrogance of his youth. The ugly arrogance I'd never been partial to.

"You made up your mind yet, or you gonna keep us in the dark?" His chin jutted aggressively.

Gray's hand reached over to cover mine. "You

talking about the farm?" he said.

"Of course I'm talking about the farm!"

"Jacks—"

"No, Wendy!" He shrugged off her attempt to calm him. "I want to know." He pushed aside his dessert plate. "I want to know if we're building pipe dreams on the farm. Wendy and I want to marry, start a family, build a future together."

A slimy thickness clogged my throat and I answered with difficulty. "I'm not stopping you."

"You won't sell. So where does that leave us?" His hand balled into a fist. For a fleeting second, I glimpsed that faint white scar.

"Back off Jacks." Gray's voice was low and deadly.

"Jacks, this is not the time," Gerald appeased.

Wendy leaned into Jacks and stroked his arm. "It's all right, honey." She looked at me, concern shadowing her face. "He doesn't mean to offend you, Zoey. We have so many plans but it's difficult for us to implement them if the sale of the farm is up for question." Her honesty and care for Jacks were clear as day.

"I'm sorry." I looked from Wendy to Jacks. "I don't mean to be selfish but it's difficult for me to let go. My family is buried here. And Magic." Gray's hand pressed down on my trembling one. "That horse made everything my family had possible. To sell the farm feels like a betrayal. I still have to get past that," I said huskily.

"This is Davis land!" Margaret's voice reverberated down the table. I flinched sideways into Gray, and his hand wrapped around my nape. Margaret thrust her chair back and rose imperiously to her feet.

"Margaret." It was a low warning from Gerald.

She didn't even spare him a glance. "This ranch. Morgan Farm. It's all Davis Land." She stared down her patrician's nose, her scornful gaze daring me to challenge her. "It always has been. It always will be."

"Margaret! That's not true." Gerald surged to his feet, fury contorting his face. "James Morgan earned that land fair and square, and you know it." He stabbed his finger at his wife.

"He stole it!" Margaret hissed. "From my father. From me." She slapped her hand to her breast.

"Bulldust! He traded Magic's breeding rights for land. A deal I'd like to remind you that saved this ranch from bankruptcy. If it wasn't for the foals bred from Magic, your father would have gone bankrupt and lost everything."

"If it wasn't for that horse, my life would have been different." Her voice was shrill.

Gerald leveled his wife with a cutting glare. "Different? How so?"

Her hand flailed in front of her. "James and I—"

"James and you!" Gerald snorted in disgust. My throat closed. "For goodness sake, woman, when are you going to accept James was never going to marry *you*? He was never in love *with you*." His tone mocked her. "From the moment he laid eyes on Mary, he was blind to any other woman." He shook his head and his gaze shifted to me. I curled my nails into my palms. Dark shadows lurked in his watery eyes. "His daughter's the same," he said gruffly. "Like her dad, Zoey's a one-horse woman. From the time she was eight years old, she only ever had eyes for our son." My lungs burned, and I ducked my head.

"For Jacks?" Surprise rang in Margaret's voice.

"Don't be ridiculous, woman!" It was a thunderous shout, as Gerald thrust his arm at Gray. "Zoey only ever had eyes for Grayson and you damn well know it."

I lurched to my feet. The age-old fissures in this family were splintering in front of me. I refused to witness another moment of their pain and vitriol.

"Excuse me," I mumbled.

And ran.

****

Gray

Gray's chest burned like holy hell. He itched to follow Zoey but forced himself to remain seated. When he heard her running up the staircase instead of the slam of the front door, his balled fists unfurled. She was running but it wasn't away from him. He slowly exhaled, his fear fading to a tingling relief. He knew exactly where she'd run.

Fucking hell!

He was still reeling from Gerald's outburst. He'd never heard him attack his mother like that before.

"I'm sorry, Gray. I was hoping your overdue visit home would be more welcoming." He dropped back in his seat with a sigh. Gray shrugged, but he needn't have bothered. His father's focus was fixed back on Margaret. "Come hell or high water, you just can't let it go, can you?" He drummed his fingers on the table.

Gray glanced at his mother. She stood with her arms cradled close to her chest, her neck rigid. *Christ*. She looked like she was braced for a punch.

"Let what go?" Her lips barely moved.

"This poisonous feud you have with the Morgans. They never hurt you, Marge. And James and Mary only ever spoke well of you." His accusing gaze shot to Gray. "What about you?"

Gray's heart hammered. "What about me?"

Gerald leaned forward, his fingers tapping aggressively on the table. "James and Mary ever speak ill of your mother?"

"No." It was true, no matter how much the Morgans were aware of his struggles with his mother, they never bad-mouthed her. "Never," he added emphatically.

Gerald's attention refocused on his wife. "So why can't you do the same? They're dead, woman, surely that's enough."

His mother's mouth gaped open, then snapped shut. Her bottom lip thinned. Darkness flickered in her eyes and Gray sucked in a shocked breath. It looked to him like fear, but then she blinked, and whatever he'd seen was gone.

"I'm going to make coffee." She turned and moved stiffly out the room.

Her departure spurred Gray. He inclined his head at his father and shoved his chair back. "I'm going to check on Zoey." He raked a quick glance over Jacks and Wendy. Neither of them had moved during the altercation. Wendy looked embarrassed at being caught up in the family ugliness. But Jacks' face was ashen, all sign of his earlier arrogance gone.

"Okay," Wendy whispered.

Gray walked out and took the stairs two at a time. When he hit the landing he looked down the hallway to his old bedroom. *Yeah. Just as he'd thought.* The door was ajar. He took several deep breaths in an effort to clear his head.

Zoey's a one-horse woman.
Zoey only ever had eyes for Grayson.

What his dad said was beautiful. And true. But he doubted it was what had driven his butterfly to flutter away in panic. There was more. Much more.

He gathered himself and nudged the bedroom door open. Zoey was at the window, her back to him. He took in the room with a glance. It had been stripped and redecorated as a guest room. The walls were now painted a pale silver-green with a darker green dado rail and trim. The pictures were nondescript landscapes. The bedlinen a plush mix of greens and florals. There wasn't a single sign that a boy had grown to manhood there.

"There's no trace you were ever here." It was like Zoey was reading his mind. He moved toward her. "When Jacks brought me here to stay, I begged to sleep in this room. It was the only place I felt safe." She turned and Gray's heart lurched. Such a sad smile tugged at her lovely mouth. "I'd hide up here for hours. And at night, I'd lock the door and jam a chair under the handle." She closed her eyes and tipped her head back. "I could still smell you in here."

Her husky voice reached inside him and wrapped around his heart. He quickly closed the gap and framed her delicate face. "You don't need this room anymore. You've got me." Her eyes opened. Liquid green and gold. His heart lurched again. "I won't leave you, Zoey."

"W-won't you?"

Gray cursed himself. She sounded so unsure. He'd done this to her when he left all those years ago. Luke questioned whether he'd left because of Zoey, or because of his own confused shit. All he knew right now was that he'd fucked up. Bad. "I won't leave you," he repeated with more force.

Her breath puffed warm against his mouth. "What if I ask you to? I've done that before." Gold-tipped lashes swept down. "More than once."

"Come here, Butterfly." He tucked her into his warmth. "I'm here and I'm not going anywhere. *Ever*."

She burrowed into him, her fingers digging into his shoulders. "Don't let me disappear, Gray. I don't want to be like my mother."

"Shhhh." He bent over her, caressing her back with long slow strokes.

"Why am I so terrified in this house?" she whispered.

His spine tingled, cold and clammy. "I don't know, but I swear to you, I'm going to find out."

****

Gray

Gray led Zoey back into the dining room, his fingers threaded firmly through hers. He stopped behind Jacks and Wendy. "We're on our way."

"Your mother's made coffee." Gerald gestured at the coffee Margaret was busy plunging. "Stay, we still have a lot to catch up on."

Gray gritted his teeth. His father was being purposefully obtuse to the awkward undercurrents thickening the air. "Sorry, Dad. A colleague's arriving from New York and we have plans."

"A colleague?" Margaret spared him a quick glance.

Zoey's fingers dug into his hand. "Her name's Eva. She works with Gray but she's coming here to help me."

Jacks twisted in his seat. "Is that the shrink you mentioned before?"

"What's this about a shrink?" His mother banged the coffeepot down.

Gray wanted to bite Jacks' head off. "The *shrink*," he emphasized sarcastically, "is a highly skilled psychologist who's helping Zoey with her memory."

Margaret sat up ramrod straight. "Helping her how?"

Gray studied his mother. She seemed oddly agitated. "Helping her to regain her memory of the attack."

His mother's lined face seemed to cave in on itself. Deep grooves marred her wide forehead as she stared at Zoey. "If I'm not mistaken, the ketamine destroyed your memory of that awful night."

Zoey's chest rose and fell in distress. "I've always experienced flashes of what happened, but my brain keeps trying to protect me." She looked down at Jacks. "I know I saw who raped me, who murdered my family. I just need to convince my brain that it's safe for me to see."

Jacks twisted back to stare at their mother. "And is it safe?"

Gray's adrenaline spiked. He inched around so he could see his brother's face. Jacks was staring unblinkingly at their mother. A silent communication seemed to be happening, but Gray was damned if he knew what the hell it was. "What are you trying to say, Jacks? You mentioned before that Zoey getting her memory back might not be safe."

Jacks cleared his throat and shuffled back in his

seat. "I'm just saying it might be less stressful for Zoey if she allows the past to remain exactly that. The past."

"I agree with Jacks." Margaret lifted her chin at Zoey. "What happened to you and your family was a nightmare. Why would you want to take yourself back there?"

"Because I want to move forward, and to succeed in that I need to face what happened." Zoey looped her arm through his and pressed into his side. "When I was alone I couldn't do that," she said huskily. "But Gray is here now and he'll make sure I'm safe."

Amen to that.

Zoey's firm response succeeded in shutting down further conversation. Gray hurried their goodbyes, and only began to breathe easy when they were in the car, and heading back to the cottage.

Nothing had changed. Being in that house suffocated him. It was even worse than he remembered. Either he was paranoid or there was a malevolent presence living in his childhood home. And it was wrapped all around his family.

Chapter Twenty
Exotic Butterfly

Granddad Davis' Cottage
Late Afternoon
Gray

Gray twisted the top off his beer before reaching for his ringing phone. It was King. He swiped connect and put the phone to his ear. "Yeah."

"Eva's not on the flight. She's flying with us in the morning."

"Us?"

"Luke and myself."

Christ. That was all he needed. "You coming to play nursemaid?"

King chuckled. "You feel the need for a nanny, Walker?"

"Fuck you," Gray said mildly and tipped his head back pouring half the chilled beer down his throat.

"Not in your lifetime. Luke's worried."

Gray walked to the porch doors and leaned against the wood frame. Zoey was in one of the cane chairs, staring vacantly out the open screen. "Luke's paranoid and overprotective," he muttered into the phone.

"Yeah, like somebody else I know." King's voice was derisive. "We're coming in on the jet. I've rented a vehicle so we'll drive to you, no need to collect us at the airport."

Gray took another swig of beer. It was a waste of time to try and change King's mind. The man had an annoying habit of taking control even when it wasn't his place to do so. "I don't have space for you in the cottage."

"Book us into a lodge nearby," King said tersely. "And Walker, make sure it's separate rooms. I'm not bloody sharing with Hunter, listening to him have phone sex with his wife."

In spite of his irritation, Gray laughed. "You're an asshole."

Zoey turned to look at him. He winked at her and felt it in his cock when she smiled back. Her eyes creased, melting away some of the melancholy shadowing her face.

"We need to shut this shit down." King's voice had lost its sarcasm, pulling his attention back to the phone. "I'm already short-handed with Mira and the twins out of play. I need you back here ASAP."

"Glad to know you got my back, *kemosabe*," Gray jibed.

King grunted indistinctly. "Our ETA is eleven."

"See you then." But Gray was talking to a dead phone. King had hung up.

The head of King Security was a complicated man, but Gray got him enough to know he was coming to help because he wanted to. The heavy weight in his chest lightened a fraction. With Luke, King and Eva in the picture, maybe he could finally sort what the hell was going on here.

And Zoey would be better protected.

He walked back into the kitchen and finished off his beer. He'd call Randy to recommend a place for the team to stay, and then it was time to distract Zoey from the blue funk she'd settled into.

He grinned to himself and repositioned his cock.

Oh yeah.

He had the perfect distraction for his fiery sweet-thing.

****

Zoey

I turned at the sound of Gray's footsteps on the wooden deck. He walked up to me and reached for the empty wine glass in my hand. "You want a refill?"

"No thanks." A fizz of excitement stirred in my belly. The sensual gleam in his eyes was the same that seduced me into stripping for him when he asked me to.

He placed my glass on the table. "That was King on the phone. Eva's been delayed."

"Oh."

"She's coming in tomorrow morning. King and Luke are flying in with her."

"Why?"

Gray moved to the side of my chair. "They think they're family so they tend to interfere." As had become his habit, he twirled a lock of my hair around his finger. "They're also worried about you." He tugged my curl, then released it.

My scalp tingled. "About me?"

He circled behind me. I shivered when he brushed my hair to the side, and his warm breath feathered against my neck. "You're mine. That makes you family."

You're mine.

It was an erotic challenge. One I couldn't resist picking up. "Is Tane coming too?" I bit my tongue and smiled up at him nonchalantly.

He exhaled sharply and nipped my ear.

"Ouch!"

"You got another itch, sweet-thing?"

Tingles spiraled down my spine. "I don't know what you mean," I said breathlessly.

He bunched my hair and tipped my head back. "You know exactly what I mean." A dark flush stained his cheeks. "Did you like getting hot and sweaty on the dance floor?" He bent over me. "Did all those tattoos get you wet and tingling?"

I squeezed my legs together. "Jeez! I only danced with him that one-time. But so what if I did like it?" Gray's eyes narrowed dangerously. I sucked in my lower lip, and then let it go. "I'm sure he'd be more willing to play than you." I felt like my pulse was going to jump out of my throat.

Gray's nostrils flared. Then suddenly he smiled. Wicked. Deadly. "Tane may think you're cute and hot, Butterfly, and maybe he'd like to play with you. But trust me when I say, he'd much prefer breathing." He dipped his head and caught my lower lip between his teeth. His tongue laved, scorching and wet. I grabbed onto the front of his shirt and tried to pull him closer. His warm breath blasted my face. "And he knows if he lays one fucking finger on you, he won't be breathing for long."

I shuddered. I was certifiably nuts because his jealousy made me hotter. "That's what Tane said," I breathed against his mouth.

His eyes wandered over my face and then his lips quirked. "You finished talking shit?" I jerked back, but he still had hold of my hair and he brought my face closer to his. "You're a one-horse woman, Zoey. You know it. I know it."

I scrunched my nose at him. "So what now?" I said huskily.

"Now you have a choice. You can relax back and spread your legs, or you can slip down to your knees and unzip my jeans."

I struggled to catch my breath. "You're telling me my choice is whether you go down on me or I go down on you?"

His eyes danced. "Makes life easy you catch on quick, sweet-thing."

His sexy drawl was like an invisible stroke between my legs. I stared, open-mouthed, as he straightened and circled back in front of me. His zipper was at eye-level. Saliva flooded my mouth. I fought not to pant at the idea of his throbbing heat filling my mouth. My tongue darted out to lick my lips.

"Good choice," Gray growled. Then he bent over me and braced himself on my chair. His mouth captured mine, his tongue demanding entrance. I looped my arms around his neck and gave him what he wanted. His tongue surged inside. *God.* When Gray kissed me like this, all my doubts melted away. I belonged to him. My tongue pushed into his mouth because he belonged to me too. He sucked hard and I squirmed, burning desire soaking my already wet folds.

"Love your mouth on mine, Zoey." His tongue flicked and teased. "But now I want it wrapped around my cock."

Oh, Lord.

"Here? Outside?" I sounded strangled.

He reached around and grabbed the large throw

cushion behind me. "I like the breeze," he whispered in my ear, then moved back, and tossed the cushion on the floor. "Don't want you to bruise your knees."

I gulped as he widened his stance and started to unthread his belt. It was impossible not to stare at his bulging hard-on.

"Zoey!" It was a primal growl.

He popped his jean button, and like an electric bolt, it galvanized me. "Stop! That's my job."

His brows shot up. I nearly bit through my lip when his mouth curved into a sexy smirk. "Then you better get on with it."

Male arrogance was stamped all over his face. For a second I was tempted to call him on it. But he was too wicked. Too delicious. I moved to the edge of the chair and slipped down to my knees. Gray's hand settled lightly on my head.

"You sure, Butterfly?"

I glanced up. All teasing was gone from his face. His eyes gleamed a gentle smoky-blue. I stroked my hands up his thighs. Powerful muscles rippled beneath my touch. Firmly, I smoothed my hand over his throbbing heat. His sensual mouth parted. My fingers curled over the waistline of his jeans. He blinked slowly and the tip of his tongue wet his bottom lip.

"Yes," I rasped. "I'm sure."

His fingers brushed my cheek. Then he reached up and yanked his shirt over his head.

Lordy Lord.

I stretched up and greedily pressed my lips to his taut stomach. The tactile warmth of his skin always surprised me. I trailed wet kisses over his defined abs to the sexy V at his hip. His fingers gently tangled in my hair but he didn't exert any pressure. I dipped my tongue into the concave valley, then slowly kissed my way back to his zipper. When I reached his open button, I glanced up. And sucked in a ragged breath. His pupils were dilated with lust. I let my lashes sweep down, and concentrated on drawing his zipper down. I stopped halfway and spread his jeans open. His erection pulsed. I slipped his jocks over the head of his cock. And licked.

"Fu-uuck!"

My mouth curved. I left his silky-smooth glans peeking from his jocks and licked my way up the fine trail of hair that ended at his navel. He sucked in his flat stomach when I wetly kissed his belly button and teased it with a stiff tongue.

"You're a witch," he groaned, his fingers flexing in my hair.

"You don't like it?" I kissed my way to the V on his other side. When I delved my tongue into the crease, his abs jumped.

"I like it just fine, but if you don't release my cock, I'm gonna have to take things into my own hands."

My eyes lowered. Pearly essence coated his engorged glans. Without hesitation, I shifted across and licked.

"Jesus Christ!" he hissed.

Salty. Musky. His taste spread like hot sex in my mouth. I yanked down his zipper and tugged his jeans over his hips.

"Easy, sweet-thing."

I didn't want easy. I wanted Gray.

Giving to him. Pleasuring him. It satisfied a need I never knew I had. For so long I'd had a gaping hole at my core. It was filled with so many tears, I'd become immune to its pain. Kneeling before Gray now, his taste filling my mouth, that weeping hole began to heal.

I pulled his jocks over his turgid length. I didn't have experience in giving blowjobs. Like kissing, and most everything else, it was an act of intimacy I'd avoided. During my darkest years I'd given away my body, but nothing else. Always, I'd been punishing myself. Pleasure had nothing to do with it. Now. It was all about pleasure. And thankfully I was a doctor with a thorough knowledge of human anatomy, including the male pleasure zones. So I wrapped my hand around his throbbing shaft, bent over him, and went for it.

Gray wasn't small. I didn't even attempt to take the length of him in my mouth. Instead, I started with small kisses. I savored the top of his glistening head and slowly progressed to his sensitive underside. I flicked my tongue gently and moaned when he jerked against my mouth. I flicked again, and his fingers bunched in my hair. My nipples pebbled and rubbed abrasively against my dress.

Oh, God!

I stroked my hand up the length of him. *Beautiful.* His cock was iron-hard but hot and silky to the touch. Drawing in a deep breath, I coated my tongue in saliva and licked all the way down to his root.

"Fuck, yeah."

Trailing my tongue up again, I stopped to suckle at that sensitive spot. Gray's breaths came harder. I did it again. And again. The more I licked, the more my nipples ached. And the more my pussy throbbed. I was wet. *God!* Soaking wet. I jacked him gently. And then gripping him more firmly, pursed my lips, and blew.

"Zoey!" His hips arched, seeking more.

I looked up. Our eyes locked and I opened my mouth and slowly sank over his delicious length. His pulsing heat filled my mouth, filled my heart, and I moaned.

Gray.

Gripping the base of his shaft, I began to move faster. With each bob of my head, he sank deeper into my mouth. His taste was erotic. Addictive. My mouth watered, and I kept on sucking. Gray's hips moved in rhythm, but I sensed his iron control.

And I loved him for it.

Because I wanted more. So much more.

I slipped my hand between his legs. His balls were big and velvet soft, but I could already feel them bunching up. Easing down to my haunches, I puckered my lips and covered his pulsating sacs with soft, wet kisses.

"Oh fuck, yeah."

My pussy sang as he tilted his hips, and urged me deeper between his legs. I tenderly sucked first one ball, and then the other, loving their velvet smoothness in my mouth. I kept one hand wrapped around his cock, and rotated it up and down, constantly stroking my palm over his silky head. Gray's panting was music to my ears. I inched my finger behind his balls, and gently stroked the satin skin.

He growled, his cock thrusting between my rotating fingers.

Yes. Yes.

I kneed up, wanting his surging length back in my mouth. But his hands cradled my head, holding me from him. "Is your pussy aching, Zoey?"

I struggled to catch my breath.

"Answer me, sweet-thing."

Did my pussy ache?

"Yes-sss." It was a raw hiss.

"You naked under that dress?"

Oh Lordy!

I nodded, my tongue darting out to wet my swollen lips. Earlier, before I came to sit outside, I slipped off my shoes. I also slipped off my panties and bra. After the debacle with his family, I wanted to feel sexy. I wanted to follow Gray's new house-rules.

"Such a good girl," he drawled and combed his fingers through my hair. "Show me how wet you are."

"What!" I gasped.

"Let go of my balls, and put your hand between your legs."

Beads of sweat rolled down between my breasts. "Gray—"

"Come on, sweet-thing. You know you want to."

Our eyes locked in erotic battle. I stroked my fingertips over his scrotum, and then dropped my hand to the hem of my dress. My other hand stayed clasped around his pulsating length. Slowly, I inched up my skirt. He thrust his shaft through my lightly clenched fist. My fingers flexed, and he thrust again. I wrenched my gaze from his and a wave of hunger swept over me. His cock was thick and rampant and coated in his essence. Instinctively, I flicked my finger and brought it to my mouth.

"Zoey!"

My gaze shot up. His taste spread over my tongue. Creamy wetness escaped my pussy and trickled down my thighs. The hem of my dress reached my hip, and a soft breeze blew. I shuddered.

Gray's breeze.

A wildness let loose in my chest. I let go of my dress and cupped my heat. "Gray," I mouthed.

"Show me."

My clit throbbed. I brushed over it, feather light. And like I'd lit a match, fire seared through me. *Yesss!* I stroked again. And again. My hips began to undulate.

"Open."

My lashes fluttered at his hoarse command. *Oh God, yes!* He was holding his cock in front of my mouth. And it was dripping. I opened my lips and sank hungrily down his length. He cradled my face, bracing me as he thrust.

"That's it, Butterfly." He plunged in and out, his cock surging powerfully, but never too deep for me to cope. "Fucking beautiful. Frick that gorgeous clit, but don't you stop sucking."

I clutched his thigh, but the fingers on my other hand obeyed, and never stopped thrumming. Waves of need gathered. It was building fast.

His hand tightened in my hair, restraining me. "Show me your fingers. I want to see how wet you are."

Crippling desire sent shudders rippling through me.

"Now, Zoey!" Steel ran through his growl.

My knees wobbled as pleasure wreaked havoc with my balance. Gray's eyes smoldered with blue fire. I sucked in a jagged breath. My pussy spasmed as I withdrew my hand and offered it to him. He grabbed my wrist and leaned down, closing his mouth over my fingers. I began to pant. His mouth was scorching hot, his tongue an erotic tease. Each lick felt like he was running his tongue over my quivering folds.

"Gray." It was a husky moan. He nipped my fingertip, and my clit jumped. "Gray!"

"I've changed my mind."

What!?

He yanked up his jeans, then crouched down and scooped me into his arms. "I want more of your taste, Zoey."

For a second the room tilted, and I clung to him. Then we were moving through the cottage and into the bedroom.

****

Gray

Son-of-a-bitch.

Her taste coated his tongue but it wasn't enough. His body screamed for more. He'd convinced himself Zoey was his kryptonite. He was dead wrong. She was the vital ingredient he'd been missing since the day he walked away from her. He hugged her closer to his chest. Fiery hair kissed the side of his face, and honeysuckle flooded his senses. *He was a damn fool.* How had he ever thought he could be happy without her?

He stopped beside the bed and swallowed a smile at her pouting face. Her lips were swollen from sucking on his cock. *Holy hell.* He could still feel the heat of her mouth. The wet seduction of her tongue lapping at him. When she stroked behind his balls, it had taken every ounce of his experience not to explode down her throat.

"You pissed?" He tried to decipher the jeweled intensity gleaming in her eyes. Fury. Excitement. Frustration. His mouth curved. A combination of all three he decided.

She slapped him lightly on the chest. "You're not

supposed to pull out just when I'm getting to the good stuff."

Keeping her pressed against his body, he let her legs drop to the floor. "You prefer to come on your hand rather than on my tongue?"

She slapped his chest again. "I was talking about you."

He felt for the wraparound tie at the back of her dress and pulled it loose. The dress opened and he slipped the sleeves over her shoulders. As the dress fell to the floor, he grinned. She was so busy being pissed, it didn't occur to her to stop him stripping her naked. "What's the problem, Butterfly?" He let her go and reached down to remove his boots.

"I wanted you to come in my mouth."

Gray swayed before he caught himself. If Zoey kept talking like that, he was going to come in his pants. He yanked off his footwear and made quick work of his jeans. His throbbing dick sprang free. *Thank fucking Christ.* He lunged forward and grasped her around her slim hips. And tossed.

"Gray!"

She landed sprawled across the bed, her hair an untamed halo framing her face. Before she could right herself, he followed her onto the bed. Her floundering limbs froze when he settled himself on top of her. Careful to support most of his weight, he buried his face in her neck and breathed deeply. He couldn't get enough of her scent. It had the duel effect of making both his heart and his cock throb. Zoey's arms crept around his neck. He nuzzled her ear and gently bit down on her earlobe. Her breath hitched. "I love that you want to finish me in your mouth," he whispered and glided his tongue over the rim of her ear. "But I'm a lot to take that way."

Her body tensed. "You don't think I can do that for you?"

He lifted his head. *Shit. That wasn't what he meant.*

"Gray?" She bucked against him. He instinctively used his weight to hold her still. Her soft breaths puffed against his face. "Tell me what's really stopping you, tough guy." A faint alert tightened his gut. Her leg curled over his, and she began to stroke her foot up and down his calf. "Gray?" she whispered huskily.

"I don't want to scare you," he murmured.

"You think your cock scares me?"

He just managed to stop his jaw from dropping. She waggled her brows. A wave of desire swept over him. *What the fuck was he thinking?* She wasn't the one confused. He was. His kitten wasn't a kitten anymore. He pressed his cock against her mound. Her breath caught, but her vivid gaze never wavered. "Nothing about me scares you, does it?" he said.

"Only that you're holding back." She cupped his face. Confidence radiated from her. And strength.

Only that you're holding back.

A sliver of guilt nudged Gray, but he shrugged it off. Arousal burned in Zoey's eyes. *Cat eyes.* He tilted his hips and teased her with his dick. Her pussy was petal-soft. And so fucking wet. "You gonna let me go down on you now?" he said against her mouth.

She bucked against him. "You gonna let me make you come with my mouth?"

The base of his spine tingled. "Whatever you want." He pushed his cock against her clit and she

299

gasped. Gray ducked his head to slake his thirst. Her moans vibrated down his throat and his balls began to contract. *Fuck. Fuck.* He caught her lush lower lip between his teeth and winced when her hands fisted in his hair.

His exotic butterfly. So fucking beautiful. He'd give her whatever she wanted for as long as he could breathe.

"Whatever you want," he repeated forcefully. Her lashes fluttered and he cupped her breast, thumbing her aroused nipple. She arched into him, her cunt searching. He squeezed her nipple hard.

"Gray!" Her eyes dilated.

Oh yeah. His sweet-thing liked a bite of pain. Gray stored that knowledge away, and regretfully let go of her breast. He stroked her damp hair from her face, careful not to tease her with his cock. It was screaming for her heat, but first, he needed something else. He cradled her face. "Before you suck me off, I'm going to love you." Her eyes rounded and she opened her mouth to reply, but he rested his thumb over her lips. "I'm going to lick and taste every inch of your gorgeous body, and I'm not going to stop until my tongue is buried in your cunt, and you're coming screaming on my face."

She bucked hard and Gray swallowed his grin. It hadn't slipped his notice how she loved his dirty talk. *Thank fuck.* Because that's the way he liked his sex. Raw. Carnal. And downright fucking dirty.

But that was sex.

Right now was about loving.

Because he loved Zoey. He loved her with every breath in his body.

He just wasn't ready to tell her.

So instead, he'd use every skill in his arsenal to show her.

****

Zoey

First, I'm going to love you.

Lordy-Lord.

The man was an expert at giving love.

He trailed hot wet kisses from my neck, where he lapped at my wildly beating pulse, to my newly sensitized toes. No matter how much I writhed and begged, he stayed the course. Kissing and licking. Savoring and devouring. Like a miner sifting for precious metals, he sought out every erogenous zone in my body. I thought I'd implode from the pleasure when he hovered over my breasts. Nipping and teasing. Laving and swirling. And then he sucked. And sucked. And the invisible thread connecting my nipples to my clit began to strum. And Gray plucked it like an expert.

By the time he had his fill, I was a wreck. A shivering, sweating, needy wreck, desperate for his mouth on my aching core. Instead, he trailed more delicious kisses down my body. Lower and lower, until he reached my mound. For a breathless moment, his gaze swept up. Bold. Feral.

Then he ducked his head and proceeded to destroy me.

My beautiful snake charmer gently pressed the lips of my swollen labia together, trapping my engorged clit. And then he massaged.

And I screamed.

Oh, Lord! I hadn't even come yet and I was screaming.

Like he lit a fuse, strands of dynamite circled my pussy, sending incendiary sparks racing all over my body. I was panting. And dry-mouthed from screaming his name over and over.

"Gray!"

"Gray!"

"Gray!"

He pressed a soft kiss over my tattoo. "Soon, beautiful Butterfly. Soon."

I shuddered. His hands slipped under my butt and his thumbs spread my pussy open. I stopped breathing. He dragged his tongue over my clit and licked his way down my center. Wet heat spilled from me. His tongue plunged inside, lapping and feasting. Circling and invading. Then he tilted my hips and slowly licked a path down. I bucked wildly. But with wicked intent, he held me in place, and his tongue flicked. Over and over again. Dark shivers raced up and down my spine. His thumb swirled over my creamy folds, sliding around and around my begging clit.

A storm was building.

And it was going to be catastrophic.

I swung my leg over his shoulder and dug my heel into his back. I couldn't speak, my voice was paralyzed with need.

Gray's sinful gaze trapped mine. "You can come whenever you want, Zoey." It was a gravelly rasp. He licked his lips. Then with lust spreading across his face, he stroked his fingers through my weeping heat. And slowly. So slowly. Sank them into my core.

I let go of the bedding and grabbed onto his hair.

He dipped his head, and his tongue swirled. His mouth kissed and licked. Back and forth. Never stopping. No matter how much I writhed, he never slowed. He also never picked up speed. The man was an artist. But it was his fingers that undid me. He fucked me with a circular motion in sync with his tongue. When I started to contract, he deepened his reach, rubbing rhythmically against the roof of my pussy. Over and over again, he hit that sublime spot.

The storm broke.

Molten heat poured from me, and I came apart. Screaming. Waves of pulsing pleasure erupted. Multiplied. I arched up. Powerful arms wrapped around me, but his tongue kept licking. I shuddered and trembled. His hands stroked and calmed.

Gray. Gray. Gray.

It was a litany of love reverberating in my head. In my heart. In my soul.

Satiated, I languished against the pillows, my limbs like liquid jelly. Gray's head rested against my thigh, my fingers drifting through his hair.

Beautiful. Peaceful.

And then he was moving. Shifting to his knees, he trapped me between his legs. Before I cottoned on to what he was doing, he lifted me and propped me against the headboard. He moved closer, and with a burst of lust, I understood. Voracious hunger flooded my mouth. Gray was holding his tumescent cock right in front of me.

"No more teasing, Zoey. I need you. Now." Carnal lust harshened his voice.

I needed him too. Only it was in a different way. I needed him buried inside the female heart of me. Claiming me. But Gray wasn't ready for that. Something was holding him back. And I loved him too darn much to push him.

So I'd wait.

And in the meantime, I'd take him any way he'd let me.

I gripped his hips. "So have me, tough guy. Take whatever you need."

And he did.

I opened my mouth. Gray pushed inside.

"Fuck, yeah."

He clasped the side of my face and flattened his other hand against the wall. Potent essence leaked from his throbbing glans. I licked and swallowed. He sank deeper. His turgid shaft was so rock-hard, I knew he was seconds from blowing. I grasped his ass, and his muscles bunched, taut beneath my touch. The tip of his cock brushed the back of my throat.

"Swallow, Butterfly."

My lashes swept up. A swathe of untamed heat washed over me. Soaking me. Feral need had turned his eyes blue. Incandescent. Breathtaking.

I swallowed.

Again. And again. Gray surged, and I swallowed.

Erotic. Primal. And so fucking intimate my eyes began to water.

His strokes shortened, his motion sped up.

Totally wild. Totally controlled.

"I'm gonna come, Zoey. You sure—"

I pulled him tighter to me.

"Fu-uuck."

He arched, his powerful body arcing over me. Hot essence exploded in my mouth. Glorious. Potent. Alive.

Perfect. But not perfect.

My core was empty. Crying out for Gray to fill me.

Claim me.

A shadow of doubt lurking in my heart unfurled.
Would I ever be enough for him?

Chapter Twenty-One
I'm Saying It

Granddad Davis' Cottage
The Next Morning
Zoey

The breakfast dishes clattered into the kitchen sink. I quickly checked over my shoulder. Gray was still on the phone, giving directions to King who had already landed. He was en route with Luke and Eva. Gray raised a brow and I smiled self-consciously, smoothing my ponytail. I was aching in places I'd never ached before. *Damn.* How was I going to cope when he finally claimed me? I envisioned his cock sliding into me and quickly spun back to the sink.

Jeez. I was an addict.

I plunged my hands into the soapy water and waited until the wave of arousal faded. Gray's voice moved to the sitting room. As I washed the dishes, I thought about how I'd woken in the early hours this morning. I'd been tucked along the length of him, his chin resting lightly on the crown of my head. Feeling hot, I'd tried to edge away, but his arms had locked. I stopped moving, not wanting to wake him. His heart had been a faint flutter against my back. Slow. Steady. Without conscious thought, I'd matched my breaths to his.

In that perfect moment, it dawned on me I was

protected. Safe.

Something else also finally clicked. Gray holding back was not about me, but about him. I remembered how he was with his mother. And how she was with him. Brutally cold. I'd recoiled inwardly. Then I'd forced myself to remember the look on his face when I accused him of causing my nightmares. How I'd begged him to leave me alone. My silent tears had soaked the pillow. But I'd vowed I would make it better. I wanted, with all my heart, to help Gray heal. But first I had to heal myself.

I pulled the plug from the sink and watch the soapy water swirl down the drain. The black clouds were shifting. My tough guy better look out because when they finally parted I was coming for him. And I wasn't stopping until I had all of him. Every beautiful inch.

I dried my hands and watched Gray end his call. He tucked his phone into his jeans pocket and walked over to lean against the island. "They'll be here shortly. I'm going to take King and Luke with me to Randy's. You going to spend some time with Eva?"

I nodded. Gray wanted to examine the original police file from the attack on my family. He called it "giving it fresh eyes." Randy was the sheriff now and had agreed to allow Gray access. I refused to overthink what he thought he might find. I had enough on my plate.

"You going to be okay, alone with Eva?" Concern deepened his voice.

"I think it's better if we're alone. I like her, trust her." I shrugged and admitted softly, "I've got a lot buzzing around in my head. I need to talk it through with her."

"Good. Just don't push yourself too hard."

I sucked in an impatient breath.

"Dammit, Zoey! I see that stubborn look in your eyes. You drive yourself too hard and it'll only set you back."

I yanked on my ponytail. "I'm not a fool and neither is Eva."

Gray closed the gap between us. I leaned back against the sink but his arms closed around me. He pulled me to his chest. I resisted—for about two seconds. I couldn't fight his protective warmth. It soaked into my bones, melting away my irritation.

"Sorry," I muttered into his chest.

His arms tightened. "You've got nothing to be sorry about."

I wanted to explain. "I feel like I'm being stalked. Like time is running out." I tipped my head back. "You feel it too, don't you?"

His eyes darkened. "I don't want you with Jacks, not unless I'm with you."

I shivered. "Please don't say that."

"I'm saying it."

My eyes filled and I squeezed them shut.

Knock. Knock.

Gray ignored the door. His hand settled warm around my nape. "Zoey, did you hear me?"

Knock. Knock. Knock.

I opened my eyes. He wasn't going to open the door until I gave him what he wanted. "Okay," I said.

His lips brushed mine. "Okay," he whispered.

Then he let me go and went to get the door.

****

Gray

Knock. Knock. Knock. Knock. Knock.

Whoever was outside began to pound their fist on the door.

"Hold your goddamn horses." Gray swung the door open. *Speak of the devil.* "Jacks. What the hell man?"

"Gray! Thank God." His fist hovered mid-air. A sheen of sweat coated his ashen face. "Wendy is missing."

"What do you mean, missing?"

He crushed the brim of his hat, his breaths coming harshly. "Um. She…she—"

"Shit. Come inside, catch your breath." Gray stepped back, holding the door open.

"Uh-yep-thanks-man-thanks." Jacks' words ran together as he stepped hesitantly into the cottage. His gaze flicked past Gray.

"Hi, Jacks." Zoey's smile was small.

"Hey, Zoey," he mumbled.

Gray closed the door and crossed the room. He put an arm around Zoey and pulled her stiff body snuggly against him. Jacks toyed agitatedly with his hat. His pupils were dilated, bouncing around like ping pong balls. Shit. He was clearly spooked.

"What do you mean Wendy is missing?"

Jacks sucked in a ragged breath. "Yesterday, after we got back to the farm, things were tense. Wendy was freaked out." He shrugged. "That lunch was darn crazy." His gaze slid to Zoey, and then quickly back to Gray. "I went riding. Wendy didn't want to come with." He dragged his fingers through his hair. Gray noted it was already spiked in all directions. "I was gone about an hour. Came back. Fed the horses."

"Then what?" Gray encouraged calmly.

"I finished in the barn. She wasn't around. I called her. Went up to the house. *Shi-iit!*" Jacks tugged at his hair. "Man, she's always around. Always helps, 'specially when we got kids coming."

Behind his thick bifocals, fleshy skin bunched around his eyes. It made them look more puffy than usual, but it didn't disguise the dark circles already bruising his skin. Gray's gut clenched. *Jacks looked seriously short on sleep.*

"I waited all night. Called her phone a million times." Jacks crushed his hat to his chest. His voice rose. "We've got kids arriving today. Wendy would never just disappear."

"Did you have a fight?" Gray's tone was flat.

"No! We never fight." Clearly agitated, he waved his hat. "We're not like that."

Jesus. The fucker really seemed to give a shit. "What did the police say?"

Jacks blinked several times. "I haven't called them," he admitted.

Gray's arm dropped from Zoey, and he stepped forward. "Why the hell not?"

"They always say wait twenty-four hours—"

"Call Randy. He'll help you."

"Heck, Gray. You know darn well he doesn't have the time of day for me." His chin jutted out.

"Fuck that!" Gray snapped. "This is different. Call him. He'll help."

"I'm gonna chase up her family first. Maybe she got spooked after that darn lunch yesterday."

"Jesus, Jacks. Maybe she had an accident or something." He tried to catch Jacks' eyes, but they kept sliding away. "How do you know something's not wrong?"

Zoey gripped his belt at the small of his back. He shifted, and lifted his hand to her nape, kneading it gently. Jacks' gaze darted between them. Gray's spider-sense began to crawl. He could smell the fear on him. *Fucking hell.* His brother reeked of it. "Did you do something you shouldn't have?"

The front door swung open. King stepped inside, followed closely by Luke and Eva. Gray tensed in irritation. "Don't you fucking knock?"

King's brow arched, but the rest of his face remained impassive.

"What's wrong?" Luke said.

Gray briefly closed his eyes. A dull pain throbbed in his jaw. He needed to chill or he was going to lose it. And then he might miss something again. Something vital that could bring an end to this goddamn nightmare. He sucked in a calming breath and flicked his eyes open. "This is Jacks, my brother." His gaze swept over King and Eva and stopped on Luke. "Says his fiancée, Wendy, is missing."

"When was the last time he saw her?" Typical of Luke, he directed the question at him and not Jacks.

"You two have an argument or something?" King's piercing gaze raked over Jacks.

If it was possible, Jacks paled further. A line of perspiration beaded his upper lip. "No. No." He shook his head, and his eyes darted wildly from King to Luke. Then he began to back toward the door.

King moved deceptively fast and blocked his way. "Wendy own a cell phone?" Jacks froze in his tracks. "Your fiancée own a cell phone?" King repeated with more force.

"Um. Y-yes."

"Give the number to me. We'll ping it. See if we can track it down."

"You okay, honey?"

Gray glanced sideways. Eva was beside Zoey.

"I'm fine." But Zoey was clearly distracted by the drama playing out at the door. His chest tightened. Her face looked clammy.

"You don't look okay," Eva said softly and rested her hand lightly on Zoey's arm.

"I'm fine, really." She gave Eva an absent smile. "I'm going to the bedroom for a while." She stretched up and brushed her lips over his. Gray recognized the expression clouding her pale face. She avoided his questioning look, and without saying goodbye to anybody, retreated to the bedroom.

"I don't like the look of that," Eva said. "She's shutting down."

"No she's not," he murmured. "She's thinking." He watched Jacks recite Wendy's phone number to King then walked over to join them.

Jacks' dilated gaze sought him out. "I gotta go, Gray."

"I'm going to see Randy," Gray said.

A flash of anger twisted Jacks' face. "You don't need to do that. I said I'd handle it."

"I'm not seeing him about Wendy. We're going take a fresh look at the case file from the Morgan Farm attack."

"What? Why?" Jacks crushed his hat between his fists. "Jesus, Gray. What do you imagine there is to find?"

Gray studied his brother's wildly blinking eyes.

He'd give a lot to know what was going on inside that head. "I don't know, Jacks. I guess we'll have to wait and see."

Jacks nodded jerkily. "I gotta go." He looked at Luke and King and abruptly shoved back his shoulders. "I gotta go." He sounded desperate.

Gray tipped his chin at King. As soon as King stepped aside, Jacks walked out. Luke joined them by the door, and they watched Jacks walk stiffly down the path. By the time he disappeared out their line of sight, he was practically jogging.

****

Gray

Gray took a last look at Zoey and pulled the bedroom door closed.

It had taken him less than twenty minutes to bring the team up to speed. Luke already knew a lot and had briefed King and Eva en route. Zoey stayed in the bedroom the whole time. Even when he came to tell her they were leaving to see the sheriff, she remained distracted. *Christ*. He ached to wrap himself around her. Protect her. But now was not the time. As much as it burned like acid in his gut, the best thing he could do for her right now was to give her space. And time with Eva.

He walked into the kitchen and joined the others gathered around the island.

"She okay?" Luke asked.

"She will be." He caught Eva's look. "You'll take it slow with her?"

"Your brother stinks of fear," Luke spat in disgust.

"Something's definitely out of whack," King added.

"Eva?" In this arena, her opinion mattered most to Gray.

She met his gaze, her eyes like blue steel. "Luke's right. He's definitely frightened. But it could be because he's scared about Wendy." She shrugged sharply. "Or because he's scared about what you might find in that file. We don't know the answer to that yet."

"You'll be alone with Zoey. I want you armed."

She frowned. "You're that worried?"

"Yes."

Luke braced himself on the counter edge. "About Jacks?"

"I don't fucking know!" Gray slammed his fist into his palm. "I just know I don't want her alone. Especially if my brother returns while we're out."

"I'll babysit."

Gray's head whipped sideways. *What the fuck?*

"I know what you're thinking." King scowled. "Bloody hell. I learned my lesson with Luke and Katya."

Anger spiked through Gray. "You fucking used her as bait and like a jackass I was complicit." He would never forget Katya bruised and bleeding in that warehouse. He knew, without doubt, a piece of Luke still blamed him for letting King put Katya in danger. Gray had never forgiven himself. And he never would.

"Yes. I used her as bait and it worked." King's hand shot up. Doubtless to stop him—or Luke—from punching him in the face. "But I admit I could have gone about it differently."

Gray balled his fist. "You think?"

"I know!" King said with force.

Gray exhaled silently. He had gone to war with

Thane Kingsley. Bled with him. And as much as the man could be a pain in the ass, he trusted him. "In case you don't already know, she's my heart."

King's brow arched sardonically. "You don't say," he drawled.

"Prick," Gray breathed, but his mouth twitched.

King slapped the counter. "Go. Look at the file with Luke. Eva and I will watch over your woman."

It was an order, but Gray couldn't resist a final dig. "Thane Kingsley. Protector of all he surveys."

"Always the fucking smart-ass."

Gray smirked, but he picked up his phone and keys and headed for the door. "Call when the intel on Wendy's phone comes in." He opened the door and let Luke pass. Before following, he looked back and caught King's gaze. "Thanks, man."

King's chin lifted. Then he turned and walked into the sitting room.

Gray smiled grimly. *Yeah.* His boss could be a first-grade asshole, but besides Luke, there was no better. He pulled the cottage door closed and walked quickly to catch up with Luke.

King had parked a black Ford Expedition alongside his sedan, dwarfing it. Luke was eyeing his rental suspiciously. Gray ignored him and hit the remote. "Let's go." He yanked his door open and climbed in. The passenger door opened and Luke slid inside. Gray quickly turned away to hide his smile. Zoey wasn't wrong when she kidded him about this shit car. Luke's large frame was crammed into the front seat. He looked like he was sitting in a kid's play-car.

"Hey, Hunt?" He fiddled with the key in the ignition but didn't start the car.

"Yeah?" His friend sounded disgruntled.

Gray swallowed his smile. "Can't say it's not good to see you, and you gotta know I appreciate the back-up." He met Luke's appraising gaze. "But not convinced there's much for you to do here, bro."

"We'll see."

"You seeing something I'm not?"

Luke shifted, trying to maneuver more leg space. "King's not wrong. Something is seriously out of whack here." He gave up trying to slide his seat farther back and looked at Gray. "Man, it's in your voice, in your eyes. And your woman looks like she's about to jump out of her skin."

Gray gripped the steering wheel. "I'm jumping at shadows. Everything in my gut is telling me there's a threat, but I can't fucking see it."

"You're blinded because you're too close to the problem." Luke's mouth set in a hard line. "Or too close to whoever is threatening you."

"I want Jacks to be guilty." Gray's knuckles whitened. "But I need him to be innocent. For Christ's sake, he's my brother."

Luke's face remained impassive.

Gray had an inkling what he was thinking. That Jacks had not been his brother for a long time. "*Fu-uuck!*" He raked his hand through his hair. "Every time that motherfucker's in front of me, all I see is that bauble on her finger. It didn't jive then. And it sure as hell doesn't jive now. Jesus!" He slammed his hands on the steering wheel. "I fucked up walking away. I fucked up huge."

"You weren't equipped to deal, Gray. Not then. Whatever happened fourteen years ago, Zoey didn't see it coming. And neither did you." Luke's voice deepened. "Look at me, brother—" Gray took several deep breaths before he turned to face Luke. "History ain't gonna repeat itself. Not on my watch. And not on King's." His navy eyes glittered with promise. "Now, start this piece-of-shit and let's go see what we can see. Fresh eyes have a habit of paying off."

Gray started the car and drove down the rutted path. Neither of them spoke until he exited the ranch and increased speed. The sheriff's office was on the outskirts of Denton, about a fifteen-minute drive.

"You working things out with Zoey?" Luke said.

"It's a roller-coaster, but I wouldn't want to be anywhere else." He shrugged. "She needs time to sort her head."

"You don't think fourteen years is long enough?"

Gray turned sharply to Luke. "I'm not leaving her if that's what you're implying."

"Then what?"

Gray looked back at the road.

"Oh, shit," Luke groaned. "Please tell me you're not giving her breathing room."

Gray clamped his lips together but not before a loud snort escaped. He remembered Luke's repeated complaints about his blue balls because he refused to have sex with Katya until he decided she was ready. He'd called it giving her "breathing room." "I'm not a fucking nut like you." He laughed.

"Thank Christ," Luke sighed.

Gray's laughter died. He shot a quick glance at Luke then looked forward again. "That's not completely true," he said softly. "I haven't taken her yet. We've been together. A lot. And it's amazing. But I haven't gone all the way."

In the corner of his eye, he saw Luke look at him. "What's wrong with her?"

"There's nothing wrong with her. She's perfect."

"Bullshit!" Luke bellowed. "Gray. Shit. Nobody's perfect, man. Not even Katya. Christ. I've told you that my woman can be a pain in my ass. But I wouldn't have it any other way." He leaned forward, searching Gray's face. "You know why—because she's perfect for me."

Gray swallowed hard. "You think Zoey isn't perfect for me?"

Luke sat back. "It's not what I think, it's what you think, bro."

Gray's mind scrambled. The traffic on the Loop was busy and he took his time before he spoke. "There's not a time I can remember when Zoey has not been mine. There is no more perfect woman for me. But she's fighting with demons, and I'm not going to take her until her head is free and thinking clearly."

"Okay. But you telling me you make love to your perfect woman, then hold back from claiming her?"

Luke's question hung in the air. Gray rubbed the back of his neck, trying to settle the unease sending chills down his spine. "She isn't ready," he said.

Luke shook his head. "Why don't you flip it around? She makes love to you with her mouth, her hands, and her tongue. But when it comes time to sink your cock in her, she closes her legs. Refuses you entry into her body. That make you feel good?"

"She isn't ready!" Gray roared.

"From where I'm sitting, brother, you're the one not ready."

"Fuck you!" The car swerved as Gray tapped the break too hard.

"Right back at you, bro."

Gray's heart pounded. His hands clenched and unclenched around the wheel.

Luke was right. He'd been going about this wrong. Added to that he was a bloody coward. Too afraid of getting hurt, rejected. His stomach heaved. *His fear was hurting the woman he loved. Again.*

Luke gripped his shoulder. "Make it right, Gray. Every time you hold back from her, you're rejecting her. You got me?"

"Fuck! Fuck!" Gray's jaw was locked so tight, his voice came out a hiss.

Luke squeezed his shoulder then sat back. "Yeah. You got me."

Chapter Twenty-Two
Paper Wasp

Granddad Davis' Cottage
Mid-Morning
Thane "King" Kingsley

King absorbed the natural wildness surrounding the small screened porch. A paper wasp nest was hanging from a branch several feet away, covered in dozens of the maroon and black insects. If he tilted his head just so, he could hear the low-level buzz emitting from the nest. He could also hear Eva close Zoey's bedroom door, but he waited until her footsteps approached before he turned away.

"She talking yet?" he murmured.

Eva stopped by his side. "She wants more time."

"Wants, not needs." He ignored Eva's thinning lips and reached for his phone vibrating in his pocket. He read the caller's name—*Hunter*—and swiped to engage the call. "You found something?" he said tersely.

"A lot of something. A lot of nothing," Luke said.

King scowled. "Break it down for me."

"We read through everything. Randy, Gray's buddy, brought in his dad to contribute. He was the ranger on point at the time. Goes by the name Shamus Sowell. Seems like a good man. Retired now. Says this case got its claws in him and never let go."

"He shed any new light?"

Luke sighed. "It was more about nuance. Shit that he thought but had no evidence to support, so it wasn't written up."

"Shit about Walker's family?" Silence echoed down the phone. The fine hairs on King's neck lifted. "Where's Walker now?"

"Getting some fresh air."

"Talk," he said into the phone. It was an order.

"You know the case in broad strokes so I'll talk detail, starting with the birthday cake. It was the way in for the perps, so the task team spent a lot of time checking it out. They visited every local baker. Nothing."

"They talk to friends and family. Somebody could have home-baked it."

"They did the rounds. Talked to everybody they thought mattered. Still nothing."

King began to pace. "A cake is personal."

"Yeah, that's what Sowell said. They were convinced it had to be somebody close to the family."

"Was the K baked into it, or added after?"

"We discussed that. Forensics concluded the K was in powder form. It was added in big quantities to the icing in the middle layer and the topping. Difficult to prove, but the consensus was the baker laced it."

"Jacks a baker?"

Luke breathed heavily down the phone. "It came up. Gray said not that he knew of."

"Jacks have a girlfriend at the time."

"Nope. From what I gather, his only focus was Zoey. But Sowell said Jacks was never a suspect. He had the K in his system and was shot point blank in the shoulder."

King's brain extrapolated the data, looking for unseen threads. "Could he have shot himself?"

"Nope. The angle of the bullet was all wrong."

He stopped pacing. "But it was a controlled shot, not meant to kill." It wasn't a question so he didn't wait for Luke to respond. "Tell me about James and Noah Morgan."

"Multiple body shots. Definitely meant to kill. Both their cake plates were eaten clean. They were either out from the K or too fucked up to stand. They bled out where they sat. The shooter was messy but ice-cold."

"And Mary Morgan?"

"Fuck!" King's hand tightened around his phone. Luke Hunter was rarely squeamish, but the revulsion in his voice was clear. "Don't know how she survived, man. Whoever it was, he did a real nasty job hacking her up. No doubt her attack was personal. Real fucking personal."

His words painted a graphic picture. King swallowed hard and forced a steel cage around his emotions. "Forensics on the stab wounds?" he bit out.

"Inconclusive. They think she was bending over her son when she took the first hit, so it was difficult to calculate the height of the perp. The depth of entry shows strength, especially the cuts she received after she fell to the floor."

King started pacing again. "You're assuming it was a man?"

Luke didn't respond.

"The depth of the cuts. It could have been rage."

It took a moment before Luke answered. "Yep, it could have been." Tension vibrated in his voice.

Hunter didn't like what he was implying. Bloody hell. Neither did he.

But King could sense the threads coming together. He hated what they were telling him, but Grayson Walker was going to hate it more. "All right. I want to hear about Gray's parents. Start with Margaret Walker."

"According to her statement, she visited earlier in the evening. Went to toast Jacks and Zoey's engagement." King heard paper flip. "Says here Jacks arranged for her to join them for a toast. He told her in the morning about the impending engagement." More paper rustled. "She had one glass of champagne. Couldn't stay for dinner or cake. Something about a sick horse."

"They ask her specifically about the cake?"

"Yeah. She stated it was on the side table when she arrived. Sowell remembers her being adamant about that."

King breathed steadily. "Jacks' statement corroborates his mother's?"

"Yep."

"Sowell say whether Margaret Walker was ever a suspect?"

"He said no but he looked squirrelly when he said it. Witness statements show they talked to the vet and he vouched for her. They were up with a sick horse most of the night. Margaret Walker left the stables for a couple of hours. The vet couldn't be more specific about the time as he was focused on the horse."

"Anything else?"

"Gray pushed Sowell but all he'd admit was since Jacks was a victim, his mother never roused their

323

suspicions."

King's heart rate spiked. "But Jacks wasn't really a victim. The shot to his shoulder was only a flesh wound."

"Sowell said he bled out like a pig. If he hadn't come to when he did, he'd have died from blood loss."

"It could have been a mistake," King mused. "Leaving him to bleed out like that could have been unplanned." King stared absently at the wasp nest. "Tell me about the father."

"He went to look at a horse in Kentucky."

"Verified?"

"Witnesses corroborated his story. His time of departure was sketchy but never pursued. Forensics found no trace he was ever at Morgan Farm."

"Gray's take?"

"He's firm his dad had nothing to do with it. Said it's not in his nature."

"But he thinks it's in his brother's nature?"

"Shit, King. I don't believe he knows what he thinks. This is his family for fuck's sake. It blows his mind even thinking Jacks was involved." Luke's voice lowered to an angry growl. "How the hell is he supposed to cogitate one or both of his parents might have orchestrated it?"

"Well somebody fucking orchestrated it," King growled back. Eva raised a hand for the phone, but King shook his head. He sucked in a steadying breath and heard Luke do the same. He changed tack. "Talk to me about motive."

Luke spoke quickly. "The house was superficially tumbled. The Morgans had a home-helper who came in once a week. She listed what she thought was missing.

But with everybody dead, and Zoey too messed up to help, they could never verify. The safe in her father's office was never touched. And there was no evidence the perps entered the bedrooms."

"Possible they were disturbed?"

"By who?" Frustration rang in Luke's voice. "Nobody reported anything until 911 got a call from Jacks at four-thirty-six in the morning. He was groggy, but appeared certain nobody else was in the house."

King followed the flight of a lone wasp as it tried to penetrate the porch screen. "A home invasion with intent to rob not the motive," he said softly.

"This was no ordinary house invasion," Luke said.

"The women?" King probed.

"Doesn't fly. Only Zoey was touched that way."

"But Mary's attack was personal. Vicious. Whoever did this wanted to hurt those women."

"Maybe. But Mary Morgan was meant to die. Zoey was raped and beaten, but she was definitely meant to live. Why?"

"That's the million-dollar question," King said. "Remind me. Red was the only one with an injection site. Correct?"

Luke paused. "Red?"

King mashed his lips together. A faint snort echoed down the line. "Correct?" King repeated, his voice cold.

Luke knew him well enough not to push. "Correct," he said. "The medics and the hospital couldn't initially rouse her. Police questioned Jacks before he was loaded into the bus. He insisted he was drugged, but knew nothing about Zoey. When doctors examined her, they found an injection site on her butt cheek."

"And Jacks?"

"Once forensics pointed to the K being in the cake, they re-examined the crime photos. It looked like his cake plate was smashed to the floor, but from the few cake crumbs found, they deduced he'd eaten most of his slice. When he was questioned about it, he said he had no recollection of the cake at all."

A thread connected in King's brain. "Luke, what if he ate the cake after the invasion? After the rape?"

"Shit. You're really going there." King didn't reply because Luke wasn't asking a question. "Okay. Let's assume Jacks was the rapist. There still had to be another perp because who the hell shot him?"

King looked at Eva. She was watching him closely, her arms folded tight to her body. "I'm going to get Eva to step it up with Zoey."

Luke's voice turned deadly. "Careful, King. Gray won't deal with Zoey getting hurt. Not again."

King's chest tightened. "She's already hurting. Every second that evil is trapped inside her, it's doing more damage. She's ready to face it." He narrowed his eyes at Eva. "She just needs somebody to kick her in the ass."

Without waiting for Luke's response, he ended the call. "It's time to push her."

Doubt clouded Eva's face. "She's deep inside her head, King."

"Then you need to push her even deeper."

Eva nibbled her lip, her fingers drumming against her folded arms. "Tell me what Luke said."

"In a nutshell, there's no doubt there was more than one perp. Evidence indicates two. Luke's hesitant to point a finger at Walker's family."

Her forehead creased. "But you're not?"

He shook his head. "Luke knows I'm right, but won't say it. He's protecting Gray."

"How is Gray?" Eva whispered.

"In a world of pain. When it comes to reading evidence, not much gets by him. He has to be where I am, and I don't think he's ready to face it."

"Of course he's not. This is his family we're talking about."

Sadness darkened Eva's eyes, and King caught a shimmer of tears. His throat thickened. "Family's not always what it represents, Eva. I know that. You know that."

She looked away, blinking hard. "I hope for Gray's sake, this is not like that."

King ran a thumb feather light over her cheekbone, and then stepped back. "Don't get your hopes up, little sister, because I think that's exactly what this is like."

Chapter Twenty-Three
Dancing On the Table

Granddad Davis' Cottage
Midday
Zoey

I was stretched out on the two-seater in the sitting room but I was far from relaxed. My mind kept trying to retreat from Eva's coaxing.

"You're at the pond, Zoey. It's your favorite place to be."

Her voice was melodic and I tried to pay attention.

"Slow, deep breaths, Zoey."

My stomach heaved. I wanted to be brave, but fear had me in its icy grip.

"You're calm, Zoey. You're safe."

I was cold. So cold. Why had I agreed to this?

"Slow, deep breaths, Zoey. Look around you. The pond is so still the trees are reflected in the water. It's beautiful."

I promised King and Eva I'd give this a chance. They needed the information buried in my head. Gray needed it.

Dammit! I needed it.

"Slow, deep breaths, Zoey."

Okay. Okay.

I inhaled deeply. My lungs burned but I kept taking in more air. More. More.

"That's it. Nice and slow."

I trust Eva. I trust Eva. I trust Eva.

"You're calm, Zoey. You're safe."

Where was Gray?

Tears gathered behind my eyes. I wanted Gray.

"Your feet are sinking into the warm earth. You can feel the water lapping at your ankles. It's so inviting."

My heartbeat slowed.

I loved the pond. I was happy there.

"A soft breeze is blowing through your hair, over your skin. It's so peaceful."

Gray's breeze.

Warmth crept over me.

"You're calm. You're safe. The pond is warm, so inviting." Her voice merged with the lure of the water, tugging at me. "Deep breaths, Zoey. You're sinking into the water. It's all around you. Holding you. Protecting you."

Roses. Scattered pink roses. Everywhere.

God no!

Their sweet scent filled my head.

No!

"Slow, deep breaths, Zoey. You're calm. You're safe."

Safe. Yes, I'm safe.

"The water's all around you. Holding you. Protecting you."

The monster's here. Inside me. I have to let it out.

"Slow, deep breaths, Zoey."

I have to let it out.

"You're calm. You're safe."

I have to let it out!

329

****

Several Minutes Later
Scarlett Eva Young

"Where are you now, Zoey?"

"At Mama's dinner table. I miss Gray."

"He's not sitting with you?"

Zoey's face creased with a frown. "No."

"Who is sitting at the table with you?"

"Noah. My dad." Her eyelids started to flutter. "Jacks is next to me."

"What's upsetting you, Zoey?"

"I miss Gray."

Eva's chest clamored. "I understand, honey. Can you tell me where your mother is?"

"Mama's answering the door."

Eva's eyes shot to King. He sat like a statue on a chair opposite. She took a silent breath and returned her gaze to Zoey. "Who's arrived at the door?"

"It's Margaret. She's come to wish me a happy birthday."

"That's very friendly of her. Has she also come to celebrate with you and Jacks?"

"Yes. It's my birthday." She shifted restlessly.

Eva carefully probed again. "Tell me about your engagement to Jacks." Zoey's arms stiffened. "Be calm, Zoey. You're safe. That's it. Slow, deep breaths."

"Harvard."

"What about Harvard?"

"Dad opened champagne to celebrate. Mama's so excited. I received a scholarship."

"Well done, Zoey. They must be so proud." Zoey's arms relaxed, but Eva remained alert. She knew Zoey's fear could return at any time. "Are they also excited

330

about your engagement to Jacks?" Again, Zoey's arms went rigid, her hands balling into fists. She began to move around, clearly agitated. Eva pressed. "Jacks proposed to you and you accepted his ring. Do you remember?"

"No. I don't know. No." She began to methodically bump her fist against her leg.

Eva's heart pounded. "You're calm, Zoey. You're safe. It's all right, honey. Slow, deep breaths. You're safe." Zoey's breathing slowly steadied. Eva could see she was still in a deep hypnoidal state. She wanted to look at King again, but Zoey was demanding all her concentration. She wet her dry lips and decided it was best to move away from the engagement. "Zoey, Margaret's arrived to wish you happy birthday. Can you tell me what's happening now?"

"She can't stay. She hugs me goodbye. She kisses Jacks. Then she's gone." Her breath hitched, and her eyelids began to flutter again.

"What are you doing now, Zoey?"

"Eating my birthday cake. I'm not hungry. I miss Gray." Her mouth suddenly quirked. "Jacks hates chocolate. He's funny. He's pretending to eat his cake, but I can see he's only playing with it."

Nausea pierced Eva's professional calm. She swallowed hard. "Zoey, do you know who baked your chocolate cake?"

"Surprise. It's a surprise—" Her voice faded. She sounded puzzled.

"It's a surprise birthday cake?"

Her hands suddenly flailed. "I miss Gray." She began to hyperventilate.

"Where are you, Zoey? What can you see?"

She shook her head, her breathing becoming increasingly distressed.

"Tell me, Zoey. Where are you?"

"I feel sick," she gasped. "Everything's spinning." She started to cry.

Eva dug her nails into her palms. "Deep breaths, Zoey. You're safe. Be calm."

"No! No!" It was shrill.

Eva moved forward to the edge of the chair and dug her fingers into the arms. She wanted to hold Zoey but knew she couldn't. "It's all right, Zoey. You're safe."

"No! I don't want to look."

"Close your eyes, Zoey. You don't have to look. That's it, close your eyes. Deep breaths…deep breaths."

Zoey's hiccupping gasps faded, but her body remained rigid.

"That's it, Zoey, keep your eyes closed."

Zoey crossed her arms over her chest and her head cocked. Eva thought she looked like she was listening for something. "You can hear something, Zoey. What can you hear?"

"He's behind me," she whispered harshly. "I can hear him breathing."

Eva sucked in a painful breath. "It's all right, Zoey. You're safe. He can't hurt you anymore. Keep your eyes closed, Zoey, and tell me what's happening."

"Everything is spinning. I feel sick. He's leaning over me." Her hand moved to press against her stomach. "The plates are falling on the floor. It's loud." She curled her hand into a fist. Uncurled it. "Glasses are smashing. I can't stop him. He's hurting me, pulling at me. Oh God," she sobbed. "He's pressing me over the table." Tears overflowed and ran down her face.

Eva forced back her nausea. "I need you to be brave, Zoey. Can you be brave for me?"

"Y-yes."

"I want you to open your eyes and look at his face." Zoey's sobs broke Eva's heart, but she knew she had to keep pushing. "Open your eyes, Zoey. Now!"

"No. No. He's behind me, holding me down. I can't breathe."

"What can you see, Zoey?"

"My roses. They've toppled over. Pink roses everywhere." Her hands shot into the air, flailing around. "They're dancing on the table. Gray's roses. *I hate pink roses!*" she screamed. "Oh God, help me, please. It hurts. He's hurting me. Mama, help me."

A tear escaped and rolled down Eva's cheek. It took all her professional control to keep her voice steady. "Where's your mama, Zoey? Can you see her?"

"She's on the f-floor. She's watching. Why won't she help me?" She began to cry harder.

"Be calm, Zoey. You're safe now."

"Mama's c-crying," Zoey sobbed, her voice filled with devastating despair. "She's w-watching, but she won't g-get up and h-help me."

"It's going to be all right, Zoey. I want you to look away from your mama. Can you do that for me? Please, Zoey, look away. Now!"

Zoey continued to cry, but her chest rose and fell with jerky breaths.

"That's it. Deep breaths. You're safe now." Eva's pulse steadied as Zoey's sobs faded. "Deep breaths, Zoey. You're safe now." She waited until Zoey seemed back in control. Then making sure she didn't look at

King in case she lost her nerve, she leaned closer. "I need you to be brave for me once more, Zoey. Can you do that for me? For Gray?" Zoey stilled. "Keep breathing, Zoey. You're safe. You're calm. Good. Now, I want you to focus on the man who hurt you, Zoey. What can you see?"

"He's pushing me into the table. It hurts." She began to hyperventilate again.

"No, Zoey. It's finished. You're safe. He can't hurt you anymore. You're safe." Eva knew Zoey was close to hysteria. And if she failed to find the answer now, all they could do was try again later. But later might be too late. "Please, Zoey, tell me what you see."

"His hand," she gasped. "It's braced on the table. It's right in front of my face." She started to pant. "The scar! Oh God! I know that scar."

"Who, Zoey? Who is it?"

"It's *his* scar."

"Tell me, Zoey. Now! Who is it?"

"Jacks! It's Jacks. Oh God, Jacks, why did you hurt me?" She sobbed hysterically. "*Ja-aacks!*"

****

Zoey

"It's all right, honey. That's it. Slow, deep breaths. You're safe. I'm here. King's here. You're safe."

I grabbed onto Eva's voice. It was a comforting litany, chasing away the monsters breathing their filth all over me.

Jacks! Jacks!

Why? Why did he do that to me?

My father and Noah pushed into my head. Bleeding. Dead.

No!

334

A sharp pain twisted my stomach.

Focus on Jacks. Focus on Jacks.

"Here, Red. Drink." King put a cold glass into my hand. I trembled violently and water splashed onto my leg. His hands clamped around mine and he guided the glass to my mouth. "Sip it slowly."

I drank. My parched throat eased.

"More."

I scowled into his face. His eyes were green. Not like mine. They were darker, like the moss that grew under the cottonwoods in the forest. And they were gentle. Knowing. King's gaze was normally intense. Penetrating. I hadn't ever seen it gentle. Tears welled in my eyes.

"Come on, Red. Drink a little more." He looked so grave, deep lines grooving his handsome brow.

I sipped the water.

"Good girl." He tipped the glass again. I swallowed. A tear escaped and trickled down my cheek.

"Mama was watching. She saw him hurting me."

King took the glass from me and reached up to catch the tear with his thumb. "She was hurt, Zoey. I can't imagine her agony, but she didn't leave you alone, did she?"

"She was crying."

"She was crying for you."

A convulsive sob burst from me. And then another. Like thick clots of dark acid, the evil ripped away and burned its way up my throat. Eva pushed closer, but I clung to King's gentle gaze. "S-she never l-looked away," I cried. "T-the whole time, her eyes were o-open." My throat was on fire, but I had to get it out. "M-Mama was crying, but she never looked away."

King's hands caught mine and squeezed tight. "It was her way of helping you. She refused to leave you alone. It was all she had the strength to do."

Mama. Oh God, Mama, I miss you so much.

"At the h-hospital—" My voice broke. I tore my gaze from King's and reached for the water. He passed me the glass, and gratefully, I drank.

"Honey, it's a lot to take in," Eva said softly. "You need to rest."

I emptied the glass and sucked in a jagged breath. "At the hospital, I visited her." I looked at Eva. "She was catatonic. But every time I entered her room, she'd start to moan."

"She recognized you, Zoey," Eva whispered.

"She'd get so agitated, the nurses would ask me to l-leave." I cleared the frog from my throat. "In the six months life clung to her, she never spoke. B-but I'd walk into her room, and she'd start to thrash."

Tears shimmered in Eva's eyes. "Oh, honey. I'm so sorry."

"I want to kill Jacks." I didn't try to hold back my own tears. They overflowed, running down my cheeks, down my neck, and soaking into my thin blouse. "I want him to die, Eva. He took everything from me. *Everything!*" I leaped to my feet.

"Take it easy." King stood from where he'd been sitting on the coffee table.

"I'm going to the farm; I want to see him now."

"Not until you calm down." His tone was hard. Unbending.

The rage in my gut exploded. "*Who the fuck do you think you are telling me to calm down!*" I threw my glass and it shattered against the wall.

King didn't move but the muscles in his neck were rigid. I panted, my throat burning and raw. My fury searched for more to feed on but King's granite face was softening. I recognized his stark sadness. It sucked up my fury and left nothing but exhausted anguish in its place. My head pounded. Dry stickiness coated my mouth. "I need to see him," I croaked. "I need to look into his eyes and ask him why. Why. *Why!*" I grabbed onto his shirt, bunching it in my fists. "Why did he hurt me? Why did he murder my family?"

"How do you know he murdered your family?"

"What do you mean?"

"You remember it was Jacks who raped you." His gaze sharpened, green flinty rocks nudging at the soft moss. "But you didn't say he shot your family. Stabbed your mother."

I yanked on his shirt. "Stop it!"

"Not yet, Zoey." His fingers circled my upper arms. "Tell me what else you remember."

A loud gushing deafened me. King's mouth moved but I couldn't hear him. "What?" I was panting.

"—need to push, Red. Who else did you see?"

"No! No!" I shook my head, but couldn't look away from King.

"Stop it, King!" Eva plastered herself to my back, her arms circling me. "It's all right, honey," she whispered huskily. "It's all right."

It wasn't all right.

It wasn't bloody all right.

"Help me," I pleaded.

King's fingers tightened, but somehow I knew he wasn't bruising me. "Somebody else was there that night, Zoey. Jacks was not alone. There was another perp, and I think that's who murdered your family."

Red flashes exploded behind my eyes. Blood. *Oh, God! Too much blood.* I couldn't breathe. Pink rose petals filled my vision. I sagged back against Eva.

"Shhh, Zoey. Deep, breaths. It's going to be all right."

Her warm body pressed closer. I squeezed my eyes shut. I yearned for a different warmth.

Gray. I wanted Gray.

I tried to let go of King's shirt but my hands were numb. He gently untangled my fingers. "Sit down before you fall down," he rumbled.

Eva guided me to the couch. My knees gave, and I sank into the soft cushions. Eva plopped down beside me. I tucked up my legs and hugged them to my chest. "What's happening?" I said.

"You have to give yourself time." Her hand rested on my arm. "Your memory is surfacing. If you push too hard, the fog will close in again."

I shuddered. "I need to see," I whispered.

"And you will."

I rested my head on my knees. "Gray found something in the file, didn't he?" I dragged in a breath and looked at King. His already hard face hardened further.

"Jacks didn't shoot himself. And he didn't bake that bloody cake."

A scent of burning birthday candles suddenly stained the air. My chest clogged and I began to wheeze. "I'm sorry. I'm sorry." I hugged my legs tighter.

I needed Gray.

I stared pleadingly at King. "I know that I know," I

rasped. "But I can't look yet. I just can't."

Gray. Oh, my God. This was going to shatter him.

I took several careful breaths. "I have to see Jacks now. I need to convince him to go to the police." It was hard to keep my voice steady. "I want you to come with me but if you won't, I'll go alone."

King's mouth set in a hard line. "If I let you go, Gray will beat me to a pulp."

My chin lifted. "When Gray finds out about Jacks, he's going to kill him."

Arrogance twisted King's mouth. "And that's a bad thing?"

"Yes!" I let go of my legs and quickly rose to my feet. "They're brothers. If Gray takes Jacks' life, it will carve a mark in him that will never heal."

"They're not brothers." Disgust hardened his English brogue.

I stepped closer and had to crane my neck to keep eye contact. "This isn't your call to make. You can either come with me or I go alone." I jammed my fists onto my hips to try and hide my trembling.

"Or I could keep you at the cottage until Gray gets back." His hawkish gaze raked over me.

Shit. He could easily do that. I glared at him. "You could try." I held my breath.

He blinked slowly. "All right, Red." His voice was deadly calm. "We'll do this your way, but first I'm going to call Luke. Tell him to meet us at Morgan Farm."

"King, no—"

He shook his head. Once. My mouth shut.

"Luke will bring the police. We'll have a head start and you can try and sweet-talk Jacks. I think it's a bloody waste of time, but I'll give it to you."

"This is not a good idea," Eva said. "We don't know how Jacks will react. And Gray's going to go nuts."

"She's not going to be alone. If that fucker even breathes wrong, I'll blow his brains out." His gaze shifted to me. I flinched. Green death blazed. "He's not my fucking brother so I really don't give a shit. He's done hurting people I care about." His hand cut the air. "Done!"

Okay. Shit. Not such an a'hole after all.

His gaze released me, and he turned to Eva. "What about Gray's parents?" she said. "Shouldn't we contact them?"

"No," King said sharply.

My stomach rolled. "But Margaret is so protective of Jacks—"

"No, Zoey."

A flash of red hovered in my mind's eye. Bile trickled up my throat. "Maybe we can talk to Gerald then. Warn him." King frowned, and I looked to Eva. "Margaret will go gonzo," I said huskily.

She shrugged a shoulder at King. "I can go and speak to Gerald."

"Dammit, Eva—"

Her hand rose. "I'll be careful to talk only to him. And I'll take a sidearm."

My heart kicked so hard, a pain shot through my chest.

"Zoey," King said quietly. "Go and get ready. I'll take you to the farm to look for Jacks. Eva will go to the Walkers and find Gerald." He reached for his phone and began to walk toward the porch. "He can decide how to handle his wife." He gave me a piercing look over his shoulder. "But Jacks is ours."

My throat burned as I watched him walk outside.

Jacks is ours.

Oh no, he wasn't. Absolutely fucking not.

Jacks was mine!

Chapter Twenty-Four
That's Not Love

En route to Morgan Farm
Zoey

"Stay alert," King said as Eva exited the vehicle.

"You too." She shut the door and King immediately rolled forward. I craned my neck to watch Eva as we drove away. She waited until we hit the gravel road, then turned and started to walk up the pathway to the Walker's front door.

Ring-ring! Ring-ring!

King hit a button on the steering wheel to connect the car phone unit. "Mira. I'm with Zoey."

"I found Wendy." Her voice was clear over the speakerphone. "She's in Fort Worth. The address listed belongs to her sister and brother-in-law."

His brows snapped together. "Okay. Good job."

"You need anything else from me?"

"You sound tired, Amirah."

"Fuck you, Thane. I've been busy. And I'm not your sister so quit playing big brother."

There was a click. Then an empty silence that said Mira had hung up.

Wendy ran off without telling Jacks?

My head already ached trying to grapple with "Jacks the monster rapist." It was beyond me right now to think about "Jacks the loving fiancé." I desperately needed a reprieve and turned to King. "Big brother?" His lips compressed. I probed again. "Um, Eva—"

"She talk to you?" he interrupted coldly.

"No!" I said hurriedly. "But I'm a doctor and that makes me observant." I studied his bone structure and knew I was right. "I can see the familial resemblance."

He nodded abruptly.

Jeez. Like pulling teeth. "Why don't you acknowledge who she is to you?"

"Why don't you ask her?"

"Fair enough," I muttered. Unpleasant tension filled the car. *Damn.* Using King to distract me was a pathetic plan. I stared out the windscreen. King made the turn into Hartlee Field Road.

"I'm her brother in every way that counts," he said evenly. "She knows that. And so do the senior members of my team."

"Okay." I rubbed my hands down my jean-clad legs. Morgan Farm was approaching fast. "But you're not a brother to Mira." It came out strangled and I felt his gaze.

"You need the distraction, don't you?" he said tersely.

My throat thickened. "Y-yes."

He smiled grimly. "I like you, Red, and I don't like a lot of people. So you get one question with one straight answer."

I didn't think twice. "What is Mira to you?"

"What is Gray to you?"

Heat exploded in my chest. "Everything."

"There you have it."

He spun the wheel and we made the turn to Morgan Farm. My family home loomed ahead. "Stop,"

I whispered. "Please stop."

King hit the brakes. The huge black SUV drew to a halt in a swirl of dust. I quickly wound down my window and hot air blasted into the air-conditioned interior. My skin was clammy and I couldn't decide if I was hot or cold. "How did I not see what he was?" Bitterness trickled down my throat. "How could I have missed it?"

King shifted toward me. "You understand enough about psychiatry, Zoey, to know psychopaths are good at hiding in full view." He leaned closer, his expression fierce. "They look like everybody else until the day they show their true colors. Then the evil is right there, staring you in the face."

I took several shallow breaths. "No matter how hard I try to remember, I have no memory of...of...*him* proposing to me."

King's eyes flared, and then went flat. "That's because he probably didn't."

"Then how—?"

"The bastard raped you," he snarled. "That he could slide a ring on your finger. Fucking lie about it. That's tame in comparison."

"But that's completely insane."

"You said it, Red." His hand lifted like he wanted to touch me. I didn't flinch but he must have seen something in my eyes because his arm dropped. "You were set up. Your system was fucked up by the drugs. You were raped, beaten to shit and you watched your family die." His thick brows knitted in a deep frown. "It didn't take a whole lot more for him to take advantageous of you."

"But why would he do that to me? To Gray?"

"That's what you're going to ask him." He straightened and released the handbrake. "And if there's a hope in hell he's going to give you a coherent answer, you need to calm your shit."

I reared back. "Jesus, King. Really?"

He pressed down the accelerator and the vehicle lurched forward. "Yes, Red, really."

Red. What was with him calling me Red?

I must be losing it because I stared out the window and my mouth curved into a small smile. *Red.* Noah used to call me Red. The wind from my open window tugged at my hair. And I had the crazy feeling everything was going to be all right.

Okay. It was going to be godawful first. But then it was going to be all right. That's what I told myself.

Totally crazy.

****

Morgan Farm
Zoey

When we arrived at the farmstead a red truck was pulling out from the stables. King waved it down. The driver wound his window down and identified himself as Hank Allens, a local student. He was helping Wendy with the kids to earn community service credits. He told us she called him and said to tell Jacks she had canceled the kids for the week. He'd been about to drive out to look for Jacks.

"Why don't you phone him?" King asked.

"He left his phone in the stables." He yanked off his hat and combed his fingers roughly through his sandy hair. "Sir. I don't wanna speak out of turn, but I'm right worried. The boss seemed out of it. He kept rushing around, shouting for the missus."

"Wendy?" King said.

"Yessir," he nodded.

"You know where he went?"

"Said he was going to find Miss Wendy. He said over and over again, he had to go look in the pond."

King turned to me. "You got any idea where he'd go to look for her?"

"There's one place—"

He turned back to the clearly nervous student. "Wait here. The police are on the way. Some friends of mine will be with them, Gray Walker and Luke Hunter. Direct them toward the pond, yeah." It wasn't a request.

The kid's mouth gaped, but he nodded vigorously. King hit the button to close his window and we did a U-turn out the drive. There was only one place I could think of that Jacks could be. I directed King along the gravel road leading to the inlet where we often went swimming as kids. I tried to focus on what I was going to say to Jacks, but hate played tricks on me. Comic book images of cruel revenge played out in my head. In them, I was always the avenging angel.

No! I was better than this.

Jacks had paralyzed me in the dark for too long. I'd allowed his evil to squat in my brain like a smothering parasite. No more. The only plan I needed was to find the truth. I gritted my teeth and pointed out the familiar narrow path leading to the pond. We turned off the gravel road and King cursed as the SUV lurched violently. The forest soon thinned, the trees giving way to a small beach. The pond glistened in the bright sunlight. Tears pricked the corners of my eyes. I used to come to this swimming spot with Noah. My heart screamed and I craned forward to see the beach.

Gray kissed me there.

"Fuck. He's got a gun," King bit out.

I went rigid. Jacks was several feet out, knee deep in the water. He was stumbling around, waving his arms. It looked like he was talking to himself. And King was right. He had a gun gripped in one hand. I clutched the dashboard as King inched the SUV closer. "What's he looking for?" I said.

"Lady of the Lake," King muttered and stopped the SUV. He pulled the handbrake and keyed the ignition off. "The man's unstable, I don't think he knows what he's doing. Until I get a handle on him, you stay in the car." He leaned over and popped the cubby by my knees. My stomach went solid when he pulled out a black handgun. Without another word, he opened his door and climbed out.

As soon as his door slammed shut, I opened mine. I was out the door and had managed two steps before King was in my face. "What the fuck?" His hand clamped around my arm.

"Let me go." I glared imaginary scorching rays at him but they were lost because his alert gaze never strayed from Jacks.

"I gave you an order—"

Fury swept over me. "You don't get to order me; I won't stand for it." I yanked my arm, but his grip didn't loosen. "Let me go, King. I mean it."

"Goddammit, Zoey!"

"No!" I spun in front of him and hissed in his face. "This is *my* fight. *My* truth. You don't get to take that from me."

"Where's Wendy!"

Jacks' frenzied scream had my skin crawling like

mutant bugs were burrowing into me. King's gaze met mine for a fraction of a second. I swallowed hard but didn't budge.

"You stay a step behind me, Zoey. You understand?"

"Yes."

"You don't get in between my gun and that motherfucker." His grip on my arm tightened and I winced. "I have a clear shot at all times, no matter what shit he spouts."

"Help me! I can't find her, where is she!" Jacks sobbed.

King released my arm and stepped around me. "Gray's going to fucking kill me," he cursed.

I exhaled loudly and rubbed my arm. My heart was pounding. Jacks seemed oblivious. He'd shoved his gun into the back of his jeans, and was now hunched over, swinging his arms haphazardly through the water. As I followed King, the sand began to thicken. At the water's edge it turned to thick mud, and for a moment I teetered, nearly losing my balance when my sneakers sank down. I glanced at King. He was holding his gun at his thigh, pointed toward the ground. The water lapped at his boots. Forcing my shoes through the ooze, I stepped up beside him.

"Zoey," he growled.

Jacks' head shot up. My stomach churned. His pupils were so dilated his brown eyes looked liquid-black.

"Help me, please," he begged. "I can't find her."

"Jacks. What are you doing?" I tried to keep my voice steady.

His head tilted sharply. "I'm looking for Wendy."

"You think she's in the pond?"

For a moment his face went blank. Then he stumbled back. "She took her. I know she took her." He bent over and began to thrash at the water again. "She killed her. I think she killed her."

My hair stood on end. Jacks continued to rant. I stared at his thrashing arms. The dark water swirled. I could see fragments of her face.

"Jacks, who do you think killed Wendy?" King said.

Wendy's alive, but Mama was dead.

Wendy's alive, but Dad was dead. Noah was dead.

"*You kno-ooow!*" Jacks' bloodcurdling screech ripped my focus from the watery depths. "You know," he croaked. "You know." His finger kept stabbing at me.

"I don't know." Nausea swirled inside me, cloying and rotten. I felt myself sway.

I did know.

Doubling over, I hugged myself until my arms screamed in pain. *I did know.* Dry heaves rattled my teeth.

"Red?" A warm hand settled on my back.

"No!" I lurched sideways and shoved out my hand. "Please. No." I stared mesmerized into the water, breathing slowly through my nose. My head ached but I could see her. Like it was yesterday, I watched her stroll into our dining room.

"Surprise," she gushed and thrust a birthday cake at me. "Jacks told me about Harvard. It's so exciting, Zoey. I can't stay but I wanted to bring you something. I baked it myself."

"It was Mother," Jacks whimpered. "You know it

was my mother, Zoey. You saw her." His anguish drifted over the murky water.

In my memory, this place held so much love and laughter. Now everything was stagnant. Dead. There wasn't a whisper of a bird squawking or a wasp buzzing. No hovering dragonflies, or grasshoppers clinging to the long grasses. Even the breeze had dissipated. It was like everything was holding its breath. Deafened by my despair. My rage.

The water rippled.

She was there, standing in the shadows. Watching.

My stomach cramped and I bit my tongue. A coppery taste flooded my mouth.

She was watching her son hurt me. Rape me.
Jacks!

I heaved violently as forgotten agony screamed awake. "It was you," I gasped. "You hurt me. You forced me." I lunged forward. King's arm shot out and held me back. *"You murdered my family!"* I screamed.

"No! I'd never do that."

"But you did." I strained against King's hold. "I remember, Jacks. I fucking remember!"

He shook his head fiercely. "It wasn't me, Zoey. It wasn't me." His eyes looked bruised. Haunted. "You know she drugged the cake. I only ate a little but I got woozy. Everything was blurry." He lifted his hands, imploring. "I didn't hear her come back. I heard the gun shots, but I couldn't see." His voice broke and he stumbled forward. "I c-couldn't see."

"Stop it, Jacks. For God's sake, stop!" I wanted to believe him but the darkness was gone. The light was shining bright. So bright it was burning everything in its wake. "You saw my mother. You had to." Grief thickened my throat. "Why didn't you help my mama?"

"I couldn't get up. I couldn't move. And you were moaning." He blinked rapidly. "I was terrified for you, Zoey. You were all I could think about."

"Then why didn't you save me?" I cried.

"I did!"

My throat closed and I began to sway.

"Breathe through it, Red. You can do it."

I grabbed on to King's voice, his faith an anchor in the madness.

I needed to know. I needed to understand.

I forced a breath. Then another. Jacks watched me, his face twisted with emotions I struggled to read. "You raped me. You hurt me. Why Jacks? Why would you do something so hideous?"

He flung his arms wide. "I did that to save you."

"You're insane," I blurted.

He dropped his arms to his sides. "She said she would kill you if I didn't claim you. Called you vermin." His voice had turned eerily flat. "She held a knife to your neck. Vowed to slice you like she did your mother. I believed her." He tilted his head, his eyes bottomless pools of black. "She wanted us to be together. To join the families, join the land." His hand half lifted then flopped down. "I did it to save you, Zoey."

I shuddered. I was suddenly freezing cold. "You raped me to save me?" He flinched and I had a horrible desire to laugh at the look of hurt on his face.

"She gave you to me." His voice rose again. "She even brought the ring. Put it on your finger."

The ring.

I could feel it on my finger. Alien. A betrayal.

351

"You took what didn't belong to you, Jacks. And you helped her murder my family—"

"No!" he yelled. "When my head cleared, Noah and your father were already dead." His hands lifted again, beseeching me. "You have to believe me, Zoey. She made me do it. And after, she cut more cake. Forced me to eat it. When I woke, I was bleeding." He sounded childlike as he gripped his shoulder, rubbing at what must have been his bullet scar. "You were hurt too. Bleeding. I called the police."

My stomach heaved with hate, but his explanation rang true. I rubbed my ring finger until the skin burned hot. "And after, Jacks. When we were safe in the hospital. Why didn't you tell the truth then?"

"The truth?" He laughed harshly. "The truth wouldn't help me. If I told the truth, Gray would have killed me himself." His face twisted with mockery. "If I told the truth, I would have lost you."

Pain crushed my chest. "Don't you understand, I was never yours to lose."

"Maybe. But you weren't Gray's either." He swayed and lost his footing. When he regained his balance, he moved back, deeper into the water. "You know what's so funny?" His dilated gaze trapped mine. "I never thought Gray would believe me, and I definitely never thought you would." He gave a macabre chuckle. "It didn't take much to convince you both, did it? Just a ring on your finger. Is that what you call love, Zoey?" His arm moved behind him and he withdrew his gun.

I stood frozen, his words an ugly tattoo in my head. *Is that what you call love, Zoey?*

"That's not love." He waved his gun in my

direction. "I don't know what that is, but it's not love."

"Drop the weapon," King snarled, his own gun aimed at Jacks.

I tried to breathe.

That's not love.

My heart shriveled.

I don't know what that is, but it's not love.

My soul wailed in despair.

"Now Jacks, or I'll blow your fucking head off."

Jacks' arm wavered. "Find Wendy, please. Find her. Tell her I love her." He brought his arm up, pointing the gun at his head. "Don't let my mother hurt her."

"Jacks, don't—" I wheezed.

His dark gaze shifted to King. "You'll find what you need in the pond." His voice was strong, clear.

Bang!

I jumped.

Splash!

"Bloody hell!" King jumped forward. Jacks was already partially submerged. King shoved his gun into his jeans at the small of his back and waded deeper. He grabbed onto Jacks and started to drag his body through the water.

A loud buzz roared in my ears. I was only ankle-deep in the pond but I couldn't move. The mud was like thick glue, holding me in place. My heart was thumping, the ends of my fingers tingling. I shook as I watched King half carry, half drag Jacks out of the water. He staggered and dropped Jacks' limp body beside me. Breath whooshed from me and I fell to my knees. Jacks' head lolled to the side. Half his skull was blown away. The mud began to change color. Darken.

Dead. I knew he was dead. But instinctively I reached out and pressed my fingers to his neck. His skin seemed already cool. And still. His pulse silent.

"He's dead," I whispered.

"No shit," King growled. "Come on, we need to go."

"We can't just leave him here."

"The police will find him." He reached out a hand. "We need to go."

"King—"

"Dammit, Zoey! Eva's at the ranch. With his bloody mother!" He gestured sharply at Jacks. "Good riddance to evil shit, I say. Now let's go and find the rest of the garbage." He thrust his hand at me.

For a moment I stared at Jacks' face. It was relaxed. Calm. It seemed death had brought him peace. But I hated him. I hated him for what he had done to me, to Gray. But most of all I hated him because he was right. What sort of love gave up at the very first obstacle?

I grabbed hold of King's hand and let him pull me to my feet. My nails dug into his skin as I tried to swallow down the pain.

Why did we let our love crumple in the face of their evil?

We hadn't even put up a fight.

Chapter Twenty-Five
The Way to Your Heart

Morgan Farm and Walker Ranch
Zoey

King drove back to the homestead as fast as the terrain allowed. I clung to the door handle as the SUV bounced jarringly. My body ached like I'd gone several rounds with the wrong end of a bat. The buzz in my ears had faded, but an annoying feeling of them being blocked remained, and I kept yawning to try and clear it.

King had his phone in one hand. He tapped a number and tossed the phone into the cubby next to the handbrake. A distorted sound of ringing filled the car interior. It rang once before it was answered.

"You find him?" It was Luke.

"You on speaker?" King said.

"No." Luke's voice had lowered.

"Good. Keep it that way. Where are you?"

"About to pass by Walker Ranch."

"Get Gray to stop, and then listen to me."

The SUV rocked wildly as King turned too fast off the rutted pathway and onto the smoother graveled road that led back to the stables. We could hear murmuring in the background and then Luke's voice came back.

"Okay. We've stopped. Gray wants to know about Zoey."

I felt King's gaze rake over me, but I stared steadfastly out the window.

"She's safe but Jacks is dead. The motherfucker confessed to raping her then blew his own head off."

"Jesus!"

"You need to divert back to the ranch."

"What—?"

"I don't have time to explain, Hunter. Eva's at Walker Ranch and she's not safe." My gaze skewed sideways. King's knuckles showed white around the steering wheel.

"Who from?"

"The mother. Margaret Walker."

"Jesus Christ," Luke hissed.

"Go," King bit out. "Don't let Gray do anything stupid."

"What about his father?"

"The hell if I know. Keep your eyes open and keep Gray clear of the poison." We crested a small rise and the stables came into sight. King accelerated. I gripped the door handle so tight my hands cramped.

"How many cars with you?" King asked Luke.

"Randy and his deputy. Another car following with two more deputies." I could hear the urgency in Luke's voice.

"Split them up. Keep the sheriff with you. Send the other car here. There's a kid waiting by the stables, Hank Allens. He'll show them where to go. They need to dredge the pond. There's something in there that Jacks wanted us to find. Might be that bitch's gun."

Without waiting for Luke's response, King cut the line. In what felt like seconds, we roared into the stables. Hank Allens was standing by his truck. King braked hard, jumped out and wasted no time briefing the freaked out student. Then he was back in the driver's seat, and we were flying up the road, a cloud of dust in our rearview mirror. We turned into Hartlee Field Road and a sheriff's vehicle roared by us. They didn't stop. Neither did King. My throat closed and I struggled for breath.

Oh God! Oh God! Oh God!

"Keep it together, Red."

A sob escaped and I clamped a hand to my mouth. *Breathe, dammit. Breathe.* I rocked back and forth, my lungs burning for more air.

"Don't you dare pass out," King threatened. "Gray's going to need you now."

I sucked in a harsh breath. "Oh God! His brother, his mother. He's going to believe he's stained with their evil." I rocked harder. "Oh my God! He's going to blame himself. Hate himself."

"You love him?"

I jerked. King's question was a barked challenge.

"Do. You. Love. Him?" He enunciated each word.

"Ye-es." It was a broken whisper. I wrapped my arms around my waist and squeezed. *Fuck you Jacks. I love him. I've always loved him.* "Yes! I love him," I shouted.

The vehicle swung wildly as King made a fast turn into Walker Ranch. The imposing gates loomed ahead, but he slammed on brakes. I lurched forward, the seatbelt biting into my shoulder. In the sudden stillness, I pushed back from the dashboard and glared at him. "What are you doing—?" My tongue froze when his eyes slammed into me.

"Firstly, that motherfucker who just blew his head

off—that's not Grayson Walker's brother. He never was." He leaned closer. I bit my lip because King in full alpha mode was scary-as-shit. "And Margaret Walker—" He stabbed a rigid finger toward the gates. "That bitch has never been Gray's mother."

I nodded hesitantly. He wasn't wrong, but looming over me, he was still scary-as-shit. "K-King—"

In a flash, he lowered his hand and brought it to my face. His grip was gentle but firm. "There's no doubt their evil has touched Gray's soul. Made him believe he's not worthy of love." His thumb brushed my cheekbone and tears surged behind my lids. "What happened between the two of you, how you let go of each other, that's in the past. Yes?" His penetrating gaze demanded an answer.

I swallowed and willed my tears away. "Yes."

"Good. Now it's today. And today is your chance to do better. And you're smart, Zoey, even smarter than I am. You'll work it out."

Shit. My vision blurred again. "I pushed him away," I said hoarsely. "He kept coming back and I kept pushing him away."

His fingers flexed. "Yes. But you're not pushing him away anymore. Today's the day you take his hand and you show him the way."

"What way?"

"The way to your heart."

My eyes widened. *Oh, my God.* A bubble of warmth nudged the ice holding me hostage.

King's mouth twitched. "While you get busy saving Gray from himself, you mind if we get moving so I can save him from blowing his fucking mother's head off?"

This time I snorted. It was nuts. "No, King." My own lips started twitching. *Totally crazy.* "I don't mind."

I held my breath when he leaned closer, his hand sliding to wrap around the back of my neck. He pulled me to him and his mouth settled on the crown of my head. "Nobody's going to hurt you anymore, Red." His voice was deep, husky. And it resounded with such intensity I knew what he said was a vow. He squeezed my neck and let me go.

I held onto the dash as the SUV accelerated through the gates and up the road. One tear rolled down my cheek, and then another. My smile slipped away.

But the ice in my chest continued to melt.

Today's the day you take his hand and you show him the way.

Yes. I could do that.

I would do that.

For Gray, I'd do anything.

****

Walker Ranch

Zoey

When we pulled up to the elegant colonial house, Gray's rental and a sheriff's vehicle were parked in the drive. Nobody was in sight.

King's phone pinged.

He grabbed it and read the screen. "Luke says the house is empty. Thinks they must be at the stables. Let's go."

"Shouldn't we wait—?"

"No."

"But—"

In a hail of flying pebbles, King accelerated out the

drive. "If you don't want Gray doing something he can't come back from, we need to get ahead of him."

Shit. I pointed to the left. "Follow that side road."

He drove silently. We passed a small grove of oaks, and then the road turned back on itself. The stables were right in front of us. My heart hammered. Nothing had changed. It was still beautiful. Peaceful. The large barn and outhouses were all buttercup yellow with dark-green trim on the windows and doors. They were built in a semi-circle around a small courtyard where, in pride of place, there was a glorious bronze of Morgan Magic. A gift to Gerald from my father. Noah once told me that we'd had one exactly the same, but Dad destroyed it when Magic died.

King parked. I reached for the door handle but he grabbed my arm. "Just like at the pond, you give me a clear shot. Yes?"

I swallowed hard, but my throat was too thick to talk.

"Zoey—"

I nodded abruptly and tugged at my arm. He let me go and we both climbed from the vehicle. A movement by the main barn flashed. Eva. Before I knew it I was running. The huge doors to the barn stood wide open. King's warning rang in my ears and I slowed. Without breaking stride, he moved smoothly past me. I sucked in a jerky breath and followed.

It took a moment for my eyes to adjust. The barn was exactly as I remembered. High-beamed rafters with wooden fans, skylights dotted evenly the length of the large space. Six roomy stalls on each side. And at the end, the tack room.

The tack room.

Nerves shrieked as flashes of memory flooded my mind. Eva was standing outside the tack room door and she gestured for us to be quiet. I pushed away the sensual echoes of a younger Gray and me, and quickly caught up to King. We stopped beside Eva. There were voices inside the tack room and I craned past her to look inside. Gerald was talking to somebody but the door blocked my view.

"Margaret's going off the deep-end," Eva whispered in my ear. "Gerald's trying to talk her down."

"It's over. You have to stop protecting him."

I gripped the doorframe.

"Don't blame me. You're always blaming me." It was Margaret. Her voice was high. Unnaturally brittle. "And what do you care anyway? It was so long ago. Nothing but a family grudge." Fury slammed into me. I must have jolted because Eva slipped her arm around my waist. "Why do you have to dredge this up now?" Margaret wheedled.

I yanked free of Eva and lurched into the room. Margaret's hand flew to her chest. "Nothing but a family grudge!" I cried, advancing on her.

"Zoey, you don't understand." She backed away but the tack room wall blocked her retreat.

"It's all right, Zoey. Eva explained about Jacks." Gerald moved to stand next to his wife. "She told us what you remembered him doing to you." Lines of pain hollowed his cheeks.

"Yes, I remember." I pointed at Margaret. "I remember you. You brought me the cake." Like a startled bird, her angular face tilted. "The drugs made everything hazy but I remember you standing there.

You watched him rape me." For a second the room spun and I sucked in a sharp breath. "How could you? You watched your own son rape me!"

Her eyes narrowed to slits, her pupils like tiny black diamonds glittering with intelligence. Or madness. She lunged forward but Gerald's arm shot out to restrain her. "James' little girl," she hissed. "Nothing but a disgusting slut."

I flinched. "What?"

"I heard you. Here. Right in this barn." She strained against Gerald's arm, her gaze flashing over my shoulder. "Fornicating with him. Begging him to take you."

"Zoey." Gray's hand circled my waist. "You okay?"

No.

But the denial died in my throat. Margaret was pulling against Gerald like a rabid dog on a leash. Her chin jutted awkwardly, a line of spittle escaping her contorted mouth. "Taking everything from my Jackson, you were. I would not stand for it!"

Gray's arm jerked around me. I bit my tongue, forcing saliva into my mouth. "Gray's your son too," I whispered.

"No! Not mine. An interloper." She twisted in Gerald's arms and glared up at him. "You! I saw your will. Leaving my land to him. Just like my father, giving it away."

"Margaret, you have to calm down—"

"Weak! You're weak!" She reared back and spat phlegm in his face.

Gerald shoved her against the wall. She flailed and grooming implements crashed to the floor. Gerald wiped his face. Her wild gaze swung to me. "You should have been mine. Mine and James'."

"For goodness sake, Margaret!"

She turned to Gerald and thrust her arm at him. He jumped back.

"Jesus Christ," Gray swore.

Margaret was wielding a hoof knife that she must have grabbed from the wall. It had a wooden handle with a sharp hooked steel blade.

My eyes squeezed shut. Drops of blood rained down in my mind, washing away the leftover fog. I sagged and Gray's arm tightened like iron around me. "It was you," I gasped. "You stabbed my mother."

"She took everything from me!" she snarled. "She had to pay."

"She was innocent!"

"She was guilty!"

"And Noah? My father? Were they guilty too?" Black spots danced in front of me. I couldn't catch my breath. "Were they guilty too?" I wheezed.

Gray dragged me back, his warm breath brushing my ear. "She's not worth it, Zoey."

My fingers dug into his arm. "Why me?" My voice was a ragged whisper. "Why didn't you kill me?"

Her mouth went slack. The glitter in her eyes began to fade, leaving behind a dazed blankness. "I saved you because of James." Gerald took a step closer to her but she ignored him. "You needed a lesson, Zoey, but you were still our little girl. My little girl." She moved forward. "You were mine to give to Jacks."

Jacks!

His voice was a scream in my head.

She said she would kill you if I didn't claim you.

363

I stared at her. Eva would analyze her in medical terms. A mother. A malignant narcissist. Pathological. But I couldn't. I refused to. Taking strength from Gray's powerful embrace, I craned forward. "You're evil and you're insane," I said coldly. "And you poisoned Jacks until he was as twisted as you are." The hooked blade waved unsteadily in her hand. "You destroyed my family and you devastated Gray." I curled my mouth in disgust. "Now your poison has killed your son."

Gerald hunched over. "*No-oooo!*" His agonized cry sent cold shivers racing over me.

Margaret stiffened, her gaze shifting manically from Gerald to Gray. "You're not dead."

Gray jolted. "Not me. Jacks."

Her jaw slackened. "Jacks?" She began to shake her head.

"Yes," I hissed. "Your son, Jacks. He's dead."

She went rigid. The sun shifted and began to beat through the skylight, catching dust motes in its beam. They floated around her head, her body, isolating her in a hazy mist.

Suddenly she lunged.

"Gray!" King shouted.

"Watch it!" Luke moved in my peripheral vision.

Gray swung me around, but not before I saw Gerald jump forward.

"Goddammit, Dad!" Gray shouted, holding me to his chest. I began to struggle in his arms. "Stop it, Zoey, please." I went still. He was breathing loudly, his head twisted to look over his shoulder.

"Look at them, Margaret." It was Gerald, his voice unsteady. "They belong together, they always have."

I shoved against Gray. His hold didn't loosen but he shifted sideways.

No. No.

"Look at them!" Gerald cried. He had one arm fastened around her shoulders, the other pressed to his side. Blood covered his hand. Margaret looked eerily vacant. She was staring at us but I had the feeling she wasn't seeing us. "They're perfect together," Gerald whispered.

King and Luke closed in on either side of them. King moved, but Gerald moved faster. He pulled the knife from where it was buried in his side and sank it into Margaret's chest. Gray's arms contracted. I hugged him so tight my arms burned with pain. Gerald clutched Margaret in his arms, and then slowly lowered her to the floor. I knew she was dead. Gerald had aimed right for her heart and he hadn't missed. He collapsed to his knees and I looked away.

The far corner of the tack room was covered with trophies and faded newspaper cuttings of Morgan Magic. In the center was a framed photo of Magic, festooned in the winning garland from the Triple Crown. On one side of him stood a smiling Gerald, and on the other, my father, grinning from ear to ear.

A miracle horse. A magical horse. So much happiness and so such pain. For James and Gerald, it was their dream. I looked down at Margaret, lying dead on the barn floor. For her, it had been nothing but a nightmare. Now, like her son, she looked morbidly peaceful in death.

Gray released me. "Need some air." He urged me to loosen my grip.

His face was blank. I let him go. There was nothing

magical about watching your father kill your mother. He needed to find his balance, and I needed to help Gerald. He strode out, Luke on his heels. I could already feel him withdrawing. I glanced at King and swallowed my doubt.

Today's the day you take his hand and show him the way. The way to your heart.

Shit. It was going to take more than a day. I sucked in a steadying breath and moved to Gerald. Gray could take as long as he needed, but in the end, he was going to be exactly where he belonged. Right beside me.

"Eva, I need clean towels." I knelt beside Gerald and pressed my hand to the stab wound pumping blood on his side. He slumped sideways and I gently rolled him onto his back. He was unconscious. And like his wife and son, he looked strangely peaceful.

I bit my lip. Hard. *What Gerald did to Margaret was probably the sanest thing to happen all day.* I silenced the crazy thought as warm blood escaped my clamped hand.

Chapter Twenty-Six
I Want My Man

Granddad Davis' Cottage
One Week Later
Zoey

I breathed in the heady aroma from the simmering pot. Home cooked Bolognese exactly how my mama used to make it. Fresh peeled tomatoes, finely sliced black mushrooms, lots of garlic—and her secret ingredient she learned from her own mama—a dash of sweet chutney.

Gray was on his way to the airport with Eva. I'd had my final session with her and she was returning to New York. The moment they left, I started peeling and chopping tomatoes.

It was a week since the past clashed violently with the present, and left Jacks and Margaret guilty and dead. We'd all breathed easier when Randy proved to be a loyal friend. Even though he was by the tack room door when Gerald took Margaret's life, he stated in the police report it was self-defense. Gray challenged him, not wanting Randy to lie on his behalf, but he refused to discuss it. Of course, King, Luke and Eva's eyewitness statements supported Randy's version. And so did mine. I think we all knew there had been enough hurt. Enough lives destroyed. There was no point adding to Gerald's agony. He was out of the woods now, soon to be released from the hospital. I hadn't visited with him. Neither had Gray. Unexpectedly, it was Wendy who spent time with him each day.

After two days of dredging the pond, the police found most of the objects stolen from my family home at the time of the attack. They'd been placed in a bag and tossed from the old jetty. The bag had since disintegrated but the objects were found buried in the pond silt. They also found a Smith & Wesson Model 10 Revolver. It had extensive water damage, but when they showed it to Gerald, he identified it as a gun gifted to Margaret from her father when she was eighteen. He recognized it from its hand-carved wooden handle. It was a family heirloom passed down by three generations of Davis'. And like most guns passed from one family member to another, it was never officially listed, so the police had no idea Margaret owned the weapon. She had most likely given the damning evidence to Jacks to get rid of.

In self-imposed solitary confinement, Gray grappled with his rage. He even refused to speak with Eva, demanding instead I talk with her daily. I didn't argue. Gray needed me to heal. And if I was going to help him, I needed me to heal too. King and Luke returned to New York. Before he left, Luke confided that Gray had shut him out. "Don't let him handle this alone, Zoey. He won't make it." The concern leaking from his navy eyes made my own sheen over. I plucked up courage and hugged his huge frame. "I promise," I whispered to him. "I love him and I promise to bring him back to you whole."

It was a promise I refused to break.

So I worked hard with Eva. She helped me break it

down. Understand it. Accept it. "Your Self could not cope with the heinous knowledge of who your rapist was," she explained. "Nor who it was that you watched murder your family." She pointed out that the continued presence of Jacks and Margaret in my life exacerbated my trauma. "Your subconscious recognized you were not safe," she said. "So you buried everything. So deep, your mind could pretend it never happened."

Our talks were cathartic, but the wounds carved into my soul were deep. Eva said each person's journey was their own. That understanding and accepting were two different things. Nobody could force me to heal; I had to confront my demons when my mind was ready.

And I was ready. I'd lived too long with the ugliness buried inside me, weakening me, suffocating me. It was time to let it go.

And time to take Gray's hand, and bring him along with me.

Even if I had to drag him.

But what if I failed to reach him?

Each time I thought this, my stomach crawled with sick panic.

And I'd force myself to take several deep breaths. The clean air would settle my nausea, and I would remind myself there was hope. Hope that came each night when Gray slipped into bed beside me. When he pulled me against his warm body and wrapped me in his strong arms. We never made love; neither of us was ready for that. But we slept side by side, his heart a protective beat against my ribs, his breath a quiet presence whispering against my neck.

Yes. There was hope.

I reached for a lid to cover the Bolognese. It

needed to simmer, and I needed to prepare. Prepare to take Gray's hand and show him the way to my heart.

****

Later That Evening
Zoey

"Talk to me, please."

"I don't know what you want me to say." His face was granite except for the erratic pulse jumping below his stiff jawline.

"Anything. Something. But you need to talk to me."

We were on the porch. It was after we'd polished off the spaghetti Bolognese and most of a bottle of red wine. If I thought home cooked spag bol would soften Gray up, I was dead wrong. So far my gentle urgings for him to open up had all failed.

He was sprawled back in one of the cane chairs. Handsome and aloof. And so filled with bottled anguish, my heart ached. I sat opposite, as usual with my feet tucked up beneath me. "You can't let their poison take root inside you."

He crossed his arms over his chest. "What, you mean the way it did with you?"

I flinched inwardly. His cold cynicism was a defense mechanism, but it didn't lessen the hurt. "That's exactly what I mean. But this isn't about me, it's about you."

"Bullshit!"

"Not bullshit." I swung my legs down and leaned forward. "I'm not the one in danger anymore. You are. If you let their evil sink inside you, then you let them win."

He bolted upright. "This is about *you*, Zoey. What

they did to *you*."

"Dammit, Gray, don't you understand? It wasn't only me. They hurt you too."

He leaped to his feet. "That's a load of rubbish. Did they murder my family? Did they rape me?" Cobalt fury blazed in his eyes. "Jesus Christ, Zoey, you were a virgin. They took that from you too. From me." He spun away, grabbing his wine glass and downing the dregs. "I want to fucking kill them with my own hands, but they're already dead."

"Gray—"

"*Fu-uuuck!*" The glass went flying, shattering against the far wall. "Fuck! Fuck! Fuck!" He punched his fist into his hand.

My eyes filmed over. His pain was a burning coal lodged in my heart.

"Thank Christ their blood doesn't run in my veins." He spun around and stared at me. "Jesus, Zoey, she weaned Jacks on poison. How did I not see this?"

I clasped my hands tightly in my lap. "Your mother wasn't only pathological, she was highly manipulative too. Jacks never stood a chance."

He stabbed a finger at me. "Don't you dare make excuses for him. She may have got him all twisted up, but what he did to you was on him. I hope that fucker rots in hell right alongside his evil bitch mother. And if that means I have to join them when it's my time to go, so be it."

I jumped up. "Gray Walker, you are not going to hell!"

"No?" His jaw jutted stiffly. "I walked away from you when you needed me most. I left you in the arms of the enemy."

"Our enemy!" I cried. "We were both victims of their lies and deceit."

"I was ripe for the picking, wasn't I? A stupid kid who was so pathetically needy."

"Of course you were needy. Your mother rejected you." I pressed a hand to my aching chest. "That goes to the core of who you are. You may be my tough guy, but you're not a superhero."

"You can say that again."

I stamped my foot. "Dammit, Gray! Stop feeling sorry for yourself. Look at what you've made of yourself in spite of them." I held out my arms. "You fought for your country. You still fight for strangers who have nobody else to turn to. You're surrounded by people who aren't only your friends, they consider themselves your family." I dropped my arms and dared to take a step closer. He didn't move. "Screw Margaret and Jacks Walker. They were never your family. They did their best to tear you down. Rip us apart." I raised my chin. "And they failed. They fucking failed." I wanted to be strong but I started to cry, tears trickling down my face. His agonized eyes tracked them.

"Did they?" he said hoarsely.

Impatiently, I flicked them away. "It wasn't all you, you know. It was me too."

"What are you talking about?"

"I kept waiting for you to save me."

"Bloody hell, Zoey, you were traumatized, grieving—"

"No, I wasn't!" I shouted. "Not two years later, or three years later." I gestured wildly. "Dammit! Six years later." Our gazes clashed. "I kept sending you away. Over and over again."

"It wasn't your fault." Emotion roughened his voice. "It was never your fault; you had no control over what was going on inside your head."

I drew in a shuddery breath. "I'm not the only one who let fear keep us apart."

"What are you talking about?"

"Fourteen years ago you used my innocence to keep us apart. Then you shoved Jacks between us." His mouth flattened, but I forged on. "Now you're making it all about me and my fucked up head. What's wrong, Gray? Aren't I good enough for you?" My eyes blurred again. "Perfect enough?"

He jerked like I'd punched him. "Jesus, Zoey. What the hell are you talking about?"

My stomach spasmed, but I'd started this now, and I had to finish. "When you hold yourself back from me, that's how it makes me feel." I hugged myself. "That you want me to be perfect. And I have to tell you, Gray, I'm never going to be perfect. And neither are you."

A shadow crossed his face. "Have you been speaking to Luke?" he barked.

I reeled back. "What?" He abruptly turned his back. "What about Luke?" He waved his hand dismissively and paced away. "Gray!"

"Never mind."

He stopped at the end of the porch and stared out into the dark forest. I hadn't noticed the night encroach, but in the sudden silence, the hum of insects seemed deafening. I shivered and rubbed my arms, feeling chilled. Gray held himself stiffly. Apart. "Gray," I called tentatively.

He turned, harsh emotion grooved into his handsome face. "It wasn't about you being perfect all those years ago." His voice was quiet, but it cut easily through the insect drone. "I wanted to be careful of your innocence, respect it. But mostly, it was about how you looked at me."

My breath caught. "What do you mean?"

"You looked at me like I was your prince, Zoey. Like I was the answer to all your dreams."

"That's because you were," I cried. "And you still are."

He shook his head. "I'm not, Butterfly, I screwed up." He walked back and dropped into the chair. Lowering his head, he raked his fingers through his hair. "I ran away to lick my wounds. I didn't open my eyes and see the evil swirling around us."

"You were young, Gray, and you were hurting." I walked over and sank to my haunches in front of him. "You'd been hurting for a long time. Protecting yourself." He raised his head and I cradled his face. "Listen to me, please." I shook him gently. "I knew that about you, but I forgot. When you finally looked at me as a woman I was so besotted with the idea of us, I forgot about your pain." I leaned forward and brushed my mouth over his. "All I could see was your gorgeousness," I whispered. "And all you could see was your innocent butterfly."

He closed his eyes. "I was besotted too, you know."

"I know." I pressed a soft kiss to the corner of his eye. And then repeated the caress on the other side. "And when you saw Jacks' ring on my finger, believed his lies that we were engaged—" His eyes opened and met mine. "Listened to your mother say I chose Jacks over you. What did that do to you?" My stomach cramped at the pain contorting his face.

"It was like acid eating through my bones," he rasped.

"Exactly. And in that red haze of pain and betrayal how were you to see the truth?"

He turned his head and dropped a warm kiss on the inside of my wrist. "You're making excuses for me."

"No, just painting a clear picture."

He grimaced. "You're gonna hurt yourself crouched down like this." He curled an arm under my knees and wrapped the other behind my back. Before I realized what he was doing, I was sitting in his lap. His solid warmth immediately penetrated my thin cotton dress and I snuggled against him.

"Jacks said what we had wasn't love," I said softly. He frowned, and I smoothed my hand over his creased brow. "But he was wrong. We had love, but it was immature. Idealistic." I stroked his jaw, enjoying the brush of his beard. "My life was close to perfect, and now there you were, looking at me like I was the most beautiful thing you'd ever seen."

Gray threaded his fingers into my hairline. "You were."

I shook my head. "I might have been nineteen but I hadn't lived. I hadn't experienced pain or loss, or learned humility, sacrifice, compromise." I shifted until I could look him full in the face. "And you—" I flattened my hands on his chest. "I cast you as my prince. My hero."

He laughed mirthlessly. "Jesus. Some kind of fucking hero!"

I smacked him on the chest. "Dammit, Gray, it's not funny!"

"I'm not really laughing, Butterfly."

I searched his face. No, he wasn't really laughing. "We failed each other. Let's not do it again."

His mouth twisted, the laughter gone. "I don't want to fail you again, Zoey."

"You won't." I pressed against him. "When the fear caught up with me and I had nowhere to turn, I came to you. And when you realized how messed up I was, you didn't hesitate to help me. That counts for something, doesn't it?"

His arms tightened around me.

"I love you, Gray. I love all of you." My hands crept up again to cradle his beloved face. "I love how you love me so deeply, exactly as I am, crazy brain and all. I love your honor and your unflinching loyalty to those you call family." I caressed the laugh lines at the corner of his eyes. "I love your humor. I love your need to protect me, to protect others. And I love knowing how much you love Lily." His arms jerked, and my vision blurred. "You're going to make a wonderful father," I said huskily. "And I can't wait to see you playing with our children. Loving them."

"Jesus, Zoey, enough—"

"I'm not finished," I snapped.

His face softened. "So finish," he said gruffly.

"I love your incredible sexiness." I pressed close until our mouths brushed. "I love your hands on me, your mouth on me." I touched the tip of my tongue to his lower lip. "And I love how my body ignites whenever you even so much as look at me."

His hands stroked up my sides. "You finished now?"

"Nearly." I pushed back until there was a little

space between us. "I can't decide which I love better, Butterfly or sweet-thing."

His brow arched. "Why do you have to choose? They both belong to you."

"How do you mean?"

He grabbed my hand and pressed it to his chest. "One comes from my heart." His hips arched and I felt his hardness push against me. "The other from my cock. And they both belong to you."

I smiled, my heart thumping. "I love you, Gray. You're so much more than enough for me. More than I could have ever dreamed." I pressed my palm harder against his chest. His heartbeat was strong. And fast. "Please let me be enough for you."

His hand flattened over mine. "You're my heart, Butterfly. I love you. So much that if I lost you again the hurt would be fatal." A single tear escaped his iron control. I leaned forward and caught it with my lips.

"The only way you can lose me, beautiful man, will be beyond either of our control. Fear has taken so much from us already; don't let it take any more." I pressed a gentle kiss to his sensual mouth. "You are your own man, Gray. My man." I slipped off his lap and held out my hand. "And right now, I want my man."

Chapter Twenty-Seven
Magic

Granddad Davis' Cottage
Zoey

I held Gray's hand as we walked through the sitting room, down the small passage, and into the bedroom. And I didn't let it go until we stood beside the king-sized bed. I loved his hands. They said a lot about him as a man. Warmth, strength, roughness. And most of all his need to protect. I lifted one and pressed a soft kiss to the center of his palm.

"Zoey." Blue-smoke captured my gaze. "You're wearing too many clothes." He slid his hand from my grasp and cradled my cheek, his thumb brushing over my lips.

"So are you," I said huskily.

He bent and replaced his thumb with his mouth. He kissed me gently, softly. "No games tonight. We've both waited too long."

Liquid warmth trickled through my veins. "Okay."

I was wearing a cotton floral skater dress that flared at mid-thigh. It had spaghetti straps and no fastenings. I bent down and lifted the hem, and kept on lifting until the dress cleared my head. Shaking out my mussed hair, I tossed the dress to the floor. Then I dared to look at Gray. And shivered.

His porn star mouth was sensually parted and his

burning gaze was tracking over every inch of my exposed skin. "It pleases me no end, sweet-thing, that you take my house rules seriously." He reached between his shoulder blades and grabbed his T, pulling it over his head. It landed on the floor beside my dress.

I was buck naked, and watching Gray strip in front of me was hotter than hot. I bit my lip as he popped the button on his jeans. But instead of finishing the job, he reached past me, grabbed the bed cover and yanked. My mouth fell open as the cover and pillows went flying. He stepped back and pulled me against his hard length. My arms circled his neck and he nuzzled the soft skin behind my ear. "Climb onto the bed, beautiful Butterfly." He stroked down my spine and my skin heated as his hand dropped to the curve of my butt. "I want you on your back, relaxed, and spread open for me."

I gulped. If I'd thought for a second that baring our souls to each other would make Gray soft, I was wrong. My heart pounded in delight. I hung onto his shoulders and ran my tongue up the taut muscle in his neck. His skin was salty and tangy and delicious. "Okay," I whispered into his ear and flicked his lobe with my tongue.

He growled and reached back to circle my wrists. His lips were twitching but his eyes were narrowed. "Careful with that tongue, sweet-thing. The more you use it, the more I'm gonna have to reciprocate." He pulled my arms behind my back and my body arched helplessly. "And the longer it's gonna take before I get to sink inside you."

Sink inside me.

I stopped breathing. And my core began to ache.

There was nothing I wanted more than Gray's pulsing length sliding inside me. Filling me.

"That's my girl." His lips settled over my racing pulse.

"You have to let me go so I can do what you want," I panted.

He pressed his jean-clad erection against my bare skin. *Lordy Lord.* For a moment I thought I was going to come. Then he gently put me from him. "Bed. Lie flat, and spread your legs."

My knees were suddenly trembling. I scrambled onto the bed before I fell onto the floor. *Jeez.* This man had a secret elixir that stirred me to madness. With everything we'd said and all the heartache we'd shared, it did nothing to diminish the raw heat he ignited with his touch.

I crawled to the center of the bed and lay down, positioning myself exactly as he'd asked. As I spread my legs, I met his eyes. Twin blue flames scorched through me. "Gray," I whispered. He already had his boots off and he wasted no time removing his jeans. I stroked my hands up my body, cupping my breasts. "Hurry, tough guy, I need you." And I did. In that moment, I felt lost without him.

The end of the bed dipped and Gray moved between my legs. His hands drifted up my thighs and over my tummy. He hesitated and lowered his head. I felt his lips caress my butterfly tattoo. "I love this tattoo," he murmured. "And I know it has more meaning than what you've told me." His lashes lifted. "And one day soon you'll share that with me." He pressed his lips to my skin again. "But I can't help loving it. It's like my mark is branded on your skin."

I threaded my fingers through his hair and pulled. Reluctantly he looked up and my heart thudded. "Don't you know, Gray Walker, your mark has been branded on my heart forever." For a moment his hands dug into my hips, then he crawled up and shifted to lay beside me. I rolled into him and settled my leg over his hip. "Every day, I used to pray you'd find a way to forgive me." I pressed my hand against his chest. "You were like this shadow living in my heart, waiting for the perfect time to come out into the light." I moved my hand to caress his face. "The light is shining now, my love, and it's so bright. There's no more darkness lurking in the corners."

His beautiful eyes searched mine. "How can you be sure you won't wake up one morning, the sun shining down on us, and remember what my family did to you?"

"Because it haunts me more knowing how much time we've lost." I reached up and ran my tongue over his bottom lip. "Make love to me, please." I arched against his pulsing heat. "I need you, Gray. Deep inside me, I need you."

****

Gray

I need you, Gray. Deep inside me, I need you.

Zoey's husky voice wrapped like molten heat around his cock. And her vivid green gaze, leaking with gold, filled his vision. Magic. She was pure fucking magic.

"Then you got me, beautiful Butterfly, you got me."

Her slim body arched against him and Gray knew without a doubt, he was the only man who could take

381

Zoey where she needed to go. Fuck. Where he needed to go. She was completely his. To love, to protect, to pleasure. And she was finally ready for him to love her how she needed to be loved.

He pressed close and caught her mouth, his tongue parting her lips and surging inside. Honey sweet. Hot and fiery. Like her hair, her taste was a contradiction he adored. Her tongue kissed against his. Demanding. Needing. She whimpered and heat pooled in his spine. He pushed his rigid cock against her seeking pussy.

"Gray." It was a whispered groan in his mouth.

"I've got you, Butterfly." He reached down and cupped her between the legs. *Christ*. She was burning up, her pussy already like hot silken lava. "Zoey, I want to take you bare."

"Okay." She undulated against his hand.

Jesus. No hesitation. "Listen to me, beautiful." He pressed his hand firmly against her heat. His balls tightened. *Fuck, he needed her.* "I want you bare. Skin to skin. Nothing between us." She shuddered and arched even closer.

"I want that too."

Her husky voice licked over him as her tongue darted out and wet his lower lip. Gray knew she loved his mouth, especially the dent in his lower lip. She was forever staring at it and it was the first place her tongue went when she kissed him. And it always sent desire curling in his stomach and arcing down to his dick. But before he lost himself in her, he needed to make sure. He gripped her hair and tugged her mouth from his. Her lashes fluttered and hungry green and gold peered at him. Impatient. He only just stopped himself grinning. "I need to know if you're protected, sweet-thing."

She blinked. Then smiled, her cat eyes giving a lazy, impudent roll. "Yes, Gray, I'm protected." She lunged and grabbed his lower lip again, biting it gently before she let it go. "But I wouldn't care if I wasn't."

For a fraction of time, his breath caught. Then he was rolling, using his superior weight to flatten her to the bed. "No foreplay, Zoey. I'm going to take you now and I'm not going to stop until I have all of you." He pushed up to his knees and pulled her to him, resting her gorgeous ass on his thighs. "And you have all of me." His voice was guttural.

"Oh God, yes," she sighed. "Please, Gray, yes."

Christ, she was perfect. So fucking perfect for him.

He clasped her slender ankles and folding her legs back, spread her wide. "Stay open for me, sweet-thing." Gray gripped his cock and rubbed it against her entrance. Silken cream coated his throbbing cock head. Her legs began to tremble and his heart stuttered. He tore his gaze from the erotic sight before him and sought out the eyes that held his soul. "I love you, Zoey." Her eyes flooded with tears. He watched them spill and roll down her temples and into her hair.

"I love you, Gray." She pressed her heat against him. "Oh God, I love you so much."

She was breaking his heart. And it felt so goddamn good because he knew she was crying tears of happiness. Of relief. Of love. He arched his hips and his cock sank inside her. Liquid heat instantly surrounded him. He groaned and pushed deeper. "Jesus, you're so fucking tight and hot." He drew back and surged forward again. And again. Her scorching pussy caught fire and started to suck him in. Inch by erotic inch. "*Fuuck!*"

"Gray!"

He moved over her and braced his hands beside her head. Then he slowly lowered his body, letting his heat settle her. Shelter her. Protect her. Zoey's arms curled around his shoulders and she arched into him. And Gray buried his cock full length inside her.

"Gray." It was a long sigh like she was welcoming him home.

And he was home. Finally. "I've got you, Butterfly. I've got you." He guided her legs around his hips. "Now hold on." He began to move. Slow and easy. She trembled but her hips undulated and she eagerly met his thrusts, pushing hungrily against him. Her pussy was like a silken fist, squeezing him tight. He shuddered, the pleasure more than he could have ever dreamed. Because it wasn't just her body he was claiming, it was her soul. And she was giving it freely.

"More, Gray, please. I need more."

Always. From now until the day he stopped breathing, he'd give Zoey what she needed. No more holding back. It was time for him to also give freely because his butterfly owned him, body and soul.

****

Zoey

I was dying. The need inside me was so great, I was clawing at Gray's back. His cock was filling me, hard and slick. Over and over again, he was burying himself deep inside me. But still, I needed more.

"Harder, Gray, please. I need more."

And he gave it to me.

Moving his weight to his legs, he began to drive his flesh inside me.

Oh God, yes!

I wrapped my legs tighter around his hips and dug my heels into his taut ass. And again and again, he slammed into me, each stroke sending exquisite bolts of pleasure streaking through me. His skin was wet with sweat, his powerful muscles sliding with animal heat against me. I stretched up and licked my tongue over his madly beating pulse. Salty. Musky. And so much beautiful man. I bucked against him and lightning crashed through me. I could feel his balls slapping against my flesh, his breath hot against my face.

"Gray! Oh my God, help me."

"I've got you." His mouth brushed mine, his wicked tongue darting in and lashing against mine. "Come for me, Butterfly. I want to see you fly apart on my cock."

He braced himself on one arm, the other slipping between us. And I lost control because his knowing fingers found my clit and began to stroke. Once. Twice.

Oh Lord.

His cock continued to thrust, stretching me, loving me, and lightning hit again. And again. I clung to him as my pussy convulsed. It was too much. I arched and shattered. Into a million burning pieces, I came apart in Gray's arms, my scream echoing around us.

"Graaay!"

"I love you, Zoey. I've got you."

And he did. Shaking and trembling, melting from pleasure, but as complete as I'd ever been. He had me.

As soon as my tremors began to ease, Gray began to move. He braced himself over me, his mouth hovering a breath above mine, and his eyes blazing cobalt fire.

My heart went wild and my soul wailed, reaching

out for his. "Come for me, my beautiful man," I whispered against his lips.

His hips slammed into me, his cock so hard and hot, I felt it brush my womb. "Jesus, Zoey." He buried his mouth against my neck.

I held him tight and he thrust again. Hard and deep. *Oh God, so deep.*

I contracted around him. Holding him. His shudders ripped through me and I swear I felt his heat fill me when he finally lost control. His strength gave and I took his weight as he poured more of himself into me. Filling me.

Nothing in my life had ever felt this good. This perfect.

I was complete.

I was home.

And I was loved.

Chapter Twenty-Eight
Unbreakable

Morgan Farm
Eight Days Later
Gray

Gray stepped around the side of the house and paused. Gerald was where Wendy said he'd be, sitting on the narrow wraparound porch. He'd moved in with Wendy at Morgan Farm to recuperate, and she said he spent hours out there, staring at the rolling fields. His chair seemed uncomfortably upright, offering little in the way of cushioning. He had a full mug of coffee perched precariously on the crooked arm. It looked cold. Forgotten.

Gray cleared his throat. "Dad," he called quietly. His father's head twitched. Gray joined him and leaned against the splintered wood railing. Gerald looked gaunt. The unfamiliar paunch he'd been sporting was gone. Deep lines cut into his face. His hair was shorter, neater. Maybe Wendy had given him a trim. Gray's mouth thinned and he looked away. He wanted to feel more compassion for this broken man. More love. More anything. Just more. But he didn't.

Gerald shifted. His elbow just missed knocking over the mug, and Gray stretched over and removed it, placing it on a small chest by the railing. As he'd thought, the coffee was cold. "They've released the bodies," he said.

Gerald blinked several times.

"I'm sorry, Dad, but I can't go to their funerals."

"I know." His voice was thin, tired.

Gray waited for his father to look at him. His jaw clenched in frustration when nothing happened. "Did you know?" he said gruffly. "About what she did?"

Gerald gave a half shrug. Gray thought he wasn't going to answer, but then he spoke quietly. "I knew she killed Magic. So did James."

"You knew. How?"

"Magic was killed during the christening of young Noah. James and Mary invited all their staff and friends to the occasion." His gaze flickered to Gray. "I was there too."

Gray's insides shriveled. "But not Margaret." He'd made a vow to never refer to that evil bitch as his mother. But even her name tasted bitter in his mouth. "She wasn't there, was she?"

"No, she refused to come." His father's weather-beaten hands curled around the spindly chair arms. "She never forgave James for rejecting her. First for that horse, and then for Mary."

"So you think she poisoned Magic to hurt James?"

His father nodded. "And she succeeded. Magic's death darn near broke James."

"So why didn't he do something about it?"

"He did. He told the sheriff to quit the investigation."

Gray's brows shot up. "Why the hell would he do that?"

"Never said why, but I knew. He did it for me." Gerald tipped his chin at Gray. "And for you. That was his way." His head dropped and he seemed to slump in defeat. "But Magic was worth a fortune so the police still poked around some. Found no evidence so eventually, they stopped looking."

Gray let out a harsh breath. "But *you* knew. Why did you protect her?"

Gerald stared blindly out. "Your mother was so filled with bitterness. Always focused on what she didn't have, not on all the wonderful things she did have."

"That's hardly an answer, Dad. Why did you protect her, stay with her?"

"Because I loved her." Conviction clung to his father's frail voice. "She didn't love me, but I loved her. And then Jacks was born. I couldn't leave you both on your own with her. And the ranch, it was my life." His voice trailed off.

Gray tried to control his fury. "You knew she murdered the Morgans." He jerked a hand in the direction of the dining room. "How could you protect her from *that*?"

"No!" Gerald bolted upright. "I never knew she did that." He shook his head at Gray. "Sweet Jesus, no. I didn't know." Gray's chest rose and fell with each of his father's pained denials. "I didn't want to know," Gerald cried, tears of remorse flooding his eyes. "It was too awful. Too awful." He hunched over, beginning to rock. "I'm sorry Gray. So very sorry. I did what Zoey did. I blocked it out. It was too dreadful to face."

Gray balled his fists, strangling his scream of rage. His father was weak. So fucking weak. If he'd been a little stronger, a little more awake, maybe he could have stopped the evil in its tracks. Gerald's breaths came harder. Gray's throat thickened and he turned his back. *Fucking hell.* His father was a shrunken ghost. "What are you going to do now?" he said softly.

Gerald took several deep breaths. "I'm going to sell the ranch." He made an attempt to square his shoulders. "Most of the profit will go into a family trust held for your children. The rest I'm going to give to Wendy. She told me Zoey wants her to stay on here."

For your children.

Gray's rage dissipated. If he closed his eyes he could almost see her laughing, a tiny redheaded toddler in her arms. He thought of where she was now, saying goodbye to her family, and suddenly he wanted this over. He wanted to be with her.

"Zoey doesn't want to sell the farm, not with her family buried here." He swung back to look at his father. "You're right. She asked Wendy to stay on, continue working with the kids."

"I'm going to work with her," Gerald said. "Help her continue the good things she and Jacks started here."

Gray shoved his hands in his pockets. "You warned her to leave the farm, didn't you? Go to her family."

His father nodded, deep grooves furrowing his brow. "After that lunch, I panicked. I went to Wendy and gave her just enough of the story." He dropped his head but not before Gray caught another glint of tears. "I promised her I'd take care of Jacks," he sobbed.

"Jacks put a gun to his head. There's not much you can do about that." Gray watched his father's shoulders shake, and his jaw clenched. "To save him you should have stepped in a long time ago. A very long time ago."

Gerald shuddered.

"We're leaving today," Gray said abruptly. "Zoey's at the graves saying her goodbye."

Gerald roughly swiped at his eyes. "You'll stay in touch?"

Gray stepped off the porch, but he couldn't ignore the soft plea. "If you want to visit, you'll have to come to New York." Before his father could respond, he walked away.

He followed the path around the house and made his way up the small hill. The closer he got to the trees standing sentry, the easier his breath came. He caught a flash of copper-red hair and lengthened his stride. She always wore it loose these days. Flowing down her back, wild and free. His pulse raced. Each day they were together, he caught more and more glimpses of the mercurial young girl he fell in love with. Every precious smile she gave him, every wicked laugh, she added another layer of richness to the beautiful woman she already was. Gray liked to think this was his gift to her. A recompense. Because with each moment of joy, he cried a silent tear for those countless moments lost. Stolen.

Cut it out, Gray!

His chest vibrated as her voice echoed in his head. His butterfly didn't miss a thing, especially the shadows that frequently darkened his mood. "Wanting to apportion blame, tough guy, is a zero-sum-game," she'd say. "They're dead, and we're alive. They're dead and we're having orgasms. Every bloody day!"

Yes. That was his Zoey. Fucking hilarious. And mostly fucking right. Mostly. Because their victory had left haunting scars. Deep slashes on their souls.

Zoey called them scars of life.

He called them scars of hate.

Zoey promised time would heal. That their love had endured their separation. That it was stronger now. Unbreakable.

Gray agreed. Mostly. Not because their love had endured, but rather because it had been forged in the pits of hell. And survived.

"Semantics!" Zoey would insist and threw up her hands.

He didn't argue.

As long as they were moving forward. Together. Gray really didn't give a damn.

****

Morgan Family Gravesite
Zoey

JAMES MORGAN
Loving husband and father
MARY MORGAN
Loving wife and mother
NOAH MORGAN
Loving son and brother

Each name was an invisible tattoo inked on my memory. Each epitaph, an invisible thread of love interwoven into every cell that made me who I was. Again, my eyes traced the simple words engraved on each headstone. They said everything and nothing at the same time. They didn't say how much I adored each and every one of them. Or how much I missed them to the bottom of my soul. But I knew there were no words in existence that could.

A puff of wind stirred the still air and I lifted my face to let it dry my damp cheeks. The pain of their loss made my heart ache. But I also felt a lightness that had been missing most of my adult life because now I felt free to remember. Remember the boundless love of my father, the deep protective spirit of my brother, and the innate love and understanding of my mother. I wasn't alone. Their love was all around me. It always had been. It always would be.

I knelt down and laid the last bouquet on my mother's grave. "Miss you, Mama," I whispered. A shadow fell over me and the warmth in my heart blossomed. "Hi." I smiled over my shoulder.

Gray crouched down beside me. "How you doing, Butterfly?"

"I'm good."

"Sure?" He reached for my hand, threading his fingers through mine. I nodded and smiled when he brought my hand to his mouth, dropping a feather light kiss across my knuckles. His gaze left mine and drifted over the graves. "I bought you pink roses for your sixteenth birthday," he said.

My throat thickened. "You gave me roses for my nineteenth birthday as well. They were on the table when—"

He shot to his feet, dragging me up with him. "Jesus! I'm sorry—"

I flattened my hand against his chest. "Don't be. Please."

He tugged me against him, but his gaze kept veering to the flowers I'd placed on each of the graves. I turned in his arms and looked at the pink roses. "In my nightmares, I hated those flowers. All I could see were pink roses spread across the table, blocking everything in my head." His arms tightened around me, and I held onto his powerful forearms. "But now I remember my mother's strength. Her love. And I remember how much I loved your roses." Pivoting in his embrace, I stretched up and brushed my mouth over his. "They mean love for me. I won't let Jacks and Margaret steal that from me. They've stolen enough."

Gray's hands swept up and sank into my hair. He lowered his head, his breath a gentle kiss against my mouth. "So you want roses for your next birthday?"

"Yes. Pink ones." My voice was husky. "Every birthday, I want pink roses." I leaned into him, stroking my hands up either side of his neck. "We're not going to bury this, Gray. We're not going to let it fester like an old wound. When it crops up we'll deal with it, together."

"Okay." His pulse beat a steady rhythm against my thumb.

"Promise me," I pressed.

He lowered his head, and for a brief moment, rested his forehead against mine. "I promise, Butterfly."

I closed my eyes and took a deep breath. *Okay then.*

Gray untangled his hands from my hair. "You ready to go?"

I nodded.

He held the small wrought-iron gate open for me. It was a new addition, as was the low, wrought iron fence that surrounded the gravesite. Wendy told me Jacks had built it years ago. Just as he'd cared for the graves and laid fresh flowers regularly. I didn't try to understand why. I didn't care.

I took one last look at the peaceful setting.

I love you. Always.

Then I threaded my arm through Gray's, and we

slowly walked along the well-trodden path, back to the homestead. "I spoke to my department chief in Boston."

Gray looked at me. "You sure about the move to New York?"

"I'm sure. I like it in Boston but I can work anywhere." I squeezed his arm. A frisson of heat tingled through me when his muscle didn't give an inch. "I told you, you belong in New York. With Luke and Katya, Eva, King—"

He snorted. "King! The bossman has ice running through his veins."

I jostled him. "Nonsense. He's got warm blood like the rest of us, and it runs even hotter for those he cares about." Swinging round in front of him, I lightly slapped his chest. "And you, tough guy, are high up on that list."

His hands covered mine. "Yeah. He really came through for me when I needed him."

"Yes, he did. And Katya swears by him."

Gray's mouth hardened. "Don't know why. He hung her out to dry."

I leaned into him. "He made a mistake. We all make them." Gray reluctantly nodded. I went on tiptoes and pressed my mouth to his. It immediately softened, and I stole a quick taste before moving back to his side. "Katya says he's got a magic wand that never ceases to amaze her." I threaded my arm back through his. "I think we could do with some magic in our lives, don't you?"

We started to walk again. Gray didn't answer, but his mouth was twitching. I felt my own begin to curve.

"So what did your boss say?" he asked.

"He'd like me to stay on until he finds a

replacement. I said yes."

"You got space for me while you're doing that?"

I stumbled, and Gray's arm shot out. "I don't think you'll fit into my shower," I said breathlessly. "It's for very small people."

Suddenly I was off my feet, the world spinning as he swung me into his arms. "I'll shower at the gym," he growled.

I looped my arms around his neck. "Will you promise me one more thing?"

Blue cobalt ignited in his eyes. "Whatever you want."

"While we're getting to know each other again. Promise you won't give me breathing room."

He threw back his head and burst out laughing.

God, he was magnificent.

Heat ballooned in my chest, but I bit my lip and managed to keep a straight face. Katya told me all about when Luke decided to give her space by not making love to her. He called it breathing room. She called it dumb.

"You heard about that, huh?" He chuckled.

I raised a brow. "Hmm-hmm."

"You don't want it?" he said huskily.

I stroked my fingers through his hair. "Not an inch of it."

"Okay, then." He smiled. "You got it. No breathing room."

My smile stretched across my face.

Gray's delicious mouth smiled right back at me. "Love you, Butterfly."

"Right back at ya, tough guy."

About the Author

Anni Fife is an exciting new contemporary romance author who has already made her mark in the popular genre of steamy romantic suspense. Her debut novel, Luke's Redemption, has been acclaimed by critics and readers and is a Finalist in the 2017 RONE Awards. Anni credits Kristen Ashley as her guiding inspiration and strives to make her characters equally as heart-wrenching and unforgettable. Anni is currently completing Book 3 in her King Security Series, Eva's Peace.

Anni closed the door on a successful career in television production to fulfill her lifelong passion, writing. In the space of a month, she shut her business, packed up her city life, and moved to a small seaside village. When she's not writing, she can be found on the beach searching for pansy shells, or drinking red wine and gabbing with her gal posse.

If you want to know when Anni's next book is releasing and be first to get regular updates and BONUS TREATS, sign up to join her POSSE: www.annifife.com.

Anni is published by The Wild Rose Press and is a member of Romance Writers of America (RWA).

~*~

To chat with Anni Fife and other Wild Rose Press authors of erotic romance, join us at www.groups.yahoo.com/group/thewilderroses.

Also Available

Luke's Redemption
King Security Book One
By Anni Fife

http://a.co/6Mh10aA

Red-hot sex. Searing betrayal. A passionate and elusive love…

Chased by her criminal kingpin father, Katya Dalca runs to New Orleans and straight into the arms of Luke Hunter. Sucked into the carnal world of the French Quarter, she succumbs to Luke's potent sexuality. He not only steals her breath, he steals her heart and the only leverage she has against her father. She is left with no choice except to pick up the pieces and rebuild her life alone.

Undercover DEA agent Luke Hunter thought his newest assignment—recover a stolen flash drive to gain the trust of the Russian mob—was like any other. But his target brings him to his knees, and after one taste of her intoxicating beauty, he's in too deep. Doing his job means walking away, leaving his heart behind with nothing but a promise to reunite. It's a promise he can't keep.

When Katya's past reaches out and her world unravels, her only hope is the one man she is most vulnerable to—Luke.

Also Read

Passion Unscripted
By Anya Sharpe

http://a.co/6b2pmVh

A celebrity playboy looking for love…

Carson Wells' heart closed up shop six years ago when his fiancée ran off with his rock-star best friend. Since then, the dancer-actor has turned his back on serious relationships, seeking no-strings, down-and-dirty sex with a laundry list of hot women. But lately, a growing loneliness tugs at his gut…along with an unrelenting desire for his co-star. When he finally acts on their smoldering mutual attraction, there's no turning back. He's hooked.

A sassy screen star putting her heart on the line…

Having spent years guarding her scarred heart, Lara Kincaid is totally out of her depth with the fiery attraction to her playboy leading man. His history with women is a deep well, and her insecurities and secrets run even deeper. Even so, something about the man tugs at her heart and soul. Carson's sex appeal and charming persuasion have cast a spell on her, but their pasts threaten to unravel that magic. She's dipped a toe in the water—should she dive right in, she just might drown.

www.ingramcontent.com/pod-product-compliance
Lightning Source LLC
Chambersburg PA
CBHW070803030726
47504CB00003B/683